# FOR THE HOPE OF IT ALL

a merrymount series

ILA SIKORSKI

For The Hope of it All



Editing by Cassidy Hudspeth

Editing and Proofreading by Kim Swiszcz

Book Cover and Art by Marissa Lussier

# Dedication

*For every girl who was ever told they were forgettable.*
*They're gonna remember our names, babe.*

# The Playlist

**August** by Taylor Swift
**Ceilings** by Lizzy McAlpine
**Little Lion Man** by Mumford & Sons
**What Was I Made For?** by Billie Eilish
**Better Together** (sped up) by Lucky Socks, Mark Ambor
**Invisible String** by Taylor Swift
**End of Beginning** by Djo
**Touch Tank** by Quinnie

## Content Note

For The Hope of it All is an adult romance novel.

It addresses the MMC's parental loss and cheating in a past relationship (not the MMC), a side character's parental abuse, the FMC's anxiety, pregnancy, open door intimacy, drinking/alcohol, and explicit language. Readers who may be sensitive to these subjects, please take note.

A *Spice Guide* has been included in the back matter of the book outlining the chapters that contain explicit sexual content for readers who wish to find or avoid.

# Prologue



*Margot*

I HAVE BEEN STARING at the "it's not you, it's me" let-down text from yet another failed first date for a good twenty minutes now. I shouldn't be surprised because failure has always been the common theme of my dating life, but this date felt *different*. We didn't have to ask each other our favorite colors (who actually cares?) or sit painfully through a conversation about the weather (yawn).

Call me a hopeless romantic. I felt the zing - the early 2000s romcom spark we're all chasing. I caught myself relating a little too much to Ginnifer Goodwin's character in *He's Just Not That Into You*. You just never know who is on the end of your invisible string, you know?

Looking back and replaying it all in my head, I still can't figure out where it went wrong, and maybe it didn't. Maybe it just wasn't enough. Lately, I've been abandoning the blind optimism and not going into first dates with much hope. I mean, how much can you really know about someone from a dating profile? And even then, how much of it is true? I've been on too many dates with 6' tall guys who suspiciously look like they are 5'9" to be positively sure about an instant connection.

A couple nights beforehand, after two glasses of wine and an unsuccessful attempt at scrolling through Netflix for something to watch, I found myself playing the swipe game on a dating app in bed. It's like counting sheep but more bleak. I was about to throw my phone across the room and force myself to at least try to get a couple hours of sleep when I landed on Sawyer H's profile.

I don't know if it was because the first picture in the carousel finally wasn't a guy holding a stupid fish, but wow, he was fucking *hot.* It got me to stop long enough not to instinctively swipe to the next dud. He was dressed up for what looked like a wedding, maybe at the cocktail hour. You could see the scruff on his face, and he didn't seem to care that his dark brown hair was slightly messy. It worked for him. He was standing in front of a gorgeous sunset, filling out a slim-fit navy suit, and holding a scotch glass. And he was wearing a maroon bow tie. I'm a sucker for a fucking bow tie.

Swiping through his photos, I was actually surprised there *wasn't* a fish-holding picture because he seemed like the outdoorsy type. There was a picture of him and a couple other guys on the water in kayaks, one of him sipping out of a coffee mug next to a campfire, and the last one of him hugging an older woman with gray hair peeking out of her beanie and who was a whole head and a half shorter than him. Her scarf covered most of her face, but from a guess, she looked like she could be his mom or maybe grandmother, and he was finally smiling with his white teeth. They were bundled up at a Christmas tree farm.

His bio was short, not giving much information about who he was beyond the standard.

*"6'3", Small town living. I hate texting. Probably watching The Food Network. Happier outside. What's your favorite type of pasta?*

And that's what made me swipe right. We matched, and I immediately sent a message saying, "Fusilli. But if yours is some basic answer like spaghetti, I'll see myself out."

He responded almost instantly, telling me he was offended that I had already thought so little of him. It was a fun back-and-forth banter that continued almost nonstop for the next few days, despite his profile saying he hated texting. When he finally asked if I wanted to do dinner, it was so easy to say yes. The next night, I had first-date jitters as I was heading out the door to meet him.

Sawyer walked into the restaurant just as I was opening the Kindle app on my phone to read at the bar while I waited. I'm not shy and not above a dramatic reveal for myself, so I started at his shoes, a classic pair of black, low-top Converse, the kind you can tell have been worn and loved. I continued up to his faded black jeans that hugged his thighs just right, paired with a loose, light denim button-up. He was putting his Ray Bans on his head when we made eye contact, and based on the smirk on his face, I knew I was caught.

He was even more handsome in person. I'm half surprised I didn't stumble off my stool. Completely opposite from what I usually go for, scruff on his face and a casual but well-put-together outfit made him look effortless. Where every past date I had looked like they were fighting to impress everyone in the room in their expensive suits and always seemed to come up a little short, he did it without even trying.

Short, Sawyer was *not*. I had to physically look up to see his eyes. At least I could already confirm he didn't lie about his height.

Betrayed by my inability not to blush mixed with the wine I ordered, I raised my glass of Pinot Noir to hide my reddening face and signaled him over. As he made his way to the bar, his genuine smile with those perfect teeth eased my nerves, and from there, everything just flowed. He let me talk with my hands without making fun of me and told me about his grandma's obsession with taking in stray cats. My face hurt from smiling and laughing by the end of the night.

Walking back to my car, I kept thinking about how I couldn't wait to do this again, and based on his pinky linking with mine as we made our way through the parking lot, I thought he felt the same.

After opening my driver's door for me, he kissed the top of my hand before letting go as I eased into the seat. The contact zapped through my skin. I remember thinking how old-fashioned it felt and how it made my stomach literally flip. I drove home listening to my happy Taylor Swift playlist. For once thinking about how this really might be the beginning of something, even if it wasn't *the* thing.

But it's not me, it's him. Or rather, it's his ex-girlfriend who apparently wants to "try again!" and who am I to compete with that as the one dinner girl from a dating app he met a week ago? Nor do I *want* to compete with that. As hard as it is living in a constant state of the talking stage, I know my worth. I know what I'm holding out for, and it's not Sawyer "I'm going to take your breath away and then send a shitty text two days later" Hale.

I decide Sawyer can still be useful as a wake up call. I can't keep doing this. I'm not going to waste my time spiraling because, technically, he owed me nothing. I just got caught up in my head. I thumbs up his text and toss my phone to the other side of the couch.

There has to be a reason I haven't had a real relationship since my one boyfriend in my senior year of high school (if you could even call it that). There's a reason my mom is my best friend and the only person I can list as an emergency contact. It has to be me. So, that means I have to make a change.

I've spent the past few years trying to make everything work, including a job I hate, going on countless first dates (sometimes second dates, but never thirds), and spending my weekends escaping reality with spicy romance books so I don't have to be alone with my thoughts and scattered take out containers. Here goes nothing… I guess.

<h1 style="text-align:center">Chapter One</h1>

*Margot*

MY LEGS ARE DEFINITELY BEING EATEN alive by mosquitoes, and there is a suspicious-looking Canadian goose staring at me from the water with eyes that tell me we have a feud I was unaware of until now, but I'm…home, I think.

Within the last month, I've walked away from essentially everything: my job in the Seaport and the apartment I sat on a waitlist for over two years for. Plus, I have purged every dating app from my phone. Not that there was much happening there anyway; I haven't been on a date in almost a full year to the day. I think a lot of people would call this a quarter-life crisis, and honestly, maybe they're not wrong. But the quiet voice in my head telling me to ditch it all got too loud, and I couldn't ignore it anymore.

"Well, that about covers it. You have the keys, and the lease is signed. I left a copy on the kitchen counter. Cottage B is officially yours, Margot."

I break my staring contest with the goose and look back at

the older woman standing in front of me, handing me the keys to my place. This is where I'm supposed to say thank you and let my new landlord - landlady? - be on her way, but I can't seem to find the words. As soon as she's gone, this will be real, and I'll be left alone with my thoughts. Cue the spiraling.

"Thank you so much again, Mrs. Rivers. Everything is perfect. I'm so grateful this worked out." I outstretch my hand to shake hers, but she waves me off and pulls me into a hug I wasn't expecting.

"Don't thank me, girl. And please, it's Beth. I'm excited to see more young kids like you back here. Us old folks have been running the place for too long. I'm sure you'll see my grandson around. He's right next door in C. He's a bit of a stormy cloud, but I can see you clearing that up." Mrs. Rivers - Beth - gives me the least subtle wink I've probably ever seen and is out the door before I can even mumble bye.

I found Beth Rivers and this perfect lakeside cottage the old-fashioned way, an ad in the paper. When I committed to uprooting my life in the name of happiness, I didn't want to do anything the way I normally would. No realtors, no apartment-finding apps. Just me, a phone, a highlighter, and a newspaper.

When I saw the listing, I had a feeling that this was it: one bedroom, one bathroom cottage on a lake, pets welcome on a case-by-case basis. I don't *have* a pet, but the idea that I *could* get one in this new life I'm creating for myself was just the thing that made me dial the number. I probably sounded way too enthusiastic on the phone, but I didn't care. Beth agreed to meet me the next day. Here we are, two weeks later, with most of my shit thrown into random boxes and reusable shopping bags and trash bags. The papers are signed, and I'm standing in Cottage B. It's mine.

My mom has been supportive. Okay, she's definitely putting on a good act and internally panicking, but it's been just me and her for the last twenty-something years, so I can pick up on when she's being genuine and when she's trying to let me lead the way, even if she doesn't fully understand it. It's why we're so close. When I laid out my plan to her a month ago, she hung out in the latter category. I'm impulsive, and she runs with it but it gives her hives in the process.

Mom got pregnant at nineteen from the lifeguard at the pool where she taught summer swim lessons. He said he wanted to stick around and step up, but they never got married, and by the time I turned four, our trio had become a duo. She never missed a chorus concert, my birthday felt like a national holiday every year, and we were happy. Now that I'm an adult, I see the sacrifices she made. She gave up everything to give me this life, and we didn't need him. Or anyone else, for that matter.

I never asked my mom for details on why my dad left because, honestly, I don't think she has many, and I don't want to put her through that. She always said no one should have to be a parent if they truly don't want to be, and that was that. My memories of him are slim to none, and the number of pictures I've seen of him over the years has been next to none. I never kept any for myself when my mom and I would stumble on one accidentally. I never felt a connection with him to need anything.

All I know is his name is Mike, and we have the same green eyes. We don't even share a last name because Mom made sure I took hers when filling out the birth certificate. I'm pretty certain the only things I got from him are my love for peanut butter cups (because we used to share Moose Tracks ice cream) and those green eyes.

Refusing to fuel the girl with daddy issues cliché, I prefer to pretend I don't care that one of the two people biologically programmed to love me and be there for me decided not to, but it still hurts. Unfortunately, he was just the first cut. My grandparents - if you could even call them that - disowned my mom as soon as the pregnancy test showed the two lines, and she's an only child like me, so besides the small circle we found from the pool, it really just has been the two of us figuring shit out.

I wouldn't say I had a difficult time making friends. I got along with everyone, and I wasn't bullied or anything like that. I've been to my fair share of birthday parties over the years. I just never clicked with anyone on the level I saw most kids my age doing throughout childhood. It's not from lack of trying. I just think I've mastered my role as a sitcom side character in everyone's life. At some point, being alone just made more sense.

When it came time to decide about college, it was Mom who pushed me to go. She dropped out of her freshman year to raise me, and I felt like I owed it to her to see it through. Don't get me wrong. I don't regret going. I spent four years learning a lot. Yes, I got my degree in digital marketing, but it was more about the experience for me. I was finally living with people besides just my mom. I partied and made friends and hooked up with boys, and it all felt good. But it also felt temporary. My roommates never became the lifelong best friends you read about. The guys were always just flings. And my major just felt like something to do. So, when graduation came and went, it was an easy goodbye.

If I'm being honest, walking away from the firm I was working for felt almost identical to leaving college and, before that, graduating high school. I had no passion for what I was doing, and my coworkers and I didn't have a relationship beyond an occasional *hey, how are you?* and the job itself... it was just another thing I was doing because I felt like I had to. When I gave my two week's notice, I thought I was going to be sick, but as I packed my office up on the last day, it clicked that I didn't care. I felt hollow, I felt numb, but I didn't feel sad.

Honestly, I wish I felt sad because it would have been better than emptiness.

I'm still standing in the middle of the kitchen in this cottage that is now mine, in this small town I've never even passed through, let alone visited for any amount of time, with no real plan aside from the three months of savings I have in my bank account to hold me over until I figure out what I want to do.

Despite me telling her I could handle it on my own, Beth helped me haul in the ten or so boxes I managed to squeeze into my car, along with my mattress I haphazardly tied to the roof before we both signed the lease. For a woman who has to be in her late sixties and is even shorter than I am (and I'm 5' on a good day), she's strong as hell. The boxes are stacked in the living room, and the mattress is on the floor of my bedroom until the new frame I ordered online arrives some-time next week.

I need to unpack. I need to grocery shop. I need a fucking job. But first, I need coffee.

# Chapter Two

*Margot*

THE GOOD OLE Google tells me the cottage is about a ten-minute drive from the center of town. While I've lived in New England my entire life and am familiar with its charm, you never get used to driving down a cute little main street for the first time.

In the short drive over, I passed a bookstore, a family-owned drug store, and a flower shop that looks like it belongs in a fairytale. The pizza place I just drove by looks like it's been here since the town was founded. I make a mental note to pick up a takeout menu at some point because there is nothing I love more than a good cheese pizza, extra cheese, add pickles.

Finally, I park my car in front of the first coffee shop I see. Checking Google Maps, I see it might be the *only* coffee shop in town, which is surprising because if you've spent any time in Massachusetts, you know you normally can't walk twenty feet in any direction without finding a Dunkin'. The window decal reads, "Red's Place: The pot's hot. Come on in!" I laugh to myself as I get out of the car and head inside.

As I step into the building, I'm hit with two things. One, it smells amazing. Like when you were a kid, and you popped the top of a *Foldger's* coffee can to take a whiff when your mom was making her morning cup of coffee before school and work. And two, there's a "Help Wanted" sign propped up next to the register. When I said I went into this new season of life with no plan, I meant it. I spent too long working a corporate job that sucked the life out of me to box myself into that being my only option again, so this might just be the opportunity I need. Could it really be that easy?

The entire front of the shop has glass windows from floor to ceiling, letting in all of the sunshine and giving the place a light and airy feeling. The floor is black and white tiled, giving a classy, modern vibe. It's a contrast to the surrounding buildings that look like they've been here forever. From a first glance, I can tell a lot of thought went into everything here.

I make my way to the counter, taking in my surroundings. There's a group of what I assume to be high school-aged kids in a booth. A few people are clearly working on their laptops at the bar-style seating that faces out the front window. My eyes go a little wide when I see four elderly women seated together having what appears to be some sort of book club because they're all holding a copy of this new, hot cowboy book that just came out. I'm already plotting how to join their spicy group when I get to the counter and smile at the most beautiful woman I've ever seen in my life.

She has to be at least 5'10" with the hourglass figure of every man's fantasy and every woman's vision board. She's wearing a pair of loose, light-wash jeans with holes in the knees and a plain cream-colored sweater that sits just off one shoulder. Her winged eyeliner looks like it would take me at least half an hour to attempt, and even then, it would be smudged and uneven. But you know it was effortless for her. Based on her long, what's best described as fiery hair that looks like it just got blown out at a salon, this has to be Red.

She looks up from the register and immediately lights up when we make eye contact.

"Hi! You're new! You're Margot. I just know it. I'm so glad you stopped in. Beth said to give you time to get settled, but you're here! How do you like the cottage? Have you met your hottie neighbor? Do you need anything? Oh my gosh, you're here, so obviously, you need something. Coffee? Tea? Seltzer? Oh my gosh, again, I'm rambling. I'm Gwendolyn or Gwen, but no one calls me either unless I've pissed them off. You can call me Red."

After a deep breath, she throws her hand across the counter. I gladly accept the handshake and a second to process all of… that.

"Wow, hi! Yeah, I'm Margot. The cottage is great, and I would love a, um," I pause to quickly glance at the menu handwritten above her head on the chalkboard. "A caramel latte."

I'm not even going to comment on the hot neighbor thing. This life change is for me. I'm not here to chase a boy. I can most certainly *look*, but my life currently has no room for nonsense.

"I totally pegged you as a caramel girl. It's my superpower. I get this tingly feeling and just know what someone is going to order. Give me two minutes, and I'll have it ready for you on the house. Call it a welcome home present." Red shoots me another beaming smile, and then she turns to get to work on my drink.

Home. I haven't felt at home in a long time. I watch Red bop around and make my latte as I work up the courage to ask about a job. I finally stop picking at a cuticle on my finger and shoot my shot. I have absolutely zero experience as a barista, but I love coffee and people so what's the worst that could happen?

"Hey, Red - the help wanted sign - what kind of help were you looking for?" I probably sound as nervous as I feel.

She places the to-go cup on the counter in front of me and hits me with another, what I'm now recognizing as a very genuine, bright smile.

"Are you looking for a job?!" she exclaims.

"I mean, yeah, but-"

"Easy enough, you're hired. I don't do interviews. They always feel so serious, and both the interviewer and the candidate are putting on this act. I hate it."

"Wait, seriously?" I ask.

"When I took over Red's from my parents, I said I was doing things differently. This place is built on vibes, and I can already tell you're gonna fit right in. When can you start?" She places her hand on one hip.

I take a sip of my coffee and almost audibly moan. "Okay, first of all, thank you. Second of all, this is heaven in a cup. You have no idea how badly I needed this. This being the caffeine *and* the job. But I should be upfront. I have next to no experience. Actually, even that's a stretch. I've only been on this side of a coffee counter. You're sure?"

Red laughs and scoffs, "Of course, I'm sure. I promise I can teach you everything you need to know. Besides, you think this is for you, but I spend every day here. Don't get me wrong, owning this business has been a dream of mine forever... My parents set me up. But I'm still in my twenties."

She leans over the counter and lowers her voice. "Between you and me, I've thrown myself in here instead of dealing with some things. Maybe this is my sign to finally face them, you know? Live my life again."

"Then I can start as soon as you need me, boss." I outstretch my arm to shake hands again, but Red jumps over the bar and pulls me into the tightest hug of my life. She's tall, and I am very much not, so my face is squished right into her chest. While this should be awkward because we are literal strangers, it's oddly a very comforting hug.

"Oh girl, we're family now. You're a part of Red's Place. Get used to this. When Beth flew through here this morning, she mentioned you came into town today. If you need help unpacking, text me." She takes the to-go cup from my hands, writes her number on it with a heart, and hands it back to me.

"Otherwise, I'll see you Monday. We open at six, so is it good for you to meet me here at 5:30? I'll have a set of keys made for you, too. John over at the hardware store has a bunch of Disney designs to pick from. Do you have a favorite character?" Note to self: Red rambles.

"5:30 is perfect for me and umm…Elsa? From *Frozen*?"

"Ooo, the Ice Queen. A little damaged, a lot hot. I'm onto you, and I like it, Margot. I'll see you Monday. Or earlier if you need help or company. My offer stands!" Red blows me a kiss, hops back over the counter, and saunters into the back.

Holy shit. Has this entire day been real? I planned on sitting at whatever coffee shop I found to scroll through job listings, but now I'm wired and have A JOB. A job where I'm *doing* something. It has purpose. Okay, it's not life-altering like brain surgery or anything, but I'm contributing good to someone's day, damn it. I'm excited, and as sad as it is to admit, I haven't felt excited about my day-to-day life for… I don't even know how long.

I'm on my way back to my car, coffee in hand, quietly singing "Show Yourself" from *Frozen 2* because even mentioning Elsa got it stuck in my head. When I get to the driver's side, I see an olive green Jeep parked inches away from my car that wasn't there when I pulled in. What a fucking asshole. Who parks this close to another car? They're lucky they didn't *hit* my car. I'm positive I can't even shimmy my ass between the two vehicles, never mind trying to open my door without denting the Jeep.

They'd deserve it, but I'm having a good day, so I have to keep putting that energy back into the universe. I head to the passenger door and crawl over to the driver's seat. I'm backing out and about to put my car in drive when I slow to look at the plate on the Jeep. I'm committing it to memory so I can avoid the car around town when I see a Millennium Falcon sticker on the bumper.

What a weird wave of deja vu.

# Chapter Three

*Sawyer*

YOU'D THINK nobody in this goddamn town has ever met a new person with the way they're obsessing over Gran's new tenant. I've been waiting in line to pick up my pizza from George's for five minutes, and I've had to endure three separate conversations about whatever her name is. Now that I think about it, Gran never even told me her name.

"Did you know she's starting at Red's?"

"I heard she's running away from some skeevy boyfriend."

"So you're saying she's single."

Alright, I've had enough. "Hey, Dean, before you go pick out a ring for the new girl, maybe think about moving out of your mom's basement," I say loud enough for him and everyone in here to hear without looking up from my phone. I definitely should not be engaging with this asshole when I'm already not in the best mood, but he makes it too fucking easy.

"Christ, Hale. Way to kick a guy while he's down. You

could have just told me you already called dibs," Dean mutters as the laughter around us dies down.

I finally lift my head and look Dean right in the eye when I say, "You can't call dibs on someone, you ass. Maybe your marriage wouldn't have fallen apart, and you wouldn't be back at your mom's instead of enjoying a life with Red if you didn't think and fucking talk like you do."

Now, along with the laughter, all conversation has halted. You could hear a pin drop in here. Alright, guess I took it too far. Wouldn't be the first time.

I've lived in Merrymount for a good chunk of my life, and I've been going at it with Dean Fitzgerald for just as long. It was easy for us to become friends when we were younger because what else do you need in common growing up aside from being the same age in the same classroom?

But as we entered high school, Dean became the classic douchebag because he thought his looks gave him a pass, and they did until they didn't. Like when his wife caught him cheating on a "work trip," and he said that since it was outside of the town lines, it didn't count.

Red threw all of his shit on their front lawn and called John down to change the locks within an hour. I wish someone had recorded it. Hell, I would have recorded it if I was there.

Not that I was always the poster child for The Good Guy, but I was raised by strong women. I've definitely messed up and broken some hearts, well, one heart that I know of, but it's never been intentional. I know the rules. You walk on the outside of the sidewalk, you hold the umbrella over a girl when it's raining, and you end it before you cheat. It's basic. But apparently, not simple enough for Dean over here.

"I forgot we were all in the presence of perfection. I'm out of here. My shift starts in ten."

Dean tries to shoulder-check me on his way out, but he

loves to forget that at 6'3", I'm almost half a foot taller than he is, and his shoulder doesn't quite line up with mine.

I finally make it to the counter and see George shaking his head, laughing as he says, "Man, you never let up on him. He needs someone to keep him in check, though."

"I really don't need it to be me," I say.

"Too much ego on that one. I have your small cheese here. You need anything else?"

"No thanks, George. That'll be it. Gran's making dinner over at her place later tonight, so this'll hold me over." I hand him a ten-dollar bill in exchange for the pizza.

George Forbes is the third George that I know of to own this place. He graduated a couple years ahead of me in school and left Merrymount to go to college, but, like almost everyone, he came back after. He said no other place felt like home. Within a year of his return, a summer tourist got lost and somehow ended up in the pizza shop asking for directions and to borrow a charger for his dead phone.

George and John have been inseparable since. They got married at the courthouse on Christmas Eve that same year, and by New Year's Eve, they were signing papers to open John's Locksmith right next door to George's Pizza. They're good people.

"Tell Beth I said hey when you see her and make sure your new neighbor feels at home. We all know Dean isn't the best spokesman for Merrymount, and we want to make a good impression. Get to her before he does, yeah?" George looks me in the eye as if there's some hidden meaning in what he says. But I'm out the door, waving a hand above my head as a goodbye and avoiding making any further comment.

Have I mentioned how unbearably nosy everyone is? I don't even know this new girl's name, but I wonder if she knows she's the topic of the entire town's conversations. I would hate to be in her shoes. While I really have no idea if she's running away from a boyfriend, I do expect there has to be a reason for her to move to a new town by herself where no one knows who she is.

When Gran said she found a tenant for Cottage B, I assumed it was going to be someone from Merrymount. I love this place with my whole heart, clearly, because I still haven't left and have no plans to do so. But, it's a small town that doesn't change very often, including the composition of residents who live here. We all know each other. It's a big, dysfunctional family. I hope whoever she is, she's ready for the welcome committee.

Backing out of my spot on the street, I head right back towards the riverside. I have a few things to finish up work-wise before dinner later. I pry open the pizza box sitting on my passenger seat and grab a slice.

▭

I NEED to stop by my place before heading to Gran's. I should probably change before dinner. I've been by the river all day, and although I didn't do too much manual labor-wise, I respect my grandmother too much to show up looking sloppy. Plus, she'd hit me on the backside of my head.

I'm not avoiding the new tenant, but I'm also not going out of my way to introduce myself. If the rumor mill is right, she'll be working at Red's, so Red can be her guide around town. That's right up her alley anyway, and I bet she'd love the distraction. Maybe the new arrival could use a friend. I don't have the mental capacity to take on that kind of project right now. But of course, to get to my place, I have to pass her cottage.

Slowly driving by, I look over to my right and notice she clearly wasted no time unpacking because what was once an old front porch, covered in dirt and cobwebs, has been transformed into… Well, the only way I know how to describe it is as… a fairy garden?

There are industrial string lights zigzagging across the top of the porch, flowers *everywhere*, and one of those egg-shaped chairs with way too many pillows shoved in it. It looks nice, I guess. It's just a lot. I can't even imagine what she did with the inside.

I park my jeep in front of my house and hop out, immediately hit with whatever Taylor Swift song is blasting out of the windows of the cottage next door. Great. We're going to have to work on noise control, apparently. Whatever. That's not my problem right now. The plan is to get in, change, and get out before I have to deal with anything related to next door.

My phone rings just as I get through my front door. I fish it out of my pocket and see Gran's face across the screen. She must have forgotten something for dinner and wants me to stop by the store before heading over to her place.

"Hey, Gran, I'm about to be on my way. Need anything?"

She jumps right into things without pause or even a greeting. "Is your new neighbor home? What do you think about inviting her over for dinner? She didn't have anyone helping her move in, so she must be some kind of alone. First night in a new place. I bet she could use the company." Subtle is not in Beth Rivers's vocabulary.

Leave it to the woman who can't say no to a single cat that finds its way on her porch to think of including the stranger next door for dinner her first day in Merrymount. We don't even know her, and from what I've seen, I'm good with keeping my distance.

"I think we should let the new tenant get settled on her own," I gruff into the phone.

If Gran wants whatever her name is at dinner so bad, she can call the woman her damn self. I put the phone on speaker and set it on the kitchen table. I toss the small pizza box with a couple leftover pieces in the fridge and head into my bedroom to quickly change into a new pair of jeans and an old Rivers' River t-shirt.

Not even two minutes later, I'm out the door, making a beeline to my Jeep before she can try to change my mind about my *new neighbor* when I stop dead in my tracks at the corner. I can barely hear Gran scolding me over the phone about being hospitable when I interrupt, "Gran, I'll call you back."

I end the call before she can respond, blindly putting my phone in my back pocket and staring at the cottage next door. Well, not the cottage. I'm staring through my Jeep's windows at the five-foot-nothing pixie girl of my dreams standing on her own front porch.

She has the biggest scowl on her face, eyebrows scrunched together, but that look that could kill isn't aimed at me, it's at my Jeep. She's barefoot, wearing jean shorts that are so frayed and so short, I'm convinced she cut them herself. It's April, and not nearly warm enough out here for shorts like that. I'm not complaining, though, because while she lacks height, her legs are sinfully long and not a sight you want to look away from.

I can't make out what her shirt says because her arms are angrily crossed over her chest, but I can see a sternum tattoo peeking out of the bottom of her faded black crop top. She has no makeup on, and freckles dot her face from cheekbone to cheekbone. Her blonde hair is in a messy bun, sitting lopsided on the top of her head.

It's the same face I've thought about for a year now. Even in her disheveled, pissed-off state, she's just as stunning as I remember her from that one night last spring. Before I went ahead and fucked it all up.

# Chapter Four

*Margot*

YOU'VE GOT *to be fucking kidding me.*

The parking asshole from downtown is my neighbor? I shouldn't even be surprised. This would be my luck. Everything was going too smoothly to let this day end on a good note.

Wait. If they're my neighbor, that means the Jeep's owner is Beth's grandson. *Fucking fantastic.* No, you know what? This is fine. I lived in the city long enough to know I didn't have to be friends with my neighbor. We can ignore each other as long as he doesn't park anywhere near my car. I can't afford any issues.

I'm so lost in my spiral I barely register the man's voice as he comes around his Jeep.

"Margot?"

Did his grandmother tell him about me? I look through the other side of the Jeep and focus on the man walking around to meet me. My brain takes a second to catch up to what I'm seeing, and then it takes everything in me not to duck and cover, as if that could get me out of the situation I just landed myself in.

No. *Nononononononono.*

He slowly steps forward and looks at me cautiously as if asking himself if I remember him. Or, based on his hesitancy, he's worried I'm going to hit him. I try to morph the expression on my face into one of indifference. Maybe I can use his hesitation and pretend I'm the cool girl who didn't get hung up on the guy who blew me off after one date. "Hey, wow. Margot, it's me. Uh, Sawyer Hale. From-"

"Dinner at Rosie's. Yeah," I say, cutting him off, deadpanned. *Okay, smooth, Margot. Way to play that off like you didn't recognize him.* I uncross my arms and place my hands on my hips. I'm about to turn around and make a run to the safety of my cottage when he starts talking again.

"Holy shit! What are the chances? What are you doing in Merrymount? What about Boston?" he asks.

He remembers? How do I respond to that when *I* don't even know what I'm doing here? Looking at my new neighbor, I'm suddenly questioning my decisions. God, the universe really knows how to fuck with me.

He looks and sounds like he's almost relieved to see me. I need time to process this, and I'd rather get away from him before his girlfriend shows up. Or maybe it's fiancée, now? I make a quick note that there's no ring on his finger so it's safe to assume he's not married, I guess.

"I just thought I'd… try something new." I manage to put together a full sentence: go me. Now, I have to get the hell away from him.

"I'm a little biased, but I think you picked the best damn place in the world if you're looking for a fresh start." He takes his baseball hat off and runs his hand through his hair. Still perfectly messy.

And then he goes ahead and puts the baseball hat back on. Backwards.

Fuck.

"I'm not running away from anything if that's what you thought." I almost shout at him and then immediately look at the ground.

"Woah, I wasn't assuming anything, but you did move to a new town alone, so I thought-  Oh, maybe you're not alone. I'm sorry. Actually, yeah. That makes sense." Sawyer starts rambling and basically talking more to himself than to me. He takes one tentative step forward.

I roll my eyes and look up to meet his. "Not that it's any of your business, but I am here alone, and I'm in the middle of unpacking. So, if you need a cup of sugar or an egg, knock on my door. Otherwise, I'll see you around, Sawyer." This time, I do manage to fully turn around and start to walk back to my door, needing distance between us right now.

*A cup of sugar? An egg? What is wrong with me?*

I hear him take a step towards me. "No, Margot. Wait. Hold on. We're getting off on the wrong foot here-"

I do a quick swivel around, interrupting him as I do.

"And learn how to park your goddamn car!" I shout at him before he can say something nice and make me change my mind about him.

I do another pivot and book it into my cottage, slamming the door before I can catch his response. I don't care what he would have said anyway. I hear him sigh just before I listen to his footsteps walk away.

Why is this happening? This is like the plot of a bad movie or something. I'm a good person. I tip well. I pay my taxes. I brake for every animal, damn it.

Maybe I'm overreacting. It was just one date. It wasn't like he broke off an engagement. Why am I so stuck on this?

I'm asking myself this like I don't already know the answer.

He's another reminder of yet another failure. And a damn good-looking one at that. I really tried to downplay how hot he was this past year, but all of that progress has been squashed.

Today, he was in jeans with holes that look like they came from hard work outdoors and not bought off the rack. They're just short enough to see his slutty ankles, a weakness I didn't know I had until right now, apparently. His scruffy facial hair and faded T-shirt are so simple that my brain must be short-circuiting if I'm reacting like this. All I can think of is how much I would climb him like a goddamn tree. And that isn't even taking into account that backward hat. As soon as the thought crosses my mind, I look down and realize I look like a fucking mess.

If I'm being honest with myself, I've looked and felt like a mess for a while now.

Recapping the last ten minutes, I realize I might have gone a little overboard, but that's not out of character for me. Mom says I fly off the handle faster and hold a grudge better than most people. But this is *my* new beginning, and it's hard to call it that when something - *someone* - from the past is making a reappearance.

What I need to do is get a grip. Clearly, I was just very right in my original assessment of Sawyer Hale. He's a good guy, but he's not the guy for me. I can wave at him in passing and be a regular neighbor.

Saving me from my continuing spiral, my phone starts vibrating on the kitchen island, and I see the picture of my mom and me on my graduation day display on the screen. She made it almost to 6:00 p.m. before calling me to check in, and I have to say, I'm impressed by her self-restraint. It took a lot to convince her I could and wanted to do this on my own. But I won't lie and say I'm not relieved to hear her voice.

"Hey Mo-" I'm cut off before I can even put the phone on speaker.

"Baby! Not one picture, text, or call from you. I've been checking my phone in between lessons all day. Are you okay?"

"You do remember I'm not one of the little guppies in the morning swim class anymore, right?" I say through a half laugh, half sigh.

"My little guppy, you'll always be. It's just how it is."

While she started out as a lifeguard, Mom ended up taking over the entire swim program at our town's community pool. I was in elementary school. Besides me, it's her entire life. As she and I both got older, she stuck to a stricter schedule at work and delegated a lot to make sure I had a routine and someone at home, but five days a week, you'll find Melanie LeClair in the water, making sure every single person who enters that pool swims like a fish. She loves hard.

Melanie LeClair is also the biggest worrier I know.

"Mom, I moved thirty-five minutes from the house. You have my location on, and we talked less than twenty-four hours ago. I'm good - I'm more than good. I found a job!" I prattle on, conveniently leaving out any mention of he-who-lives-next-door.

"Having your location on and hearing your voice are two entirely different things. I am your mother. Actually, enough of just your voice. Switch it to video. Give me the grand tour! Oh, and tell me about the job! Jackie's on her way here to set up for Sophie's birthday party, but I have time."

We switch to video, and I can see my mom in her office. I actually watch the tension leave her face when she sees I'm in one piece. Coming up on her forty-fifth birthday, my mom looks great. More often than not, just like it is today, her hair is in a braid to keep it off her face, practical for being in the water all day. She's wearing a red lifeguard zip-up over one of her dozens of plain black one-piece bathing suits. She has no makeup on because she doesn't need it. The only things on her face are the clusters of freckles across her cheeks and nose, just like mine. She's been mistaken for my sister more times than I care to count, and she eats that shit up every single time.

When I went through an art phase in high school (one of my hundreds of phases), she let me paint an underwater mural on the wall in her office behind her. Don't get me wrong. It's not bad. Painting is just another thing I either failed at or didn't stick with. But true to who she is, Mom will never paint over it or change it because even if I'm failing or flaking, she's cheering me on.

"Well, it's a cottage, so this is basically it." I flip the camera on my phone so she can see.

I'm not saying that to downplay the place or throw myself a pity party. I already love the small space. I'm standing in the kitchen and you can see everything from this one spot, which is one part terrifying and one part comforting. I don't have any art hung up yet, but while the walls are empty, I currently can't see my kitchen table under the mountain of just about every knick-knack and home decor item I've acquired throughout my life, plus a few shopping bags and boxes.

After I left Red's, I jumped on the highway and headed to Target. I haven't figured out the laundry situation yet because I forgot to ask Beth, and I'm afraid to rely on my ability to unpack properly for clean underwear. While I was there, I splurged on a comfy chair for the front porch, so I can read and look out on the water, and picked up some other random things as a treat.

I found one of those metal baskets farmers had to store hay at an outdoor flea market last summer, and I've secured it to the wall above the couch to house all of my fuzzy blankets. Living alone made me a master of the power drill a long time ago.

The coffee table is already set up with coasters and a stack of books, some well-loved and read dozens of times. I know some people are very particular about book handling, but I like to write little notes in my margins and highlight my favorite parts. I'll admit I've even dog-eared many pages on late nights when I'm too tired to find something to bookmark where I stop.

The guy from the cable company is scheduled to come out tomorrow to set up the Wi-Fi, so my TV propped up on the floor is fine where it is for now. I'll figure out how to get it mounted another day, and if I can't, I'll just squirrel money away every week from my paycheck at Red's until I can get a TV stand. And then pay someone to build it for me.

I bought a ridiculously overpriced, fancy cloud couch when I first signed the lease to my apartment in Boston, and I set up movers to have it delivered sometime in the next week. Once that's here, the living room should be just about perfect.

The door to my bedroom is to the right of where the couch will go and, thank god, shut. I cannot have Mom on my ass about the state of it right now. Every single article of clothing I've ever owned is thrown across the entire room, clean and dirty clothes now mixed together to the point where I know I'm just going to have to wash all of them. I really didn't mind the idea of downsizing until I thought too much about the lack of closet space I now have.

After panning around the room so Mom can see everything *except* my bedroom, I look back at the screen, anxiously awaiting her reaction.

"Oh honey, it looks like something you would find in a book! I love it. Do you love it?" Mom looks so happy for me, and it makes me forget about everything that has gone wrong and could still go wrong. I don't want to admit how much I need her approval on this, but this feels good.

"I'm really happy, Mom. I think this is going to be good for me." I switch the camera back to me so she can actually see I mean what I say. I don't need her worrying as much as she does.

"Well, now that I know you're not homeless, tell me about the job. What glamorous establishment gets the honor of employing my girl?"

"Okay, one, you're the most dramatic person I know. Two, I don't know if I would consider a coffee shop glamorous, but the owner, my boss, Red, is probably the coolest woman I've ever met. She didn't even interview me; she just told me the job was mine if I wanted it. I don't have a set schedule yet, but I'm starting on Monday, and I'm excited. I know it's not…" I trail off. I forgot about the guilt for a minute.

When you're raised by a young, single mom, and that mom pays your way through college, and now you're throwing away the degree to essentially run away… you feel really fucking shitty.

"Margot Dorothea. Don't even start with me." The softness has left her voice. "I am so proud of you. I'm going to say it again. I'm proud of *you*. Not your job title or degree. Not some fancy apartment in Boston with no personality. If you're happy, everything was worth it, and I've done my job. Hell, I can't wait to get off the phone with you and brag about my barista baby to anyone who'll listen! Just let me know when I can head down to harass you for a drink."

There is no use in arguing with her about this. I'm the one beating myself up. "I know, Mom. I know. It's all good here." I quickly look up and hope she doesn't see me trying to will the tears back into my head.

I hear a faint knock and the click of a door opening before Mom says, "Oh, hey, Jackie! No, come on in. It's just Margot. She's showing me her new place. Our girl's a barista, Jack! Can you believe it? Baby, Jackie's here, so I'm gonna go help her set up. Text me your schedule when you get it. I love you, my girl." She scrunches her nose in a wiggle and blows me a kiss.

"I love you too, Mom. Tell Jackie I said hi!" I hit end on the screen and plop onto the couch.

Well, that took up barely ten minutes of my time, and I have no other plans for the rest of the night… or the foreseeable future other than work at this point. With no Wi-Fi and my e-reader dead in a box somewhere, I'm out of options beyond continuing to unpack. It's not exactly the exciting, fresh start I was looking for, but nonetheless, it *is* a fresh start. I could go grocery shopping, but that feels like a tomorrow project.

I throw back on my *Best Bridges of Taylor Swift* playlist, and *The Best Day* starts to play. I head into the kitchen and grab the first box I see on the table. I open it up and smile, again holding back those tears that have decided to try to make a reappearance. Of course, it's my box of framed pictures. Right on the top is one of my favorite pictures I've taken of my mom in a frame I found at a flea market a few years back.

We were on a road trip from Massachusetts to Nashville because we once spent a weekend watching every single food channel show about places to eat there, and we were committed to crossing off as many as we could on that list. It was her graduation present to me when I finished high school. We decided to stop in Virginia Beach for the night and were walking along the water.

Mom was just a little up ahead of me, searching for sea glass. She must have seen something especially good because I remember hearing her excited "Oh!" as she bent down to pick up whatever it was. I picked up the camera hanging around my neck and caught her big, giddy smile when she turned around to show me her find.

In the picture, her hair is almost completely out of the braid she put it in that morning. Her long, curly brown strands were being blown around from the ocean's air. She had her sandals in her left hand, holding up the small ivory clover-shaped shell with the right, and wearing a sheer white sundress to cover her classic red one-piece bathing suit. She looks so beautiful.

That's how the entire trip went. Small, silly, happy moments. When it came time for me to choose which picture to frame to encapsulate the trip, I couldn't think of a better one.

Some would argue the little moments don't deserve to be captured in photos for the rest of forever because they're not as important. But to them, I proudly say, "You're wrong!" People deserve to see and remember what they looked like and how they felt during the quiet happy just as much as the big happy.

I place the frame next to me to start a pile for the gallery wall I'm going to put together in the living room and get started on sorting through the rest of the box.

# Chapter Five

*Sawyer*

"ALL I'M SAYING IS it wouldn't kill ya to make friendly with her."

Gran has been going on about Margot since I walked in the door almost twenty minutes ago, and honestly, I don't blame her. Margot is the kind of woman I knew Gran would love instantly. I almost told Margot that on our date and then realized that might have been weird. In my defense, I've only been on two first dates in my almost thirty years of life, and the one with Margot was the second.

Gran still thinks I'm going to be the asshole next door who pays Margot no mind like I do with every woman that Gran tries to get me to latch onto. She does it with every woman she meets who is even remotely close to my age, so she doesn't see me back with Katie. But this is different because it's Margot, and *I know her.*

Okay, we went on one date, and I royally fucked it up almost immediately after, so I don't *really* know her, but she's still different from the others. This is the first girl who didn't know me from Merrymount and didn't look at me with pity when I mentioned my parents. She didn't question why I never left my small town or why I didn't need more out of life. I've replayed that night in my head so many times over the last year and wondered what the hell I was thinking when I agreed to give Katie another chance. Again.

Katie St. James and I were first seated next to each other in the sixth grade when I moved in with Gran after my parents died, but I recognized her from my summers spent in Merrymount before then. When you grow up in a place like Merrymount, the kid you befriend on the first day of school sticks with you for life. It only made sense as we got older that we'd end up together, and it worked until it didn't. She was my first and only everything. As shitty as it sounds, I stayed with her longer than I should have and then kept coming back because I felt like I owed her.

We fought about everything. She wanted to move to the west coast and couldn't fathom why I wanted to stay in Merrymount. It had always been my plan to stay, and I had been upfront with her about that, but she always acted surprised when I reaffirmed that desire. She thought I was too close to my grandmother and was always discouraging me from helping Gran out.

I wanted to spend time with Katie, but it constantly felt like we never wanted to do the same things. I'd suggest a cooking class, and she'd suggest a luxury spa day. I'd ask to do some hiking or walking trails in the area. She'd want to go to a popular club in the city. For her, the flashier, the better. I'd ask for pineapple on pizza, but she'd say it's vile. I'd say Star Wars is one of the best cinematic universes ever created, and she'd blanch and refuse to watch a single movie. She wanted a whole pack of Goldendoodles, and I was perfectly fine helping take care of the stray cats Gran collects. You name it, we disagreed on it. I think, at some point, the drama just felt familiar, and when we would break up, it was basically a given we'd get back together after we cooled down.

Whenever we went out to dinner or a party, someone would jokingly ask when there would be wedding bells for us. Katie would smile and wave them off, saying we were in no rush. We were meant to be regardless. She always knew how to put on a show.

But as soon as we were alone, it was World War III. She'd scream and cry, but she was also cruel and manipulative. Honestly, she was just really fucking mean. She loved to remind me if it wasn't for her, I'd be alone. She'd remind me that she was doing me a favor by staying with me since nobody would ever want a small-town bumpkin like me. She'd tear me down until I was convinced I was as worthless as she said.

Sometimes, the fights would last a few hours, others a couple days. But eventually, one of us would cave, and we'd be back to doing the same shit on repeat.

And then she cheated.

One time, apparently. *Only one time,* she had said.

She said it was because I didn't pay enough attention to her. I wasn't building for a future with her. She needed to blow off some steam. I wasn't exciting enough. She thought I wouldn't notice. It wasn't a big deal. It was something she had to do and something the two of us could get over together. I didn't say anything. Not a single word. She was screaming and crying and asking me to do something, but I couldn't.

After telling Gran and Gus I needed time away, I took off for a whole week and left my phone on my kitchen table. It was a no-questions-asked, check-in-when-you-can situation. I packed a backpack with some clothes and my wallet and bolted.

I found myself driving south with no destination in mind. If I found a decent enough hotel, cool. If I had to sleep in the

Jeep, fine by me. I was at the point where I cared about nothing.

Maybe Katie was right. If I didn't have her, I'd be alone. I couldn't tell if that was a good or a bad thing anymore. Like I said, I didn't give a fuck.

A few weeks passed, and I still refused to speak to her, even once I came home. I ignored every call and text. I didn't answer the door when she showed, and I crashed at Gus' more times than I'd like to admit to avoid her. I told myself I was better off without Katie, and that's the life I was supposed to live.

Until Gran fell and broke her leg. The femur, too. The fucking big one. So she was in the hospital for a few days and caught pneumonia, she declined so fast, and I was a fucking wreck.

I took it all back. I didn't mean *alone* alone. There couldn't be a life without my grandmother already. We had more time. I didn't think I could do it all over again.

And then Katie showed up at the hospital. Looking back, she used my weakest moment to slide her way back in. I see that now. But then? It seemed safe to say yes to her when she walked into the waiting room where I was pacing. She seemed genuinely concerned for Gran and me, bringing me food and just being there, I guess. I wanted to forget the issues for the time being, and she clearly felt the same.

So, as soon as Gran turned the corner and was discharged, the cycle continued. The fights started back up, mixed in with a new layer of trust issues that neither of us even tried to resolve. We talked nothing out.

The last break-up was brutal. I mean, none have been pleasant. Katie's not… quiet. But I just knew this last one was something we couldn't come back from. *I* couldn't come back from.

*We've been back together for about six or seven months. Katie is* staying at my place more often than not, so I had a key made for her over at John's. I think giving her a key would help hold off a conversation about what we are doing and where we are heading for a little while longer. It sounds shitty, but I need time.

I'm not ready for her to actually move in, nor does she want to. She's always sending me listings for houses for sale and rental properties, all of course, outside of Merrymount. Katie always says the cottage is mine and we need something that is ours.

After wrapping up work over at the Riverside, I head home. As soon as I walk in the door, I can tell it's going to be a long night. The cottage is filled with the kind of tension you physically feel almost immediately. It's dark except for my bedroom light spilling into the living room, and I can hear Katie sniffling.

"Katie? You in there?" I call out as I walk through the house but get no response other than shuffling and a drawer closing.

"Katie, I can see the light on. What's going on-"

I walk into my bedroom doorway and see Katie, tears streaming down her face, holding my mother's engagement ring, the ring my dad gave my mom when he promised her forever. I stand there, not moving. Not sure what to do next.

"Were you ever planning on giving me this, or were you just stringing me along for fun?" she snaps.

The funny thing is I did plan on giving her that ring. Just a long fucking time ago, before we entered our toxic cycle of fighting, breaking up, and getting back together. Before she felt comfortable fucking someone else because she knew I'd come back around.

"Katie, what the fuck are you doing with my mom's ring? What are you doing snooping through here, period?" I quickly shoot back at her.

"I can't believe I wasted my entire life on you, Sawyer! I've given you everything. I've stayed in this shitty, good-for-nothing, middle-of-nowhere town. I've waited for you to come around to the idea that we're getting older and it's time for the next step, but I'm TIRED OF WAITING." She screams it at me, tears still pouring out, her hand still clutching my mom's ring.

*I wish I could say this is the first time something like this has happened. Or even the third time. But if I'm finally going to be completely honest with myself, this has been unraveling for a while, since before the last break up, before anything that happened in the last couple years between us.*

*"You know you sound insane, right? Can you maybe chill for five minutes so we can rationally talk about you looking through my stuff while holding my dead mother's ring?" I'm seeing red at this point. I walk over and pluck the ring from her hand, placing it in its small, black velvet box and putting it back in my top drawer, where it belongs.*

*I try not to yell in arguments. I don't think it ever gets your point across and it makes it difficult for the person on the other end to see where you're coming from, but I'm beyond being rational with her.*

*"I don't think it's insane to question why you haven't proposed after a decade together!"*

*"Do you not remember me finding out you fucked your coworker in a bar bathroom?"*

*She sucks in a breath, too stunned to respond. We haven't talked about that night since.*

*Katie St. James is a smart, talented, gorgeous woman. She always had been. I loved her for a long time, but standing there looking at her, makeup running down her face, it finally hits me, and I realize that there is never going to be a right time for us. I'm never going to be able to promise Katie forever. I don't want this.* Fortunately for my well-being, and unfortunately for the fate of our relationship, *I finally realize being alone is the better option.*

*I keep going, "Say we even pretend to forgive and forget that bullshit, we've been back together for barely half a year. And you know what? No, I haven't thought about proposing. Not fucking once. You know what I have thought about? How tired I am of THIS."*

*And I mean it. I'm tired of the fighting, and I'm done apologizing for living the life I want to live because it's not fitting the St. James's plan. I'm never going to be good enough. I wake up every day asking myself what the hell I'm doing, and it finally hits me: I've loved Katie out of obligation, and that's not fair to either of us.*

*The shitty thing is, she's right. It's kind of insane that I haven't proposed over the last ten or so years before the cheating. From the outside and on paper, we should be married and happy with a kid or two in a town like this. Hell, we should at least have gotten a dog together. But I can't see it. That's not the big picture for us.*

*Everything becomes scary quiet. "You don't mean that."*

*I let out a sigh I think I've been holding in for the last decade. "Yeah, Katie. I definitely think I do."*

I shake my head to come back to the present. I tuned Gran out, getting lost in my memories, and now I'm about to face the repercussions of that decision. She's staring at me like she's waiting for a response, and I don't have a fucking clue what she could have asked.

"I take it you think it's a shit idea." She looks at me like she might be just a little disappointed in me.

I don't think Gran has ever said a negative thing to me about how I live my life, but I can tell I'm starting to hurt her. I've noticed it more and more lately. She had to bury her only daughter and son-in-law and got stuck with the emotionally stunted grandson because of it.

I've been this way - *distant* - since my parents died. Though, my solitude is not from her lack of trying to help me. After the accident, she found me a therapist who could help me cope with joining the dead parents club at twelve years old. She made sure I was signed up for sports so I would have non-school contact with other kids (even though nothing really stuck). She threw me a birthday party every year, inviting every single resident of Merrymount. I'm pretty sure she threatened their lives if they didn't come. Gran wanted me to know that while she couldn't bring my parents back, she'd make sure there would always be people showing up for me.

This isn't to say she failed. I just think I'm better off alone.

"Gran, I'm gonna be honest, I haven't been listening to a single thing you've been saying, but if it's your idea, I'm sure it's a great one. And you'll go ahead with it whether you have my approval or not." I wink at her to try to lighten the mood.

The disappointment vanishes from her face, and it's replaced with something I hate even more, a curious look that I know will lead to a mile-long list of questions.

"You met her," Gram says matter of factly, a sly smile creeping out.

"I-"

"Don't lie to me, Sawyer Hale. You met our new girl, Margot, and you like what you saw."

This all could have been avoided, and I wouldn't have been blindsided if Gran had told me her name at least once. Then again, what would I have done? Told her to pick a different applicant to avoid seeing Margot? Would I have reached out?

I briefly give lying a thought. But if I pretend I don't know Margot, Gran will try to make introductions. I won't have a chance to clue Margot in about pretending to be strangers, so she might throw me under the bus without meaning to (or on purpose. She didn't seem too pleased to see me earlier today), and then I'll have to admit I lied. While I've done my fair share of shady shit behind Gran's back as a teen, we don't lie about stuff like this to each other.

"It's her, Gran." I let out a sigh.

Her smirk disappears, replaced by an expression that implies I've just formed three heads. "I missed something. I'm confused. Who?"

"Margot is the girl."

"The girl…" she trails off. She puts the fork she was using to eat dinner down, clearly deciding this is a conversation that needs her full, undivided attention. Maybe her grandson has finally cracked.

She's not getting it, and I'm going to have to explain that

I've embarrassingly thought about a girl that I had one single date with for over a year. I told Gran about the date, but how often Margot has been on my mind is something I've actively avoided telling anyone. I even refused to tell my best friend, August, and he knows more about me than anyone.

I take a deep breath. This is going to extend dinner, and I was really hoping for an early night. "I went out on a date with Margot last spring, during the last break Katie and I had. I might have mentioned it." I look down, pushing the shepherd's pie around my plate in an attempt to distract myself.

"Margot is the girl," Gran quietly states.

"Okay, I think we've established that. But also, Gran, before you start, and I know you're gonna start - I can practically hear the gears in your head warming up - I'm gonna ask you to pump the brakes. I ran into her on my way over here. She's freaked the hell out, and I need to respect her space. She just moved to a new place alone. Do we even know why she moved?"

"I can't say I wouldn't be freaked the hell out, too, if my past fling was my new neighbor… but your mom would have said this was a sign."

"I'm not a 'past fling,'" I huff. I knew she'd be difficult. "We went out one time. You know what? Not important. Gran, seriously. Do we think she's running from something? Maybe someone?" I point my fork at her. The more I think about it, the more I think it's weird Margot would just show up in a random, small town by herself.

"Well, don't you sound like a regular ole Merrymounter with your theories on the new girl?" She smiles at me, tilting her head to the side slightly. "I can't be sure, but I don't think she's running. When I saw her earlier today, she didn't mention anything, and the town gossip hasn't picked up on any red flags yet. Maybe this is just a right place, right time situation."

"Yeah… Written in the stars or whatever Mom would say, right?" A quick, sarcastic laugh escapes me.

Gran apparently doesn't appreciate my humor because she drops her smile. "Actually, my boy, yes. Written in the stars *is* something Nora would have said, and she would have followed it up with the same question I'm going to ask you. What are you going to do about it?"

I have no fucking idea.

On the drive over here, I purposely threw my music on shuffle and cranked it because I need to clear my head before getting to Gran's. I had no plans of bringing this up tonight.

Margot is here in Merrymount. Not only that, Margot is my next-door neighbor, in my family's cottage, and alone. I'm assuming that means she's single. I won't lie and admit a part of the reason that I didn't reach back out was because I was embarrassed and actively trying to avoid getting a drink thrown in my face. Which I wouldn't have blamed her for.

We had a great night together, and even that's an understatement. She's so animated when she talks, always using her hands and making different, dramatic facial expressions when she's telling a story. I could have let her read me the menu word for word at dinner and would have been entertained. I remember the waiter, for the third time, asking us if he could help us with anything else, clearly trying to politely shoo us out of the restaurant, after the table had been cleared and the check paid for, I don't even know how long before. I realized that I didn't want to leave. She just made me feel lighter.

I remember walking her to her car and grabbing her hand to hold without even thinking about it. It was so small in mine that we ended up just linking our pinkies. I kissed her hand and wished her goodnight before shutting her driver's door. I didn't even unlock my Jeep until I watched her drive away.

Gus had told me before I left Merrymount to play it cool and not immediately text her after, and I thought that'd be easy. It was dinner with someone I met online. I had a better chance of walking away with a funny story to tell Gus when we got beers after work the next day than finding anything special. But on my ride home, I couldn't stop thinking about how I wanted to see her again. I should have told her to text me to let me know she made it home safely. I had to figure out how to go about this without making myself look like an idiot.

And yet, somehow, I got roped back into the toxic cycle with Katie, and that was my own fault and a decision I had to live with. So, reaching out to Margot after Katie and I ended things again, potentially making her feel like someone's second choice, just wasn't an option for me. I couldn't be selfish just because I made a bad call. Besides, Margot was incredible. I didn't know why she was on a dating app to begin with. In my mind, there was no way she'd be single for long. I just hoped whoever she found was appreciating her and not fucking blowing it like I did.

But clearly, things have changed. Maybe my mom really is calling some of the shots from up there because from what I can remember and what everyone around here tells me, she wholeheartedly believed in fate, a real *everything happens for a reason* kind of person. It's something that I refused to buy into because what twelve-year-old is going to hear and believe that when he just buried both of his parents?

If Margot is in Merrymount and planning on staying (and judging from the signed twelve-month lease sitting on Gran's counter, she is) and if she's single, this is my chance to right my wrong. I realize I have no idea how to do that and reluctantly admit to myself that I'm going to have to enlist some help from my sixty-eight-year-old grandmother and my shut-in of a best friend. The odds are stacked against me, but I'm working with what I've got.

"Can I fix this? *Should* I fix this?" I ask Gran.

"Oh, Sawyer, your worst quality is your inability to see the good you bring to the table." She gets up from her seat, walks over, places her hand on my shoulder, and looks at me. "That girl, any girl, would be lucky to have you care about them. You don't let most people in, and I understand your pain is something I can't erase. I also can't promise easy. You say she's freaked, and I can't say I blame her. But you always have to try. Sitting back and watching others live their lives is just punishing yourself for no good reason. You're asking me the wrong questions."

"You want me to ask you *how* to fix this, and I can't lie. I'm a little scared of whatever idea you think you've come up with." I stand up, pick up both of our plates, and head to the sink to start cleaning up. She cooks, and I clean. Those are the rules.

Gran immediately starts laughing and heads over to her couch, picking up her Sudoku book - another post dinner requirement. She says it keeps her brain from going to mush.

"Just ask her out, Sawyer. You're not planning a proposal, and for as much as you beat yourself up, technically, you didn't do anything wrong. You didn't cheat. You didn't leave her hanging. You made a bad call, but you're a good guy. Margot will see that and give you another chance. And if she doesn't, well, you have a new neighbor that you'll actively try to avoid. It's the same thing you were going to do until you found out who she was."

Well, shit. She's… not wrong. I did try to do the right thing last year, and I would have continued to try to ignore her if it was anyone else living next door. I finish washing the dishes and walk into the living room to say goodnight to Gran before I head home to think things through about a hundred times.

"Do you want me to start the teapot before I leave?" I ask her.

She places her puzzle book down, "No. I'm tired myself and probably heading to bed as soon as you're out the door.

Felt like a big day, huh?" She lifts her head to give me a kiss on the cheek as I bend down to do the same.

"That's an understatement, Gran. Thanks for dinner. And thank you for everything else. I- I have a lot to think about." I head over to the door and put my work boots on. I open the front door to step out when my Gran says,

"I love you forever, my boy! Margot Hale has a nice ring to it, don't you think?!"

I knew I wasn't escaping without one wild comment from her. I throw out a "love you," and I'm out the door, refilling the cat food dish on her porch for the strays like the sucker I am.

———

I PULL into the shared driveway a little after 11:00 p.m. I spent some time driving around, giving everything Gran said some thought. The kitchen light at Margot's is still on, and before I can talk myself out of it, I'm putting my Jeep in park, hopping out, and walking over to her place. I have no plan and no idea what I'm going to say, but she didn't give me any time to get a word in earlier. So I'm going to make it up as I go.

For as much decorating as she did on the front porch, Margot clearly did not prioritize curtains because I can see right into the kitchen from the third step. I get to the top and stop dead in my tracks. Wearing the same shorts, shirt, and bun on the top of her head from earlier, Margot is slumped in a chair. The top half of her body is folded over the small kitchen table we've had in this cottage since before I can remember. Her arms are sprawled out on top of what looks to be piles of pictures. She must have fallen asleep while unpacking. I'm watching her back rise just a little with slow, rhythmic breathing when it hits me that I'm being a fucking creep.

I should turn around and get the hell in my house before she wakes up, catches me, and presses charges for stalking. I don't even think I'd blame her. But then I think about how uncomfortable she has to be, sleeping at the table like that. I didn't even think to ask Gran if she had someone helping her move in earlier or if movers were coming. Did she even have a bed set up? The cottage had some furniture already, like the table, but not everything somebody would need.

Without thinking, I gently tap on the window, trying to avoid scaring her but wanting her to wake up. She finally startles after my fifth or sixth tap and when she lifts her head and turns to see me in the window, she shrieks. Within half a second, she's up and flinging the front door open.

I can tell she's still half asleep because, suddenly, she's stumbling over nothing. Before she falls face-first down the stairs, I catch her with my hands on her hips. Her arms shoot out, and her hands reach up to find my shoulders.

I look down at the same time she looks up, and I suddenly forget how to breathe. I'm looking into her sleepy eyes, completely caught up in how green they are. They're a shade of sage I don't think I've seen on anyone before. Her lips are parted just a little bit, and her freckled cheeks are stained a bright pink. The lines on the left side of her face must have formed from sleeping on the pictures she had scattered on the table. Strands of blonde hair have fallen out of her messy bun, framing her face. She's breathing heavily, and I can feel goosebumps break out on her body where my hands are still firmly locked on her.

She's so goddamn beautiful.

I don't know how long we've been standing like this; it could be seconds or minutes. I'm sure as shit not going to be the one to let go. I can see when the realization of our situation finally dawns on her face, and she jumps back to the doorway, holding onto the frame for purchase.

"You're lucky I didn't kill you! What the hell are you doing here?" she yells, even though I am barely two steps away from her.

"Kill me? With what? An empty cardboard box? Or maybe you thought you'd strangle me with your fairy lights?" I gesture to the porch lights wrapped around the railing.

"Maybe I would have. You have no idea what I'm capable of, and I'm not about to give away all of my secrets. Answer the question, Sawyer. What are you doing here?"

"Margot- Listen. I- This is- I'm-" Wow. Maybe I should have given this some thought on the drive home or the walk over.

She lets out a sigh, sounding defeated, looks up at the sky and then back at me.

"Sawyer, don't. Please, I swear I had no idea Merrymount was yours. I sure as hell didn't know I was moving into your grandmother's cottage. We're neighbors, and I work at Red's. I'm so embarrassed, and I'm just asking you to show me one bit of mercy and just leave it at that. I'm here for the next twelve months, and then I promise I'll be out of your life. I don't want to cause any problems."

*Hold up. Embarrassed? What is she even talking about?*

"What are you embarrassed about?" I ask her.

She does the thing where she looks back up at the sky before looking at me again, this time leveling me with a glare that says I'm about to be kicked off this porch.

"I'm not explaining shit to you. In fact, I don't need to talk to you, period. I have one year here, and I'm going to make the best of it, okay? You fish on your side, I'll fish on mine. No one fishes in the middle. Now go home, Sawyer." She backs into the kitchen and slams the door shut. After a moment, I hear the click of the lock.

I'm standing on the porch, debating banging on the door until she opens it up to hash this out when everything goes dark. She managed to shut off the kitchen, front porch, and fairy lights almost simultaneously. Message received, Margot.

I'm not going to press this tonight. It's her first day in town. Never mind the surprise of me being in Merrymount, she just uprooted her life to move here. I'm man enough to admit defeat when it comes my way, and there's no sense in pushing her when it very well could lead to her taking off. After all, our interactions today both ended with her bolting and then slamming doors.

I need a game plan. I head down her stairs and make my way over to my cottage, pulling my phone out of my pocket and bringing up Gus' text thread. I shoot him a message saying I need to talk to him tomorrow at work. I'm not fucking this up again.

# Chapter Six

*Margot*

THE SUN HASN'T EVEN STARTED to rise, and yet here I am, yawning repeatedly in my driver's seat with the heat cranked, waiting to meet Red at the coffee shop. I could see my breath on my walk from my front door to my car this morning. The cold is not super common, but it is also not out of the question for early spring in Massachusetts.

It's not that Red's late. She told me to meet her here at 5:30. I just found myself unable to keep my brain quiet and eyes closed long enough to not show up unreasonably early for my first day on the job.

The clock on my dash reads 5:17 a.m., and, shit, I am not above counting down the seconds until Red gets here to unlock the doors so one of us can start a pot of coffee. I don't remember the last time I was awake in time to see the sunrise. I'm not *not* a morning person. But I'm also not going out of my way to beat the birds.

I didn't get much sleep this weekend. After my two unbelievably embarrassing interactions with Sawyer on Friday, I've successfully avoided him since, but that doesn't mean I haven't been on edge and in my head about the whole situation the entire weekend.

I still haven't braved the grocery store in town for fear of running into him or, worse, his girlfriend. I also held off on doing an online deep dive to find out anything about her or them together. I didn't look up her name or try to figure out how serious they'd gotten. Nothing. I'm proud of myself because, normally, I'd be throwing my FBI hat on to get every detail I could find. I am assuming they don't live together, though, or maybe she's out of town because Sawyer's Jeep is the only other vehicle I've seen in our shared driveway in the past couple days. Not that I was, like, keeping tabs or anything.

The anxiety of how this all could play out over the next year has made me pick up my phone to dial Beth to somehow get out of this lease too many times to count. I always manage to stop myself, though. I owe it to myself to see this through. I was serious about committing and doing this *for me.* And I'm not going to let a man get in the way of it. Even if said man is stupid hot.

I keep replaying Friday night in my head. I can still feel his hands splayed on my body, from the tops of my thighs to the bottom of my ribcage, and his shaky breath against my face. My entire body lit up like a fucking Christmas tree, the pins and needles causing goosebumps to break out everywhere, all because he was being a good guy and making sure I didn't faceplant and knock out my front teeth on the stairs. Apparently, I have no sense of balance when I'm jolted out of a dead sleep on my kitchen table.

I picture myself looking up at him, my hands gripping his shoulders like my life depended on it. For half a second, I felt it. That weird electric spark that disappears just as fast as it makes itself known. It happened a year ago when we locked pinkies, too.

*No, Margot. It didn't happen then, and it didn't happen the other night. Get out of the fantasy in your head.*

I spent the rest of my weekend holed up in the cottage, surviving off of the road trip snack box I usually keep in the trunk of my car. One would argue bags of chips and seasonally shaped Reese's peanut butter cups do not make well-balanced meals, but to hell with them.

I managed to unpack every single box I brought and fortunately accomplished getting my TV mounted in the living room. Margot LeClair, mover extraordinaire. Add it to my resume. Tell my mom.

Speaking of my mom, I might be half-avoiding her. I haven't completely ghosted her, because that would backfire on me and have her showing up at my door without notice to make sure I was alive, but I've kept texts short and only sent a few pictures to squash her worry. It seems to have placated her. She's responded with ridiculous GIFs and told me to call again once I was settled. She's really good at letting me know she cares without smothering me. And for that, I'm thankful.

I'm avoiding that call because I haven't made a decision on how to fill her in on the Sawyer situation. I wish I could say that when she eventually comes to visit, if he just happens to be around, I could casually introduce him as my neighbor, and things would be fine. But as soon as his name leaves his mouth, I know Melanie LeClair will whip her head towards mine with a knowing look.

*The* look. The "Oh how funny, your new hot neighbor has the same name as the hot guy you last went out with" look. She'd do it because she would think it was a crazy coincidence, an inside joke between the two of us, and I'd give myself away because I wear every emotion I've ever felt on my face.

And then shit would get awkward, and I would feel guilty,

and I'm about ready to break out in hives just thinking about it.

I'm sure most adult children are not as close with their moms as I am, and while I manage to remain insecure about most parts of myself, my relationship with my mom is sacred. It's something I'll never take for granted or feel embarrassed about. She always has made me feel like I never have to face anything alone. If I do, it's always by choice. I also never felt the need to keep secrets from her because she always taught me nothing could be worse than a lie between us. So, she knows all about my pitiful dating life.

I know I have to tell her. Just like, not right now. It's on the list of things I need to deal with. I'm just getting exceptionally good at procrastinating with some specific items on that list, it's fine.

Red never gave me a uniform or guidelines for dress code, nor did I really expect there to be one, seeing as how there was no formal interview, and Red was the only employee until I came along. So, I showed up this morning in a pair of black leggings, my comfiest running shoes, as I imagine I'll be on my feet a lot today, and a plain, black long-sleeve top. I put on some concealer and mascara to not scare away the customers with the bags that definitely have formed underneath my eyes, and French braided my hair down my back to keep my hair back, aside from some loose pieces in the front.

The coffee cup Red wrote her number on Friday afternoon is still sitting in my center console cup holder. I haven't put her number in my phone contacts yet and wanted to keep it there in case of an emergency. I'm debating finally giving her a call to make sure everything is okay when I see a Mini Cooper practically drift around the corner, flying down Main Street. The red car comes to a halt, stopped in the middle of the road, behind where my car is parked, and I can see Red, her long hair thrown up in a giant messy bun, rolling down her passenger side window.

"Ohmygosh-" Red yells out in a rush, "I'm *so* sorry I'm late! We have a few spots in the back for parking so we can keep the front clear for customers. Follow me around. I'll explain everything once we're inside, and I can get coffee started. I'm falling apart. Some first impression as a boss, huh?" She laughs to herself and rolls her window back up. I can see her rubbing her hands together and blowing into them. She must not have even given herself a minute to get her car warmed up.

Looking at the clock again, I see it's only 5:32. I would hardly call that late, but Red must really pride herself on being punctual. I guess you need to be when you're supplying the town with their morning coffee - people heading to work, school, or wherever. I'm not one of those people who is constantly late for everything. I just consider myself... realistically chill.

I throw my car in reverse and follow Red around to the back of the buildings that line Main Street. Each business has three designated parking spaces, plus a dumpster. The doors are all labeled with a business name and *"employees and deliveries only"* in script below. Red's area has two doors, though the second is unmarked.

I pull up and park in the second spot next to Red. I get out of my car, grabbing my tote bag that holds my wallet, a half-eaten bag of turkey jerky, a phone charger, and my keys. Clearly, I packed the necessities for my first day on the job.

Red is unlocking the labeled door on the left when she looks back at me smiling. "Let me try this again-" she says in a mockingly serious voice. "Good morning, Margot. So glad you made it, Margot. Welcome to the team, Margot." She salutes me and heads inside to start turning on the lights. I follow her in.

Even in her disheveled state, Red is still drop-dead gorgeous. Aside from her fiery hair that I'm pretty sure cannot be tamed, everything else about her today is tight. She has on black leather ankle boots, giving her a couple extra inches in height, and her high-rise dark wash jeans look like they were painted on or stitched perfectly to her measurements. They literally mold to her legs. The black long-sleeved top she picked cuts off just above her belly button, showing about half an inch of skin around. I notice she has the same two gold chains on she was wearing the other day. It seems as though Red also went minimal on makeup today, too. She has freckles dotting all over her face and down her chest, which I didn't see the other day. I look like her dorky, frumpy, younger sister standing next to her.

Red swoops through the space, like opening up requires no thought, and she's doing it from muscle memory, flicking on lights, lighting candles, and flipping what I can only assume are the on switches for multiple machines. I suddenly hear the soft piano version of one of my favorite Disney songs. When I look at Red, she turns away from a laptop on the counter that must be connected to the speakers.

"I swear I'll get my shit together and go over all of this in more detail on your next shift. But it's Monday morning, and I apparently am a poor planner when I'm working on two hours of sleep."

I've just been standing here in the middle of the space, my tote bag still slung on my shoulder, like an idiot. "No! It's fine! You're fine!" I say.

Red places her hands on her hips and levels me with a look. "Seeing as how my phone did not receive a single phone call or a text from you this weekend, we have a lot to go over, both professionally and personally. Don't think I'm letting you get out of this without a friendship. Unfortunately for me, luckily for you, I'm behind. I normally try to get here a little after five, but clearly, that didn't fuck- freaking happen this morning," she huffs.

I laugh. "Red, you don't have to worry about swearing in front of me. I can handle it."

"Oh! Oh no. Oh my gosh, no. I have the worst mouth. Dean says it's unattractive, and I'm trying to work on it."

"Dean?" I question. What kind of asshole cares if a woman swears?

"Shit. I mean- no, I meant shit. Dean is my hus- *ex*. He's my ex-husband. He's also why I'm late, and I'm embarrassed about it. This is a whole can of worms I wasn't planning on opening before the morning rush, so let's agree to backburner this, and I promise you can grill me on the nitty-gritty later, okay?"

"Well, fuck him for thinking he can control how you talk *and* fuck him for making you late. Although, I'd argue you're not doing so bad on time. Put me to work, boss." I match her earlier mock salute.

"I love you already." She winks and claps her hands together. "Alright, let's get this shit show on the road then. Let me show you where we ditch our stuff, and we can get started on filling the pastry cases while the coffee brews. Doors open at six, so we're in a bit of a time crunch."

I put my bag and phone in Red's small office in the back and get to work alongside her. We work well together. I ask questions about where things go, and we both hum along or sing the lyrics to the music playing throughout the shop. I'm placing the last of the cinnamon rolls in the case when Red heads over to the front door, flicks on the neon open sign, and unlocks the door.

Within minutes, residents of Merrymount are floating in and out of the coffee shop. Almost everyone already knows my name and introduces themselves. I have no idea how long it's going to take me to learn their names in return, but something tells me no one will mind. I manage to only spill one drink, and I think I'm getting everyone's order right. If I'm not, they're being polite and not telling me. It's like they called a town meeting over the weekend without my knowing and collectively voted to show me only grace and patience today.

And that's how the rest of the day goes. Everyone seems so genuinely happy that I found myself here. They tell me I fit right in, and they can't wait to see me tomorrow. It's over-whelming, and I'm very much used to being in the back-ground. All this isn't to say Merrymount hasn't already decided to start showing its quirks. It's the kind of small-town weirdness you only dream about experiencing in real life. I'm obsessed.

The elderly ladies I saw the other day started waltzing in around noon today. I'm able to confirm they indeed call them-selves a book club, and they do actually read, but that's not their sole purpose. You see, there are six of them in total. Judy runs the show, and she gives me the scoop. They're all retired along with their spouses and have been for almost ten years now. Around the five-year mark, the couples got together for some sort of a summer barbecue, and the women were lounging by Judy's pool when Cheryl blurted out that she needed a break from her husband, Marv.

It snowballed from there. All of the women love their husbands dearly, and they felt like they all finally *made it*. They have successful careers behind them, kids who grew into contributing members of society, grandchildren to spoil, the house, the dog, the yard. But they needed to break up the day-to-day. Anya had admitted she borrowed a few of her daugh-ter's books the last time she was babysitting her granddaughter and had been very surprised. They were romance novels, and she warned the women that they would be blushing. They all jotted down author names and book titles, and by the following week, they agreed to meet at Red's to discuss.

The once-a-week meeting turned into twice-a-week meetings and so on until they finally declared themselves an official book club meeting every Monday through Friday because they were burning through contemporary romances so fast. The meetings include book talk, but mix in conversations and debates about anything and everything in between. They just want more time to be together.

Honestly, if I think about it for too long, I'll start crying. Seeing girlhood live on like that is so fucking magical. And I love that they meet at Red's, so I can sporadically participate.

Red has thought of everything when it comes to this place. You can tell each detail is filled with love and passion. It's inspiring to see someone care about something so much. I've spent the lull after the lunch rush organizing the kid's area she's put together in the corner of the shop by the front window.

The space has a custom built table and four chairs sized just right for tiny humans. There are stacks of supplies, including construction paper, lined paper, and a pile of Disney character coloring books. A desk organizer sits next to those, holding colored pencils, markers, crayons, safety scissors, regular pencils, pens, and a glue stick. Along the wall is a small bookshelf that houses a few picture and chapter books, a bucket of green army men, and Barbies, some new and some that looked like Red must have grown up with them.

I'm pinning a picture of a cat a preschool-age boy drew onto the corkboard Red has on the wall for the kids' artwork when she breaks through my peaceful inner monologue.

"Sawyer built me that table set. Have you met him yet?"

I must have whipped my head around too fast because she starts laughing. "I'll take that as a yes. I forget he brings that kind of reaction out of women. He's more than easy on the eyes, but Sawyer's always been the grumpy brother I never had."

Attempting to play it cool so as not to give myself away, I swallow and force my face into what I hope is a neutral look.

"Yes! Yeah. Yep. I met Sawyer. That's his name? Cool. Cool. Yeah, he was… cool."

*I'm an idiot.*

Red does me a solid and glosses over my unique ability to be awkward literally at all times, especially when I really need to be cool.

"He *is* cool! Like I said, he's like a brother. He's saved my ass too many times to count. He's also usually in here at least once a day, so it's weird we haven't seen him yet." She looks around as if she'll find him walking in on cue.

The bell on the front door jingles, and I practically dive behind a barstool to hide. Within two seconds, my irrational brain has convinced itself that Red has somehow summoned Sawyer. I peek out and thank fuck, it's just another Merrymount regular who Red greets. She lets the man know she'll get his coffee in just a minute and then looks down at me.

Because now I'm hiding behind a barstool.

"Uh, Margot? You okay?" Red tilts her head to the side, taking one tentative step towards me.

"I'm good! Just uh, I thought I dropped a crayon over here." I pretend to look around the floor. "Nope, all clear! Phew, wouldn't want anyone to slip on it and fall, right?"

Red walks over to me, skepticism all over her face. "Right, babe. Hey, it's after one, and I haven't seen you take a real break yet aside from scarfing down a bagel in between helping customers a couple hours ago." She reaches out to gently place her hand on the top of my arm. "You're fucking killing it, but I have, like, labor laws to follow, and I don't need you getting burnt out on day one. I'm already attached."

I let out a sigh of relief. "Thanks, Red. For… all of it. Today felt good."

She links her arm with mine, guiding me around the counter to the back. "Your first day was a smashing success, Margot. Take off for the rest of the day. Go explore town or something! You can't hole up in that cottage forever, and if you try to, don't be surprised when I barge in to break you out of there." Red lightly smacks my ass. She blows me a kiss as she heads back out to help that man. I can hear her asking him about his day.

I grab my tote bag and head out to my car. I get in, start the car, and think about heading home, but I want to take Red's advice. I want to get out and discover more of Merrymount. I decide to start now before I can talk myself out of it, and when I find myself back on Main Street, where I would normally take the left to head towards the cottages, I go right.

I'm driving through a wooded area, listening to some random radio station, thinking about how I need to make a playlist for exploring, when I notice the quantity of trees start to taper off, leaving more space between the trunks. Even though they're less dense out here, there are still enough trees for the tops to create a canopy over the ground. It looks like the perfect kind of spot to pull off for a picnic.

As soon as the thought passes through my mind, I see a cabin come into view on my right. A hand-painted sign is staked into the ground next to the road that reads *"Rivers' River, Merrymount's very own outdoor recreation center."*

I almost drive my poor car into said sign when I see none other than Sawyer fucking Hale coming around the side of the cabin, carrying a goddamn two-person kayak over his head like it's nothing to him. A bag of fucking sugar. His T-shirt is riding up just enough to see some of his stomach, a happy trail of hair, and a *very* defined V pointing directly towards-

*Nope. We're not going there, Margot. Stop that.*

I don't even check to see if he saw me. I pray to whatever higher power is in the sky that he didn't and drive by, taking out my phone to GPS myself back home. Exploring is most definitely done for the day.

It's when I throw myself on my couch, not even bothering

to take my shoes off, that I realize unless I venture back out to a store, I'm surviving off of the turkey jerky in the bottom of my tote bag. My stomach lets me know that's not a viable option with a growl so loud I'm self-conscious the bitchy goose outside heard.

Well, I guess I'm going to finally pay a visit to the grocery store.

# Chapter Seven

*Sawyer*

I AVOIDED Red's like the plague for the first time in my life to give Margot some space just to be caught off guard by her driving by the riverside of all fucking places.

I kept my distance from her all weekend, too. I was up and out before the sun, keeping myself busy here and not coming home until well past dark. I've gotta say, the riverside hasn't been this organized in a long time. Now, this isn't to say we don't normally keep things in good working order around here, but since I forced Gran to take a step back and Gus and I have taken over, it's been more *chaotic* organized.

When I moved in with Gran after my parents died, on top of the mandatory therapy, she also thought some good old-fashioned manual labor would help out, too. And as usual, Gran was right. She threw me into the family business that she had been manning on her own since my grandpa Dale passed away a few years prior, and I got to be a part of something that felt really good.

Rivers' River was my grandparents' baby before they had their only actual baby, my mom. They got married without either of their parents' blessings at seventeen and knew they had to make things work, out of one part their love for each other and one part spite, as Gran loves to tell the story. Despite their parents not approving their marriage, my grandpa's grandparents had left him a small trust fund to be made available to him when he got married. It was just enough to buy property and spend the summer figuring the rest out.

Knowing they had to make the money count, they had to come up with a plan to invest. In what? They weren't sure until they found this old, decrepit cabin for sale with a plot of land along the town's river in the Merrymount Daily Mailer. They just had this feeling that this was it for them. They put in a cash offer, and it was immediately accepted because the place had been sitting vacant for years.

Grandpa got to work on fixing up the cabin for them to live in and clearing out the land around it while Gran came up with a business plan. They both loved the outdoors and exploring and realized Merrymount didn't have much to offer in that department other than a few hiking trails. So, they decided to be the much-needed outdoor hub for it all. On the weekends when Grandpa was taking a break from renovations, they'd drive around surrounding towns and states, checking out different flea markets, buying used kayaks (singles and doubles), canoes, life jackets, oars, and fishing poles until they felt like they had enough inventory to open their doors.

They kept things simple in the beginning, renting out the equipment and selling worms for bait out of a wooden farm stand Grandpa built. Eventually, they started selling snacks and camping gear and offering tents for rent that customers could pitch along the river.

Merrymounters show up for their own and spread the word outside of town, so my grandparents profited enough during their first year in business that they were able to upgrade the farm stand to a second cabin, this one within sight of the road and the river. It became the new and official Rivers' River main building.

The following year was even better. They continued to put their money back into their business, and just before Nora, my mom, was born, they purchased their second property a few miles down the river. My grandpa and a few of his friends came together and built the cottage cul de sac that I live in now. It has three small, one-bedroom cottages for the less adventurous campers to rent, and one cottage that still houses the washer and dryer units and extra miscellaneous outdoor equipment from the riverside.

My mom, like my grandparents, met my dad young. Thankfully, *unlike* their parents, Gran and Grandpa were more than supportive. Once everyone realized things with them were serious, they put my dad, Drew, to work. He fit right into the family business like there was a spot waiting for him all along. My parents got married only a couple days after my mom's eighteenth birthday on the sandy shoreline of the cottages.

It was actually my dad who came up with the idea to combine both properties in some way. He had a landline set up in the cottage with the extra equipment and laundry so when customers rented kayaks or canoes at the main riverside, they could take their time traveling down the river. Whenever they decided to come ashore at the cottage's location, they could call up the main building and someone would come around with a truck or a van, loading up the kayaks or canoes and guests, bringing them back to Rivers' River so nobody had to worry about coordinating rides or dealing with the equipment return.

By twenty, my parents had me. They were living in Cottage B and knew that they had to move us somewhere with more space. They easily could have built something or made an addition to an existing cottage, but I think despite how happy my mom was with their life, she was feeling claustrophobic within the town lines. So, they packed up and moved the three of us to a townhouse in Rhode Island. We were still within an hour's drive of Merrymount, giving my dad the ability to commute to the riverside to continue working with my grandpa. But it gave my mom the space I really think she needed to be her own person.

On the last day of school every year, the three of us would pack up and cram ourselves into Cottage B for the summer. We'd do the same for every school break and holiday, too. It was my mom's way of showing my grandparents we were never really far from home. I'd spend my days exploring both of our properties and downtown, when I wasn't following my grandpa practically everywhere. He coined the nickname Little Shadow for me before I could read and write.

Nora Hale was made to be a mom. Not just a mom - she was made to be *my* mom. There isn't a second of my childhood that wasn't touched by her in a positive way. She had crafts and activities planned for almost every day. She insisted on reading to me every night, and when I learned how to read, she would sit there and listen to me instead, helping me sound out the hard words. When I started school, she volunteered for anything a parent could participate in. If there was a sport or program I wanted to try, she'd enroll me and be my biggest fan.

And then there was Drew Hale, "Nora's husband and Sawyer's dad." It was the first thing out of his mouth every single time he introduced himself. He was so proud to be ours. Where Mom could burn boiling water, Dad was our very own MasterChef. He had a tiny notebook he kept in a kitchen drawer where he would scribble down, almost illegible to anyone else, our favorites of everything. He would make sure to include something we loved along with something new every time he cooked.

In my wallet, I have the tattered newspaper clipping of that old, decrepit cabin for sale that my grandpa saw his future in, the thing that started it all.

I keep my mom's copy of the *Grimms Fairy Tales* she used to read to me on my bedside table, along with her engagement ring tucked into a drawer.

And I have my dad's tiny notebook of recipes in the silverware drawer in my kitchen.

It's all I have left of the three most important people in my life who were taken from me before I even had the chance to experience real life with them. It's not fucking fair, and it never will be, but I have Gran. I'd hate the world a lot more if I didn't have her.

As if I summoned her with my thoughts, Gran's old beater of a truck that she refuses to trade in pulls up alongside the main cabin as I'm putting away the kayak I was carrying over when Margot drove by. The thing has well over two hundred thousand miles on it, it's questionable whether it ever had air conditioning, and it gets only one radio station to come in clear that exclusively plays Christmas music all year round. But it's the last truck she and Grandpa picked out together, so I don't fight her on keeping it. When it dies, we'll use it as a lawn ornament if she wants.

I start my walk over to try to beat Gran in opening her truck door, but she's too quick. She says I'm too old-fashioned, but we both know I learned from Grandpa, who would never let Gran touch a door handle. She's just stubborn.

"I didn't think you were coming in today." I call out to her.

"Since when do I have to run my plans by you, my boy?" she shoots back playfully.

"Woah, alright. Sorry. I'm happy to see you, just surprised." I put my hands up in mock surrender.

Gran places her sunglasses on the top of her head and reaches out to bring me in for a hug. "A little birdie told me you've been spending too much time here lately, so I came to investigate."

"I'm gonna fucking kill Gus," I mumble as I hug her back.

"Tsk tsk, you'll do no such thing to my favorite employee. He's worried about you." She levels me with a look that tells me she's also worried about me.

I sent Gus that text Friday night telling him I needed to talk to him the next morning and then blew him off like an asshole because I didn't know how to unload everything. I'm not too surprised to hear he ran to Gran to get to the bottom of things because he knows me. I've gotten pretty good over the years at avoiding all conversations that dive into emotions and feelings. Gus will pay for this interrogation he brought upon me.

Gran and I begin walking to the main cabin, and she's doing this thing she loves to do where she lets *you* fill the silence. She won't crack either, I've tried. Honestly, she'd probably make a great therapist.

I let out a sigh. "I'm fine, Gran, really. There's always something to do around here, and I had the time to get a lot of shit done. You should be *happy*, not skeptical that your only grandson has taken such an interest in the family business. And don't think I missed that you called Gus the favorite."

"Okay, let's play the game your way. You were here, putzing around from sun up to sun down, ignoring everyone, avoiding everywhere, because...what? You're on a one way track to employee of the month?" She stops and pretends to ponder. I choose to ignore the question.

"Funny, I just left Red's, and she said you didn't even stop in this morning - or at all this past weekend, for that matter. Can't remember the last time *that* happened." She squints her eyes at me.

"I wasn't…thirsty." Yeah. That's the best I could come up with.

"Sawyer Fern Hale, what the hell is going on? You left my place Friday night, and you seemed genuinely excited and, god forbid, maybe even a little happy. Emotions I haven't seen pour out of you in a long while, and now I find out you're hiding away like the town hermit. You're acting worse than Gus."

"I'm not hiding away. I'm giving her space!" I snap.

We walk into the cabin, and Gran sits behind the desk we still have set up for her in the main space, even though she's not in here for the day-to-day like she used to be. It makes her happy. She shuffles some papers around on the desk and then picks up the framed picture that's sat on this desk for as long as I can remember.

I don't have to look at it to tell you it's her, Grandpa, my parents, and me. It's the last picture we have all together. I don't remember who took the photo, but the five of us were huddled around the firepit outside of the cottages, roasting marshmallows. We're all mid-laugh at something I think my dad said. I was just about to turn nine, and it was our last hoorah of the summer. Gran and Grandpa invited everyone and anyone in Merrymount to come out for smores and drinks. Everyone was talking about how they couldn't wait to do this again next year.

Grandpa had a heart attack in his sleep right after Christmas. There was nothing anyone could have done. He was gone.

And not even three years later, the universe decided to throw up another middle finger and took my parents. Suddenly, I was an orphan and a shadow with no one to follow. My gran lost the love of her life and her only daughter.

So much has changed since that photo was taken.

"I want to see you happy again, Sawyer. They'd want us to

be happy." She gently sets the picture frame down and looks up at me standing on the other side of her desk.

I don't know what to say because we don't do this. Gran and I goof off and shoot the shit. It's how we've gotten through the last eighteen years together. We don't talk about my parents and Grandpa. It's too hard for both of us. We didn't get enough time.

I muster up a smile, albeit a pathetic-looking one. "I *am* happy, Gran. I stayed in Merrymount because I wanted to. I have you and Gus, even if he is the lamest mother fucker running to my grandmother over something stupid like this. Am I freaked about Margot being here? Sure, I guess. But I swear I'm just giving her space because she's freaked too."

She let what I said sit for a minute, probably deciding in her head if it was a sufficient answer for her to let this go. I must have been convincing enough because she sighs in defeat while opening her laptop. "Alright. I'm dropping it for now because it's still fresh. Gus is over at the cottages waiting on a family of four with two canoes to finish up so he can transport them back here. How about you head over and help him with the load."

"I'm sure Gus is more than cap-"

Gran looks up from her laptop and cuts me off. "I *said* how about you head over and help him out? And when you're done, you're done for the day. I don't want to see you here again today. I love you forever, my boy." She sits down behind the desk, messing with the papers again, pretending to look busy.

"I love you too, Gran."

I have to pick my battles with her, so I walk around the desk, kiss her on the head, and start my journey to my Jeep to make my way over to the cottages. Gus'll be lucky if I don't drown him in the fucking water when I'm done reaming him out for bringing Gran into this.

AUGUST BURTON HAS BEEN my best friend since he moved to Merrymount our sophomore year of high school. As a fellow latecomer to town, I got what it was like to show up in a close-knit community as the new kid so I wanted to make sure he didn't feel alone.

Gus, however, was hellbent on making sure I thought he didn't care if he was alone. He even said he preferred it. I'd sit with him at lunch, and he'd immediately grumble something I couldn't quite make out and then get up and leave the cafeteria entirely. I noticed he never brought anything to eat nor did he line up to buy something the lunch ladies cooked up.

Katie always told me I was wasting my time with him. She would get so annoyed when I would tell her I'd catch up with her later so I could chase Gus down the hall to talk in between classes. She really didn't like when I'd blow her off before homeroom to try to catch him before the school day started, but something deep within me was bugging me to keep trying.

It wasn't until our spring semester, when our schedules lined up for gym class, that I noticed the bruises. Gus tried hard to hide them, and whoever put them there tried even harder to make sure they were in spots no one would normally see . But it was mandatory for us to change for class, and the bathroom stalls weren't always open for him to change in private. So, one day, I saw the black and blue spots on his back and ribcage. Some were smaller, yellowing, and healing. Others were fresh, so purple they were almost black, and they covered so much of his skin.

I cornered Gus at the end of that same day. I lied and said I needed his notes from another class we had together. I told him I was already failing, and I knew he was my best shot at turning things around. I felt bad lying, but every other time I tried to crack this kid, he bolted. I was out of options, and I couldn't ignore what I saw. He took pity on me and told me he could stay after school the next day to share his notes and maybe give me a few pointers to help move me along in the class.

Gus didn't show up for school the next day, and I panicked. Again, I don't know why, but I had this nagging feeling I needed to check in with him. The office ladies knew who I was because of Gran. I told the secretary I needed to bring Gus the schoolwork he missed.

I still didn't have my driver's license, but a perk of living in a small town is that I could bike just about anywhere within town lines. When I pulled up to Gus' house after school, he was out front mowing the lawn. He had headphones on, and he must not have heard me over his music playing because when he just so happen to look up, I could see the shock and horror in his left eye that I'm sure as shit matched mine. His right eye was completely swollen shut and almost totally black.

Now, I'm not what someone would consider a small guy. Even in high school, I was fairly tall for my age and was on my way to filling out just fine, thanks to the work I did at the riverside when I wasn't in school. But August Burton has always been a big mother fucker. He had a good two inches on my 6'3" height and about a hundred, if not more, pounds of muscle on me. So when the initial shock of me showing up on his front lawn passed, he charged at me, yanking me across the yard to the other side of his garage like I weighed nothing.

He tried to tell me I couldn't be there, and I told him I refused to leave until he told me what the hell was actually going on. For some reason, he finally cracked. He put his back to the garage wall, sank down to the ground, and told me everything.

His biological dad up and left when he was a kid, but he didn't really remember too much of him because, within the same year, his mom had remarried his now stepdad, Roy.

Roy fucking sucked. He was a useless drunk who managed to pull himself together only to go to work during on weekdays as some sleazy lawyer. But he took care of Liza, Gus' mom. So, she turned a blind eye to everything that happened under their roof. And when things got too loud for her to ignore, she started drinking herself into a coma every night to drown it out.

Roy made sure Gus and everyone else knew that Gus wasn't his kid, so he had no obligation to Gus. Liza could never peel herself out of bed in the morning to make Gus lunch or give him any money, and fucking Roy locked the fridge and cabinets. It didn't matter if it was a good day or a bad day for Roy. He always found something to get pissed at Gus about. Gus confirmed what I had assumed: Roy was normally smart enough to only leave a mark where it could be hidden, but he was out of control the night before, triggered over nothing, and had wailed on Gus like a punching bag.

Gus told me he was waiting it out. He'd turn eighteen in less than two years, and he'd be out of here, never looking back. He had no plan, but he didn't care. I asked where his mom and stepfather were, and he told me they were inside getting ready for some work event of Roy's in the city. They'd probably get a hotel room for the night. Earlier that morning, his mom had called him out sick from school so no one in the building would start asking questions about his eye.

I told Gus to give me his phone. I input my number, and sent myself a text so I had his. I told him to text me once they left, and I'd be back. I showed up that night with an empty backpack. I helped Gus pack all of the shit he wanted to take, only enough to fill the bag I brought and his own. Then he got on his bicycle and followed me back to my house.

I'll never forget how Gran opened the front door, took one look at Gus, and pointed to the spare bedroom. After she fed us both, she sent me upstairs to my bedroom. To this day, I don't know the specifics of what was said between her and Gus that first night, but when I came down the following morning, Gran declared Gus was a Rivers now, and if anyone approached either of them about it, to direct them to her.

And that was that. The spare room became his room. Gus started working alongside me at the river, quickly learning the ins and outs of the business. We went to school together, he started hanging out with our group of friends (despite his and Katie's immediate mutual hatred for each other), and we eventually graduated together.

Both Gus and I opted to skip the college experience - well, aside from me dragging him along to crash in Katie's dorm after parties on the weekends. I never felt like I was missing out by being an only child, but I'm always going to be grateful I gained Gus as a brother.

I pull onto the dirt driveway and see Gus laying on top of the picnic table that sits smack dab in the middle of mine and Margot's cottages. He must hear my Jeep come around because he jumps up and yells, "Before you shoot, just know I was only worried about you! Because you're my best friend!"

"You play dirty, August," I say as I get out of my Jeep and walk towards him. I notice Margot's car isn't here, and I wonder where she is off to this afternoon.

"Oh, it's August now?" He laughs.

"You sicked Beth on me, man."

"And *you* told me you needed to talk then not even ten hours later told me you forgot what you wanted to talk about. And *then* you left me on read the rest of the weekend. What the hell?" He lets out a breath and looks up at the sky. "Listen, I'm just gonna outright ask, is Katie back?"

"Fuck no." I say, barely letting him finish his sentence.

The look of relief that washes over his face is priceless. Despite his rough upbringing, Gus is hands down the nicest guy I know. He never says no to helping out and always makes sure everyone around him feels good. He's quiet though. You're one of the lucky ones if you get him to let you in. But all of that goes out the window when it comes to Katie.

Gus shakes his head, laughing. "Alright, well, thank God for that. Honestly, that's why I brought Beth into this. I don't have it in me to deal with her again. I've paid my dues."

I roll my eyes, but I know he's right. I'm not going to get him out of here unless I tell him what's actually going on and while I'm not embarrassed by being almost thirty and only having been with one woman my whole life, I don't really want to talk about it in detail with him or anyone, preferably ever.

With the canoers still out on the water and Margot not being home, I decide this is my chance to get it all out, hopefully painlessly and quickly.

I take a seat next to him on top of the picnic table and let out a sigh. "Okay, so you know Margot? Beth moved her into Cottage B."

"I haven't met her yet but yeah, obviously, everyone in town is talking about her. I stopped by George's for dinner the other night, and he and John both wouldn't shut up about her. Apparently Red hired her, too?"

"Yeah. I don't know when she starts, but yeah."

"I think it's a good thing. Red's been throwing herself into work too much lately. I was thinking of asking her if she needed any help pretty soon."

"I know her." I say.

"Well, yeah. No shit you know Red, man. Wait." He stops. "Oh, you mean Margot?"

"Fuck!" I take my baseball cap off and run my hands through my hair. "Yeah, I mean Margot. Remember when I stupidly downloaded one of those lame ass dating apps last year when Katie stormed off about whatever and broke things off again? And I ended up going on a date with that girl, and I finally thought things were gonna change?"

"But then Katie came crawling back," Gus finishes my story for me.

"Yeah."

Gus blows out a breath that turns into a whistle. "Shit, Sawyer. Did Margot know you live here? Is this a stalker situation?"

I laugh. "No. Not stalking, I told her I grew up in a small town but she had no idea. It's just this weird coincidence. Life's fucking with me."

"I'm guessing she wasn't too happy to see you."

"That's an understatement. Every time I try to talk to her, she bolts. I mean, she will literally stop mid-conversation, turn around, run away, and slam a door in my face. It's happened twice now."

"I mean, do you blame her? I'd probably hate you, too. No offense."

"That's the thing. She doesn't seem... angry? It's like she's embarrassed or scared. I'm not trying to make her uncomfortable, but, fuck, if I don't want a chance to just talk to her."

"So you're giving her space to let things settle."

I don't know why I held off on talking to Gus. I feel like even more of a dick now because I should have known he would have gotten it. We both sit here, looking out at the water for a minute in comfortable silence. It's another thing I appreciate about Gus, he never minds sitting in the quiet, and he doesn't feel the need to fill it with bullshit.

"Do you think I have a shot?" I ask.

"If you want the cookie-cutter answer, yeah sure, of course you do. But the reality is you fucked up, man. You say you had this great night with her. That's awesome. I'm happy for you, but you kind of ditched her. Now it's a year later, and she looks like the second choice because your first plan didn't work out."

The realization hits me like a fucking truck. If I posted this in one of those Reddit threads, I'd be the asshole.

"Based on that dumb look on your face, you're connecting the dots. That's great. Step one is acceptance or whatever those programs say. Now, I think you made the right call giving her some space this weekend. Ignoring everyone else was a weird choice, but it's you so I get it. You're neighbors though so you can't avoid her forever, and I don't think Beth is too keen on you moving into the Rivers cabin, or worse, her place. And there's no room in mine, so don't ask."

"I wasn't going to ask to move in with you, Gus. Jesus."

"I'm just covering all my bases here. I think you should stop by Red's when Margot's working and play it cool. Ask her how the new job is going. Work your way up to maybe asking her out again."

"You don't think it's a bad idea to corner her at work?"

"Is it cornering? You go there daily. Or do you really plan on abandoning your morning coffee and Red entirely forever? Come on. At some point, you were heading back there."

He has a point.

"Look, Sawyer. In the years we've known each other, I've never even seen you look at another girl besides Katie. No matter how bad things got with you two, no matter how many times I tried to take you out to introduce you to new women, you seemed content in your misery with her. It sucks that it played out like this but just give it a shot."

I get up from the table we're both sitting on and take a few steps towards the water. I find a stone on the ground, pick it up, and attempt to skip it across the shallow waves, scaring the ducks that were casually floating by.

"You're right." I turn to Gus and ask, "So… you wanna get some coffee before work tomorrow?"

He gets up from his spot and claps a hand on my shoulder. "A front-row seat to the shit show? Wouldn't miss it for the world, brother."

# Chapter Eight

*Margot*

I'M NOT USUALLY someone who talks to herself. Actually, that's a lie. But normally, I manage to contain the dialogue in my head. This time, I've been sitting in my car for the last fifteen minutes arguing out loud with myself about whether to chicken out and jump on the highway just to get what I need from the food section at Target or grow up and shop at my new town's little grocery store.

"Okay, Margot. You're an adult with a 401k. You're starving, and it's literally just a grocery store. Unbuckle and go the hell inside," I mutter to myself.

I'm about to commit to the cop-out when there's a tap on the window. I jump out of my seat, and the seat belt locks. It hits me right in the throat, and I'm coughing, choking on air, when I look to my left and see Beth Rivers smiling at me on the other side of the door.

"Honey, why are you so jumpy? Are you heading in, too?

Walk with me!" She holds up her reusable shopping bags and points to the storefront, where the window decal literally reads *The Store.*

*The Store* is three doors down from Red's Place on Main Street. In between are the flower shop, which I've learned is named The Fuzzy Leaf, and Village Tavern, which I'm assuming is the local bar. Red told me earlier today she'd take me on her personal tour of Merrymount at some point soon, so I'm guessing she'll fill in the blanks for me, seeing as how my one attempt to explore today ended embarrassingly quickly.

Well, I guess Beth has made up my mind for me because there's no way in hell I'm telling this woman I've been considering hightailing it out of here for an unreasonable amount of time.

Unless she already saw me sitting here in my car, which is so fucking embarrassing to think about. I'd rather do just about anything else than let my thoughts wander with that. So I unbuckle the seatbelt that almost took me out, grab my keys and tote bag, and hop out to walk with Beth into the store.

"Hey, Beth! *Crazy* running into you here, huh? Did you just get here?" I ask, just a smidge too quickly. Why am I so fucking awkward around this family?

She laughs and links her arm in mine as we walk up onto the sidewalk and into the store. "Yes, my girl. Just pulled up, I'm running low on some of the essentials so thought I'd pop over. You've been in yet and met Chris?"

The door has the same jingle as Red's when we walk in. The store is only four aisles wide, and a yellow plastic sign hangs from the ceiling by fishing wire at the front of each identifying where to find everything by section. There are multi-colored Christmas lights wrapped around the perimeter of the store, seemingly there year-round given the fact that it's currently April. One single cash register is up in the front by the window, with a conveyor belt lane that couldn't be more than a foot and a half long. Beside the door, along the bay window looking out on Main St, there's a self-bagging bar with brown paper bags stacked on the end in case you didn't bring your own.

"Nope, first timer! I, uh, actually didn't venture out much this weekend and worked my first shift over at Red's this morning, so here I am. Now brav-" I cut off, trying to catch myself before I make more of a fool of myself. "Going grocery shopping."

Beth laughs again. "Well, alright then. I'll let you get on with your journey. If you get lost, just holler. I'll hear ya." She winks and heads right towards the refrigerated section. I grab a shopping basket and go left down the first aisle, looking around and trying to mentally mark where everything is for future visits.

I grab a couple Margot house staples like pickles, pasta, and oatmeal creme pies, along with other necessities, and round the corner of aisle four to head to the checkout. So far, I haven't had any other interactions besides with Beth on the way in, although I can hear her humming along with the music playing light over the speakers to herself now. The cashier at the front was playing on his phone when we walked in. Another good mental note: *The Store* is apparently dead on Monday afternoons.

I make my way to the counter and start loading my small pile of groceries up, startling the cashier. "Hi! Sorry!" I say as his phone fumbles to the ground.

He quickly snatches it up and inspects it to make sure the front screen isn't shattered. Thankfully it's not. "Hey, Margot!"

"You… know my name?" I ask. Slightly confused, slightly concerned.

"Oh yeah. Welcome to Merrymount. Don't be surprised if

there's a feature on you in the paper. My grandma actually runs the book club that camps out at Red's. I'm Chris." He reaches out his hand, and a deep purple polish is painted on his nails.

I laugh, accept the handshake, and brush off my nerves. He can't be older than eighteen. His patchy facial hair and puppy-dog eyes are almost a dead giveaway. He has long, light brown hair pulled into a low ponytail. Thick, black-framed glasses take up a big portion of his face.

"Your grandmother is a hoot. It's nice to meet you, Chris."

"Yeah, we hear that a lot. Did you find everything okay?" He scans my items and pulls out a canvas reusable bag to fill up. *The Store* is printed in a black, cursive font across it.

"I did! I think. I'm not sure. I'll probably be back for snacks more than I care to admit right now."

"No judgment. Hey, how cool is it having Sawyer Hale as your *neighbor?*" His eyes light up like he's talking about a celebrity. "Sorry. Not to be weird. He's just… He's a cool guy, you know?"

I try to hide how just hearing Sawyer's name makes me jumpy, and quickly look over to make sure Beth isn't listening in. "Oh. Sawyer? Yeah. Haven't seen much of him. Are you guys… friends?"

"Don't I fucking wish- I mean. No. Not really. I'm about to graduate from Merrymount High. He's kind of a big deal."

"Is he?" I'm making an attempt to be coolly half interested. Not positive it's translating, though.

"Have you *seen* him? He looks like he could model on the cover of a magazine, and he could throw me across a football field. I'd let him."

My eyes go wide at his explanation. He's not wrong, though.

Chris continues. "Besides all that, he's kind of the best.

He's got that sweet, hometown, tortured thing about him." He stares longingly out the window as if Sawyer's going to walk by at any minute.

Honestly, knowing I'm not the only one around here delusionally crushing on Sawyer Hale from afar made this whole trip worth it.

———

"IT IS with deepest pride and greatest pleasure that I award you *Employee of the Month*." Red bows and ceremoniously hands me a to-go cup, most likely filled with a caramel latte, with "employee of the month" written on it in her cursive and surrounded by hearts all around.

"Why, thank you, m'lady." I curtsy and accept my trophy of coffee.

"Have I told you how much better things have been since you got here?"

"Only every day, Red. Thank you, I mean it. This is, hands down, the best job I've ever had."

"Now, when are you going to let me take you out? Eat something not from the cafe? Go have a drink? Maybe even, dare I say, *shop*. Come on. I've been patient. I've let you get settled. Be my friend, Margot." She finishes her sentence with a mock whine and shakes my shoulders, laughing, before walking to the back.

"We *are* friends. But you're right. Let's plan something."

"I'm holding you to it!"

It's the end of April and Red tells me she has been the sole recipient of this prestigious award for the last few years running, so I should feel proud. And I am, but I'm not going to tell her I'm also really proud because this marks one whole month of being a Merrymount local.

Nothing totally monumental has happened, but I've loved every single day. The rest of the furniture and stuff I ordered was finally delivered. I've video-chatted and texted my mom enough that she tells me she's finally sleeping through the night again, no longer waking up in a panic that her baby girl is all alone and lost. Dramatic, that one, I'll tell ya. I've blown through a lot of books, surpassing my reading goal of the year, only eight months ahead of schedule.

I've worked as many shifts as Red will give me at the coffee shop. I don't think I could have found a better job to start out in a new place. I get to talk to so many people every day, learning different things about the town, who's who, and who does what. It's just been fun.

There's this one guy who comes in around two o'clock most weekdays. He looks like he might be a few years younger than me. He waits for who I'm guessing is his daughter, or little sister maybe, to get off the school bus.

He never says much, and Red normally has his order handled. The first time he came in, though, I almost dropped the coffee I was making, caught off guard by how similar his eyes were to mine. It felt like looking in a mirror. I have this weird thing with noticing green eyes since they're so uncommon. I don't know how to explain it, but he feels familiar.

Sawyer came into Red's on my second day of work, and it was fine, normal, even. He introduced me to his best friend, Gus, and they've been in most mornings since like it's a part of their regular routine. Because it probably is. I mean, I'm the newcomer. They've been here forever.

Sometimes, in my head, I can pretend Sawyer is making it a point to stop by when I'm working just to see me. Even if our conversation is always simply friendly and surface-level. Sometimes, I also pretend he looks forward to our quick exchanges just as much as I do.

Sometimes, when one of us is leaving their respective

cottage as the other is coming home, we wave and say hi to each other, and I can hope to myself that he's about to ask me something, anything, to keep me outside with him for even just a minute longer. But then he catches himself before a single word is said. The moment passes just as fast as it began, and we go on with our days.

# Chapter Nine

*Sawyer*

AN ENTIRE MONTH has gone by, and I've made absolutely zero progress with Margot. I guess that's not entirely true. She's not sprinting away from me mid-conversation like she was when she first got here, but shit, this is tough.

We're *neighborly,* as Gran mockingly put it at our Friday night dinner. Gran thinks I'm stalling… due to the fact that I'm stalling.

I don't want to make Margot uncomfortable. I don't want her first instinct to be running away from me when she sees me coming. I want to go back to our date when the conversation flowed so easily, and neither of us wanted to say goodbye. But I realize it's not productive to want that because it's not happening, and that's on me. I need to come up with a plan aside from having her make me coffee at Red's in the morning or passing by on my way to or from work.

So that's why I'm sitting in my living room, listening for her footsteps or waiting for the light sensor to go off outside of the laundry and equipment building. I have my own basket of dirty clothes next to me, ready to go. I've noticed that Margot loves a routine, and she does her laundry every Tuesday night. Normally, I bring mine to Gran's to do in-between jobs at the riverside, but this might be my only opportunity to talk to Margot alone without the risk of her slamming a door in my face. Okay, the risk is still there, but it's low, and I'm taking it.

Before the light sensor picks up movement or I hear foot-steps, I hear… singing? At least, I *think* it's singing. It's just… not good. I get up from the couch and peer through the blinds to see Margot, donning big-ass hot pink headphones, walking down her porch steps, and holding her laundry basket with detergent and dryer sheets on top. She's really into whatever song she's listening to because she's belting out lyrics like she's putting on the performance of a lifetime. She's clearly clueless to me being home, watching her from my window like a goddamn creep.

I watch her balance the basket on her hip with one hand while using the key Gran must have given her to unlock the building, and head inside. That's my cue. I grab my basket and quickly make my way over to ~~talk to Margot~~ do my laundry.

As I open the door, Margot has her back turned to me and is bent over, putting her clothes in one of the two washing machines we have in here. She's still singing along to her music, headphones firmly in place with the world tuned out. I smile to myself as she does her own thing.

I'm stuck standing in the doorway, and I try.

I try so fucking hard not to look.

But she's wearing those fucking cut-off shorts that I haven't seen her in since the day she showed up, and her ass is slightly peaking out.

I snap out of it quickly, and right as I'm about to clear my throat or purposely knock something over so Margot doesn't get freaked out when she turns around, she does that very thing.

"*I will fucking cut you!*" she screams and throws her headphones straight across the room as I try to yell sorry as fast as I can.

Margot takes a second to process and register that it's me. I can see her chest heaving from the initial shock. "Sawyer." She holds a finger up to tell me she needs a minute.

*A better alternative to the other finger she could have been giving me.*

I stand there gaping like a fish when she walks over to where her headphones now lay on the floor, hopefully still intact. If they're broken, I'll buy her a new pair. I don't care. It's the least I could do at this point. "Sawyer, holy shit. I thought I was dead. I thought *Merrymount is too good to be true. Of course, there's a serial killer living in the woods, and I'm just another victim that will be swept under the rug.*" She places her arms across her chest, imitating a corpse in a casket.

*This fucking woman.*

"You thought all of that up that fast? I'm impressed." I place my laundry basket on the floor next to me and lean against the cabinets on my right, raising an eyebrow at her. "I'm here to do my laundry, same as you. I live next door, you know."

"I'm painfully aware. I mean- Not that I've been paying attention. I just mean you live next door. Obviously."

"You keeping tabs on me, Margot LeClair?" I walk over to the empty washing machine and start to load my clothes in.

"No. No, I'm not. I literally do not care what you do with your time. In fact, I was here first, and I'm just going to continue my routine. So, if you'll excuse me," She puts those obnoxious bubble gum headphones back on her head and hops up on the table in the middle of the room we have so people can fold their clothes. The headphones look almost too big, and she's swinging her dangling, perfectly tan, insanely smooth legs. It's fucking adorable.

I shake my head and laugh to myself as I pour some detergent into the machine. I can hear her music seeping out. It sounds like a sped-up version of a popular song that I've heard too many times on the radio. She pulls out a book she must have stacked in her laundry basket and pretends I don't exist.

This version of Margot is fun. Not that I know all of her pieces *yet*, but I've seen a few now, and I'm into them all.

On our date, she was so animated and passionate. I really felt like I was watching something spark in her.

At Red's, she's so aware and attentive of everyone in the shop. I never hang around too long because I don't want to make her uneasy but during the time I do spend there, I see her memorizing orders and names and making sure the people sitting are getting refills when needed. She's always organizing or cleaning something too. You can just tell she cares, and it's paid off.

Everyone loves her. She fits right in our little town without even trying. Watching her get comfortable here, even from afar, feels like magic.

I'm not proud to admit I'm jealous of everyone else getting to know her better around here.

But this side of Margot? The one who's flustered but manages to still snap at me? I kind of love it.

Besides Gran and Gus, everyone in Merrymount tiptoes around me. They're either afraid I'll snap in anger or break down because, apparently, I'm the only kid here whose parents died young. It's frustrating, but it's fine. I get it. They care, and I can deal. But someone like Margot showing up? It's refreshing, and I can't pretend I don't want more of it.

Once I see the water start to fill up in the washing machine, showing me everything is all good, I hop up right next to Margot. I make sure I leave enough space so we're not touching, but she knows I'm there without having to look up from her book that she's pretending to read to avoid talking to me. Unfortunately for her, that's not gonna happen.

I sit here and wait a few minutes, tapping my fingers on the table along to her music. Then I can't help myself, I reach out and pull one of the muffs away from her ear, "Must be some dedication for you to have been rereading it over and over this entire time."

She stiffens. I see the blush start near her collarbone and watch it work its way up her face until those pretty freckles on her cheeks have a pink background. She snaps the book shut, taps her phone to pause her music, and moves the headphones around her neck. "What are you talking about?"

"You've been on the same page for as long as I've been sitting here. It has maybe six words on it. You're telling me you're actually reading?"

I don't know how it's possible, but her blush darkens, almost red. "I- No, you know what? I'm ignoring you."

"Why?" It's a simple question but I have a feeling the answer won't be as easy.

"Why? What do you mean *why?*" She looks completely dumbfounded.

"No hidden meaning behind it, Margot. I want to know why we have to pretend the other doesn't exist."

"We don't. I make you coffee. You accept it. I tell you to have a good day, you tell me the same, and we move about our days. It's a system that I think is working just fine. Well, it was until *this.*" She gestures with both of her hands to us, sitting here together.

She continues. "I'm going to sit here and listen to my laundry playlist and pretend to read this stupid book until the wash is done. Then I'm going to switch my clothes over to the dryer and continue sitting here, not talking to you. Then I'm going to fold my clean clothes in silence, and then I'm going back to my house to keep avoiding you in perfect, neighborly bliss. Got it?"

"You have a laundry playlist?"

She looks caught off guard. "I have a playlist for everything."

"Really?" I ask. It's not something I've ever thought to do, but I'm intrigued.

"Yes, really. And maybe it's stupid, but-"

I stop her, "No, it's not." I think for a second, "It's like you get to be the main character in a movie or something. That's actually really cool, Margot."

"That's… exactly why I make them." The shock is still lingering on her face.

"What's on this one?"

"Uh, okay, well. I've never had to explain them, so now this *will* sound dumb."

"Sorry, I gotta stop you there. I'm not about to call anything you say or do, stupid *or* dumb. Got it?"

She takes the headphones off, looking down and holding them in her hands. I get the feeling she has a hard time sharing anything about herself for some reason. "Yeah, okay, got it. So, there's no formula to the playlists, and I don't even know if some of them make sense to anyone but me. Especially this one. Laundry is sped up songs only. Think like, chipmunk voice level fast."

She gets her phone out and scrolls through the song list, leaning over just a little bit to show me. She smells like lavender. "In my head, the sped-up songs make the chore go by faster, and that keeps things upbeat and fun. It's silly."

"Can I listen?"

Margot's lips move into a tiny O shape, and she silently hands me her big-ass headphones. I take them and put them down in between us on the table. I pull out my earbuds case from my front pocket, holding them up. "We can share?"

After about a minute of connecting my earbuds to the Bluetooth on her phone, we sit together and listen to a couple of the songs, neither of us saying anything as we nod along to the music. It's not bad. I actually get what she was saying.

I pop the bud out, "This is cool."

"Yeah?" There's a soft smile on her face.

"Yeah. You'll have to send me a link. I'd probably blow through some of my work at the riverside faster if I had this."

She nods her head, and her soft smile turns into a full-blown beam of joy. She's so pretty it hurts. "I could do that."

"Cool. But Margot-" I watch the light drain from her face. "If we're being honest, I still don't get why you think you need to avoid me."

"You're really gonna make me say it?" Margot looks at me and pauses, practically wincing.

Normally, I'd tell her to nevermind, and I'd let her have her peace. But I'm choosing to be selfish right now because I don't know the next time I'll get a chance like this.

"Please?" I look at her and give her a small smile.

She opens and closes her mouth, seemingly trying to put her thoughts together before speaking. I think she's about to finally crack when her machine starts beeping. She jumps off the table and with her back turned, she finally starts talking.

"I don't want to step on her toes," she quietly says, her back still turned to me as she switches her clothes from the washer to the dryer.

I'm confused. "Whose toes?"

"Jesus Christ, Sawyer. Your *girlfriend?*" Margot finally whips her head back around and looks at me like I'm a fucking idiot.

Which is well deserved. I am a fucking idiot because I still don't really get what she's trying to say. Is she talking about Katie? Does she think I'm still in a relationship? Why has Red or no one told her? Has she even asked anyone?

Margot doesn't leave me room to respond and turns back

to the dryer. "Do you know how embarrassing it is to move to a new town, completely alone, and find out you're now neighbors with the last guy you went on a date with? And I'm not blaming you for it. I respect it, I do, but you ended things before they even really began to get back with… drumroll, please." She actually imitates a drum roll on the top of the dryer. "Your girlfriend."

She still doesn't let me get a word in. "I'm not self-absorbed enough to think that I could rock the boat, but I'm a girl's girl, Sawyer. If there were a chance my being around could upset her, causing issues for both of you, I'd feel so guilty. I just wanted a fresh start."

She finally hits the start button on the dryer and fully turns around. I feel like I'm being punched in the stomach when I see the look on her face. She's not looking for sympathy. She doesn't even look sad. She's used to this, and I contributed to it.

My washing machine starts beeping, so I get up and take a few steps until I'm standing next to her to start switching my clothes, she doesn't move.

"I don't have a girlfriend, Margot," I say. I take a deep breath because this sucks. "We ended things about six months ago."

"Oh," is all she says. Silence fills the room.

I don't look at her or try to continue. I give her a minute to process while I load the dryer. I give myself a minute, too. How the hell am I the last guy she's been out with?

She makes her way back to the table, and hops up, sitting crisscrossed. Once my clothes are tumbling, I meet her, opting to lean against the table, instead of sitting.

"I'm sorry," she says quietly.

I can't help it, a laugh escapes. "Don't be, I'm not."

Suddenly, her face morphs into shock, and I just shake my head. "It was never going to work for me and Katie, and I'm a jerk for not accepting that sooner, but I'm not sorry it ended."

I can tell she wants to ask more questions. I'll tell her anything she wants to know.

But of course, Margot surprises me. "Well, that's… good, I guess, right? To be sure of something."

"Yeah, it is."

Suddenly, she jumps down from the table. "Do you want a water or anything? I'm so thirsty."

"Uh, no, I'm okay-"

"I'll be right back!" She's out the door before I can offer to walk with her. Maybe she needs a minute alone.

A minute turns into ten, and then twenty, and I'm honestly starting to get a little nervous, so I peek my head outside to see Margot pacing on her front porch. She seems to be  talking to someone on the phone or maybe to herself because her hands are noticeably empty. I wouldn't judge either way.

I head back inside the building to wait out the dry cycles and to give Margot some space. I'm scrolling aimlessly on my phone when another twenty minutes go by, and her dryer starts beeping, letting me know it's done. I don't know how long she's going to be, and I don't want her clothes to sit and get wrinkly, so I open up the dryer door, grab her clothes, and dump them onto the table so I can start folding them. My machine's timer goes off a few minutes later, so I throw my pile next to hers to start once I'm done.

I have a t-shirt of hers in my hands when she walks back in with two water bottles. "I know you said you were fine, but I grabbed you one too, just in ca- What hell are you doing?" She looks mortified as she places the two bottles on the table.

"I'm folding your clothes so they don't wrinkle. You're welcome." I wink at her.

"You're touching my clothes. Oh my god. Sawyer, *stop.*" She runs around the table and snatches the t-shirt out of my hands before attempting to cover the pile by throwing her entire body over it.

"You gonna tell me why you just disappeared?" I ask her, ignoring her flailing. Instead, I get to work on folding my own pile of clean clothes.

Margot starts quickly and haphazardly folding her clothes, throwing them in her laundry basket, basically defeating the purpose of folding them to begin with. "I got us waters. Duh."

"For forty minutes?" I ask.

"Not that it's any of your business, but yes. And my mom called so I was just, you know, catching up with her."

"Funny. Kind of looked like you were talking to yourself on your porch there for a little bit."

"Were you *spying* on me?" She stops her folding and stares at me.

"No, Margot. Despite your multiple attempts to accuse me of stalking when I live here, I was just making sure you were okay. It's after 9:00 p.m., and you ran off."

I thought she was flustered before, but it has nothing on the incredulous look on her face now. "Oh. Well. Got it. Anyway, it's been a real treat, but like you said, it's late. So, I'm off, goodnight!"

I try to stop her so we can continue our earlier conversation, but she throws all of the stuff she came in with on top of the pile in the basket and quickly tries to lift it off the table. She loses her balance and the basket starts to tumble. I grab one side, and she grabs the other before everything falls out onto the floor.

Well, almost everything.

Unfortunately for her, a black, lacy scrap of fabric is now on the ground in between us. We both reach down to grab it at the same time, but she screams and swats my hand away. "Don't you even *dare.*" She stuffs the thong deep in the basket as if it's about to try to jump out to make a run for it.

Now that I know why she avoids me like the plague, I have a little more hope that this is actually going to work out in my favor. I'm not giving up, despite how feisty she is. Besides, I haven't had fun going back and forth like this in a while.

"Same time next week?" I ask before she's out the door.

Margot doesn't turn around, but I hear her laugh, and it's so fucking sweet to have earned that. She hikes the basket up on one hip again and throws a peace sign up with the other hand. "Catch ya on the flip, Sawyer Hale."

I can't lie. Hearing her say my full name does something to me. I feel a shiver down my spine. I'm in an almost daze, continuing to fold my clothes when I realize… *She didn't say no.*

# Chapter Ten

*Margot*

HAVE you ever looked at someone's face and just known they deserve to be punched? Like, they deserve to be absolutely and completely laid out? And it's been a long time coming?

These thoughts pass through my brain every single time Dean Fitzgerald walks into the coffee shop, and I have to put on a fake smile and the performance of a lifetime to not spit in his peppermint latte and tell him to fuck off.

And you know what? Who the hell drinks peppermint lattes year-round? It's basically toothpaste-flavored coffee. The guy is criminally insufferable in every way.

Red hasn't told me everything that happened between them, just that they got together in high school, married almost right after graduation, and divorced last year. I can't imagine how hard it must be to start from scratch like she did, but I'm thankful she did.

While he never does anything outwardly offensive, it's like

he's found the line and mastered how to walk along it unscathed. But the little things add up. He *sucks*.

I count to three and take a deep breath when I see Dean, self-proclaimed *Merrymount's Finest*, walk in the door. I throw my happy barista smile on just as he gets to the counter.

"Morning, Dean. Same as usual?" I move to grab a medium hot cup to get started. The faster I get this made and in his hands, the faster he's out the door.

"Hey there. I'm actually here to see Red, but I'm also not going to say no to a pretty lady like you offering me a coffee. That'd be silly of me, wouldn't it?" The flirty smile he plasters on while he leans against the counter actually makes me want to puke.

I manage to swallow the urge to gag in his face and ignore almost everything he said besides the basics. "Sure thing. Give me two minutes. Red's in the back. I'll let her know you're here."

"No need," he says, waving me off. "I can find her." Dean starts to move toward the door behind the counter.

Before he makes any progress to get to the back, Red walks out. She blocks his way, arms crossed over her chest, and she doesn't look happy. She never looks happy when he's here, though. Not that I blame her. It's not every day - I think even he knows that's crossing a line - but he's been in here enough that in the month and a half that I've been in Merrymount, I've caught onto his bullshit.

I just can't figure out why *Red* puts up with his bullshit. I get he's a cop in town, and I get they were high school sweethearts gone wrong, but from what I've seen of her in the short amount of time I've known her, she is, and likely always has been, infinitely better than him.

Red sighs. "Please. I don't have time for this today."

"Spare a minute for an old friend? I come in peace. I promise." Dean sheepishly smiles.

The act is insufferable, and I roll my eyes as I finish pouring his coffee. "You're all set, Dean," I say flatly as I place his cup on the counter.

"You're the best, Mar-go-go." Add that to the list of things I hate about this guy. He winks and grabs the cup to take a sip. I hope he burns his tongue.

"Her name is Margot. Don't start that with her. I'm giving you two minutes." Red starts to walk, not to the back, but a small table we have in a corner with two mini bar stools. I've always thought they looked uncomfortable, and now I can't think of a better seating option for someone to pick to get themselves out of a conversation quickly.

Red thinks of everything.

I smile to myself, knowing she can handle Dean, but I also keep one ear open, just in case I need to jump in for whatever reason. The front door jingles, and in walks Sawyer.

God damn it, he looks good. He always looks good. It's unfair. The rugged, dirty jeans, work boots, and worn t-shirt thing works for him. He also usually has a baseball cap or knit beanie on his head, and I catch myself with my mouth open, visibly staring every time he walks in.

Today, he's in his normal weekday uniform, opting for the black beanie I've seen him in a few times now - not that I'm keeping track or anything - and his jeans have holes, like always clearly from wear and tear. I can see a tattoo peeking out on his thigh. I can't make out what it is from here, but this is the first I've seen or heard of him having any ink. Surprisingly, he hasn't asked about mine.

Any guy I had been even remotely into or involved with has always been  the clean cut, following in Daddy's footsteps, finance-business type. And they *always* had something to say about my tattoos. They were never outwardly insulting, but you get enough *Oh they look nice but I could never get one*, and you're over the conversation entirely.

The past two Tuesdays, Sawyer has met me in the laundry building wearing some sort of hoodie with fucking *grey joggers.* And they sit *low.* They leave *very little* to the imagination. I'm starting to wonder if he does it on purpose because he knows it's what most women with a pulse are secretly drooling over. And unfortunately, I am, and will always be, one of those women.

I thought about switching the night I do laundry. I thought I should keep my boundaries and continue avoiding Sawyer as much as possible. It was working just fine. But something snapped in me when he said he wasn't with his ex-girlfriend anymore, causing me to bail and hide out on my front porch for the entire dry cycle. And then something snapped again when he asked about meeting me at the same time the next week.

Like he wanted to see me.

I don't want to admit how much I look forward to Tuesday nights now. He brings a cooler, filled with water bottles and a couple cans of some local beer. He tells me it's so I don't get lost again, and we just talk. I brought a bag of chips for us to share last week. Turns out salt and vinegar is his favorite too.

We volley questions between each other, topics spanning from our favorite childhood vacations to what our middle names mean and everything in between. He really pays attention to everything I'm saying, and when I start to get self conscious about rambling, lost in my head, he shoots out another question. If I'm being honest, it feels a lot like that one night we had together last year. He flirts, but it never goes further than that. I think it might just be his personality.

But I don't let myself dwell on it very much. At the end of the day, the spark I felt then and the jitters in my stomach I feel now are one-sided. I'm a forgettable person, something I've been told and reminded of multiple times. The only reason we're doing all of this now is because life just had to play a sick joke on me, and now we're making the best of the time I have here in Merrymount. We're neighbors, maybe even friends.

I was adamant about not asking Red about his relationship status before. I didn't want to have to explain why I was asking about him. I knew Red wouldn't say anything or make it uncomfortable, but it would have been too much for me. It's not like it could go anywhere.

Did I think it was weird no one had mentioned her, and I hadn't seen her in the time I'd been in town? Yeah, I guess. But I assumed she was away, traveling for work or something. For some dumb ass reason, it never crossed my mind that they weren't together.

I check to make sure I'm not drooling as Sawyer strolls right up to the counter with the biggest smile on his face. He has really nice teeth. I learned earlier this week he had braces his entire middle school experience, and felt guilty his Gran had to pick up the bill after his parents passed. He hasn't told me what happened, and I'm not pressing the topic. It doesn't feel like something I have the right to ask about.

Just as I'm about to greet him, I hear Red raise her voice - not loud enough for the few customers hanging out here to be bothered, but enough for both Sawyer and me to notice. It's as if he was making a mental note to pay attention as soon as he walked in and saw Dean here.

I look over, and I can tell they're arguing. I can't pick up what they're saying, but obviously, it's not good. Sawyer waves to me and pivots to make his way over to Red and Dean but stops when he sees Red hold her hand up. "No need, Sawyer. I appreciate the mediation-" She looks at Sawyer and offers him a half smile. "But Dean was just on his way out." She turns back to Dean with a look that shows she's leaving no room for discussion.

"Whatever, Red. I'm not dropping this, but I'll fucking see you around." He storms out, tossing his barely touched to-go cup in the trash, not even bothering to put on an act to say bye to anyone else. What a fucking waste.

Red shakes her head and walks over to the counter, a defeated and tired look on her face. "I'm so sorry, guys. Margot, are you good up front here for a little? I just want to finish up the cinnamon rolls I have going in the back."

I don't want to press her now, but this conversation has been brewing for some time. Coffee pun not intended. I've loved working alongside her since I've been here, and we obviously talk all throughout my shifts. I even finally saved her phone number in my contacts, and we've been texting when not at the shop. It feels really good to finally have a girlfriend. But we haven't addressed the elephant in the room that is her ex-husband, and I haven't worked up the courage to bring up anything Sawyer related.

Before I can respond, Sawyer looks to Red. "Hey, you sure you're good? He doesn't need to be hanging around here."

"You know Dean does whatever he wants. I'm fine. It's nothing I can't handle."

"Never said you couldn't."

I interrupt before Sawyer can answer. "But you shouldn't have to."

Red looks at both of us, blinking any tears that were even thinking about forming back into her head. "Well, aren't you two the perfect pep talk team? Thanks, guys." She rubs her hand on Sawyer's upper arm and turns around to walk back to what she was working on before Dean ruined the vibes of the day.

Why did her referring to Sawyer and me as a team make my stomach flip?

Once Red's out of earshot, Sawyer mumbles to himself. "God, I fucking hate that prick. Sorry-" He sheepishly looks at me, "I didn't mean to come in here and start off like that."

"Literally, no one who has said sorry in the past ten

minutes was the person who should have been apologizing. He's the fucking worst. Do you know how hard it is to put on a fake smile and pretend to give a shit about every dumb thing that comes out of his dumb mouth? It's hard, Sawyer. And I hate it." I start aimlessly restacking to-go cups to keep my hands busy. "Why does everyone let him act like that? Actually, what I really want to ask is *how* Red put up with that?" I ask.

"Where do you want me to start on his entitlement list? We'll be here a while." Sawyer laughs. "But seriously, you're right. I haven't really checked in with Red lately when I should have. If shit's getting bad with him, can you let me know?"

There goes my stomach, flipping around like a gymnast again. It's nice to see how much he cares about the people around him.

"Yeah. Yeah, of course I can. But hey, you came in, you want your usual?" I move to the hot cups to pick out a large for him.

Suddenly Sawyer's easy smile morphes into something I can't exactly pinpoint. Nervousness? But that's ridiculous, he has nothing to be nervous about.

"Uh, a coffee?" He takes his beanie off, running his hand through the short, brown curls that were hidden beneath it. I've wanted to run my hand through them the same way. "No, I'm good. I shouldn't have any more caffeine. I had an energy drink this morning, and it made me wired. I actually hate those things, but I was running late, and we had an early reservation, so instead of coming here, I just grabbed one from the fridge in the main cabin at the river. So no, no coffee. Thanks." he takes a deep breath and raps his knuckles on the countertop.

What the hell?

I take a moment to see if he's going to elaborate.

He doesn't.

"Okay, so no coffee. Got it. Would you like… anything else?" I ask him gently, speaking as if I'm approaching a bear.

"Are you busy later?" he blurts.

"Wha-" I start.

"Do you want to take a walk along the river tonight?"

Now it's my turn to look like I'm panicking because I am. "Who?"

"You, Margot. Well, and me. Me and you, walking along the river. Tonight."

"Why would we do that?"

"Because I want to talk to you. I want to hang out with you, spend time with you. There's only so much time here when you have customers waiting, and I'm sick of fitting all of our conversations into a wash, dry, and fold cycle on Tuesday nights. I don't know if your number has changed, and I'm honestly too fucking nervous to text you to find out and get shot down because you've put a pretty big wall up. And I get that." He holds his hand up. "I understand you owe me nothing. You can tell me right now to go pound sand, and I'll do just that, but I have to try."

I try to quickly look around the room. There are a few stragglers from the book club still finishing up their drinks, deep in their own conversations about gossip, thankfully seemingly unrelated to this. Chris from the grocery store is sitting on a bar stool at the front, paying Sawyer and me no attention. Other than that, there's no one. It's a surprisingly quiet afternoon. On any other day, I'd be thankful for a chance to breathe and catch up after a lunch rush. I doubt Red will be emerging from the back in time to save me from facing this unexpected invitation, too.

Sawyer's still looking at me nervously. He's not even a little impatient, as if he knows I'm internally arguing with myself, expecting it, and being more than fine with it.

"I- don't get what you're trying to do," I finally respond.

"I want to start over and do this right. I'll explain everything later. Call it an incentive to say yes."

Deflect. I need to make a joke or say something ridiculous so I don't get my hopes up. When he says start over, he means a friendship because we're neighbors who do laundry together. We exchange breakfast orders and money. We coexist in this town with a small secret that's not even really worth calling a secret. It doesn't mean anything.

"Are you planning on murdering me?"

This gets Sawyer to bark out a laugh, I see his nervousness melt away. "Hey Red!" He calls out.

What the hell is he doing?

Red comes out from the back, holding a tray of freshly baked cinnamon rolls. The scent wafts in, and I can't stop myself from groaning. "What's up? You want one of these before you head out? I just have to throw some icing on them." She holds up the tray in offering.

"No. Wait-" Sawyer looks at me. I mean, he really looks at me. His eyes darken for just a moment. I'm sure my cheeks are beet red from realizing I just audibly *groaned* about baked goods in front of him. "Actually, yeah. Can you box two of those up for me? I'm taking Margot on a date tonight. Those'll be perfect." He never breaks our eye contact.

Thankfully, the tray doesn't crash to the ground when Red jumps in the air, screaming. She tosses the tray on the back counter and runs over to grab me by my shoulders, shaking me from behind. The few people in here who were minding their own business a couple minutes ago? All eyes on us.

"A *date?!*" Red screeches the same time I shout, "It's not a date!"

Sawyer smiles triumphantly. "A date. That Red knows about now so you can feel comfortable that I have no plans to murder you. I have a couple things to wrap up with Gus but I should be done before five. I'll meet you at your place around... six?"

Red is still standing very close behind me. I can feel her

shaking with excitement. Whatever sour mood Dean left in his wake is completely forgotten. "Six is perfect. She'll be ready." I guess Red has taken it upon herself to answer for me.

"Margot?" Sawyer asks me to confirm. I think he meant what he said earlier. If I say no right now, he'll walk away. It's the sincere respect of it that makes me finally answer.

"It's not a date." I look at him pointedly and hold out my hand, waiting for him to shake on it.

Instead of taking my hand, he holds out his own. "Give me your phone," he says.

"What? Why?"

"Do you still have my number?" he asks as I grab my phone from my back pocket and hand it over to him.

"Yes." There's no sense in lying. He can check for himself.

He must have scrolled and found his contact. "*Sawyer H.* Wow, so formal." He smiles and starts to quickly type something out, and then hands it back to me.

"Um, yeah. Okay so. Well, since you aren't thirsty, I'll see you later. For our non date. I'll bring the buns." I point with my thumb to the tray of cinnamon rolls.

He grabs my hand and it takes everything in me to not pull away from the electric shock that jolts through me when our skin connects. "Whatever you say." He firmly shakes once and then does what he did that one date a year ago. He flips my hand, still in his, bringing it to his lips where he leaves a quick, soft kiss. Tingles shoot right up my arm.

I quietly gasp, snatching my hand back. At this point, I must look like I applied an entire compact of blush to my face permanently.

*I did not just say that.*

"Oh yeah, she's bringing her sweet buns all right." Red laughs and smacks my ass as she walks away, grabbing the tray.

*Yep. I definitely just said that.*

She looks over her shoulder at us. "Sawyer, I don't know

what's going on but I'm here for it. Seems like we're overdue for a chat. I'll be seeing you." She winks and she's gone.

Saved by the literal bell, the door jingles as a customer walks in and gets behind Sawyer to wait to place their order. Sawyer must take this as his cue. "I'll get out of your hair now. I didn't mean to make this a scene but well, it got your attention, right?" His smile spreads across his whole face. He waves, turning to nod at the man behind him in greeting, and he heads out the door.

I don't have any time to recover from everything that just happened, but I've been doing this barista thing every day now, so I go through the motions of greeting this man, taking and making his order, and sending him on his way all while spiraling about this date I just signed myself up for with Sawyer. Except, it's not a date. Right?

# Chapter Eleven

*Sawyer*

I'M STANDING on Margot's front porch, rocking back and forth on the heels of my boots and holding tulips I picked up from The Fuzzy Leaf after I left Red's this afternoon.

Daisy was working the counter at the flower shop and insisted these were a safe option when you don't know exactly what type of flowers a woman likes. Plus, she added, it was the end of their season, and it would be a shame to see them go to waste. I didn't think it mattered, but she again insisted it did. I'm not going to be the one to argue with a florist named Daisy.

I'm not *not* nervous, but I'm trying really fucking hard to keep that shit locked down. I might be a man with a dating history that would take up next to no space on one piece of paper, but I hope I can pull this off.

These are the times when I try my hardest not to think about the what-ifs with my parents. What advice would my dad have given if he saw me in this situation? How would my mom feel about the choices I've made and the ones I'm trying to correct? We never got the chance to do this season of life together, and when everyone tells you it gets easier, they're lying. I miss them, but it hurts to talk about them. I can visit their headstones at the cemetery where they're buried and talk to them, but I get no response. I can always try to bring it up with Gran, but why would I want to open up that wound with the one person who has probably been in more pain than me this whole time? It doesn't seem fair.

The walls of the cottages aren't exactly thick, and I can hear inside. It sounds like she's listening to heavy rap, which is very different from the upbeat pop music I normally hear coming from her speaker in the cottage or her big-ass headphones or her car when she's pulling up, all ridiculously too loud. I'm surprised she doesn't already have hearing damage. I recognize the next song that comes on as one of my favorites to put on when I'm working out, but before the song gets to the chorus, it's cut off and replaced with a ringing sound, a call must be coming in.

I take it upon myself to knock on the door now to show her I'm here and *not* eavesdropping. I hear Margot answer the call with a "Hey, Mom!" as she opens the front door. "What's up? I only have a couple minutes." She says it while waving at me and putting up her index finger to tell me she'll only be a minute.

It seems as though the rambling and stumbling over words Margot I've gotten used to over the past couple weeks is gone, replaced by what I can only describe as… chill Margot. She's wearing a pair of running sneakers with black leggings and a gray hoodie - I think from a college - with holes on the end of the sleeves that look like they appeared after years of wear and wash, where she has her thumbs looped through. It looks like she washed her makeup off from earlier. Her freckles are on full display, and her hair is down, tucked behind her ear on one side. She looks so cute and comfortable that I'm half tempted to ditch the plans and ask if she wants to hang around and watch a movie instead.

But then I remember I asked her on a date to walk along the river, and we haven't known each other for long, even though sometimes it feels like we have. I can't forget I need to be impressing her in every way I can to make up for being an absolute idiot before. If I play my cards right, we'll have plenty of time for movie dates. I just have to keep chipping away at her armor.

I'm standing in the doorway, unsure if I should go in or wait here, ultimately deciding to keep my feet planted right where they are. She finishes up the call with her mom, telling her she'll call tomorrow morning to check back in while organizing pictures on the kitchen table. I realize this is my first time back here since the day she moved in, and looking around, it seems like she's fully moved in, except that the table is still stacked with frames and photos. It doesn't look messy or dirty. I'd call it organized chaos.

She places the phone on the table and looks over at me. "Hey, sorry about that. If I ignored her call, she'd just keep trying. Just give me a minute to grab a water bottle. Do you need one?" She makes her way over to the fridge.

"Don't apologize. I'm early, I think," I say. "And I'm good. I actually have some drinks and snacks for us and umm…these."

Margot turns back to look at me and finally notices the tulips. I hold them out for her. "Are those… flowers? Sawyer, I told you." She walks towards me. "This isn't a date." Despite what her mouth is saying, she takes the tulips and brings them up to her face to smell, trying to hide a smile behind them. She thinks I don't notice. I'll let her believe that for now. She heads over to the cabinets, opening one and revealing a vase on the top shelf. She reaches up, pretending she'll be able to grab it when we both know she can't.

Before she has a chance to drag a chair over or climb, I'm behind her. I feel her back stiffen against my chest as I reach up and over her head to bring the vase down. I put it down on the counter, placing one hand next to it and the other on Margot's other side, caging her in.

I bend down so my mouth is level with her ear. "You keep saying this isn't a date. Do you believe that yet?" She shivers and I smile to myself as I push off the counter, giving her space back. I don't want to push her buttons too much just yet. These quick moments will have to do for now.

Margot takes a second to morph her face back into that chill look she had on when she answered the door. "We're going for a walk. It's like a workout. Just two pals getting their fitness on." She gestures to her outfit, which I now recognize as something I'd see girls wear to the gym.

I can't help but laugh and shake my head. "Listen, Margot. I'm gonna lay this out for you and then we're going to get in my Jeep and get this night started. M'kay?"

"I mean-"

I stop her before she can start to argue. "Sorry, no. I walked on eggshells for over a month, giving you the space I thought you wanted because I thought you hated me for being a dick, and I was cool with that. But then I found out you were just trying to respect my non-existent relationship. Fuck out of here with that, Margot. I'm taking you on this date. It's low stakes, so you don't sprint off on me, but we're doing this."

I think I've surprised her again, although I can't for the life of me understand why. "We're doing this," she says quietly and looks down at her shoes. She sheepishly looks back up at me. "Can I change?"

"No." I take my time looking at her from her shoes to the top of her head. "I happen to like this comfy look you have going on. Grab your phone and your keys. Let's go." I turn, grabbing the clear to-go box that has two of Red's cinnamon rolls from earlier, and head back to the door.

"Yes, sir," she jokingly says. I hear her follow behind me, and it takes everything in me not to stop dead in my tracks. Now is not the time to explore what that just did to me.

Shaking that off and walking over to the passenger side of my Jeep, I open her door. I motion for her to hop in, holding out my hand in case she needs a boost.

Margot scoffs. "I can manage just fine on my own, thank you very much." And she does, which I expected. But that's not going to stop me from continuing to be a gentleman. I shut her door and make my way around to the driver's side, getting in myself to see her snooping through my glove box, unashamed. "Just checking for weapons. A lady can never be too safe. Wouldn't you agree?"

I huff out a quick laugh. "You're something else, Pixie girl."

She's moves on to search my center console but stops with a pack of tissues still in her hand. "Pixie girl?"

I put the key in the ignition and start the engine, putting the Jeep in drive to head out towards the road. "You're telling me no one's ever told you that you remind them of that fairy from *Peter Pan*?" I question.

"Why would anyone do that?"

"Margot, you're five foot nothing, with blonde hair that I've seen you keep in a bun on the top of your head more times than not, and, well, I mean this in the best way-" I take a chance to look over at her and see she's eyeing me skeptically. "You've got an attitude." I finally say.

"I do *not* have an attitude!" She yells while pouting.

"I didn't mean it in a-"

She cuts me off. "A bad way? What other way could I possibly take *Hey girl, you've got an attitude. So bad, you remind me of that bitchy fairy from the kids movie?* This was a stupid idea. Can you just turn around and take me home? Better yet, I'll just tuck and roll out."

She has a point. It came out wrong, but I'm not about to dig myself into a deeper hole on this.

"No. And buckle up." Without taking my eyes off the road, and while keeping my left hand on the steering wheel, I reach across her to grab her seatbelt and click it in place. My knuckles brush against her. She doesn't say a word, and I take it as a win.

We continue driving in silence other than whatever is lightly playing on the radio. I don't dare take a chance to change the station or connect my phone to Bluetooth. This is fine for now.

WHEN WE GET to the main cabin at the riverside, Margot is still keeping up the silent act. I'm happy to play along because she's here with no distractions and without actively trying to run away or make up an excuse to avoid me.

I take it upon myself to give her the grand tour while no one else is here to interrupt us. As we are walking around the main building, I rattle off every fact I can remember, pointing out Gran's house and Gus' cottage, detailing how Rivers' River came to be, and my parents' roles in expanding it. It feels like rereading a favorite book from my childhood.

As much as Margot acts like she isn't paying attention at first, I can see the interest on her face. The joy, excitement, and awe of seeing a family business being built from the ground up are obvious as she takes in all of the work my grandparents did to make this place what it is today. It makes my heart fucking flip to see someone new learning about the people I love and lost. I know even though they're gone, and nothing can change that, they can still live on in some way.

We make it inside, and I watch her run her fingers over the newspaper article we have framed on a wall detailing the grand opening of Rivers' River, my grandpa holding the town's giant pair of scissors that are only brought out for such occasions, Gran tucked in next to him, her smile beaming from ear to ear. They were so proud.

She moves over to the next frame, where she reads another article about their second grand opening at the cottage location. This time, my grandpa is holding my mom, only a few months old with a gummy smile on her face, giving my Gran the honor of cutting the ribbon with the giant scissors. They look just as happy as in the first picture, if not more so.

"It's beautiful," she finally says quietly.

Normally, I avoid this wall, just like I try to avoid anything related to the past. It hurts. But I have these articles and pictures memorized. I walk over, standing just behind her, and I sigh. "Yeah, they built a pretty beautiful life."

"I'm sure they're so proud of what you and Beth are doing here."

"I hope so," I sigh.

Margot looks over her shoulder, up at me. I think there are tears in her eyes, but she blinks them away just as quickly as I saw them. The only tell is that those bright, green eyes are shining, just a little. She claps her hands together like a gym teacher would right before they tell you to run suicide drills. "Okay, a walk is what I was promised. Where to?" She starts making her way towards the door to head outside. She looks back over her shoulder, a small smile on her face. "Come on, show me more."

I want to show her everything.

# Chapter Twelve

*Margot*

"WHAT MADE YOU PICK MERRYMOUNT?" Sawyer asks, jolting me out of my aimless thoughts.

So far, he's been letting me soak up everything without forcing me to respond, continuing to rattle off random facts about Merrymount. My silence started because I was just being a pain in the ass and purposely not speaking, but after seeing the emotion on his face and the love poured into this place by his family, I kept my mouth shut out of fear I'd say something stupid. I also just really like listening to him talk.

He sounds really sure of himself in everything he says and not in some cocky, know-it-all way. It's comforting and attractive as hell. I feel like I'm safe when I'm with him. Hearing about the history here as told by him makes the gaping hole in my heart that longs for something like this crack right back open.

After the tour of the main building, we start along a walking trail, marked with a green arrow for easy identification

I notice. It hasn't been too bad, but I've barely looked up from the ground, afraid I'm going to trip over a rock or a branch and break my ankle or worse. I'm not built for the outdoors, and for some reason, I think Sawyer remembers that.

The last thing this night needs is me ending up in the emergency room and Sawyer having a guilty conscience, thinking he owes me anything more than he's already doing.

"It's honestly so dumb, you're going to laugh."

"I bet I won't," he says very seriously.

"Okay, sure. What do I win when you laugh?" I shoot back at him.

He gives it some serious thought. I see the *aha* moment in his brain happen. Then he says, "When *I* win, you have to go on another date with me. Tomorrow night."

My nervous laughter escapes before I can help it. I slap my hand over my mouth. "I'm sorry." I gather myself and say, "I thought this wasn't a date."

"You keep saying that-"

I cut him off and point my finger at him. "But, fine. You don't let a single chuckle leave your mouth, and I'll go out with you tomorrow." I do realize I just gave in ridiculously too easily but whatever.

He holds three fingers up. "Scout's honor."

"I found an ad in the paper," I blurt out. "And I don't know… I just had this feeling, so I highlighted it, and I kept thinking about it all day. When I went home that night after work, I called the number in the listing. Beth answered on the second ring and said she had just listed the cottage earlier in the week and was surprised someone was already showing interest. I know it sounds a little crazy, but her voice was just so refreshing and comforting. Like I knew her, or she could be my grandma, but I don't even know what that's like. It's so ridiculous. It just felt-"

"Right," Sawyer finishes for me. He shakes his head, very

much so *not* laughing at me, "It just felt right. I know that feeling."

"You do?"

"It's why I'm still here. My mom-" He pauses. "My mom really believed in everything happening for a reason. Every time I've thought of packing up and getting out of here, something in me tells me to stay. So I do."

I'm surprised he's mentioning his mother. With everything he's told me about his life, the family business, and Merrymount, he always skims over his parents. Understandably so, but still, I'm startled. I want to tell him I feel the same way she did. Fate is real, and I do think everything happens for a reason. But I stop myself before I do. It doesn't feel right saying it to someone who has lost so much.

"Yeah," I say. What else *can* I say?

"Come on, there's a spot up here I want to stop at." He holds out his hand, and when I go to take it, he locks his pinky with mine.

"Do you think you still would have eventually moved here? If... you know... Oh god, is that a dumb question?" We continue walking along the path, and I shake my head at my own stupidity.

He chuckles. "No such thing as a dumb question coming from you. You can ask me anything. It's okay, I promise." He sucks in a breath, seemingly thinking about what I asked and how to respond. "I wanna say yeah, I probably would have still ended up in Merrymount. I loved coming here every summer. If we kept up with it, I would like to think we all would have wound up here."

When we get to the spot he told me he was bringing me to, there's a cooler waiting filled with drinks and snacks by a tree stump perfectly sized and shaped to make a bench for two.

I notice the two sets of initials carved into the side before he says anything. I run my fingers over the ridges, admiring the love that must have gone into them.

"My grandparents and then my parents. They added theirs the night my dad proposed," he says softly, handing me a bottled water.

"That's beautiful."

"My mom used to tell me, '*You know, one day, Sawyer. One day, you'll get to add your initials with your person, whoever that may be,*' and I'd laugh because no eight-year-old kid who's really only inter-ested in jumping off shit is thinking about who they're gonna carve a tree stump with. But she'd just smile and ruffle my hair."

His voice trails off, lost in a memory. He looks out through the clearing in the woods. We can see just a glimpse of the river from here.

"You will," I say more to myself than him.

His head turns to mine, and he smiles softly, knowingly. "I will."

▭

AS MUCH AS I don't want this night to end and, as much as it pains me to admit how much I'm getting my hopes up with him already, I'm so tired. I leave Sawyer at the front of the cabin to lock up, heading towards the passenger side of the Jeep. I don't remember the last time I checked my phone, so I don't even know what time it is, but I do know I'm going to crash on my bed the second I get through the door. Hopefully, *after* Sawyer kisses me goodnight.

*Wait. What?* No. Don't go there, Margot.

"Don't even think of opening up that door," I hear Sawyer call from behind me.

"Or what?" I say as I pick up speed on a jog to try to beat him. Before I can register him approaching, his arms are around my waist, picking me up, spinning me around, and placing me back on the ground so now I'm behind him. I'm giggling, and I can feel his laugh just as much as I can hear it.

Sawyer opens the car door, dramatically bowing, gesturing for me to get inside. "We'll never have to find out. When we're together, you do not open doors, Pix. Got it?"

I'm supposed to hate the nickname thing he's doing, but I secretly love it. No one, aside from my mom, has taken the time to get to know me well enough to give me a nickname. It's always been just Margot. I don't count Dean's bullshit.

"Yeah, yeah, boss man. Got it." I grab onto the handle to hoist myself up. I feel Sawyer's hands on my waist again to balance me. He shuts the door to make his way around to his side, and I quickly buckle myself in. As hot as it was to see him reach over one-handed earlier, I do not trust myself with him that close to me again. And it's dark out. I'm always braver in the dark.

Before Sawyer showed up tonight, I told myself I was setting a hard boundary of friendship. I took all the pressure away by not putting thought into my outfit and by washing off my makeup. Plus, I purposely didn't shave my legs. Absolutely no temptation. I'm a genius. I even went as far as finding an insane playlist with rap I literally never listen to because I knew it was a sure way to make sure I didn't get in my feelings about anything beforehand. I can totally handle this friend thing, and honestly, I need it. While I've loved every moment in Merry-mount so far, my social life has tanked, not going past the inter-actions I have while working at Red's.

But between my body catching on fire every time his fingers even brush me and the glances that make me have to quickly look away, my boundary line has started to blur. Of course, Sawyer's attractive. It's perfectly normal and natural to have a physical reaction to him. I mean, there's no harm in appreciating his looks, right?

The line became pretty much nonexistent when he started pointing out constellations after the sun had set. When we started laughing about nothing in particular but everything at the same time, both out of breath, unable to speak in between the hysterics. After he kept giving me glimpses into his past and his hopes for the future.

I went from not speaking to telling him about the time I agreed to go to prom with my eleventh-grade biology partner, and he ditched me after the dinner to get high with his friends. And how I spent the entire first year at my job going by Mary instead of Margot because I never corrected anyone.

He told me about how he accidentally adopted a possum family he found behind the cabin when he was a teenager. His Gran didn't have the heart to kick them out in the winter, so they raised them until they could release them in the spring.

I kept thinking to myself, *this could be more, you know.*

I want him to kiss me, but not badly enough that I would kiss him first. I would rather live in this pretend world in my head where I tell myself we could harmlessly flirt than ever put myself back out there with the opportunity for him to throw me away again. As fun as this night is, as fun as more could be, he'd get bored, he'd forget, he'd get busy, and he would move on. It's just... how it is. I'm not even going to bring up tomorrow night. The bet was just a silly thing. There's not going to be another date.

This time, once he gets in and starts the Jeep, I decide to break the silence with something that's been on my mind for a little while now, a confession I've been holding in. "I hate beer."

He sneaks a look over at me as he pulls out of the small parking lot. "What?"

"You've been bringing beer to laundry night, and I take one when you offer because I don't want to be rude. I'm trying to seem like the cool New England girl who can kick it with a brew or whatever, but it's gross. Like, it tastes like ass."

The first night he offered, I thought it might be a one-time thing and could play it off for a minute. But then the one night turned into two, and I don't know why I thought I couldn't just say *no, thank you*. I have a hard time saying no. I'd rather make myself uncomfortable than inconvenience anyone else.

His laugh fills the entirety of the car, but he pulls himself together and says, "Don't do that with me, Margot."

He's called me some variation of pixie all night, so the sudden serious change in tone and use of my actual name catches me off guard. "Do what?" I ask.

"Make yourself small like that."

"I'm not-"

"You are. And what I hate is that I think it's second nature for you now because those around you have benefited from it for far too long."

Well, he's not *wrong*, but how would he know that?

"You came to that conclusion just because I drank piss water with you?"

"You avoided me for over a month when we're next door neighbors. I can throw a rock from my bedroom window and hit yours. You did it all because you thought you might accidentally cross a line with my hypothetical girlfriend."

Okay, so he's got me there. "Fine, I sometimes have a bad habit of appeasing others to my displeasure, but doesn't everyone?"

Sawyer turns the radio on at a low volume and changes the station to something country. "To a point, yeah. I guess you're right. But I still think it's more than that with you. Which, speaking of, tomorrow night…"

Oh god. "We don't actually have to go out, Sawyer," I try to get out as fast as possible.

"What? Yeah, we do. I was just going to ask if you had

anything you wanted to do or try in town in particular or if you wanted me to plan something."

"I, uh. No, I just thought-"

"Nope, all good. You thought I'd plan something we'd both love, great. Can't wait." He turns up the volume on the radio. It's an old Taylor song about riding in the passenger seat of a boy's car and falling hard, and it's like the butterflies that had been caught in a net in my stomach are set free.

If I were alone in my car, I'd start singing along. I'd put on my own sold-out stadium tour concert. But I'm in Sawyer's Jeep on a non-date, so that would be weird. Right?

But he did say I needed to stop making myself small... *He was saying that to be nice, Margot.*

As if I need to prove a point to him, and maybe more so to myself, when the chorus comes around, I start belting it out. I fully expect him to laugh at me, make fun of me, or tell me to stop.

But he doesn't. No, Sawyer Hale smiles so fucking big as he joins in with me, turning the music up for a second time. We finish the song together as we pull into the driveway of the cottages, and I'm dancing in my seat to the next song that comes on as he parks next to his house, laughing at how crazy I must look. But holy shit, this is *fun.*

"Feels good, doesn't it?" he says when he cuts the engine, turning the radio off. "I had a lot of fun with you tonight too, Pixie girl."

Did I say that out loud? I look over at him, gearing up to get out and head over to my place, the temporary adrenaline from the ride home fading and the tiredness seeping back into my body.

We make eye contact, goosebumps break out on my entire body, and suddenly the silence is deafening. "Me, too."

I say it so quietly that if there was any ambient noise, you wouldn't have been able to hear it. But currently, all I can hear are my heartbeat and Sawyer's, every breath each one of us takes, and a pin drop. So, I might as well have said it into a megaphone.

He moves his hand next to mine on the center console, barely brushing my fingertips. I find myself leaning just a little bit forward, unintentionally. He matches my movement.

"Can't wait to do it again tomorrow." He inches just a little bit more.

"Me… too." Against my will, I feel myself moving closer.

His other hand comes over and quietly unclicks my seat belt. "Let me get that for you."

I place my hand over his to grab the belt to guide it across my body and up back into place. Neither of us makes any movement to get out.

My eyes flutter closed. Just when I think our lips are about to connect, and I can feel his shallow breath on my face, his citrus and pine scent filling my nose, bright headlights cut through the rear windshield. Whoever is behind the wheel of the new arrival lays on the horn, making both of us jump right out of the moment.

Sawyer's out of the Jeep before I can pull myself together. He's trying to see who's pulling in when we're the only two who live here, and clearly, neither of us were expecting anyone. I turn around and see Red jump out of the driver's side of her Mini Cooper, tears streaming down her face.

"Sawyer, are you still with Margot? I'm so sorry. I didn't know where else to go." Red throws herself into Sawyer's arms, shaking in between crying and trying to catch her breath.

"Red, woah, slow down. Don't be sorry, Margot's right-"

"Here!" I finish his sentence for him. "What's going on?" I make my way over to them. We're standing between Sawyer's and Red's cars, her headlights still shining on us. She lets go of Sawyer, embracing me next.

Since I've met Red, I feel like I've come to know her pretty well. She's loud, but not in an obnoxious way. She loves to plan things, take control, and talk a lot, not because she's full of herself but because of how much she cares. With caring so much, comes big emotions. But I've never seen her so rattled, and I can only think of one person that would cause this to happen.

"What did he do this time, Red?" Sawyer asks, already visibly angry. He must have gotten to the same conclusion as me.

"This is supposed to be your night where you guys finally fucking stop being weird, and I'm here ruining it. I'm so sorry." She finally lets me go and takes a step back, wiping her face with her sweatshirt sleeve.

I hate Dean so much for doing this to her. "Stop apologizing. We were just saying goodnight, weren't we, Sawyer?" I look over to him for back up. We both recognize whatever moment we were in earlier has fully passed.

"Yeah, I was about to head inside and crash, but hey, go shut your car off. No sense in standing out here. It's getting cold. Come on."

"No, no, Sawyer. You just said you were going to go to bed. It's just Dean bullshit. You know, the usual. But, I, uh, honestly, I came here to talk to Margot…" Red suddenly looks nervous, as if I would send her away.

She literally gave me a job with a steady schedule and income without batting an eye. She makes sure I always go home with something extra from the back so I don't forget to eat. She always asks how I'm doing and follows up on things that I honestly wouldn't have even put much thought into if she didn't mention it. I hate that I haven't made more of an effort to talk and do much outside of work, but I've really started to consider Red a friend. To know she feels the same way back does something to my heart.

As much as I wish this night was ending differently, I can't help but feel good that I can be here for Red like I know she would be for me if the roles were reversed. I feel guilty for having kept my Sawyer secret for so long. Now is not the time to dive into it obviously, but I'm going to make it a priority going forward.

Sawyer's right. I *do* tiptoe around everyone, and if I'm being honest with myself, I think I kept a wall up with Red to avoid getting attached. I already love so many little pieces of Merrymount, but I meant what I said to Sawyer: when my lease is up, I'll move again. This was his place first, and I think everyone can agree it's the kind of small town where you can't comfortably avoid someone forever. But there's no logical reason as to why I can't make friends.

I grab her hand. "Can an adult woman invite another adult woman over for a sleepover, or is that weird?"

"Oh, thank fucking God." She laughs. "Lemme go grab my overnight bag. I packed one just in case." Red heads over to her car and moves it into the spot next to mine.

"So…" Sawyer starts.

I look over at him and smile. "Thank you for tonight, Sawyer. I meant it. I had a lot of fun. I'm just sorry it's ending like this."

"I'm not." The look on my face must give away the shock of what he just said because he laughs. "I mean, I am. But I'm happy to see Red has a friend who'll drop anything to be there for her. She's that person to everyone else. She needs it."

The wave of relief that crashes into me is downright embarrassing. "You get it."

Instead of coming back over to us, Red waits on my front porch. Her duffel bag is on the ground, and she's attempting to curl her body into the wicker egg chair. "Kiss her goodnight, Hale! Use your tongue. I'm the bitter divorcee over here. Live a little for me!" she yells.

I give him absolutely no time to react or respond. I sprint

away, already more than halfway to my stairs. Red is laughing her ass off when Sawyer calls out, walking towards his place. "Tomorrow night, Pixie!"

"Pixie?" Red asks while trying to catch her breath in between cackles as I fish out my keys to unlock the front door.

"Don't even ask." I open the door and flick the kitchen light on.

Red follows in behind me. "Oh, I'm asking, and you're spilling. Do you have coffee here, or do we need to make a late-night trip to the shop? We're gonna be up for a while, and we need proper sleepover supplies."

I turn around to face her, happy to see her tears have, even if only temporarily, dried. She's smiling, already looking towards my cabinets, presumably ready to inspect them. "Tonight you will learn, my friend, that I do not know how to properly sleepover. But I have always and will forever know how to properly snack. Go ahead, snoop away."

Red finds a bag of salt and vinegar chips. She's already mid-chew when she looks back over her shoulder and says, "What do you mean you don't know how to properly sleepover?"

"I- Shit. This is embarrassing. I've never really had… friends like that."

"But you're normal." She holds up a hand with a chip in it, signaling she needs a second, talking in between bites. "I don't mean that in a bad way. I just mean, you're not some weirdo loner. I don't understand."

Red looks genuinely so confused, and it's sweet. I guess I should take it as a compliment that she thinks it's unbelievable that I'm this much of a loser.

"I don't know, it was never intentional. I had my mom, it was just the two of us, and it made sense. Jesus, saying that out loud makes it sound so fucking lame." My self-deprecating laugh is the only sound in the room aside from Red's chip chomping.

"It's not lame. It's good you have her." She folds the bag back down, clips it shut, and begins licking her fingers. "But you have me now, too."

Before I start to cry, because I will, I pick up her bag from the kitchen floor. "Likewise, Red. I'm just gonna go put this in my room. My house is yours. Take whatever you need."

I love this. I mean, I hate that something with Dean must have gone so bad that Red felt like she didn't have anywhere else to turn, but I'm so glad the dam is finally broken. I think about what Sawyer said earlier about his mom and her *every-thing happens for a reason* faith.

# Chapter Thirteen

*Margot*

RED ASKED if she could shower before diving into everything. So I've been laying on top of my bed, aimlessly scrolling on my phone for the past twenty minutes. I'm mid doom scroll when a text notification pops up across the top of the screen. I smile at my phone, Sawyer must have been changing his contact name when he had my phone earlier at the cafe.

YOUR LOST BOY:

Food delivery incoming. Just letting you know so you don't get spooked and threaten to murder whoever is delivering for George tonight. ;)

I type. I stop. I repeat this three times before finally settling on,

ME:

Why?

YOUR LOST BOY:

Because if you two are planning the long
overdue Dean Fitzgerald takedown, you'll need
fuel.

ME:

But why?

ME:

Also, thank you.

YOUR LOST BOY:

Just let me know if you need anything else,
Pixie girl.

I hear the shower turn off and tires on the gravel out front at the same time. I jump out of bed and head to the front window to take a look. I see George from the pizza shop hop out of the driver's seat of a car, his husband, John, already standing on the passenger side.

Sawyer meets them both at their car, shaking hands and, I'm assuming, giving them cash for the two very large bags of food John is holding. Sawyer motions to my house and all three heads turn to see me peeping from behind the blinds.

I jump back as if I can pretend they didn't see me. I was so distracted I didn't even hear Red leave the bathroom, and I back right into her. "Oh shit! Sorry!"

"Who are you hiding from?" she asks while adjusting the towel wrapped around her body.

"Sawyer. No- Wait. I'm not *hiding*, but Sawyer is outside with George and John. They brought food." I point to the window.

"For us?" She makes her way over to the front of the cottage, pushing aside the blinds to get a look outside.

Red taps on the window, waves, and then scurries over to

the front door. She opens it, completely unphased by the fact that she's only covered with a towel, right as John is placing the bags on my front porch. He picks them back up and hands them to Red.

"Sawyer called right before we were about to close up for the night. Red, it's everything you like. Margot," John peers around Red to make eye contact with me. "Sawyer wasn't sure what your favorites are, so it's a little bit of this and a little bit of that. It's like a Merrymount pu pu platter."

"Wow, thank you guys. This wasn't necessary," I say. I'm taken aback, honestly. It's in a good way, but this kind of community hasn't ever really existed to me.

"But it's appreciated," Red adds, walking back into the cottage and placing the bags of food on the kitchen counter.

I stick my head out the front door. "Thank you, George!"

"Anytime!" he yells back and waves.

I make eye contact with Sawyer, and he quickly winks at me before looking back at George to finish what he's saying. Red and I say goodnight to John, and he heads back out.

A few minutes later, Red is changed into pajamas, and we hear George and John drive away. We break open the takeout containers packed with chicken tenders, french fries, mozzarella sticks, all the dipping sauces you can think of, and more. We lay everything out on the counter, buffet style, and I grab two plates out of a cabinet for us to pile high with whatever we want.

It's too much food for two women. We do not care.

We've set up camp in the living room, sitting on the floor around the coffee table when Red finally breaks the silence in between the both of us devouring this food. "Dean wants my house."

I drop the fry I'm holding. "He *what?!*"

"He wants the house back. He says he wants me and our life back, but I know better. He's just bitter and embarrassed about living with his parents again. He thinks enough time has passed where I've forgotten, and I'll forgive if I haven't already."

"But it's *your* house, right?"

"Damn straight. When my parents signed everything over to me,- the coffee shop, the apartment above it - and the house, they put everything in my name only. They never fully trusted Dean, even though they've known him his whole life." Red giggles. "I guess that's exactly why they never trusted him. The judge who finalized our divorce felt the same. They saw the real him and tried to warn me, but I had to learn the hard way."

I swallow my bite of an onion ring. "Sorry, I'm playing catch up… I'm totally on your side, regardless, but what did he do exactly? You know, besides just existing as a piece of shit."

I slap my hand across my mouth. "Oh my god, that was fucked up. I'm sorry. He might not be a piece of shit. Just like-"

Red almost chokes on her drink from laughter. "No-" She catches her breath. "You were right. He's a piece of shit. Normally, I tell people it's a long story, but in reality, I'm just embarrassed and don't want to get into it most of the time. I mean, look at me, divorced before thirty. But," she huffs. "He cheated."

Someone like Dean cheated on someone like Red? *Seriously?* "I'm so sorry."

Her laughter quiets. "I don't even know how many times or how many women. How sad is that? I spent my birthday at Planned Parenthood getting a full STD panel because my husband couldn't keep his dick in his pants, and I was too much of a baby to ask for details."

"You never deserved that."

"I don't even know why he did it, you know? It's not like we were this old, married couple with no sex life. I loved him for what felt like my whole life, and it just wasn't enough." The deep sadness I saw on her face when she first showed up tonight has creeped back out.

"*Fuck* that, Red. I know I've only known you for a little while, but that couldn't be further from the truth. You're in your twenties running an entire business, owning a whole ass house, while, respectfully, being hot as hell. To quote the queen, Dr. Christina Yang, you're the fucking sun."

She wipes the tears that start to fall with a napkin, and a light laugh escapes from her. "Thanks. It's hard to see it that way sometimes."

"I have to ask… Do you *want* him back?"

"No!" she yells, barely letting me finish my question. "Sorry, that was aggressive. I miss feeling wanted and loved. I miss coming home to someone. I miss holidays and traditions, and I think about *what could have been* probably way too often. But I'll never know how much of it was or would be real. I would never feel safe and secure in my own life again if I let him stay. I'd rather be alone than lonely in company."

I reach over the coffee table and grab her hand, squeezing it once. "Well, you don't have to be either here."

WE FINISH EATING our first round of food, and I grab a bottle of red wine from the top of my fridge, which we both drank from coffee mugs. Red tells me everything about her and Dean from childhood till the divorce hearing. I can't imagine having so much history with someone and then having to see them everywhere, practically neighbors in a town this small. It makes me feel ridiculous to have been overthinking Sawyer and me as much as I have.

I then tell Red everything about me and Sawyer. I think her jaw was going to become unhinged when I tell her we matched on a dating app.

"Sawyer's a hermit crab. He doesn't... date." She says.

When I finally catch up to tonight's nondate and the almost kiss, I think she's to throw herself off the couch.

"You're telling me I interrupted a *first kiss?!*" she shrieks.

"For good reason!" I shout back. "We're uh, actually supposed to be going out again, umm, tomorrow."

Red picks up her phone, checking the time. "Seeing as how it's almost 1:00 a.m., you're going out today." She raises her cup in cheers.

I clink my mug to hers. "Holy shit, when did it get so late?"

"Probably around when we emptied the bottle of wine and went back for seconds on the nachos. So, what are you two doing?"

I feel my cheeks heat. "I have no idea. He said he's going to plan something."

"Do you know what you should wear?"

"Not a fucking clue." I laugh.

"Hmm." She hums to herself while taking the last sip of her wine.

"I'll figure it out. My closet isn't exactly lacking." I say, yawning and causing Red to do the same.

"Is it okay if I go to bed?" she asks.

"Oh god, yes. I'm fighting sleep so hard right now."

"I'm... so tired, both physically and mentally. But this - *you* - turned my whole night around. Thank you so much, Margot." She gets up and walks to the kitchen to set her mug in the sink.

"Of course. I'm sorry it was under shitty circumstances, but I really did have fun tonight. You should get some sleep. I'm probably going to clean up and head to bed too." I get up and follow her into the kitchen.

"Oh, no! I can stay up to help-" she starts.

"Bed, Red. Goodnight!" I say, pointing to my bedroom.

Red doesn't argue but also doesn't head right into my

room. Instead, she walks over to me with a giant smile on her face and grabs me into a tight hug. "It's nice to have a friend."

# Chapter Fourteen

*Sawyer*

"WHY CAN'T you just take her out to dinner again?" Gus asks as he throws a kayak onto the rack beside the cabin.

We just brought in one of the last families that reserved equipment today. It's been a good business day at the river, with a nice steady flow of people and things to get done. I've tried to keep my brain busy rather than think too long about the what-ifs of tonight's date with Margot.

Gus and I have tackled the tasks together, pretty much working side-by-side all day. I told him about last night, our walk, and everything that happened with Red. I'm not sure if asking him for advice with Margot was a good idea or not but regardless, this is where we're at.

"We've already done the dinner thing. I want to wow her. It's new, and it's a fresh start."

"Yeah, one you better not fuck up." Gus levels me with a look that says he has little faith.

"Says the guy with a steady string of one-night stands," I quip back.

"That's by choice, ya fucking idiot. That's all I'm looking for, no strings." He grumbles and throws a lifejacket at me, but I catch it before it hits me in the face.

"Yeah, yeah. Whatever." This is nothing new to me. Gus might have let Gran and me in all those years ago, but the circle didn't really grow beyond that for him. He gets along with everyone in town just fine, and he has no issue bringing women home when he wants. I've witnessed it during our nights out at the bar when the tourists are here in the warmer months, but he has those walls up and guarded, probably permanently.

"Listen, I think you're overthinking it. You have nowhere to go but up. As long as you don't ditch her for Satan herself again, I think you'll be fine."

"You're no fucking help, man." I jokingly punch him in the arm as he passes by me.

He might have a point, but I don't want it to just be fine. Margot deserves more than that. She needs to see how wanted she is and how much I really care about getting this right.

We turn the corner around the cabin, and both see my Gran's car parked in her spot up front. "Hey, maybe Beth has some advice for you," Gus says as he reciprocates the arm punch.

As if on cue, Gran walks out the front door, seemingly holding it for someone behind her. "Never a good sign when you two need help from me. Advice for what, my boys?"

Beth Rivers might be getting older, but her hearing is unnaturally strong. It's a sense Gus and I have tried to evade while getting into shit we shouldn't be for years now.

"This wouldn't have to do with the bouquet of tulips I arranged for you the other day, would it, Sawyer?" Daisy Stiles emerges from the door Gran was holding with a curious look on her face, tucking her long, black curls behind one ear.

Daisy is another Merrymount lifer, born and raised here by her parents with her younger brothers, identical twins. I think they're around ten or eleven now and were a surprise to everyone when they were born. The family owns the town's flower shop, The Fuzzy Leaf. Gran never really got along with her parents and never explained why, but she never took it out on Daisy or her brothers. She and Daisy have a special relationship they don't share details on with anyone else, and I respect that.

We've been friends since before I got to town officially. We'd skip rocks in the river when I visited with my parents during the summer. She used to hang around Katie when we were in school too but, like everyone, Daisy got tired of Katie's games, and they eventually drifted apart.

"As a matter of fact, it does, Daze. Haven't seen you out here in a while." I bring her in for a hug. Gus is the brother I never had, and Daisy feels like the sister version, along with Red.

"What the hell are *you* doing here?" Gus rolls his eyes, the question directed at Daisy.

"Don't even start, August." Gran snaps at him, the use of his full first name shutting him up quickly.

"Glad they're still letting the stray dog eat scraps," Daisy says, focusing on something on her hand like she can't even be bothered to look up.

"Daisy, you watch your mouth, too." Gran's glaring at her for continuing what Gus started.

It wasn't always like this with them. They used to get along just as well as everyone else. At one point I really thought we'd all see August Burton and Daisy Stiles together, like me and Katie. But a switch flipped sometime right after high school graduation and both, together and separately, have said it's nothing worth talking about. So, we don't. Instead, Gran and I get to play referee on the occasions we begrudgingly force them together.

Gran takes a deep breath, probably counting to three and questioning why she deals with all of us when she could be fully retired somewhere warm. "Daze is here to help with the business."

"What?" Gus and I ask at the same time. I ask because I genuinely wonder how she'll be helping. Gus asks it like he's about to throw up or quit. Probably both.

"It's time we started exploring that social media shit you kids are into. We need to build out and expand our marketing online. Get the youth out here. Summer is just around the corner."

I have to admit, it's a great idea. Daisy has always been creative. I guess growing up learning about floral arrangements helps, but it goes beyond that. She knows how to make those videos you always see going viral, editing them perfectly so everyone who watches them wants to do whatever she's posting about.

I'm not good with that kind of stuff. My online presence is basically nonexistent. Gus is the same way, and Gran can barely find the button to get on the internet, nevermind work out a strategy for the business, so this sounds great to me.

"That's awesome, Daze. Crazy we didn't think of it sooner," I say, holding up my hand for a high five. She meets me in the middle.

"Thanks! I have some really cool ideas I think will work. I'll be around here and there shooting content to edit, batch, and post, but I promise I won't be in the way too much."

"Great," Gus sarcastically grumbles, kicking around a rock on the ground.

"It *is* great, August. And there won't be a fucking peep out of you about it. Daisy here agreed to the same. You both will be professional about this. Got it?" Gran points her index finger right into the middle of Gus's chest.

He nods his head in understanding, then looks down at his feet. Being cowed is a product of a Beth Rivers scolding. "Yeah, yeah. Of course, I got it."

"Now, what's going on with our girl, Margot?" Gran redirects her attention to me.

Guess I'm roping everyone into this. "We have a date tonight, and I'm not sure what we should do."

"Most people just go out to dinner, Sawyer." Daisy says, giggling.

"That's what I said! Fuck, now you have me agreeing with her." Gus chimes in.

"Yeah, and *like I already explained to you,* I want to try something different."

"You want to wow her!" Gran yells.

"*Exactly!*" I exclaim back. This feels ridiculous.

Daisy's standing there, thinking. I hope she has something for me because I'm really feeling screwed right about now.

"Have you talked to Red?" she finally asks.

"What do you mean? About Margot? God no, she's with her almost every day."

"Uh, yeah, Sawyer. That's kind of my point. Red is probably your best bet for ideas relating to Margot, as she is the only person in town close to her besides you."

Oh. *Why didn't I think of that before?*

"Well, based on the 'lightbulb just went off' look on your face, it seems like you're picking up what I'm putting down. I gotta head back to the shop to get the boys off the bus, but you've got this Sawyer." She kisses Gran on the cheek, ignores Gus completely, and makes her way over to her car. "No matter what you and Red plan, Margot will love it. You're one of the good ones. Remember that."

Daisy drives away, and Gus and Gran get going on some

TV show they've been binging together. I'm left here standing with my thoughts. I don't feel like one of the good ones. I feel like the asshole who has been going through the motions for so long with things and people that weren't really right for me that I don't actually know what I'm doing.

I pull out my phone and shoot a text to Red, telling her to meet me in the back of the coffee shop so I don't chance running into Margot just yet. I tell her I need help, and without going into detail, she immediately responds.

RED:

I was wondering when I'd hear from you. See you soon, loverboy.

# Chapter Fifteen

*Margot*

SAWYER TOLD me to be ready for six. He also texted me earlier and said to dress cozy. It's currently 5:55 p.m., and I'm standing in my bedroom in my underwear with my hair in a messy bun on the top of my head. I think I have to commit to today's leftover mascara as my makeup for the night because I'm obviously going to be late.

Red and I set alarms early this morning and slept through them. We rushed out of here, tripping over everything and tumbling into whatever clothes we could find, and only made time to brush our teeth.

The work day flew by with - thankfully - no surprises from Dean before Red kicked me out early to get ready for my... date. I ended up coming back to the cottage and starfished on my bed, staring at the ceiling and contemplating how much I could and would embarrass myself tonight.

Sawyer and I clearly have different versions of cozy because mine would not be appropriate for a date. I can't walk out in his t-shirt that I'm pretty sure he hasn't realized I stole the last time we did laundry together with no pants. It was an accident to take the shirt, but I haven't exactly made an effort to return it yet because it smells like him, and it's comfy. I've also worn it to bed the past three nights in a row, but he doesn't need to know that. I mean, I could walk out like this. But, like, societal norms would tell me I shouldn't.

Do I need a sweatshirt? Should I wear my hair up or down? Is this date going to be indoors or outdoors? Sneakers? Oh god, he doesn't think I would like a night hike, right? Pretending to enjoy hiking in the daytime would be enough torture as it is. Did I set a shitty expectation with the walk?

Speaking of torture, when do dates stop feeling like *this?* Technically, if we're counting the *first date that shall not be named,* this would be number three, and I'm in dumpster fire mode, panicking. Now that I'm thinking about it, I've never made it to a third date before.

Oh my god, I've never been on a third date with anyone.

You know what? Maybe we'll keep that record going. I can cancel. I should cancel. I'm already going to be late. It's just easier this way, so he won't feel bad about letting me down a second time. Because he's going to let me down again. He'll get bored, or Kathryn or whatever the hell her name is will come back, and he'll realize again he's supposed to be with her. We'll be right back to where we were before all of this, except worse.

I don't think I can handle that type of rejection a second time from him, especially now that we're neighbors, and I quite literally cannot afford to break this lease. Plus, Beth would find out, and she'd take pity on me, and yeah, you know what? I'm all set with this.

I'm pacing back and forth in my room, still not dressed and not even a little bit closer to being ready, when I hear my phone ping from my bed. I walk over and begrudgingly pick up my cell.

Great. It's probably Sawyer canceling because I'm always late and frantic and just not worth the effort. This is exactly why I've never made it to third-date status.

I see his name on the screen, swipe to open the text, and try to laugh at the ridiculous name, but my stomach drops. Yep, this is it. He's going to bail.

> **YOUR LOST BOY:**
>
> I'll have you know I planned for your inability to be on time. Whenever you decide to stop stressing over what to wear or whatever else you have swirling around in that big, beautiful brain of yours, all you have to do is walk outside. See you soon, Pixie girl.

Hold on. He knew I'd be spiraling, and he seemingly... is okay with it? Accepts it? Accepts *me?* Jesus Christ. I'm doing it again. I'm getting ahead of myself.

Well, looks like I'm not backing out now. I see my favorite cut-off shorts sitting on the pile of clean clothes I folded with Sawyer last Tuesday and then never got around to actually putting them away. They'll do. Sawyer said to dress cozy.

He thinks I haven't noticed him checking out my ass every time I wear them, but I have. I tuck his t-shirt into the front of my waistband after I pull the shorts up and swipe a flannel from the laundry pile to tie around my waist.

Since I'm committing to this homely look, I quickly check my messy bun in the mirror and deem it acceptable. I'm about to head out the door when I see twinkling lights out the front window.

Pushing the sheer curtain aside to get a better look, I see it. The picnic table in the front is covered with a tablecloth and long-stem candles, lit and flickering. There's champagne, pizza, a fruit platter, and a bowl of candy. I can't get over how beautiful this all looks with the water in the background and the sun just barely starting to set.

Next to the table, there's a plaid blanket set out with fluffy couch pillows. Laying back on one of the bigger pillows with his eyes closed, phone placed beside him, looking so insanely at peace, and holding a bouquet of wildflowers, is Sawyer Hale. Waiting for me

# Chapter Sixteen

*Sawyer*

I KNEW she'd be freaking out. She overthinks everything, and I fully blame every piece of shit who made her think she wasn't worth it all, myself included. I'll be making up for that for as long as she lets me. The fact that she's still showing up and giving me this second chance says everything about who Margot is, and she doesn't even see it.

I'm not going to mess this up this time, and I told Red that when I went down to the coffee shop earlier today begging for her help to plan this date. Thank fuck she saw how serious I was because I know I wouldn't have been able to put this all together without her.

Margot is basically allergic to physical outdoor activities - like most of the shit to do around here is. I thought about taking her to Boston to walk around and grab food, but Red made a great point: Margot came to Merrymount to get away from the city. And while we could do the same thing downtown here, I really don't need everyone in our business. Yet. I have to realistically set my expectations with the nosiness of this town.

At least I know Red won't spread our business; she grew up here just like I did and after her very public divorce from Dean, she knows how important privacy is to me. She's a good fucking friend.

I hear Margot's front door open, and it takes everything in me to stay put here on the blanket with my eyes shut. I thought she'd yell out to me, but she must make her way down her steps quietly because I can only hear the sounds of the river and her footsteps. I open my eyes, and there she is.

"Sawyer..." she says in a whisper, looking around at everything I set up.

She's standing there looking incredibly nervous, mirroring exactly how I feel on the inside. All five feet of her in *my* shirt with those fucking shorts, showcasing those smooth, long legs for such a tiny body, unlocks something in me. It's one of those primal, caveman-like reactions that makes me want to get to know every fucking inch of her.

I sit up and hold out the bouquet of flowers. Clearing my dirty thoughts, I manage to keep my arm steady. "These are for you. I let Daisy pick the tulips yesterday, but I picked these out myself."

She takes the flowers in her hands and raises them to her face to smell them. She breathes in deep, closes her eyes, and smiles on the exhale. She's fucking perfect.

"They're beautiful. Sawyer, *all of this* is beautiful. How did you manage to pull this together in less than twenty-four hours?"

I stand up and gesture to the table. "It's just a picnic, Margot. And as much as I want to take all of the credit, I can't. It was a group effort. But I'm glad you like it."

"Like it?! I love it. No one has ever done something like this for me."

She steps to the picnic table, setting the flowers down on top. Margot's inspecting all of the food and pops a raspberry in her mouth when I make my way around to the bottle of champagne I grabbed at the store earlier. "You thirsty?" I hold up the bottle.

"Yes, please!" She's beaming. The light in her eyes that I remembered from our first date is back, and it's making that caveman part of my heart swell with pride. I did this for her, and she loves it.

"Aren't you polite this evening?" I joke.

"It's not every day a handsome man puts together a whole picnic in my front yard." Margot sits on the bench, criss-crossed, and continues to pick at the fruit.

The champagne cork pops off, and I make quick work of filling up the plastic flutes I brought out before handing her one. "Well, I'll cheers to that. And I'll also cheers to beautiful women who make outfits out of my missing shirts." I wink and clink my glass with hers.

Margot's face goes red but, to her credit, doesn't shy away as she holds up her glass and then proceeds to take a sip. "You said to dress cozy. This happens to currently be the coziest shirt I have."

"Looks a hell of a lot better on you anyway." I take another sip of my champagne.

Her face flushes again. "I swear I was going to give it back."

I move to sit beside her rather than on the bench across the table. I just want to be close to her. "Nah, keep it. Didn't even know it was gone." That's a lie. It's one of my go-to shirts, one that's been washed so many times that it's perfectly broken in. And it's a Rivers' tee. Gotta support the family business.

"Thanks, neighbor. So how was work today?"

God, how good does it feel to have someone ask me how my day was at the end of it? Something so simple that millions

- probably billions - of people do every single day. But hearing it come out of her mouth, asking because she really gives a shit? I love it.

"It was good. Gus and I had a pretty steady flow of stuff going on. Gran brought Daisy in. Have you met her yet? Her family owns The Fuzzy Leaf."

"I have not. But apparently, I have her to thank for the small garden that will now be my kitchen counter at this rate."

"Hey, every girl deserves flowers. We'll have to introduce you, she's good people. Anyway, Gran's bringing her on to help with social media. We're trying to get more tourists in from online. Daisy's really good at that kind of stuff."

"That's awesome!"

"Yeah, I haven't gotten too much info from either of them yet, but I trust those two know what they're doing."

"Smart to trust the women in your life. We know best." She winks, and I laugh.

"Don't I know it. I probably wouldn't be here if it wasn't for Gran."

"I think it's really cool you're so close with her. I'm the same way with my mom. Not a lot of people... get it. I know it's not the same, but... I'm just saying-"

"You get it." I cut her off.

She exhales a sigh of relief. "I'm sorry. I don't want you to think I'm comparing having a deadbeat dad to- Oh my god." She lowers her head onto her arm resting on the table, trying to stifle a laugh.

"A deadbeat dad to dead parents?" I chuckle.

"Sawyer, I'm *so sorry.*" She peeks up with one eye.

I'm still laughing when I say, "Margot, don't. I... don't talk about them. And, in turn, no one else around here does because they think it'll send me over the edge or something. And it might have before, but not anymore." I place my hand on her arm, squeezing so she has to look up at me.

"I promise I'm not going to make a habit out of jokes about your childhood trauma."

"I can't lie. My dad probably would have gotten a kick out of that. He had a wonky sense of humor. My mom was always swatting him over the head for saying fucked up shit around me while laughing right alongside him. My grandpa would always egg him on, too. I picked up on too much too young. But it was fun."

She stops picking at the food on the table. "Can I ask you a question?"

"Anything."

"What was it like?" she asks, almost in a whisper.

But I'm not sure what she means. "What?"

"Having a family like that. And I know. I have no right to ask that when I know somehow you lost almost all of it. But what was it like? To be surrounded by so much love and family? To feel so sure there was always a place for you?"

I don't know how to respond to that. She's not asking to hurt me. I can see the look on her face. She's genuinely curious, and I can't explain it, but it almost hurts more to know she's never known that feeling than to have had it and lost it. Neither situation is ideal, and I'm starting to see that we might be two broken pieces that just so happen to fit together.

I take a minute to think about how to answer. I don't want her to think I'm upset with her for asking, but I want it to be right.

I finally settle on "It was everything."

"It's not fair." she responds.

"Nope." I say, grabbing a piece of cheese to eat. "I spent a lot of time lost, a lot of time angry, and it never changed anything. I still had to move on and I still had to miss them. But at some point, I finally felt sure again that there was a place for me."

"Oh yeah?"

"I thought I'd leave. That Merrymount would always be this hard reminder of everything gone, and I'd have to get out of here. I was even planning a move, ready to commit. Told Gran I had to go. Then some shit went down with Gus - it's a long story - and I don't know how or why the switch flipped, but it did."

"And you stayed." Margot finishes for me.

I nod my head while I chew, trying not to talk with my mouth full. Once I swallow, I clear my throat. "This place is home. I haven't questioned it since."

▭

"IT'S LATE, HUH?" Margot says sleepily. Her eyes have been fluttering for the past half an hour but I'm being a selfish man and have made no moves to disrupt her. Lying here next to her has made this one of the best nights of my life.

"I haven't checked the time, but yeah, I'd say it's pretty late, Pixie girl. You ready to head to bed?"

"No," she says on an exhale and then opens her eyes. "Ugh, I probably should though. I'm supposed to call my mom tomorrow morning. And you're probably thinking, okay? So? But she has the morning off so it'll be a whole thing. It's something we used to do when I was in college."

"Oh yeah?" I ask.

"Yeah. We'd set up video and phone calls in like two-hour or more blocks to catch each other up on everything. Sometimes we'd talk, sometimes we'd watch a TV show at the same time. Like, virtual hangouts."

I move to a sitting position, holding out my hand to help her do the same. "That sounds great. Has she been out here to visit yet?"

She shakes her head. "Not yet. I was thinking about asking her if she would want to spend the weekend soon. Maybe for that Blueberry Festival Red and everyone else has been talking about around town."

"I couldn't think of a better way to introduce someone to Merrymount. My parents and I-" I stop myself. This isn't the first time I've willingly brought up my parents with Margot. I'm normally never in the mood to talk about them, even the good memories.

She places her hand on top of mine, a small smile on her face. We're both still sitting on the picnic blanket, facing each other. "Tell me." she says quietly.

I clear my throat. "My parents and I spent every summer in Merrymount… before…" Margot squeezes my hand, and I shake my head. "Just before. And the Blueberry Festival was always the best part. You know those American flag shirts every family has for the Fourth of July? Well, my mom had custom ones made every year with blueberries for the stripes and our names on the backs for herself, me, my dad, Gran, and Grandpa."

Margot laughs, and I join her. "Oh my god, I love that."

"We'd spend the whole day visiting each booth. They're just about the same every year, but Mom would chat up every single booth shopkeeper, try samples, take business cards, and buy anything and everything. Dad would happily hold all of her bags. We'd watch the parade, and my grandpa would enter the pie-eating contest. And at the end of the night, everyone would gather on the high school football field for the fireworks display."

What I don't tell Margot is that while Gran and I still help the town prepare every year, we haven't actually been back to the festival since my parents' accident. I normally grab Gran, and we take off to the beach for the day, avoiding any tough conversations and memories. It felt like their day, and I don't know how anything there without them could measure up.

"Wow, it sounds like a dream."

"Sometimes it feels like it was."

A few minutes of comfortable silence passes, the two of us just looking up at the sky with the stars bright and twinkling. The only light around us comes from each of our porch lights. "Would you maybe want to show us around?" Margot nervously asks.

If there were ever a reason to get me back at that festival, it'd be for her. "I'd be honored, Pix."

She seems shocked I said yes that fast, the startled look on her face giving her away. Doesn't she get that I'd agree to just about anything to spend time with her?

"Wait, really?" She stands and stretches her arms out, and I take that as my cue to walk her to her front door. I know it's only a couple steps away but I'm not missing the opportunity to pick up where we left off last night before Red showed up.

Margot heads over to the table and starts picking up our discarded remnants of the picnic. "Yes, really. And hey, you're not on clean up duty. Let's get you inside." I place my hand on the small of her back, guiding her away from the mess.

"You did all of this. The least I can do is help."

"Not a chance." She begrudgingly lets me lead her up her porch stairs.

"So…" Margot begins and turns to face me as we step up to the front door.

"I had the best time tonight, Pixie girl." That blush creeps up her neck again. I knew she was putting up a front pretending to hate the nickname. She secretly loves it. I would also love to find out where else that blush creeps.

"Enough to do it again?" She slaps her hand over her mouth. "I did *not* just fucking say that," she says, sounding muffled with her hand across her lips.

I burst into the loudest laughter at the look of pure mortification still plastered on her face. I don't want her to be embarrassed. "I'm not laughing at you." I get out in between laughs.

"It sure feels like you are." She moves her hand up to her forehead, clearly distressed.

"I'm not. It's just-" I make sure to wait until she looks me in the eye, tucking a strand of her hair that fell behind her ear. "Yeah. I really wanna do this again."

I pull myself together and take one step closer. I'm in her space now. Close enough to count the individual freckles on her face. Something I plan on doing one of these days. I hear her suck one breath in, my eyes immediately focusing on her mouth. I lean down slightly. She's looking up at me with heavy-lidded eyes, and just when I'm about to move so we connect-

"Imgonnasneeze!" Margot yells as she jumps back into her front door. And on cue, she sneezes. Five times in a row.

The blush on her face might as well be permanent at this point. She's beet red, her eyes are wide, and she's fumbling with her hand behind her back, trying to find the doorknob without looking. I'm nervous she's about to-

"Allergies. Must be allergies, season changing, the outdoors, you know, the usual. So sorry, I'm *not* sick, though, so you don't have to worry. But on that note, I should go. Get some rest. Goodnight. Best night, Sawyer!" She turns the knob, opens the door, and before I can even say *bless you* she's inside, locking up.

She's bolted.

My hand is still reaching out to try to stop her. She slipped away so fast I barely had time to register it was happening. I'm about to knock on the door until she has no other choice but to open it again when I hear her from the other side, barely, so quietly, maybe more so to herself than me. "I really wanna do this again too."

Then we will. And again after that. She'll get used to this. I'm going to take my time with Margot LeClair.

I turn and head back to the picnic. We demolished most of the food, and I tucked an empty trash bag under the table when setting everything up for an easy clean after. I'm throwing everything that has to go into the plastic bag and keep looking over my shoulder at Cottage B to see if there's any movement behind the curtains.

There's still a soft light on in her living room, but I'm hoping she went to bed. I'm not mad about how tonight ended. Margot needs time to see how this is different, and I'm going to give her that and more. I turn and start the short walk back to my place, humming to myself when I hear the sound of a door clicking unlocked and opening behind me.

I twist my head in time to see Margot practically leaping off the last of her porch steps, running towards me. I toss the garbage bag on the ground and catch her without a second thought as she jumps into my arms. Her hands grab each side of my face, and she lowers her head. I have next to no time to register what's happening except Margot's lips are pressed against mine.

She's that first rush of cold when you get into the water on a hot summer day. She's a song you haven't heard in years but remember every lyric to, no matter how much time has passed. She's spotting a doe with her babies, getting to peacefully watch them from a distance in a clearing. She's the calm quiet in the early mornings.

She pulls back to look at me, eyes wide, as if she's just as stunned as I am. Her hands snake behind my neck. Her ankles are locked together around my waist, and I'm holding her up in the air. I'm not anywhere near ready to let her go. Not sure if I ever will be after a kiss that felt like that.

"Was that okay?" she breathes into me.

*It was everything.*

My brain short circuits and all I can manage to say is *more* before I bring my face back to hers. I kiss her again, my tongue lightly grazing her bottom lip, and she opens in answer for me.

My heart is pounding in my ears, heat rushing everywhere, and I can taste earlier's champagne on her. This is already so addicting, and I need more of it. I need more of her. Right here in my arms is everything I ever fucking needed.

A shudder of breath escapes her, just slightly breaking us apart. "Holy shit."

So she feels it, too. Good. I capture her mouth again with mine, both of us taking what we need, throwing our everything into this moment, this kiss. I feel like I was starved for touch before, like nothing compares and she's ruined me from here on out.

I'm ready to dive in headfirst to any unknown from one fucking kiss, starting to dream of a future with her when we've barely had real time together.

But that's okay, we have time.

# Chapter Seventeen

*Margot*

"THE KIDS ARE ADVANCING SO FAST this season. I'm really excited to see the progress by summer's end. You'll still make it out for the family show, right?"

"Wouldn't miss it, Mom," I say into my phone that's currently pinned between my shoulder and the side of my face as I finish washing the dishes in my sink.

"Everyone will be so excited to see you. I don't remember the last time you went this long without coming by the school. Or home for that matter," she says with a tone that tells me she's less than pleased about my lack of appearances.

After I woke up this morning and was hit with each wave of consciousness of yesterday's events, I pretty much threw myself into a downward spiral, something I'm very familiar with. It started with me reorganizing the one closet in the cottage. When I moved in, I kind of threw just about anything that could fit in there haphazardly until I had to hurl my body into the door to get it closed.

My thoughts started to creep in as I was finishing that project, so I decided to get to work on deep cleaning my kitchen. But midway through that, I couldn't stop replaying the end of the night and realized that if I didn't talk it out with *someone*, I would lose my mind by the end of the day.

Naturally, I called my mom. In typical Margot fashion, I have avoided what I actually should be talking to her about for the past hour and a half, happily listening to every story she had to tell me about the kids in her classes, the helicopter parents she has to deal with, and her neighbor's vendetta against the garbage man that comes on Tuesdays because he hit her mailbox. It's been nice to catch up like this. While we text and send pictures daily and really try to sneak in phone calls when we can, it's been different from what we're both used to.

Now would probably be a good time to invite her to stay for the Blueberry Festival, but I'm going to have to tell her about Sawyer first. Not that there's much to tell, I guess. I'm just going to lay it all out there, rip it off like a bandaid.

This is one of those moments where I don't know how things will go because it's new territory for both of us. I never dated anyone long enough to introduce them to her, and if my mom ever dated, I was never privy to that information. Will she think I did all of this and moved out here to chase a boy?

"Ha, I miss everyone, too. You the most, though, of course. Speaking of… any plans for Fourth of July weekend?" I ask. There. That's a good opening.

"Hmm.." I hear her rustling some papers. "Nothing on the calendar. Jackie's probably having family and friends over for a cookout like usual, but I haven't made any commitments. Why? Big happenings in Merrymount for the holiday?"

"Actually, funny you mention it-"

"You're the one who brought up the Fourth of July," she points out.

"You're so right. Anyway, there's this Blueberry Festival. It's a big deal. Small town cute kind of thing you'll probably love, and you can stay with me for the weekend. And Sawyer, my friend Sawyer, said he'd show us around. And I thought that'd be fun. Me, you, and Sawyer. My friend." I try to get it out as fast as possible.

There's an extended beat of silence on the other end of the phone. I pull it away from my ear to make sure she didn't hang up. She didn't.

"Margot."

"Mom," I retort.

"You want to try that again?"

I sigh. It was worth a shot. "Sawyer *is* my friend. I think. But he also lives next door and is my landlord's grandson. He's also stupid hot. He *cares*, Mom. Like, about *everyone* around him. And he's also a guy I went out with a while ago. A small, silly little date. It didn't mean anything. But I swear I didn't know he lived here. Life is just weird, and I-"

She cuts me off. "Margot, *slow down*, honey. How come this is the first I'm hearing of any of this?"

I take a second before I respond, not sure how to admit it. "I was embarrassed."

"Embarrassed about what? I'm not following."

"I didn't want you to think I did all of this for him. I mean it. I had no idea this was his hometown or that he lived here. When I figured it out, I was hellbent on avoiding him like the plague until my lease was up, and then I would start over again somewhere new or come home."

"Oh, honey," she says quietly.

"But then we started doing our laundry together and he pops into Red's a lot. It turned out to be a lot harder to avoid him than I thought, and then I didn't *want* to avoid him anymore. It's just-" I catch my breath. "You spent your entire adult life taking care of me and building a career out of something you're actually passionate about, and your daughter is making out with the neighbor. She spends way too much time thinking about it and not doing much else."

"I must have failed you somewhere along the way."

I pull the phone away from my ear again, taken aback by the sudden seriousness of her voice. "Mom, what the hell? No, you're the *best*. That's literally what I'm trying to tell you."

"You're telling me you're seeing this man. He's great, you have history, and he's making you happy in this new place. And you're telling me you have been living in fear, *hiding* it all from me. Why? Because you thought I wanted you to be alone? You thought that was the life I wanted for you?"

I try to cut in. "No, it's not that."

"That's exactly what it is, and I'm hurt. And I only have myself to blame." I can hear her stifle a sniffle. I let the silence hang, anticipating she has more to say.

"I kept you to myself for too long. You were - you still are - my everything. I selfishly never wanted to have to share. When your… *father,*" The way she pauses and says the word sends a second wave of shock through me. We never talk about him. She continues.

"When he left, I took it as a sign. It was supposed to just be you and me against the world. And it was. But things are different now. You've grown, and I'm so proud of who you are. I want the rest of the world to see what I've gotten to keep to myself for the last twenty years. I'm sorry it took me so long to say that."

And now we're both crying. I wish I could reach into my phone to grab her, hug her, and never let her go.

"I love you, Mom," I manage to get out.

"I love you more, Margot. Always. Now-" She clears her throat, putting these big feelings back into a box to dive into at a later time when we're together, I'm sure. "Blueberry Festival. Me, you, and *Sawyer.*" She puts some emphasis on his name, letting me know that's another conversation to revisit.

I follow her lead. "Yes. Fourth of July weekend. I'm not sure what you have going on class-wise that Friday, and I know I'll be helping Red prep, but you can come anytime. I'm… excited. To show you everything - *everyone* - here."

"Putting it on the calendar now. I'm looking forward to this too, Margot."

I glance at the time on my phone. "But hey, I have to finish getting ready for work. Can I text you later?"

"You better." She makes a kissy noise into the phone, and she ends the call.

▭

IT'S BEEN A RELATIVELY quiet day at Red's. She didn't have me come in to open, so I missed that rush and have just been making myself busy cleaning and restocking things from the back. A few regulars have made their way in, and we've talked about random stuff happening in town, but my mind has been elsewhere.

The conversation with my mom this morning distracted me enough to get me to this point, but now I'm stuck overthinking Sawyer and how last night ended. I jumped into his arms like a crazed spider monkey.

Thankfully, there was no sign of him this morning when I left for work. He was out well before I was, probably trying to avoid me. Not that I would blame him.

He did kiss me back, though. Hard. It felt so good, his hands gripping me firmly against him. My body lit up like a fucking Christmas tree with every touch. And when he set me down after God knows how long we spent tangled together like that, his smile was so big it took up his whole face.

But that could just have been the heat of the moment. It's

not like one kiss is a big deal. It doesn't mean anything. There's no sense in getting my hopes up. I'm chill. This is cool. Friends kiss, right?

I'm putting coffee mugs away when the jingle of someone coming in the door startles me out of my thoughts. I slam my head on the bottom side of the counter when I jump. "God damn it, that hurt," I say to no one but myself, rubbing the top of my head. When I rise out of my crouching position, I see *who* made their way in here and my eyes go wide.

He's covered in dirt. From his boots to his worn jeans, to the flannel that's unbuttoned over an equally dirty t-shirt. The only things that seem like they survived whatever caused this mess are his face, hands, and very wet hair, his short, dark curls dripping with water. Despite all that, the same smile from last night is plastered across his face.

Sawyer glances at the clock on the wall as he makes his way over to the counter, tipping an imaginary hat on his head. "Good afternoon, Pix."

"Hi. Umm, why are you wet?" My voice sounds like it belongs to a squeaky mouse.

"I'm not even gonna touch the joke I could make there." My eyes go wide, and the nosey book club ladies across the room snicker. "Couple of college kids flipped their kayaks on the river, and I had to jump in to help. The bank was still pretty muddy from the rain showers. I managed to throw my head under the hose before getting over here to see you."

"Me?" I didn't think it was possible for my voice to go that many octaves higher.

He huffs out a laugh. "Yeah, Pixie girl, you. How's your day going?"

"It's uh, it's good. You know, regular degular, nothing to report." I wave my hand, gesturing to the near-empty cafe. Aside from a few stragglers from the book club and the mystery man over in his usual spot, it's just me and Sawyer in here. Even Red stepped out to run some errands.

I jump into making his regular coffee, not even bothering to ask what he wants or *if* he wants anything. Clearly, he needs a pick-me-up, and I need to keep my hands busy.

"Well, I'm glad it's going better than mine. Although I have to say, there is next to nothing bringing my mood down today." He says it loud enough to re-pique the interest of the ladies closest to us. I swear I can see them physically lean in to eavesdrop.

I make myself busy with the machine, avoiding all eye contact. "Love that for you. Any plans for the weekend?"

"Yeah, actually, I wanted to mention that. I'm taking off with Gus. We're gonna hike some trails and camp and shit. We try to do it before the official summer season starts here because it always gets busy, and then we never make time. But I'll be back late Sunday afternoon. We're not venturing into the middle of nowhere, so I'll have service if you need me for anything."

I secure the lid on the coffee cup and slide it across the counter and I say, "That sounds fun. You've been doing it for a while now?"

"Since he moved in with me and Gran, yeah." Sawyer lifts the cup to mouth, taking a quick sip. I'm sure it just burned the shit out of his mouth, but he gives me another one of those mega-watt smiles and winks. "Don't tell Red, but you make the best cup of coffee I've ever had."

I'm sure I'm blushing, but I manage to pull myself together. "Yeah, yeah. I'm sure you tell her the same thing."

Cheryl from the book club decides to chime in. "He does!"

We both laugh, and Sawyer sets the cup back down so he can pull out his wallet.

I wave my hand to swat it away. "Nope. Caffeine is on me today. You look like you need it."

He ignores me by taking a five-dollar bill out and placing it into the tip jar. "Thanks, Margot." He grabs the hand that I had on the counter and brings it to his lips, placing a small peck on the top. I feel the fuzziness of pins and needles at even the smallest touch from him, and goosebumps break out along my arm.

Sawyer picks up his coffee cup, and he looks like he's about to leave. I'm standing here like an idiot, brain short-circuiting over a kiss on the freaking hand. "It's nothing. Um, have fun this weekend."

But then he leans down and quickly captures my lips with his own. It's a small, casual kiss goodbye. I could have imagined it. I think I did.

"I'll text you, but I'll see you Sunday, yeah?" he says as he makes his way to the front door. He waves to the women, blatantly staring from their table.

"Yeah," I say more to myself than him. With his hand on the door, he finally turns and walks out, and I let out a breath I didn't even know I was holding in. I bring my hand to my mouth, my fingers lightly grazing where his lips just touched.

"Oh, you got it bad, honey," Cheryl says in between chuckles, shaking her head at Judy across from her at their table.

"Didn't book club end, like, an hour ago?" I jokingly snap, shaking off the haze I'm left in and grabbing a plastic bin to come around and bus a few tables.

"Yes, but I'm *so glad* we decided to stay for the show." Judy giggles.

I shake my head and leave them to gossip amongst themselves, deciding that's not a battle I want to get into today. Partly because there is next to nothing going on with me and Sawyer and partly because I know I'd lose.

I make my way over to the table next to the mystery man, who still has some plates and mugs left out. He looks up from the book he's reading, and we make eye contact. God, there is something about him that feels so familiar, but I can't place it.

"Hey, how's it going?" I ask him as I clear the dishes and wipe down the table.

"Good!" he responds quickly and looks back down at his book.

I should leave him be. But my options right now are listening to my internal monologue, torturing myself by discussing my barely there love life with Judy and Cheryl over there, or talking to him.

"You know, you're in here pretty much every day, and I don't even know your name."

He looks up at me, seemingly surprised I kept the conversation going. I don't blame him. Out of everyone I've met since working here, I've talked to him the least out of the regulars. I've said nothing really aside from normal niceties as he orders and telling him to have a good day.

"It's uh, it's Miller," he says shyly.

"Nice to officially meet you, Miller. I'm Margot." I reach over and extend my hand. He takes it in a firm but quick shake.

"I know." He looks embarrassed. "I mean, I know you're Margot. I should have introduced myself earlier. That's my bad."

"No worries. If you, ah, caught any of my earlier conversations, then you know I'm not the best at communicating either."

He laughs and seems to relax a bit. Looking at Miller, I would say he's a few years younger than I am, but he doesn't act like those early twenties frat boys you see fucking around Seaport or Southie. I'm guessing it has something to do with the little girl I've seen him get off the school bus. Just as I finish my thought, the school bus pulls up to drop off a herd of kids.

Miller quickly folds the corner of the page he was reading

down to mark his place in his book, closes it, and gets up. "Nah, you're fine. Believe me, I've always been awkward as hell. I gotta run though, it's the last day of school for my daughter. It was really nice to meet you."

He jogs out in time to see a little girl with long brown hair with perfect bouncing curls, hop off the last step of the bus. She's wearing a backpack that looks like it might actually be bigger than she is, but it doesn't stop her from doing a full sprint into Miller's waiting open arms.

Daughter. Well, that explains his maturity. I smile to no one but myself when I watch them walk off, hand in hand. I can't hear their conversation from inside the coffee shop, but I can see her animated face, probably rattling off everything that happened during her day. Miller is visibly listening intently, giving her his full attention.

I feel a small pang in my chest, the one that only makes itself known when I'm caught off guard by a father and daughter together. But, just like every time, it's quickly replaced with a warming sensation, knowing there's a little girl out there whose dad loves her very much. I'll always want that for everyone.

# Chapter Eighteen

*Sawyer*

I FUCKING HATE JUNE.

The bugs have defrosted and are crawling back out, traffic is picking up with school being over for the summer, and people are coming in from all over to start their summer vacations.

It's also the anniversary of my parents' death.

I don't keep track of the years because there's nothing to celebrate or honor. I like to remember them on their birthdays and their wedding anniversary. I never should have lost them. They never should have died. We still had so much to do. They should be here.

*They should be here.* I keep repeating it over and over in my head as I swing the axe over my head to chop some wood. A storm the other night blew a couple of the bigger branches off one of the trees aside from the main building, so I'm getting it all cut and sorted to make bundles for campsites to sell.

I've been at it for a few hours now, losing track of time and not bothering to check my phone or even play any music. It's been quiet today with Gran out visiting someone or doing something. I'm not too sure because I was half-listening when she rattled off her plans to me this morning. She knew I wasn't paying attention, but she didn't call me out for it. I know she doesn't want to talk about it just as much as I don't. We just handle it differently.

The camping trip helped, I guess. It usually does. But this time, I found myself counting down the minutes to get back to town. I thought about calling Margot more times than I can count but ultimately chickened out, and only ended up texting her to let her know we made it to the campsite safely.

Gus has been trying to give me space, finding other shit to do around the property, and handling customers as they come through. But I think my solitude is about to come to an end. As the axe cracks into the piece of wood I have lined up, I see him approaching from the corner of my eye, and he doesn't look too pleased. I'm not sure what could have pissed him off.

"Alright, we're getting the fuck out of here," he calls out.

"What the fuck are you going on about?" I pull the headphone out of my ear, acting like I was listening to something.

"I said we're done here. Pack it up. We're going out," he growls. Gus rips the axe out of my hands, and throws it on the ground a couple feet away.

"Dude, what the hell is your problem?" I snap at him.

"I'm not the one with the problem. It's you. I tried to let you handle this your way for years now, but it sucks. The whole situation sucks, and I get that. But walking around like an angry prick isn't going to fix shit. Beth tells me to leave you be, but nah. I texted John and George. They're meeting us at the bar."

"I don't know what you're fucking talking about." I walk over and pick up the axe.

"No? Just a brooding bastard for no reason today?" Gus lifts an eyebrow at me.

"I don't want to talk about it," I grumble, making my way back to the storage shed where we keep all the tools. Gus follows behind me.

"I'm not gonna make you. I'm telling you, we're taking the night off and going out to get a few beers with the guys. This sulking shit is done."

"Fine." I put the axe back on its hook and walk right back out. Guess I'm not getting out of this.

Gus plasters a big, fake smile on his face. "Great. Leave the Jeep. I'll drive you home tonight." We walk over to his car parked next to mine.

"I'm not planning on drinking that much." I side-eye him.

"Humor me." He flips me off before hopping in his truck.

▭

"I'M gonna run to the bathroom, you good here for a couple minutes?" Gus asks me as he gets up from his barstool.

"You're acting like a fucking babysitter, man," I say, except I think my words are starting to slur. I don't know which number beer I'm on, and I think I called for a round of shots one, two, maybe three times. Was it vodka?

Gus shakes his head with a tight-lipped smile. "Because I am fucking babysitting you at this point, asshole. I'll be back. We're heading out after this." He takes the last sip of his beer, places the empty glass on the bar, and walks off toward the back, where the restroom is.

*I wish Margot was here.*

No, wait. I don't think I want Margot to see me like this.

She's probably home at the cottage. Reading a book in her silly fucking egg chair on the porch. I don't think there's any way an average-height person could sit comfortably in that fucking thing, but Margot's pixie sized. It's cute. She always looks cute sitting out there.

Actually, she's probably in bed sleeping. I don't even know what time it is. I should be in bed sleeping. I'd be in bed sleeping if Gus didn't drag me out here.

I look around the room, noticing that most of the people who were here when we walked in earlier have started to phase out. John and George are attempting to slow dance to a song that's definitely not meant for slow dancing in between the pool tables. They're quietly laughing and whispering to each other, not a care in the world.

They remind me of my parents, back when my dad would spin my mom around in the kitchen when she was in the middle of making dinner. She would pretend to be angry, saying he was messing up her flow. But she could never hide the smile on her face.

It hits me right in my chest. A strong longing for something like that.

That feeling jolts me into digging my phone out of my jeans pocket, pulling up my text thread with the one person I could see myself dancing like that with. Telling her that sounds like a great idea, probably heightened by the alcohol. Not sure I care, though.

ME:

Pixel

ME:

NO I meant Pixie

ME:

I hate tht your not here I wanna dance. Do u dance???

MY PIXIE GIRL:

Are you okay?

ME:

Great jus thinking about stuff. I wish I didnt fuck it up the 1st time u know

MY PIXIE GIRL:

Sawyer Hale, are you drunk?

ME:

Onlny a little

# Chapter Nineteen

*Margot*

I LEFT SAWYER ON READ. I didn't know how to respond. I'm not good at this stuff.

But drunk words are sober thoughts, right?

Except I'm not entirely sure what Sawyer's drunk words really mean, and I don't know if I'm brave enough to ask. I mean, I'm definitely not asking right now. But tomorrow? I don't know. I should talk to Red.

I hear the sounds of a car pulling into the driveway, and I jump up from my spot on the couch to make sure it's Sawyer getting home safely. I breathe a sigh of relief when I see August behind the wheel as he pulls up in front of Sawyer's house.

"Well, at least he knows better than to drink and drive," I mumble to myself.

I let the curtain fall back closed and walk away from the front window to mind my own business, mostly so I don't get caught staring like a weirdo. I'm refilling my water bottle when I hear shouting.

"Dude, if you don't get in the *fucking house…*" I can hear August trying to keep his voice low.

"This *is* my house!" Sawyer yells, his words sloshing together. Oh yeah, he's more than a little drunk.

But then I realize his voice sounds really close. Like, on my porch close. I stop and hold my breath. I'm not even bothering to lie to myself about not eavesdropping.

"Sawyer, I swear to god, I will kick your ass. Let's *go.*" Now August's voice has moved closer. I hear his heavy footsteps come up the stairs. They're both definitely on my porch.

One of them is now fumbling with keys. "That's what I'm fucking trying to do! Jesus."

"You're about two seconds from me hauling you over my shoulder and throwing you into your own bed." There's no room for argument in August's voice, and I have no doubt he wouldn't struggle even a little to pick Sawyer up. He's massive. I'm short on a normal day, but next to him, it's comical.

I decide that while August can physically handle this, he might still appreciate a little help anyway. I quickly put my water on the counter and make my way over to the front door. Unlocking and opening it, I see Sawyer hunched over, keys in his hand held up to his face, looking for what I can only assume is *his* house key. August is behind him, his face a mixture of annoyance and apology when he looks down at me.

"Is everything okay?" I ask apprehensively.

Both of them attempt to respond at the same time.

"I'm so sorry, Margot," August says with a sigh.

"I just want to fucking go to bed." Sawyer looks up at me, his cheeks pink from the alcohol. "Can I go to bed?" His voice cracks, and I look him in the eyes, a deep sadness pooling there. Even though I'm confused as hell, both with Sawyer's current state and where we stand, I wouldn't turn him away right now.

"Why don't you go get comfy on the couch." I fully open

the door and move slightly out of the way so Sawyer can get past me. "Water's in the fridge if you need it. I'm just going to talk to Gus for a minute, okay?"

He stumbles into the kitchen and pulls me into a tight hug. With his cheek resting on the top of my head, he takes a deep breath. "You smell nice. Like a garden. A fairy garden."

I giggle while I try to pry myself out of his grasp, not at all mad at the physical contact or compliment. But I need to talk to August. Something is definitely up with him.

"Thanks big guy, head on in." I manage to separate us and give him a pat on his back. He heads straight through the living room… into my bedroom. I'll deal with that after I talk to Gus.

I turn back to August who's now leaning just enough so his head doesn't hit the top of the doorway. His frame takes up most of the space and he's shaking his head. "He's good to crash here. It's not a far walk for him in the morning," I say with a laugh.

"You sure? Because I have no problem dragging his ass back home."

"Yeah, it's really no big deal." I hear what sounds like Sawyer bumping into something in my room, and I lower my voice in case he can hear. "But I have to ask… is he…"

August finishes my question, "Okay?" He sighs. "No, probably not. This is… a tough time of year for him. He's normally not this much of a mess, but- I should let him be the one to tell you everything."

"It has to do with his parents, doesn't it?" I ask.

August doesn't say anything, but he shallowly nods his head.

I nod back in understanding. "You're good to take off, Gus. I can keep an eye on him." I place my hand on his arm and give him a gentle squeeze. "You're a good friend."

"Sawyer's the family I never got to have. Beth, too. They

never gave up on me. Those two deserve only good things coming back to them at this point, you know? Thanks again, Margot. Tell him to call me after he's done nursing that hangover tomorrow, okay?"

"You got it."

August gives me one more half smile and turns to make his way over to his truck. I close the door once I see his headlights turn on. I put my back to the door and lean against it, needing a minute to collect myself.

There is absolutely no sense in trying to talk to Sawyer right now beyond making sure he's okay and comfortable. We can talk about whatever we need to say tomorrow.

Walking through the cottage, I clap my hands together and call out, "Alright, big guy. You need water and Tylenol before bed. Are you hungry? I can make you a-" I stop short at my bedroom doorway and have to throw my hands over my mouth to keep myself from letting out a yelp.

In the few minutes I was talking to August, Sawyer managed to get his shirt completely off and thrown onto the floor, and only one leg is left in his jeans. Both of his boots are sitting next to the bedroom door. He's face down, spread out on my bed, snoring.

"Sawyer?" I try to see if I can stir him awake.

I'm met with a *humph.*

I walk over and sit on the edge of the bed, I put my hand on his back and try to gently nudge him. "Sawyer? How about we get you into the bed instead of just spread across it. Does that sound okay?"

Another humph comes out of him. Well, I guess I can handle this on my own. I get back up and walk around to shimmy his jeans off him completely. That gets him to stir just a little. I give myself to the count of ten to admire the near-naked Sawyer Hale in my bed. His tanned back muscles are on full display. He's wearing black briefs that do absolutely nothing to hide the toned ass and thick thighs he earned from years of manual labor.

"I'll be right back," I say more to myself than him before I head into the kitchen and grab him water from the fridge. I pop into the bathroom, grab two Tylenol from the cabinet above the sink, and hurry back into my room.

I place the water and medicine on the nightstand and try to shake Sawyer awake with a little more force than I used before. "Sawyer, hey, wake up for just a minute. Let's get you settled in properly."

His eyes slowly crack open. "Margot?" he half mumbles. "This bed is comfy." He rubs his face into one of my pillows.

"Yeah, it's me. Can you sit up?"

He manages to get himself into a sitting position. That sleepy, sad look is still in his eyes, but he gives me a soft smile as I hand him the glass. He takes a few sips and accepts the two pills in my outstretched hand, downing them on the next sip. Neither of us says anything.

He places the now empty glass of water back on my night-stand and says, "Would you believe me if I said I'm normally not like this?" His words are still slurring, but he's starting to sound a little more like himself.

"Everyone's entitled to a few drunken nights here and there." I laugh and lift the comforter and sheet, motioning for him to climb under. I climb in next to him, moving a pillow to my back so I can sit up against it on the headboard. "Do you want to talk about it?"

He doesn't answer, but instead of sitting up alongside me or laying back down next to me, Sawyer lays his head on my lap. My hand instinctively moves to his hair, and I run my fingers through it, as if this is normal and we do it all the time. I want to feel weird about it but the contented sigh he lets out causes the butterflies that were dormant in my stomach to take flight, and I forget every insecurity that was taking up space in my head.

We sit like this in comfortable silence for a little while. Sawyer's breathing starts to even out, and I'm starting to think he finally fell back asleep when he quietly says, "This used to be our house. When we would come visit Gran and Grandpa."

I stop playing with his hair, but my hand doesn't leave his head. "You and your parents?"

He sighs again. "Yeah. My mom liked the view of the water from this cottage best. We spent every summer here, and when they died…" He stops, but I don't say anything. He gets to decide what he wants to share. This is all on his terms. I pick up where I left off, moving my fingers through his curls.

"When they passed, I couldn't come back here. I knew it would still smell like them, and I'd see them in the corner of my eye or something. We ended up using it for storage and occasionally would rent it out to tourists or if someone in town needed a place temporarily. When the time came for me to move out of Gran's - my decision - not hers," he laughs. "She'd have kept me at her place forever, I think. But when I left, I picked the cottage next door. It's smaller, and my mom was right. The view isn't as good, but it was my version of a fresh start."

"That makes sense," I say softly.

"I guess I got confused tonight and somehow ended up at your door. I'm sorry. I can go."

"Stay." It's out of my mouth before I even finish the thought.

"Stay?" Sawyer peers up at me between his thick, dark lashes from my lap, his eyes barely open. His scruff is the only thing keeping him from looking like a lost boy. He's on the cusp of sleep.

In what world would I kick him out?

"I think we're both just fine where we are right now." I reach over and turn the lamp off. Sawyer makes a deep hum sound that I can feel vibrate in his chest as he dozes off. In the dark, where I'm brave, I lean down and kiss the top of his head. I continue playing with his hair until I finally drift off to sleep myself.

# Chapter Twenty

*Sawyer*

LIGHT STREAMING in my face where my black-out curtains should be keeping the sun out wakes me up from the deepest sleep I've had in years. I've had trouble sleeping since I was young, and that felt damn good. I barely remember getting home last night, so the alcohol must have knocked me out cold.

All of a sudden, right before I stretch out my body, I'm deeply aware I have a sleeping Margot tucked in my arm, her head lying on my chest.

My bare chest.

I take a quick look down. I see blankets cast aside from moving in my sleep. I realize quickly that I'm laying in Margot's bed in my fucking underwear, whereas she is fully clothed in fuzzy socks, oversized sweatpants, and a hoodie.

*What the hell did I drink last night?*

I stay exactly where I am, careful not to wake her, except to move my head and look around Margot's bedroom as the memories from last night start blurily coming back to me.

*Pissy mood at work. Gus and me meeting up with John and George at the bar. Drinks. Shots. Jesus Christ, why did I do so many shots? Texts to Margot. Showing up at Margot's. Fuck.*

I am a grown man, and I acted like a frat boy one minute and a baby the next with a woman who did not sign up for this. I'm wondering if there's a way I can slide myself out from under her without waking her when her hand, draped over me, starts roaming my stomach lazily, and she sighs.

"Good morning, big guy," she says in a sleepy, raspy voice that shoots right through me. Margot lifts her head. She rests her chin on my chest, and I think I stop breathing. Her eyes are still heavy, the green in them almost sparkling with the sun coming through the window. Her freckles look like they're dancing across her skin. She's got this lazy smile on her face, and all I wanna do is-

"Can I kiss you?" I ask instead of think.

Those pretty, sage eyes that were just barely awoken go wide as can be, and so quickly, so quietly, she replies. "Yes."

I don't waste a second. My mouth is on hers, and my hand is reaching up to cup the back of her neck. I pepper her with small kisses, waking up her soft lips with each one. It's slow and sweet, almost nervous - the opposite of the kiss from the other night. Neither of us is in a rush. I'm playing with her hair while her hand explores my torso. I completely forget all of the bad in the last twenty-four hours.

She pulls away, looking me dead in the eyes. "How are you feeling, Sawyer?" The way she asks hits me in the chest. I can see in her face she's asking, yes, physically, but more so because of what I think I told her last night about this cottage and my parents.

"A lot better than this time yesterday," I answer honestly.

She smiles and then doubt flashes across her face. "Is this-" She motions her hand in between us. "Okay, too?"

"More than okay." I lean back down and kiss her again. I'd

be good to spend the rest of today doing exactly this. But first, I need to apologize.

I break the kiss. I hold her arms in place so she knows I'm not trying to get her off me, but I readjust myself and the pillow behind me so I'm sitting up a little.

"Margot, I want to say sorry for last night. I don't really know what I was thinking, but you didn't ask to take on this baggage. You should have let Gus haul my ass out of here." I let out a laugh. "I can't even blame him. This is on me. I shouldn't have shown up here to begin with."

"You don't need to apologize. I was fine. I *am* fine. So what? You showed up at your neighbor's house sloppy drunk, it happens."

"You're not just my neighbor," I grumble.

"That's beside the point right now." She waves her hand flippantly as she moves to get up.

I don't know what she means by that because it does fucking matter that we're more than just neighbors, and I don't know why she's leaving this comfy spot we've made for ourselves so soon.

"Do you have work today?" I ask her.

Margot reaches the doorway and turns around, drowning in the hoodie and sweatpants she's wearing. She's so fucking cute. "Nope, but I'll make you a coffee anyway." She winks, and she's gone.

She's acting… odd.

I manage to sit up to take another look around the room to find my clothes and see them neatly folded on the top of Margot's dresser. God, this is fucking embarrassing. I hear the coffee starting to brew out in the kitchen, and ceramic mugs clinking together when the headache I knew was bound to hit at some point today comes crashing through my brain.

After I take a couple minutes to sit here with my head in my hands and process how much of a fucking idiot I've been, I grab my shirt, socks, and jeans. I put them on to attempt some sense of normalcy when I walk into Margot's kitchen.

I find her perched on the counter, stretching her arm for the sugar on the top shelf above the fridge, maybe - most likely - seconds from falling with the way she has to contort her body to reach.

"You're the only one who lives here. Why would you put something so out of reach that it's a hazard for you to get it?" I ask, leaning into the doorframe between the kitchen and the living room, arms crossed over my chest.

To Margot's credit, she doesn't startle like I thought she might. I was ready to rush and catch her if she did, but she manages to grab the container with two fingers and moves to quickly jump down.

"Cabinet space is limited. I do just fine on my own, thank you very much," she says, pursing her lips.

I hold my hands up in mock surrender. "You're right, you're right. My bad, Pix."

She ignores me and, humming to herself, bounces around the kitchen. She grabs creamer out of the fridge to place on the table - three different flavors - and sets two ridiculously tiny spoons down next to two mismatched mugs. One is shaped like a pair of tits, and the other has a pattern on it that looks like it was crocheted by someone's grandma in a nursing home. I also noticed two Tylenols laid out on a napkin.

I walk over and pick up the boob mug, holding it up to her. "Nice rack."

Margot turns, coffee pot in hand, and lets out the biggest laugh. Mixed with her sleepy smile, it makes me forget everything I was worried about, head pounding included. I want to pick back up where we left off before she broke our kiss this morning.

She pours coffee into each mug. "Every time my mom and I travel, I try to embarrass her in the gift shops by finding the most outrageous souvenirs. I was still in high school when I walked up to the checkout in Key West one summer with that one. The cashier could barely keep his shit together while we paid. My mom apologized to him at least three times."

I laugh with her. "Damn, my dad would have loved that." I pick up the mug, the black coffee steaming, and skip adding anything to it to get that first sip. It burns down my throat, but that feels so fucking good right now.

"If you were wondering, the pain meds aren't for me. I'm not a guest at the Hangover Hotel today. You are." She eyes me over her own mug.

"Thank you," I say, scooping up the pills and tossing them in my mouth. "And sorry. Again. I'll be out of your hair in a couple minutes."

"Oh, I'm not kicking you out or anything." She sets her coffee down. "It's just- Do you want to talk about it?" Margot nervously starts fidgeting with the sleeve of her hoodie.

I avoid making eye contact. "My parents died eighteen years ago yesterday."

"Sawyer…" She reaches across the table, putting her hand on mine that's holding my mug.

"I don't- I don't talk about it. I don't like to remember them for that."

"You don't have to, I'm so sorry I asked-"

I cut her off. "But I want… to tell you. If that's okay," I say quietly. I finally look up and take in Margot's face. It's full of concern and patience, and I know it's okay for me to keep going with this.

"I was twelve. It was the first weekend of vacation, and we had just shown up in Merrymount for the summer. Gran was still struggling without Grandpa, but when we were all together, it was better. My Gran kicked my parents out for a date night, and I was happy to hang back with her to order takeout and watch scary movies my mom was still saying no to.

I remember falling asleep on Gran's couch, excited for whatever we had planned for the next day. There was always something to look forward to."

"The doorbell woke me up. I'll never forget it because it sounded like wind chimes in my dream. No one ever rang the doorbell at my grandparents' house. They had an open door policy. I remember seeing flashing lights through the window and being so confused."

I've only said all of this out loud once, at the beginning of the therapy Gran put me in after the accident. I never even told Katie the details, not that she asked.

When we were younger I used to appreciate the fact that Katie could easily gloss over my parents being dead, but as time went on, I started to realize she maybe just didn't want to deal with talking about emotionally difficult subjects, aside from her own. I had thought she was being considerate by avoiding the topic, but she actually just didn't care.

I'm doing everything to make my body not shake. Margot squeezes my hand once, I didn't even notice she never let go, but it feels good to have her here, just listening.

"Gran was just as discombobulated as I was, shuffling to the door from her spot where she also fell asleep on the couch. She even shushed herself because she probably thought I was still sleeping. But I peeked my head over the backside of the couch and watched her open the front door. The next thing I knew, she dropped to her knees right there, wailing. It was the worst sound I ever heard."

I can't stop the shiver that goes through me. Margot squeezes my hand again, two times. It feels like she's saying *I'm here* and it gives me the push to keep going.

"Apparently, they were on their way home from dinner, and Dad was driving. The cops assumed he swerved to avoid an animal in the road but they were on a bridge and went over. The... the windows didn't open. They couldn't get out."

Without removing her hand from mine, Margot, at some point, managed to move from the seat across the table to the chair right next to me, pushed close enough that her knee is touching mine.

"There's nothing I could say to make that better, but God, Sawyer. I'm so sorry."

"I know." This time, I squeeze her hand back. "I don't remember much after that. I mean- They told us my parents were dead, and we planned their funeral. We packed up my things at my house and moved them into Gran's. She put me in therapy, and we tried to move on. Neither of us has ever been good at talking about it, but she's tried her best."

"You both deserved better," Margot says.

"I try not to be a miserable son of a bitch, but, yeah… we did. I normally don't let it consume me, though. This year felt harder for some reason. Like the more time that passes, the less they were ever here. I don't know. I can barely remember how I got here."

It's going to take some time for the Tylenol and coffee to kick in so my brain still feels like it's rocking inside my skull and I'm fighting through a fog to stay awake. I wish I could go back to sleep in Margot's bed. Preferably with Margot next to me if she's the reason I slept as good as I did.

"I can't pretend to know how you feel and maybe it's a little selfish, but I'm glad you're here." She winces, just a little bit. "I don't know… if you remember everything that happened last night, but I have to think you ended up here for a reason."

It's my turn to wince. "The details are hazy, but I told you this used to be our summer cottage, right?"

She nods her head. She's not glossing over any of this, asking too many questions, or trying to relate any of it to something else. She's just here and listening and it's made a weight that has been sitting heavy on my chest for as long as I can remember lift, even if just a little bit.

"It took eighteen years and a fiery pixie girl to get me to walk across the driveway in here to talk about all of this. So yeah, my mom would say it happened for a reason too." I snort.

A small smile breaks out on Margot's face, and I get hit with the need to kiss her again. I go to lean in when she breaks our contact after one final squeeze of her hand. "That's what neighbors are for."

Did I read the moment wrong? Why does she keep saying weird shit about us being neighbors?

She gets up to walk over to the sink. I notice there are a few dishes, I'm assuming dirty; She turns on the faucet and grabs a sponge. Hangover forgotten, I'm over there quickly to hip check her out of the way. "Let me help."

"Wash my dishes?!" she yells, giggling.

"Yeah, it's the least I can do after you babysat me and then listened to my sob story. Go sit your comfy ass on the couch or something." She looks at me like I've lost it.

"First of all, I didn't mind taking care of you. You take care of like, everything around here. And second, more important-ly-" Her tone switches to serious. "It wasn't a sob story. Don't say that. What you went through… it's unimaginable to a lot of people. I know I don't know how you feel. But being alone with those thoughts gets you nowhere. That's something I do know about."

I nod. Everything she said is right. It's just hard for me to accept.

"I meant it earlier, no rush for you to be out of here." She picks up her coffee from the table, taking it with her towards the bathroom. "I'm gonna take a shower. I have a couple things to do today, but either make yourself at home or head out whenever. Thank you for the help with the dishes and… I'm sorry, Sawyer. I'm really sorry about your parents."

It's the first time someone has said that to me, and it didn't immediately make me angry. The *I'm sorrys* are never going to bring my mom and dad back, and it always sounds like something people feel like they have to say to a grieving kid, but when Margot says it, I don't know. It feels different, like she'd fight to get a different outcome for me if she could.

I realize saw it the night she took Red in, too.

I finish up cleaning the last bowl in the sink. "Thanks. For uh, for everything."

Only Margot's head is now sticking out of the bathroom. "Like I said before, anytime, neighbor." She closes the door before I can respond.

If I never heard the fucking word neighbor again, it'd be too soon at this point.

# Chapter Twenty-One

*Margot*

RED HAS BEEN RUNNING around the coffee shop like a chicken with its head cut off since five o'clock this morning. It's the week of the Blueberry Festival, and she is… stressed. That's actually a huge fucking understatement.

"If you don't slow down, you're gonna run out of gas before we even make it to the weekend!" I bark out to Red as she zooms by me for the fiftieth time.

The current task of rearranging the seating that absolutely cannot be wrong under any circumstance has taken up most of our morning. She's been trying to work around customers, but everyone has an opinion and none of it looks right, according to her. It did look perfectly fine before this morning but that's a battle I'm choosing not to pick today.

"I'm rechargeable, baby!" she yells back to me, scraping two chairs across the floor.

Apparently, the Blueberry Festival is a huge deal to Red, specifically this year. Her parents aren't able to make it back for the weekend, so she's in charge of it on her own for the first time. The town shuts down all of Main Street so locals and tourists can walk through, visit each booth, shop, and, you know, do the usual small-town festival stuff. I guess.

A board of people runs the festival, but Red's is the only business on Main Street that stays open for the day. The only difference from our normal day-to-day is the whole menu switches to blueberry-flavored items only. Oh, and we decided on a booth out front rather than keeping the cafe open. We've been going over the logistics together for the past couple of weeks. I can't lie. While it's kind of hectic, it's also a lot of fun.

We alternate between my cottage, Red's house, and even staying camped out in the shop into the early hours of the morning planning, putting together decorations, and trying out new ideas for the menu. Our text thread never stops when we aren't together. Daisy has popped over a few times now too, joining us in the chaos, also busy getting the flower shop prepped.

It's all left little room in our lives for much else. After Sawyer's impromptu sleepover, we've seen each other here and there and stuff, but not much more. I have no one to blame but myself. Our communication over the last few weeks has been reduced to exchanging memes and selfies via texts throughout our days.

Last night he sent me a picture of him on his couch, holding up my Key West boob mug that he apparently stole the last time he was over while I was in the shower. The mug covers his mouth, but from the crinkles around his eyes, I can tell he's smiling. He wrote, *Holding the rack hostage until you return my shirt.*

I sent him back a selfie of me from Red's living room, tongue sticking out, conveniently wearing his shirt, middle finger in the air. *Hmm, after careful consideration, I will have to decline. Much too comfy. Enjoy the boobs.*

He responded almost immediately. *Maybe we can meet face-to-face to negotiate?*

I ultimately chickened out, saying, *Perhaps.*

Even though I'm not avoiding him like I was when I first got here, I can't say I have been the *easiest* to get a hold of. It's not entirely on purpose. A little, but not wholly. I don't want to let Red down, and more so, I love hanging out with her and Daisy.

Having girlfriends is so new to me, and they've made it feel so easy. I don't leave the room and wonder what they're saying, and I don't go home at the end of the day and obsess over every little thing I said. I feel so lame being this old and doing this all for the first time, but gaining Red and Daisy is something my heart was ready for. I was just always too scared to act on it.

My mom will be here sometime Friday. She's been sending me pictures of her packing progress as if it's not just a thirty minute ride, but I don't care. I'm so excited to have her here, show her everything I love about this place, and introduce her to everyone. Even if I'm terrified for her to see Sawyer. She's given me space with it but I know she's just saving it to corner me in person so I can't blow her off.

I'm sure she'll be disappointed to hear there has literally been no progress on that front, and she'll quickly discover it's my own doing, but I'll cross that bridge when I get there. I know she's going to love Red and Daisy, though. I can already see her fitting right in. In the meantime, I need to talk Red off this cliff.

"Red, come on. We're taking a break," I call out over the counter.

"I just need to get this set up." She then pushes a table over to where she moved the chairs. "Just right. There. That looks good."

The two tourists who were still in the middle of eating

sandwiches at the table Red moved don't dare to complain even though they're now sitting out in the open without a table. Their silence is probably wize. I run around the other side of the counter just as they move to get up. They have confused looks on their faces but still choose not to question things.

"Thanks so much for stopping in! Hope to see you Saturday at the festival!" I call out as they leave. The door jingles, signaling their departure, and I turn back to Red. It's just us in here now, as the day gives us a lull that we both need. "Red, what the hell?"

"I'm sorry!" She finally crashes into a booth. "I don't want anyone to think I can't handle this."

"*No one* is thinking that. You run this place day in and day out, all on your own. What's one festival?"

She slaps her hands over her eyes. "I know it sounds dumb, but the Blueberry Festival has been a Merrymount thing for, like, ever. I don't even know how many years it has been, and my parents always crushed it. It's one of those things you look forward to all year. It feels so important, and they should be here, but they're not."

I walk over to the booth she's lying in and mirror her on the other side. It feels good to lay down like this. If someone walked in and caught us, I don't think either of us would care.

"Do you think you're throwing yourself into all of this to avoid that?" I ask.

Red turns her head to face me under the table. "Yeah. Just like you're doing the same with your feelings about Sawyer."

"Ouch," I laugh.

"But I'm right, aren't I?"

I sigh. "Ugh. I guess."

"I don't know why you're holding back, Margot. He's a really good guy and clearly into you. It doesn't make sense. I've been trying to give you space with it, but come on."

"Oh no, we're not redirecting the conversation-"

"Yes, we are," Red interrupts. "My issue is easy. I'm being a neurotic perfectionist with abandonment issues. But you're purposely avoiding something that I think could be really amazing for you, and I can't for the life of me figure out why."

"We're just… friends. And neighbors." It's even less convincing out loud than in my head.

"Wow, you really sold me on that one," she deadpans.

"It's just safer this way. Besides, with my mom coming on Friday, I don't need to make things weird."

"That's bullshit, and I'm allowed to say that as the bitter twenty-something divorcee. Sawyer Hale has walked through life half dead playing it safe, and he threw that out the fucking window when you blew into town. He's shown up. At least meet him halfway."

"He might get bored. He hasn't exactly said what he's looking for."

"Have you?" Red asks.

"Well, no. But-"

"Nope, that's what I thought. You need to DTR." Her face is serious, but I burst out laughing. I have no idea what she's talking about.

"Don't you laugh at me, Margot LeClair! DTR! Define the relationship!" She sits up and throws a loose napkin that is sitting on the table at my head, and then she joins in my laughter.

"You want me to just ask him, *Hey, Sawyer. What are we?* People don't do that."

"Maybe more people should. Miscommunication sucks, and I've learned it's an easier issue to avoid if you're just upfront."

I stay lying down, looking at the ceiling. I know she's right, and the fact that she's taking the time to try to help means a lot. Red cares so much. It's why this place thrives. I feel my phone vibrate in my pocket beneath me. I move to get up so I can reach it. Glancing at my phone, I wonder if Red and I summoned him. I see a text from Sawyer.

YOUR LOST BOY:

Did you know Key West was originally called Bone Island?

Red reaches over and plucks the phone out of my hand before I can type out a reply. "Lemme guess, it's him now." She reads the text and peers over to me. "I'm begging you to put this man out of his misery. Talk to him and figure it out."

I sit up and grab my phone back. "I- Fine. I will. If *you* promise *me* you'll chill the hell out and stop scaring everyone away. Why do you think it's so dead in here right now?"

Red lets out a cackle. "Touche, M. Okay, you have a deal. I think… I think we have everything handled here. Have I mentioned none of this would have been possible if it wasn't for you?"

I've never been a hugger. I think it comes with the territory of being relatively alone for most of my life so I'm not sure where the instinct comes from when I walk over and wrap my arms around Red's waist. "You might have said it a time or two. But the feeling's mutual."

She doesn't miss a beat and embraces me just the same.

Even if Red's wrong about Sawyer and it all blows up in my face, this will have been worth it. I have a friendship I'll be able to carry with me wherever I end up. It's a quiet happy I never allowed myself to long for because it hurt to think something was so fundamentally wrong with me that I couldn't make the connections with other girls or women that I read about in books or saw in movies.

I don't let myself dwell too long on the fact that Merrymount is starting to embed itself in me in more ways than one.

# Chapter Twenty-Two

MARGOT + SAWYER

*Sawyer*

I CAN'T GET my knee to stop fucking jiggling. It's like my body isn't my own while I'm sitting here on my porch, watching my knee bob up and down and up and down. I've been checking my phone just about every other minute to look at the time that's barely been moving, and to see if Margot has finally responded to my texts.

Texts, because I've embarrassed myself by sending a couple in a row now without a reply. It started with me sending her another dumb fact I found scrolling through my phone and then I followed up asking if we were still meeting to do laundry tonight. We'd discussed switching laundry day this week because she'd been busy doing festival prep on Tuesday. With her mom coming into town tomorrow, I'm guessing she and Red are working late again tonight.

At this point, I'm basically looking for any excuse to see her. She's been caught up with helping Red get ready for Saturday, and I get it. This is huge for Red and, honestly,

Margot, too, with it being her first year here. But I think a part of her is still holding back and avoiding me.

I've been patient, and I'll keep up with that for as long as she needs, but I really need to know where her head is at. Are we really just neighbors with a lot of chemistry and a small blip of a past? Because that's sure as shit not where I'm at with us.

Headlights turn into our shared driveway, and I'm up before I can even think about it. I manage to keep myself firmly planted on my steps as Margot parks in her usual spot next to her cottage. She's out of her car with her head down in her bag, searching for her house keys. It's clear she's actually pretending she doesn't see me standing here.

Okay. We're not going back to this. "Margot." I take the few steps down to the ground but make no moves to get closer to her beyond that.

She doesn't even bother to act surprised or startled, slowly looking up until our eyes meet. "Who, me?" she calls out, pretending to look around.

"Get over here!" I call.

She mumbles something I can't make out, but she thankfully starts walking towards me. She's in her normal work outfit, black leggings and a t-shirt with an unbuttoned flannel over it. She has her tote bag slung on her shoulder. Her hair is in a classic Margot bun, barely being held together, loose waves falling everywhere. The closer she gets, the more clearly I can see the exhaustion on her face and what looks like a coffee stain going right down the front of her shirt.

"Hey. Look, I'm really tired. It was a long day. Good - but long. I *really* need to shower. Can we raincheck this?" She stops in front of me, keeping about a foot of space between us.

I watch her reach up with one hand, pulling the ponytail holder out of her bun and letting her hair come crashing down. She shakes her head and runs her hand through the strands, like them being tied up for that long gave her a headache. I'm hit with a wave of the smell of coffee and her shampoo. It smells like rosemary and mint and that familiar lavender scent I've caught every time she's near.

I've gotten my hands tangled up in that hair twice now. The scent, combined with the memories, has my dick stirring in my jeans. I try to adjust my footing without her noticing.

"What do you think *this* is?" I ask.

"I don't know. Talking or whatever. Laundry?" She's refusing to look me in the eyes.

"Why are you acting weird?"

"I don't know what you're talking about." She stares at the ground.

I take a small step towards her. "Margot." I take her chin in between my thumb and finger, directing her to finally look up at me.

"Sawyer," she says, barely above a whisper.

"Talk to me. Please."

She breaks our contact, taking a step back and throwing her hands in the air. "I don't know what we are! What we're doing! Red told me we need to *define the relationship*, and okay, it makes sense. But I still feel so fucking stupid. And yeah, we went on a couple dates, and they were great - amazing even. Sure, there's chemistry and attraction there. But what now? What happens when you get bored? I'm... I... I don't know where to go from here."

"Is that all?" I close the distance again.

"I... I guess, yeah." She blows out a breath.

"Let's go down your list together, okay?" I move, putting my hands on her hips and backing her up another step. "What are we? Margot and Sawyer, the pixie girl and lost boy. What are we doing? I guess we can combine that and *define the relation-ship* thing, right?" I walking forward, guiding her back, until her back is against the side of my house.

A nervous giggle leaves her lips.

I move to the side of her neck, leaving light kisses between her collarbone and throat. I feel the shiver rake through her entire body. "You're mine, Margot." I nip at her sensitive skin, and a breathy sound escapes her.

"That's awfully presumptuous of you."

"Is it?" This contact is driving her just as wild as I am. I can tell by the way she's arching her back. She angles her head to give me more access, and I don't hesitate. I make my way up the column of her throat with my tongue, and she moans. It's the sexiest sound in the world.

"You still haven't answered me." I whisper, nibbling her ear.

"If I'm yours.." She's breathing heavily. "Does that mean you're… mine?"

"Have been since the day you showed up, and I saw you in this driveway." I take the opportunity to finally really kiss her, and I glide my tongue along her lips. She opens up for me and meets me with equal need and want. Her hands are exploring everywhere on me, not finding a place to settle.

My palms find the bottom of her perfect ass, and I lift her up in my arms. It requires no effort to carry her around the side of the house, not breaking contact. We're intertwined and both moaning into each other's mouths. Everything about her feels so fucking good. I set her down on her feet, our tongues still twisting together.

"Sawyer…" she says in a breathy voice.

"Yeah, Pixie?"

"Is this for real?" She pulls back to look me in the eyes. I can see her chest rising and falling. There's lust and wary happiness all over her face, causing something in my chest to swell. I don't want to see that doubt on her face again. I'm in this.

"We're doing this, me and you. I have no plans for boredom or whatever other doubt you have swirling in your head when it comes to us." I find my hands playing with the ends of her hair, needing to touch her in any way I can.

She raises up on her tiptoes. "Okay." I've said it before but one day, I'm going to count each freckle that dots her pretty face.

I drop another peck on her lips. "Okay." I reply. As soon as the word is out of my mouth, we're practically fusing together again. It's not delicate. Her hands make their way under my shirt somehow, and the feel of her nails scratching along my back brings a deep groan out of me, the slight pain almost immediately canceled out by the pleasure that follows from her touch.

I don't know how long we're like this, my body pressing into hers, her back against the siding of the house. I don't remember the last time I felt like this. Both of us are exploring and taking what we need. Before I can think it through, I reach out my hand to the left, feeling around for the lever that I know is there. I feel the cool metal and turn until water from the showerhead above starts pouring out a few inches from where we're standing. Droplets splash on us.

"Ohmygod!" Margot shrieks.

I can't help but laugh, and she asks, "Since when has *that* been here?!" Her voice is still raised.

"Since my grandparents built the cottages. Every decent vacation spot needs an outdoor shower. And you said you needed to shower. I'm happy to help." I guide her arms out of her flannel, letting it fall to the ground. I move my fingers to grab the hem of her shirt. "Arms up, Pix."

She surprisingly doesn't put up a fight, though her mouth is ajar, lifting her arms in the air as I pull the shirt up and off, letting that fall too. She's standing in front of me in her leggings and a lacy black bra that's pretty damn see-through, her pink nipples hardened underneath. The only light casting over here is from the front porch around the corner so it's dark but not enough as to where I can't see the blush creeping on her face, down her neck, across her chest.

She fights through whatever nerves are spinning in her head, and I watch Margot kick off her sneakers, flick off her socks, and step onto the shower's wooden platform, just out of reach of the water. She doesn't break eye contact. She hooks her thumbs on either side of her hips and peels the leggings off, taking the matching black thong with them. She's completely bare for me, aside from the bra I plan on getting off within the next two seconds.

I struggle to find words as my eyes roam her body. She has a bouquet of flowers tattooed right in the middle of her breasts that I can't stop staring at. More tattoos pepper her ribs and arms. I notice more flowers, seashells, a small birdhouse, and a few words that I can't exactly make out in this lighting. I walk towards her slowly and see her breathing hitch.

Her hands move around her back, unclasping her bra. The only sounds are coming from the wildlife by the river, the water running out of the showerhead, and the bra falling to the floor.

"You're fucking stunning, Margot," I manage to say, my hand wrapping around the back of her neck. I kiss her deeply, and I can feel her fingers trembling at the bottom of my shirt. I break away to pull it up and over my head, throwing it carelessly to the side so I can get back to worshiping this woman.

"You have too many clothes on," she says, now moving to unbutton my jeans.

"Nope." I grasp both of her hands with one of mine and guide them up and over her head, pinning them against the wall and stopping her from going any further. "This is just about you tonight."

I back her up into the water, not giving a fuck how soaked I get. All I care about is making her feel good right now. I slowly make my way down her neck, over her chest, til I can finally suck one of her perfect nipples in my mouth. I flick it with my tongue, loving every sound I can pull out of her.

I'm nipping with light kisses as I go further down, stopping to admire that bouquet right between both perfect tits. I want to know if any of these tattoos mean anything, but I'll save that conversation for later. "Your tattoos are so fucking sexy. I'm gonna trace every single one with my tongue someday," I say into her skin.

Her breath catches. It's shaky when she whispers, "Thank you." Her eyes flutter closed, and her head falls back when I suck a nipple into my mouth, grazing it with my teeth.

Her hands are in my hair and I'm hit with the reminder of her doing the same thing in a much different setting a couple weeks ago in her bed. I drop to my knees and, I slide my hands up and down her legs, loving the feel of them.

My face is exactly where I want it to be. I hike her right leg over my shoulder, and she yelps.

"Sawyer!" she says, half laughing, half in shock.

I look up at her. I want to see those green eyes. "Is this okay?" She shallowly nods her head, and that's all I need before I dive in.

"Such a pretty pussy, Pixie," I say in between playing with her sensitive clit with my tongue. She quietly gasps, her hands tightening around my hair, pulling at my scalp.

Some guys - boys - out there do not fully appreciate the act of eating a woman's pussy. They rush through it, treating it like a chore when it can be the whole fucking meal. I don't have that problem, I fucking love this.

*** 

*Margot*

.  .  .

THE WAY his tongue is working me in between the dirty talk is enough to send me over the edge too soon. Never mind that it's been over a year since I've even been touched by another person. No one has ever made it feel like *this.*

It's not that I've had a lot of bad sex. I just haven't had a lot of sex, period. And when I did, it was fine. I guess it was good. Have I ever been able to come when I'm not alone? Well, no. But it's hard for a lot of women according to my late-night scrolling online after another less-than-satisfying hookup.

I'm not really worried about having that problem right now as Sawyer works two fingers into me while continuing to play with my clit with quick flicks of his tongue. He hitches his fingers to a spot I've only managed to find with one toy, causing me to moan so loud that if we had neighbors, I'd never be able to show my face again. I can't manage to stay still. I pull his hair and arch my back against the wall. The hot water from the showerhead combined with the cool breeze that comes through at night this time of year is driving me insane.

"You taste so fucking good," he murmurs into me.

"Holy shit, Sawyer," I pant.

He looks up at me. The sight of him in between my legs, nothing but pure heat in his eyes, is making me actually insane. "Fucking love when you say my name like that. You gonna come for me, baby?"

My leg starts to slip, but he immediately puts it back on top of his shoulder, holding it there. His other hand is thrusting those two fingers inside me in perfect rhythm to get me to what feels like the top of a cliff. I don't want to take my eyes off him, but I tilt my head back, seeing the stars twinkling above us. His tongue starts making slow circles on my clit. I let out a cry as I then see another set of stars in my head.

The orgasm makes its way through my entire body. Tingling from my head to my toes. I lose track of time and the ability to properly function.

"That's it, Pixie girl." Sawyer slows his rhythm as I come down, whimpering. He moves without breaking our contact, moving his hands to my ass to again lift me up. I wrap my legs around his waist. My clit is still sensitive as I feel it hit his bare skin.

With no hesitation, his mouth is back on mine. I can taste my release on his tongue, and while it should feel dirty, it doesn't. I unclench my fingers, letting go of the grip I have on his hair and touch him, making my way down. My hands trace his face, his shoulders. Jesus Christ, the muscles aren't just for show. I break our kiss to turn my head, kissing his neck, letting my hand go lower in between us, palming his hard cock in his very wet jeans. I whisper, "Do I get a turn now?"

He laughs as he groans into the crook of my neck and shoulder. "I told you, I just wanted to take care of you tonight, Margot."

I whine. Yep, I whine like a fucking toddler being told no.

He laughs again. "I'm not having the first time I fuck you be against the wall of an outdoor shower." With that, he pushes his hips into me so I can feel all of him pressing against me, still sensitive, still begging for more. A fucking tease.

"Then let me just... return the favor," I say with a smile.

"Nope, the first time my cock is inside you, it won't be in your mouth either." He taps my lips with the same finger that was just buried in me.

"You know, I didn't take you for a dirty-talking type of guy."

"Can I tell you a secret?" he asks.

I nod my head yes as he reaches over to turn off the shower. Because he still hasn't put me down, he walks us both to the basket and chair I didn't notice earlier in the corner. He sets me down on the chair and pulls a beach towel out of the basket, wrapping me in it.

"I'm not usually... like this." He sighs and attempts to

readjust his pants, but it's a lost cause. There is nothing worse than wet denim. Considering his huge - I'm guessing based on the outline and what I felt through his jeans - cock, that's gotta fucking suck. "I don't know where that came from." The lack of lighting isn't helping, but I think I see his cheeks redden.

"Well, you fooled me. That was fucking hot."

"Yeah?" He leans down, taking my chin in his hand and kissing me again. The butterflies in my stomach manage to break free again except this time, for the first time, I don't fight it. One arm swoops under my bottom, the other on my back, and he picks me up, cradling me against him. We leave the shower, clothes, and shoes forgotten and discarded on the ground.

I'm giggling as I lightly kick my feet, the towel falling to the sides. "I can walk, you know."

"If you think I'm letting you walk home naked, you're out of your goddamn mind," he says into my ear.

"It's like five steps away," I argue.

"Not happening." He walks up my porch stairs and sets me down. "So, your mom gets here tomorrow?"

"Yep. I told her anytime, so I expect her to be here bright and early and not a minute later. I'd hide if I were you. Pretend you're not home or something."

He plays with the ends of my hair like he can't help but touch me. I don't mind. I feel the same way as one hand keeps the towel wrapped around me, and the other lightly explores Sawyer's chest and many abs. I'm going to explore them someday.

He shakes his head. "Nah. I'm excited to meet her. We're gonna have a good weekend." He kisses me on the forehead.

I thought he'd be more nervous, honestly. I mean, I've never been introduced to someone's parent as anything more than a casual friend, but I would think meeting the mom of someone you're… *something* with would spark some nerves, but he seems completely confident. That makes one of us.

"Oh shit, my bag. It has all my stuff." Before I can even finish my sentence, Sawyer's turned around and is jogging around the side of his house. He comes back with my discarded tote bag and hands it to me so I can find my keys.

"The clothes got wet. I'll grab them later if that's okay?"

"No worries. Thank you." I fish the keys out and turn to unlock the door. "So.."

"So go get some rest, Margot." He moves the piece of hair that fell in my face behind my ear. "I meant everything I said. No more questioning it. We're doing this." Another kiss. Another flutter.

I lift up to my tiptoes and wrap my arms around his neck, letting the towel fall to the floor. Where I would normally let my self-conscious thoughts consume me, right now, I don't care. I don't try to hide the smile on my face; I kiss him back. "Okay." I let my head lean into his chest, and he rests his chin on top.

"Goodnight. Get some sleep," he murmurs into my hair before releasing me to pick up the towel and hand it to me.

"Night, lost boy."

He gently slaps my ass as I turn to go inside. Sawyer doesn't move from the porch until I shut and lock the door. I know because I'm holding my breath and listening from the other side, my bare back against the door.

If today is any indicator of how this weekend is going to go, I better buckle the hell up.

# Chapter Twenty-Three

*Margot*

I THINK I clocked maybe three hours of sleep last night, but I was up with the sun, and now I'm standing in the kitchen waiting for my coffee to brew. Normally I just wait until I get to Red's, but I need all of the caffeine help I can get today. Between my mom showing up at any given moment this morning and everything that went *down* with Sawyer last night, my brain is going a million miles a minute.

Is he my boyfriend? I'm his girlfriend? What does *mine* mean? After my insane outburst about *defining the relationship*, did I even accomplish anything?

He told me no more questions. Well too bad, so sad for him because ya girl is asking them. In fact, I move the curtain to the side and look out the window to see if Sawyer's Jeep is still there. It is. I grab my phone from the counter, ready to send him a text seeing if we could maybe talk before he heads off to work.

The sound of tires on the dirt driveway makes me pause. I

look at the time on my phone. It's not even 7:00 a.m., and my mom's here. I bet she paced in her driveway in the dark, arguing with herself over whether it was too early to make her way out here. Her maternal side definitely won.

I can save the Sawyer conversation for later. I put my phone back down and bolt out of the cottage, not bothering with shoes, and reach her before she can even get her car in park. The driver's door flings open, and I throw myself in her arms.

"Mom!" I yell, practically in her ear. I can't help but let the tears that well up in my eyes fall, and as we pull apart, I see her cheeks are already wet from crying, too. What can I say? We're emotional.

"My girl, my girl," she says, still holding me, rubbing my arms up and down. "I missed you so much."

I take in my mom's face, so much like mine. She stands a few inches taller than I am. So, average height. She has the same smatter of freckles on her nose and cheeks. The crinkles around her hazel eyes remind me of every night we stayed up laughing too much over something stupid. Her long, brown hair is thrown into its usual braid. The one tattoo she ever agreed to get - a birdhouse that matches the one I have - is peeking out on her collarbone behind the zip-up swim center sweatshirt that's hanging off her shoulder.

"I missed *you*," I tell her. It really hits me how true that statement is. I was always hyper-independent and able to handle anything on my own. But my mom was always right there, cheering me on, never letting me see her confidence shake. She's my rock, and not having her as close the past couple months left an empty feeling inside me. I'm so fucking excited to show her my little world here.

"Well, no shit, there's no cooler mom than I." We both cackle.

She pulls me in for another hug and then lets me go to

grab her bags - she brought three for a weekend trip - out of the backseat. I help her carry them in, asking, "So, are you moving in?"

"One of these bags is filled with your stuff, you know. So maybe don't start with the jokes that'll end with something like Blankie going missing." She raises her eyes at me.

I gasp, clutching the bag I'm holding, not even knowing if it's the one that has the blanket I came home from the hospital in. I slept with it every single night until college, when I had my mom store it in her house in fear I would get made fun of, and it would hinder my ability to make friends. Jokes on me, though, because that didn't work anyway.

"You wouldn't dare," I snap at her.

She squints her eyes. "Try me."

Dropping the bag in the kitchen, I hold my hands up. "Okay, okay. I fold. So," I raise my hands above my head and twirl. "This is Cottage B, home of Margot Dorathea LeClair."

Mom looks around, taking everything in. She takes her shoes off at the door, like she always does, and places her other two bags on the floor next to them. I won't lie. I'm holding my breath. I tried to clean up my version of organized, and I hope it's enough. I also took all of the trash out, did the dishes - normal stuff you do to keep your mom off your back.

My eyes go wide when I notice the towel from last night still discarded on the kitchen floor. Hopefully, she doesn't notice. It's just a towel. I'm overthinking things. There's no way she could know.

Right?

I watch as she eyes the stacks of pictures I'm still making my way through on the table. She walks over, picking up one from the top of a pile, smiling at it. She places it down and walks towards the living room, peering in from the doorway. She still says nothing as she peaks her head into the bathroom that's right off the kitchen. The silence is deafening by the time she makes her way into my bedroom. I throw a silent thanks to whatever higher power is in the sky that I managed to remember to make my bed this morning.

Instead of awkwardly waiting for her to unload every thought and opinion she has, I get started on making us each a cup of coffee. She comes back out as I'm setting the mugs on the kitchen table.

"There's magic in here, Margot."

Okay, not the first thing I thought she was going to say. "Huh?"

"I felt it when I bought the bungalow too. I just had this feeling that it was the right place for the two of us, a fresh start. It's an almost identical feeling to what you did here." She sits down and sips her coffee. "I love it."

The relief that floods out of me is definitely unnecessary. I wasn't giving her enough credit by being nervous about how she would take all of this. She gets it. "Thanks, Mom. I really love it, too."

"Now, I did notice there was a certain neighbor, *a friend even,* you might call him, not present when I thought he might be. Oh, and the ridiculously large pile of laundry sitting on your bedroom floor. I didn't miss that."

I feel the flames of heat on my cheeks when I remember *why* there's a ridiculously large pile of laundry and how it has everything to do with that certain neighbor having his head in between my legs last night.

"Some things never change," I reply with a shrug of my shoulders, trying to look as normal as possible so she doesn't sniff out the secrets I'm trying to hide.

"Speaking of!" She sets her mug down and gets up to grab the bag I brought in. She unzips it and pulls out my camera. I snatch it out of her hands in shock and inspect it, reassuring myself it's still in its normal condition.

*My camera.*

This little beauty is a birthday gift she saved way too much money for. I have loved this camera for years now. It's documented all of our travels and holidays, all of the loud and quiet happys I've captured in every single picture that's sitting on this kitchen table. Getting to click through every raw memory on the small screen has always been one of my favorite feelings. Uploading them onto my laptop and getting to relive it all through editing feels like a kind of magic I couldn't put a price on. Why I left it behind is beyond me.

"Yeah, I thought you missed that thing." She looks at me with so much love in her eyes.

"Thankyouthankyouthankyou!" I grab her back into an aggressive hug. "It was dumb not to take it in the first place. Wait, this is perfect! I can take pictures at the festival this weekend. Your first time here in Merrymount. Did you happen to bring-"

"Your memory cards, chargers, and lenses are all in there." She points to the bag.

"You know you're, like, the best mom ever?"

"Is the best mom ever entitled to get more details on Sawyer, the neighbor?" She actually wiggles her eyebrows.

As soon as the question is out, there's a knock on the door. I see Sawyer trying to look through the small glass window at the top of the door, a smirk on his face that says he most definitely just heard that.

"Shit," I say quietly, more to myself than anyone else.

"And who could that be?" As if this is her house and she didn't just show up here, my mom goes to the door and opens it. "Well, I'll be. I'm assuming this is Sawyer the neighbor. Hi. I'm Melanie, Margot's older sister." This woman has the audacity to turn back and fucking wink at me.

I practically jump in front of my mom to put any space between her and Sawyer. "Aaaand that's my cue. Hey, sorry. My mother is clearly having an *episode*." I look at her and, in a mocking singsong voice, say, "How about you go sit back down and finish your coffee before I sign the papers to put you in a home."

Sawyer seems unphased, chuckling to himself as he holds out his hand to my mom. "It's really nice to finally meet you, Ms. LeClair. You can call me Sawyer the neighbor, but I also go by Sawyer Hale. Or just Sawyer."

She takes his hand, shaking once, and then pulls him in for a hug. Sawyer stiffens for just a second and then his arms wrap around her. "A pleasure, Sawyer."

"So, what are you doing here?" I interject.

"Margot! Is that seriously how you greet people?" My mom shoots me that *I raised you better than this* look.

Sawyer laughs it off again. "Not everyone, but I get special treatment." It's his turn to wink. I don't think I like the two of them in the same room. "But I swung by because I saw a new car in the driveway, assumed it was you, and wanted to introduce myself before the chaos of blueberry weekend."

I open my mouth to say something, but Sawyer continues, "Plus, Margot and I normally do our laundry together. She ditched me last night, so I came to grab hers to throw in."

Mom turns to me, jaw practically unhinged. "You're joking."

"He's joking."

"I'm not joking?"

I sigh. "Okay, yes. We do laundry together. But he doesn't do *my* laundry-"

"I mean, I did fold it that one time-"

"I'm stopping you right there." I push my index finger into Sawyer's chest.

Mom's head is swiveling between the two of us, and a smile is creeping onto her face. I need to find a way to get everyone out of this cottage as soon as possible.

I walk over to the counter, and grab my phone to check the

time. "Alright. Mom, I'm supposed to be at the cafe for eight. I have all of the streaming services logged in on the TV if you want to hang around and catch up on some shows. Sawyer, uh, don't you have river stuff to attend to? I really don't need you doing my laundry."

"Yeah, don't worry, Sawyer. She'll ask me to do it."

"Wow, you two do kind of act like sisters."

Simultaneously, we say, "We get that a lot."

He shakes his head again. "Woah."

"Anyway, Margot. I'm coming with you. I didn't come out here to sit around and watch reality TV. Your boss won't mind me hanging around the cafe, will she? I can help, too!" She finishes what was left of her coffee and meets me by the sink, immediately picking up the sponge and soap to wash the one mug. Typical Melanie shit.

"Red's going to absolutely fucking love you. I'm not worried about that." Sighing, I say, "Alright, yeah. Let's get a move on."

"Who taught you to use such language?"

"Uh, you did. Every time you yelled at someone to *get off the fucking road* while I was growing up," I remind her. I, unfortunately, also inherited her road rage. That's neither here nor there right now.

"Oh, whatever. You turned out fine." She waves a hand at me. "Gimme five to go change. It'll give you a chance to kiss or flirt or whatever you're doing."

Sawyer manages to choke on air. I contemplate bashing my head into the wall.

She grabs her remaining two bags and pats Sawyer on the shoulder as she passes. "I'm sure I'll be seeing more of you?"

Talking over each other, I say, "At this rate, *no.*" while Sawyer gets out, "Absolutely. Can't wait." in between coughs.

My mom shuts my bedroom door, and I motion for Sawyer

to get out on the porch. We walk out, and I shut the door behind me. "Oh my god," I breathe.

"I get it now," he says, still laughing it out.

"I'll just be drowning myself in the river."

"Margot, she's great." He hooks his pinky in mine and tugs me towards him. "Good morning, by the way." He dips down to kiss me, and I let go of his pinky to wrap my arms around his neck to pull him closer.

"Morning," I say into his lips. Damn, I could get used to this.

"I really was here to grab your laundry. I don't mind," he says.

"Yeah, well, I do." I laugh. "It'll get done at some point. Besides, I didn't really mind *ditching* it last night."

He backs me into the wall, caging me in with his hands landing on the sides of my head. "Oh, believe me, me too." He doesn't move any further, leaving me wanting more from him right now, but there's a small part of my brain reminding me my mother is only a couple feet away, on the other side of this wall.

*Fuck it.* I reach up to kiss him again, his minty taste from what I'm guessing is his toothpaste mixing with my coffee. We break apart when I hear Mom loudly cough from the inside, politely, not subtly, giving us a heads up. She pokes her head out of the door. "Your car or mine?" She's holding up both sets of keys.

"Mine is fine." I grab my set from her and look at Sawyer. "We'll be at Red's I'm guessing for most of the day. We have just about everything set and ready to go but you know her. We don't have plans for dinner, but I was thinking of pizza from George's, wanna join? I was going to ask Red, too."

"Yeah, sounds great. You mind if I invite Gus?" he asks.

"No, of course not! I'll text you, okay?" I start fidgeting, not knowing what to really do with my hands. Do we hug? Maybe a wave? A high five would be normal, right?

Sawyer makes the decision for both of us by taking a step forward and quickly kissing me on the cheek. I suppress the urge to jump and dart my eyes to my mom, who's standing there with a shit-eating grin on her face. "See ya later, Pix. You too, Ms. LeClair." He turns and heads to his Jeep.

My mom calls out to him, "It's Melanie! Just Melanie, Sawyer the Kissing Neighbor Hale!"

I roll my eyes, passing her to get back into the cottage to grab my bag. I can still hear Sawyer's laughter.

"I like him," she says. I don't respond but think to myself a loud thought I didn't allow myself to form until now. *I think I like him too.*

---

TO ABSOLUTELY NO one's surprise, Mom and Red hit it off before we could even make it into the building. She somehow managed to calm Red down from the DEF CON five-level meltdown she has been in for the past week, and everyone who has stepped foot into the cafe has been thankful.

I think Red was really missing a maternal figure around here. She knows what she's doing, but I get wanting that reassurance behind you. I'm happy I can share mine.

We let everyone know it was going to be a late opening today to give us some time to sleep in and let the last pieces fall into place before the actual festival tomorrow. And true to her word, my mom offered to help as soon as Red and I got everything up and running. She's currently rolling silverware behind the counter while listening to George over the counter give her the history of Merrymount, all gossip and drama included.

I'm wiping down the space in front of the register, and I look up when I hear the door jingle. Miller holds the door open for his daughter, who comes barreling through, talking to her dad and leaving no breaks for him to respond. Her curly, brown hair is in two pigtails atop her head today, and she's wearing the cutest pair of overall shorts with a hot pink t-shirt underneath. She has to be one of the most adorable kids I've ever seen.

I hear my mom loudly gasp, and I turn to her to see what George could have said that got that reaction out of her when Miller and his daughter make their way to the counter to order. I tilt my head at her in question, but she waves her hand at me, silently telling me to forget it. Her face is pale. Confused as hell, I look back to the front and see the little girl shoving in front of Miller to get my attention.

"Hi! I'm Penelope. It's a long name though so you can just call me Penny if you want, that's what my friends in kindy call me. I have the same last name as my daddy. Caswell. C-A-S-W-E-L-L. Can I please have an iced hot chocolate?" She takes a deep breath and smiles up at me, her two front bottom teeth missing.

Miller interjects, shaking his head and smiling down at his daughter. You can tell she's his entire world. "She just needs a couple ice cubes in it. Thanks, Margot."

I wave him off and bring myself down a few inches to get eye level with her. "Hi Penelope, I'm Margot." I hold out my hand, and to my surprise, she grabs it with a firm shake, like a tiny businesswoman. "It's very nice to meet you."

I grab a cup and a hot chocolate packet from under the counter, emptying it into the cup. I pour hot water in and mix it, finishing it off with a couple ice cubes so it cools to a temperature safe for her. "Here you go, m'lady," I say, handing her the to-go cup.

"Thank you! So, are you Auntie Margot? I've really wanted to meet you but Daddy always says *not yet*, and I don't wanna wait anymore. The only family I get to have is my daddy.

Everyone else in kindy has moms and dads and uncles and aunties and brothers and sisters. I don't even have a cat!"

All at once I hear silverware clanking onto the floor and Miller goes white as a ghost while trying to throw his hand over Penelope's mouth.

"Um, I'm sorry, Penelope. I uh…" I look up at Miller, confused and slightly panicking that I gave the wrong impression or I'm about to say the wrong thing to this poor child.

"I'm *so* sorry!" I hear my mom call out, but she sounds far away. My brain is scrambling and the room kind of feels like it's spinning. This is just some weird coincidence. I'm not this kid's aunt. I don't even know Miller. I just learned his name for crying out loud.

Miller's eyes dart behind me, I turn and see he's making panicked eye contact with my mom, confusing me even more. She just got to Merrymount a couple hours ago. Nothing is making sense.

It's like a record scratched and everything in the cafe stopped, the only sound coming from the light music playing through the speakers and Penelope attempting to speak under Miller's hand.

Red, noticing something is about to go down - what I haven't the least fucking clue - quickly makes her way over from whatever she was doing and whisper shouts to all of us standing here, "Margot, Melanie, Miller - upstairs *now*. I have coloring books and crayons to keep Penelope occupied." She turns to Penelope. "Hey girlie, wanna help me out with some artwork for these walls?" She reaches out her hand and Penelope immediately takes it, following behind Red.

Miller looks like he's about to object but Red stops and faces him. "I got her. She'll be right here when you're done with whatever this is, I promise."

He looks to Penelope, then my mom, and then me. I can

tell whatever is going on is really hard for him, but he doesn't stop Red.

George awkwardly clears his throat. "Well, uh. I better get back to the restaurant."

Red sticks her head out. "George, I'm calling in that favor you owe me. Man the register." She disappears to the back again.

None of us have spoken. I guide the three of us through the back to the door leading to Red's upstairs apartment. Miller kisses the top of Penelope's head when we pass by, whispering to her to be good for Red.

I notice my mom's hands are shaking. I take one into mine and squeeze, letting her know I'm right here. She squeezes back in answer. I have no idea what we're about to walk into, but I have a feeling it's going to change everything.

# Chapter Twenty-Four

*Margot*

I GET to the top of the stairs, my mom and Miller following behind me, and open the door into the small apartment above the cafe. We walk into the living room. The room has a green L-shaped couch against the wall, a coffee table, and a TV. It's an open floor plan, so the living room flows into the tiny kitchen, big enough to fit an island with two bar stools tucked under the lip. There's a door on the left side of the kitchen leading to the bathroom, and two on the other side for bedrooms that overlook Main Street.

I walk over to the kitchen island and smack my hands on the butcher's block, a lot louder than I intended to. The tension in here is too fucking much. I'm about to say just about anything to break it, but thankfully my mom does that for me, looking directly at Miller.

"Michael is your father."

Miller lets out a deep sigh. "Unfortunately. Please don't hold it against me."

"God. You look just like him." My mom shudders.

The room is spinning again. It's my turn for my hands to shake. Actually, I think my whole body is shaking. She couldn't mean- He can't be-

"We have the same dad?" I manage to choke out. I look between the two of them, waiting for someone to let me in on the joke.

"Again, unfortunately," Miller says quietly. But quickly adds, "Not that it's unfortunate that we're related. That you're my…"

"Sister," I finish for him. I face my mom, and she has tears in her eyes. "Did you know?" I ask.

"Yes." My ears start ringing, and I don't think I want to hear the rest of this. "I'm so sorry, Margot. Can we please sit down and talk?"

"I'm good here," I quickly say.

"Margot. Please." I watch tears fall down her face, but she doesn't try to get any closer. I don't know how to feel right now. I don't know who I'm mad at, or if it even makes sense.

Miller sits down on the couch and puts his head in his hands. "This is my fault."

My mom walks over to sit next to Miller and puts her hand on his back. "Is this okay?" she asks. He nods his head yes, and she starts rubbing small circles. It's something she always used to do to calm me down. "This isn't your fault. Oh honey, with all of this, I didn't even get your name."

"It's Miller, ma'am. Miller Caswell. I'm sorry, I would have introduced myself…"

"Yeah, but would you have told her who you *were?* Or just pretend you were a perfect stranger like you did with me," I snap. I didn't mean for it to come out as angry as it did.

He lifts his head to meet my eyes with his own. They're same shade of green. His daughter's are a carbon copy, too. I don't know how I missed it.

His long hair falls in his face, and he brushes it away. "I was going to tell you. I *wanted* to tell you. I didn't even know you existed until a couple years ago when I ran into my - *our* - father with P. He was drunk like he always is. He was going on and on about how Penelope looked just like his daughter. Except he didn't have a daughter… or so I thought."

My mom and I both say nothing, waiting for him to continue.

"I brought Penelope to daycare the next day and hunted him down to force him to tell me everything. He told me about you, Melanie. And how you had a daughter named Margot. And how he just *abandoned* the both of you to pick up this life with me and my mom. I don't even know why." He laughs, but there's no joy in it. "He hated her. He put her down any chance he got, and reminded her every day she could never do better. She died when I was ten. And I was his biggest failure, never living up to his expectations."

My mom takes his hand in hers. "I'm so sorry, Miller."

"Don't be. You know I was honestly happy when she died? At ten years old I realized it was the only way she was going to find peace. She never would have left him. He brainwashed her into believing all of the bullshit he spewed."

"Where is he?" I ask.

"Hell if I know. That was the last time I saw him, and even that was a one-off. As soon as P was born, I cut him off and went no contact. I didn't want him anywhere near her."

Mom pats his knee. "Smart. But a hard decision. You're doing right by her."

He nods his head. "I know. But Margot, I'm sorry. I had no idea who or where you were until I walked into Red's, like I always do, and saw you behind the counter. I just got this weird feeling that I knew you. Then I heard you say your name and it clicked. I was working up the courage to say something. I didn't know what you knew. When you introduced yourself to me like anyone else, I froze."

I take a minute to let everything sink in. I have a younger brother. My dad is a heaping pile of dogshit. My brother has a dead mom. Oh, he's also a dad. I have a niece. My mom kept a giant fucking secret from me for the majority of my life.

I thought we didn't keep secrets.

"I'm sorry about your mom. And I'm sorry about your dad, too," I finally manage to get out. I leave the island and sit crisscross on the floor in the living room. I begin fidgeting with the loose string on the area rug and look up at my mom. There's so much pain in her face, and it hurts me so bad. She doesn't deserve this, but I need answers. "I'm listening," I say.

"I was wrong, Margot. I want you to know that. When your fath- *Michael* told me he got another woman pregnant and it was a boy - what he always wanted - I let him go completely. I helped him pack his bags. As long as he walked out that door and promised to never re-enter my or your life, I didn't care. I hoped he would at least be the father he should have been for his son. I'm sorry to hear he wasn't."

"Would you have ever told me?" I ask.

"I honestly don't know the answer to that. I would like to think I would have, but as time went on, you never brought him up… I let myself hope it would never need to be talked about. I'm ashamed of that now." She wipes her eyes with the sleeve of her sweatshirt and it kills me to see her like this. But I'm hurt too.

"But life is funny like that," she continues, a small smile growing on her face. "How you both ended up in this small town at the same time, looking for fresh starts. Looking at the two of you is overwhelming, I have to admit."

I get up and reach out my hand so she takes it, and I squeeze once. "Okay. I'm- I'm overwhelmed too. I don't know how to wrap my head around all of this, and I don't want to say the wrong thing." I look at Miller, taking in all of the features on his face that remind me so much of my own. "I just need some time. Is that okay?"

Facing me, Miller stands up. "Of course. it's more than okay. I'm here whenever you want to talk. I know P freaked you out. She's so smart, but she has zero filter, and we're working on it-"

"Penelope is perfect, Miller. I just need to sort myself out." I take a deep breath and say, "Mom, do you want me to bring you back to the cottage?"

She clears her throat and stands. "I was actually thinking of hanging around the cafe to help. If that's okay with you."

"Oh," I say. "Well, okay." I really need to get out of here.

I feel a heavy weight land on my chest. One that normally shows up when a storm comes through. I could go back to the cottage. But the thought of sitting in there alone with my thoughts makes bile rise in my throat. Instead of second-guessing my next move, I quickly crash into my mom with a hug and tell her I love her. As hurt and confused as I am, she has always done everything for me to protect me and to give me the best life. I'm not going to damn her for it.

I pull my phone out of my back pocket and bring up my contact list, handing Miller my phone. "Siblings should have each other's phone numbers." He doesn't say anything but punches in his info and passes the phone back to me.

I head towards the door leading back to the cafe when Miller calls out goodbye. I wave to both him and my mom, and make my way down the stairs. There's only one thought playing on a loop in my head.

*I need to talk to Sawyer.*

# Chapter Twenty-Five

*Sawyer*

"IT'S JUST CRAZY, YOU KNOW?"

Margot showed up about an hour ago, sobbing, and threw herself into my arms. She pulled into the parking lot like a bat out of hell, and I immediately went into panic mode, dropping everything to meet her, head spinning about what could have been wrong. Nothing prepared me for the multiple bombs she dropped.

But she came to me, no questions asked. I got to be that person for her, and it feels fucking good. Another wall feels like it came crashing down, and in place of it is another sign showing me she's supposed to be here. She has *family* here. She fits.

She brought me up to speed for the most part. Is it an ideal situation? Well, no. And while I don't really know Miller beyond a nod hi here and there, he doesn't seem like a bad guy. His daughter is cute as hell, too.

We've been sitting next to each other, our knees touching,

by the sandy area where people enter the water with their canoes and kayaks. Gus didn't need an explanation when we both saw Margot get out, and jumped right into taking over everything so I could be here.

I toss another rock into the water. "I mean, a surprise half-brother and niece? Yeah, it's pretty nuts. But…" I trail off. I don't want to upset her more than she is.

"But?" She glances at me.

"But Miller seems like a good guy, and that little girl is sweet. I've seen them both around town the past couple years. It's not ideal that it played out like this, but it did. And I don't think it's something that can't be salvaged."

She blows the pieces of hair that fell into her face away. "I know. Like, I *know* you're right, and the bigger part of me sees that, but I didn't think my mom and I kept secrets like that. I have family, Sawyer. She didn't tell me."

"I'm not saying the way she handled it was right. You get to feel exactly how you need to about that."

"I need to talk to her."

"You do. But that gets to be on your terms. I'm in your corner, Margot." I put my hand on her thigh. I always find myself needing to touch her in any way I can.

Her head leans on my shoulder. "Thanks," she says softly. "Is it bad I just kind of want to forget the heaviness of it all to just enjoy the weekend?"

"Nope. All on your terms, I meant that. Besides, from what I've seen of your mom… I don't think she'll let this blow over now that it's all out in the open. She'll want to make things right. She'll be waiting when you're ready."

Margot hums to herself for a second, letting everything settle in again. We've sat in this comfortable silence a couple times since she got here. I hope having me with her brings her the same peace it does me. I felt the same way when she held me on the weekend of the anniversary of my parents' death, despite how drunk and sloppy I was.

"Thank you." She lifts my hand from her leg and kisses the top of it. I turn my head to kiss her hair.

"You down for something to take your mind off everything?"

"God, I thought you'd never ask." She laughs. It's the most beautiful sound in the world to hear. I can see the weight of today lifting off her.

"Go grab two life jackets from the wall. I'll get the canoe situated."

"Sawyer! I'm not dressed for that!" I look her over. I check out her sneakers, black leggings, and a sweatshirt zipped up over some sort of athletic tank. She has her hair tied back into a ponytail. I'm not seeing the problem.

"Yeah, not gonna work, Pixie. Grab the jackets. Let's go." I don't leave room for argument. I get up and walk towards the rack of canoes. She tries to protest, but there's no heat in it, and she's giggling over her objections.

▭

"OKAY, NOW PULL YOUR OAR UP," I guide her.

Margot does the opposite. She plants the oar lower into the water, hitting the sand at the bottom. It causes the canoe to rock. "Oh shit!" she yells.

She tries to correct herself, but that only triggers more movement. I reach over to grab the oar from her, but the shifting of my weight does us in.

The canoe flips.

I stand up in the river, frantically looking around. We're close enough to the shore that the water only comes up just past my stomach. I've flipped anything that goes in the water plenty of times to know how to right myself pretty quickly. Margot, on the other hand...

Her head pops out, and she starts treading water. It takes me less than a second to see she's okay. A surprised laugh that sounds like a bark comes out of her mouth.

"Margot, stand up. You can touch the bottom." I wade my way over to her, pulling her up on her feet.

"I can't believe I did that. I'm *so* sorry." She's still trying to catch her breath as I brush my thumb across both of her cheeks, droplets of water falling everywhere.

"Your first flip. I'm proud." I drop a quick kiss on her wet lips.

Thankfully the only things floating in the water are the two life jackets we brought and the canoe. I grab hold of the canoe to drag onto the shore.

Before we took off on the water, I sent Gus a text letting him know I'd need a ride back later to grab one of our cars, and we left everything else back at the main building.

We floated down the river for a couple hours, switching between exchanging stories and that comfortable silence. It was nice to forget the rest of the world. It's something I've only been able to do with Margot despite how new this all still is.

After I get the canoe up and out of the river, we both crash on the grassy area aside the sand.

"That was fun. You know, for outdoor shit," she says, turning her body to face mine. I mirror her.

"I'm going to convert you. This was just all a part of my master plan."

"Well, if your plans continue to include us ending up wet like this... I can't say I'll complain." Her fingers start gliding down my chest. My shirt is soaked and stuck to my skin. There's a heat to her gaze that wasn't there earlier.

The sun has started to go down, and looking over at

Margot's dark cottage, it seems like Melanie isn't back from Red's yet. Margot texted her earlier, confirming Red was going to give her a ride back here later. No one specified what time later was, and we've had no way of reaching anyone. Like I said, it's nice to be disconnected from everyone and everything else for a little bit.

"Oh yeah?" I ask, reaching over to touch her cheek. I brush my thumb over her bottom lip and slowly bring my mouth to hers. She parts her lips, and I take full advantage to tangle my tongue with hers. I thread my fingers through her wet hair and move myself so I'm on top of her. I brace one arm on the ground, so I'm hovering, and not crushing her.

A whimper escapes her, and the sound shoots right through me. Suddenly I can't picture anything else except her mouth wrapped around my cock, making that same noise. I let out a low groan. She breaks our kiss, looking up at me with those wide, green eyes. They've gone hazy, and I realize I gotta get the two of us off this fucking ground, and into my house as soon as possible.

"Should we…" she trails off, those pretty eyes trailing down my body, pausing at the outline of my dick, already hard, and getting more uncomfortable by the minute in these wet jeans.

"Move this inside? Yeah. You read my mind. Up you go." I push myself off the ground and scoop her up, almost identical to the position we were in last night, and carry her onto my front porch.

I gently set her down so she's standing while I grab the hide-a-key I have stashed under the welcome mat. She's laughing when she says, "Kind of an obvious spot, no? Seems a little dangerous."

I get the door unlocked and motion for her to walk in ahead of me. She's still giggling. "Merrymount isn't really known for its crime," I answer.

The air becomes electric again, and we press back together. She gets a hold of my shirt and yanks it over my head in between kisses. I unzip her sweatshirt while she peels her tank top off. We're a mess, throwing our sopping clothes onto the kitchen floor.

I'm fumbling to kick my boots off, and now she's messing with the button on the front of my jeans. We're still so fucking soaked from the river that it's making everything difficult, but there's a lightness to it. We keep laughing into each other's mouths.

It's hot, and it's fun. It's the most natural I've ever felt with someone.

We manage to both get stripped down to our underwear, and she pauses while I'm kissing along the side of her neck. I hesitate, breaking contact to face her so she knows we can stop this at any time.

I might need five minutes to go jerk off in the bathroom like a teenager, but I don't want this going any further if she's not ready. "You okay?" I ask.

"Oh god, yes," she breathes into me. "I just realized this is the first time I've been in your house. Please proceed." She pulls my bottom lip down with her teeth, and it sends a shiver down my back.

"The first of many," I respond before picking up where I left off. I leave open-mouth kisses in a trail down her neck and shoulder. Goosebumps follow along her skin, and I reach around her back to unclasp her bra, letting it fall to the floor.

Her round, pink nipples are already hard from the water and air as I suck one into my mouth, remembering the sounds I coaxed out of her last night when I flicked it with my tongue in a fast motion. She moans, and I lift her up, hands firmly grasping her perfect ass. I guide the two of us back from memory, and toss her onto my bed.

I take a second - maybe a few - to admire her. Margot is lying, almost completely naked, in *my* bed, cheeks flushed, breathing heavy, desire and want has her eyes on fucking fire. Not a drop of makeup is covering a single freckle on that face thanks to our dip in the river. Perfect. She's fucking perfect. I open my mouth to tell her, but she stops me.

"I have an IUD," she blurts out. "That wasn't sexy, sorry. I just wanted you to know. I'm also clear of everything. I got tested at Planned Parenthood. And uh, well. It's been a while."

"I disagree," I say, crawling back over her. "I think birth control and safe sex talks are *very* sexy. And, to add, I was also clear at my last physical, and there hasn't been anything going on since. But I also have a box of condoms Gus got me as a joke for Christmas stashed in my bathroom cabinet that I'm happy to go grab." I move to get up, but she pulls me back down.

"I really want to feel you inside me," she whispers, cupping my face in her palms.

A chill goes through me at the thought of me buried, bare inside of her. "Thank fuck," I breathe.

I press my hips into her heat, grinding my cock against her. The lace of her thong and the cotton of my briefs are the only thing separating us. I move the scrap of fabric covering her to the side and slide my fingers along her entrance, already wet. She shivers when I press into the sensitive bud at the top.

I start slowly playing with her pussy. Letting my fingers glide in and out, switching between that, and her clit. She dips her hand into my briefs to grip my cock, and she gasps. "Oh my god," she says more to herself than to me and shudders. I dip my head down to place my mouth back on hers.

I have two fingers fucking her while my thumb continues to play with her clit, and she's stroking the length of me up and down. I don't remember the last time someone else's hand was getting me off other than my own, or when something this simple felt so good. I could come just like this, but I need to hold off.

I need to taste her again. I want to feel her come on my tongue with my fingers buried inside her before anything else. I want to tell her all of this, too, but my brain feels like it's short-circuiting. My confidence from the other night has dissipated and words are hard to find.

She seems to have a similar idea to mine because she starts wiggling. She's trying to make her way down, but I have her trapped under me. "Isn't it my turn?" Margot whines.

"I need you to come for me first." I pick up speed with my fingers. She's tight as fuck, but I guide a third finger in, stretching her, and she cries out.

I vaguely hear tires on dirt in the distance. I try to tune it out because, frankly, anything going on anywhere else is none of my fucking business right now. But then I hear a car door shut. It sounds kind of close. I hear a voice that sounds distinctly like-

"RED!" We both yell, jolting out of the bed. I tuck my still-hard dick into the band of my briefs.

"What the fuck is she doing here?!" Margot whisper screams as I fly around the room, looking for anything I can throw on her that will pass as half-presentable.

"Oh, I don't know. Probably dropping *your mom off?!*" I retort.

"Shit, you have a point. Okay, *shit.*" She stops pacing and looks at me. Her lips are pouty and swollen. "It's not happening today, is it?"

I toss a pair of my sweatpants and a hoodie on the bed for her to get into, and cup the back of her neck. I pull her into me as I sigh. "No. But that's okay. Let's get you home to your mom. We have a big day tomorrow, and regardless, the first time I have you, I want you in my bed all night. I want to wake up to you. I want to make everything so good for you, Margot." I kiss her forehead.

She wraps her arms around my waist and squeezes tight. "Fine. Raincheck."

I lean down and she cranes her neck up so our foreheads are touching. "Raincheck."

# Chapter Twenty-Six

*Margot*

I LOOK into the bathroom mirror and point at my reflection. I repeat the mantra I've had on a loop in my head since I woke up this morning. "Today is going to be a good day with no surprises, and I will not cry."

"Did you say something, honey?" my mom calls out from the kitchen.

"No!" I quickly yell. *Shit.*

She's trying. I'm trying. We're… fine. When she came back to the cottage last night, I saw a nervous look on her face I'd never seen before. She was almost hesitant to talk to me. The remaining anger melted away from me. I ran right into her arms, ignoring the shocked look on her face, and Red's *you're going to give me every dirty detail* look on hers.

Once everyone said goodnight, when the two of us got inside my place, I told Mom the same thing I told Sawyer. I wanted this weekend to stay light and fun. The heavy could come later.

228

I wanted to ask how the rest of her afternoon went at Red's, but I couldn't bring myself to get the words out. My mom, being how she is, must have seen it on my face. She said she and Miller talked a lot and then they joined Red and Penelope back in the cafe. She said exactly what Sawyer said: Miller is a good guy and Penelope is the sweetest.

I don't know what I was looking for when I ran to Sawyer yesterday, but he somehow made everything seem lighter and easier to digest. He listened while I sobbed and probably snotted all over his shirt. He let me sit in the silence, something I've only ever been able to do with one other person... my mom.

And yeah, sue me. I didn't hate the canoe trip down the river. It was actually peaceful, and seeing Sawyer in his element like that was such a goddamn turn-on. I could have done without the bugs - I now have too many mosquito bites, - and I didn't exactly plan on flipping us into the water, but it was the perfect distraction when I just wanted to shut my brain off for a little.

You know what? I take that back. The perfect distraction would have been finishing what Sawyer and I started before Red and my mom showed up, but he's right. I think I would have been disappointed if I had to leave right after sex. I don't think my heart could handle another one-night stand situation. Not that that's what it would be- but... ugh.

"You almost ready to head out?" My mom pokes her head through the doorway.

"Yeah. I just need a minute."

She nods her head and blows me a kiss. "You look beautiful. I'm going to test out that chair you have out front. Whenever you're ready, my girl."

I smile and then look back at my reflection. I took extra time to do a full makeup routine today and cleared out my entire closet to find the perfect outfit. I love a good theme, and wanted to make sure I matched the blueberry vibe.

I found this navy sundress, covered in cream polka dots, on the clearance rack in *Nordstrom* a while ago, and apparently never wore it because the tags were still attached. It hits a couple inches above my knees, and comes down low enough in the front where you can see my tattoo peeking out, which I love. Am I also hoping Sawyer loves it? Yes.

I let my hair do its own thing, my natural waves falling and only being tamed by some random hair cream my mom packed that I stole out of her toiletry bag. I ended up showering last night, and had to wash it because the thought of river water sitting in it and *on my sheets* grossed me the hell out. I can only handle so much mother nature.

I feel pretty. Today is going to be a good day. No surprises. I will not cry.

Voices - plural - float in from outside, and I throw up a peace sign to myself in the mirror before grabbing my camera and heading out. I walk out to see Sawyer leaning against the railing - looking, as usual, good as hell - talking with my mom, who looks comfy as ever in my egg chair. I make a mental note that it could be a good Christmas present.

This is a new version of Sawyer. He has on crisp, white sneakers and navy shorts that stop about two inches above his knees. There are black roman numerals tattooed on his right thigh peeking out that I somehow missed before right now. I feel my smile take over my entire face when I see he's in a white T-shirt with an image printed on it. It's a faded American flag with blueberries as the stripes on the front, just like he described. His brown waves are tousled and loose on his head, no hat to cover them today.

I watch him open his mouth to answer whatever my mom just said, but then he looks over at me and stops. He pushes off the railing to stand up straight, towering over me. His mouth falls open again, then closes. I feel the heat creep up my neck, and I know that no matter how much makeup I put on this morning, it'll do nothing to hide my blush.

"Good morning," I say. I glance over at my mom, who has a knowing smirk on her face.

"Beautiful," Sawyer whispers.

"What?" I ask.

He clears his throat. "I mean- You look beautiful, Margot."

My mom snickers. "That she does." She gets up and smooths out the bottom of the floral maxi dress she's wearing as it falls just above her feet. She looks fantastic, not that it's a surprise. As much as I hated the sister joke growing up, she really has always looked amazing. "Sawyer here stopped over to let us know he's our chauffeur today."

"Oh. You don't have to do that, I mean, we have my mom's-"

"I'm driving you. Melanie," With that, he holds out his arm, my mom links hers with his, and they walk together to his Jeep, leaving me no choice but to lock my door and follow behind them.

▭

WE SET up the coffee shop to be to-go simple coffee and tea orders today until eleven. I'm on the register, Mom and Sawyer are hauling the baked goods out for the festival, and Red is running the show. It's been surprisingly smooth, given the chaos this week brought. Even Red is uncharacteristically mellow.

There's only about an hour left in the morning before we have to head out. As the clock ticks by, I get more and more jittery. There's just something about a silly, little festival in a small, loving town.

"What's got you smiling like that?" Sawyer asks as he passes by, carrying another tray of muffins out to the table set up on Main Street.

"Does it always feel this magical?" I answer with a question.

He slows, placing the tray on a table, and clears his throat. "Uh, it's hard for me to remember."

"What do you mean?"

"I haven't exactly… attended the Blueberry Festival the past couple years," he admits.

The smile falls from my face. "How many, Sawyer?"

"The summer before they died," he looks down and mumbles. I gasp, bringing my hand to cover my mouth.

"Why did you agree to take us today?"

He walks towards me, abandoning the muffins. The counter still separates us, but he grabs the hand I still have against my face. "I don't know. It was an easy yes. Because you make me want to live life again, Margot. I'm sick of being stuck in the past like that."

"That's… I wouldn't have asked if I knew."

"Why? I could have said no. I know you would have understood. I want to do this with you. Besides, it got me to finally break into my dad's collection of shirts." He turns to show me the back of his T-shirt. *Drew* is printed in a now faded navy blue ink.

Sawyer faces me again with the proudest smile on his face. He leans over the counter, plants a kiss on my cheek, and walks back over to retrieve the tray he'd left behind.

"And believe me, I'm glad I'm here. Even if everything else went to shit, seeing you in that dress…" He looks me up and down, shaking his head. "Yeah. That made all of this worth it."

I shiver on the spot. I've never been looked at like that.

As he walks out, he holds the door open for Miller and

Penelope, who makes a beeline for me while I stand here like an idiot.

"Hi, Auntie M! Is it okay if I call you that? Daddy said I had to ask. He said yesterday was a crazy day for the grown-ups." She's talking a mile a minute, bouncing in front of the counter in a seersucker dress with tiny blueberries embroidered on it. Her hair is done in a braid, hanging off her shoulder. She's looking up at me with those bright green eyes that match her dad's and mine. Miller walks up behind her, putting his hands on her shoulders.

"P, we talked about this. I said maybe we could work our way up to that. Her name is Margot." He blows out a breath, and his eyes meet mine. "I'm sorry," he mouths.

I wave him off and walk around to their side of the counter, bending down to her level. Looking at her, I can't imagine how my mom felt yesterday. She's me twenty years ago.

"You can call me whatever you want. I think Auntie M sounds nice. But, I feel like I need a nickname for you."

"Can I tell you a secret?" she whispers. "I know I said the kids at kindy call me Penny, but I *hate* it," she admits with the most disgusted look on her face. "So, anything but that."

"You got it, Lil P." I bop her nose with the tip of my finger, and she opens her arms and falls into me. It has to be, hands down, the best hug of my life. I look up at Miller and it hits me hard to see the tears in his eyes match my own.

I wait for her to let go first - the first rule of hugging a kid - and stand up. "So, you guys excited for the festival?" I ask Miller.

"Yeah. Melan- Your mom told us to stop by before everything started to say hi. I wanted to see if you needed any help."

Red chimes in, startling me because I didn't notice her come out from the back. "No, we're good here!" in a *really* high-pitched voice. At the same time, I say, "We'd love that!"

Thankfully, Penelope is here to break the awkward silence that follows. "Can I color again?"

I side-eye Red in a *why the fuck are you acting weird* look and turn back to Penelope. "Of course. Let's get you set up." I take her hand, and she happily follows me through the cafe, grabbing what we need, and settling her in a booth.

I watch my mom and Sawyer make their way back into the cafe, greeting Miller, while Red pretends to be very interested in watering a very fake plant by the front window. I clearly missed something yesterday when I left. But again, this weekend is for light and fun. No surprises.

And as if I summoned the demon myself with my positive thoughts, in walks Dean to ruin the mood. He must be on duty for the festival today. I internally groan, so I don't raise any questions from Penelope.

Sawyer makes his disdain a little more obvious, though. "Don't start with your shit today."

He quickly looks down at Penelope. "I mean- I didn't say that."

"Daddy says shit, too," she whispers, tugging on my hand.

"Since when do you crawl out of your cave today?" Dean sneers at Sawyer.

"I said don't fucking start," Sawyer snaps. His eyes dart over at me and Penelope again, apology on his face.

Red whips her head around, finally registering that something is going on. "What are you doing here?"

"Came to see if you needed any help." He walks toward Red, and she takes a step back.

"Not today, or any day for that matter. I thought I made that clear." Red stands a little taller, making herself eye level with Dean.

"When will you let it go? I'm here as a friend, Red." He takes another step forward, and Red again backs away.

Miller places himself just slightly in front of Red. "Did you miss the part where she said she didn't need your help?"

Red's eyes go wide.

Dean lets out a humorless laugh. "Who the fuck are you?"

Alright. This needs to end. Now. I'm about to get up when my mom takes control. "Officer… Fitzgerald, is it?" She squints at his badge.

Dean looks to my mom, and we all watch his demeanor change. He's probably realizing he just acted like an asshat in uniform. He nods his head. "Yes, ma'am. Sorry for the scene. Just some small town history." He puts on a mask of sincerity, smiling at her.

Someone give Melanie LeClair a fucking award because she puts on the show of her life. "Of course. I completely understand." She pouts her lips. "But maybe it's best we not do this right now?" She tilts her head to Penelope, now oblivious and coloring princesses contently.

Dickwad looks over and at least has the decency to look surprised there's a kid in here. "Of course. I want to apologize again. Please enjoy the festival today. I hear the fireworks show is going to be amazing." He leaves without another word, and everyone holds their breath until the door shuts and the jingle stops.

Miller breaks the silence, "Okay. Who's going to tell me what that guy's fuck- freaking problem was?"

Red answers him with her head down. "The biggest mistake of my life."

After about five minutes of awkward shuffling and clipped conversations, things in the cafe return to just about normal. My mom takes over hanging out with Penelope while the rest of us keep moving baked goods out to our booth and ringing up the last of the customers that come through.

Beth came in about ten minutes ago - to Sawyer's surprise - and latched onto my mom like a long-lost best friend. I have a feeling I'm going to have a hard time separating them when-ever my mom comes into town now.

"Well, that just about does it, gang!" Red cheers. "We ready to head out there and blow the blueberries off every-one?" She claps her hands together like the captain of the cheer squad.

I can't help but laugh as I stretch to reach up and put my arms around her. "Yeah, boss. Let's do this."

Red grabs my face and plants a loud, smacking kiss on my cheek, both of us giggling.

Once we're all outside and Red locks up the front, I notice Miller guiding Penelope to say bye to my mom, who has already walked off with Beth. She's already busy introducing my mom to others as they stop and pass by.

Penelope has a pout on her face, like the last thing she wants to do is leave. As I walk over to them, I hear her arguing with her dad. I stop a few steps away.

"Daddy, why can't we all walk around *together?*" she asks, tugging on his arm.

I watch Miller take a deep breath, collecting himself to respond as he crouches down to her. "I'm sure we'll see Miss Melanie and Margot soon, baby girl. We can do our own thing. It'll be fun. C'mon, I think the popcorn stand is open. We both know it's your favorite." He tries to sound positive, but it doesn't exactly land, and it doesn't exactly change Penelope's mind.

I see the tears welling in her eyes from where I'm standing, and next thing I know, I'm interrupting.

"Hey, Lil P." She lifts her head up and quickly wipes her eyes. God, this kid already owns me, and it's been less than twenty-four hours. "A little birdie told me the popcorn stand just opened. Do you think you'd wanna come get some with me?" I look up at Miller in question as I stand up, suddenly not sure if I just overstepped.

He hesitates, "Oh, but we wouldn't want to just barge in our your day-"

Sawyer comes up behind me, wrapping his arm around my waist. Like it's the most normal and casual thing in the world. Like we're just the same as any other couple you've seen. "Popcorn?" he asks. "That's my *favorite*. I'm in."

I look at Miller. "Spend the day with us?"

My mom must have overheard because she chimes in, Beth beaming next to her. "We're not taking no for an answer."

And that's that. Penelope grabs hold of my hand, yanking me in what I'm assuming is the direction of the popcorn, and I pull Sawyer along with me. We leave Miller shaking his head with a smile on his face. He glances over to the cafe's booth where Red is readjusting the display of blueberry tarts and walks up behind her.

I hear him ask if she could use a hand, and I watch Red jump a foot in the air, caught off guard. She tucks a piece of her fiery red hair behind her ear and blushes. I don't know why she's so flustered. Maybe Dean threw her off. She bites her bottom lip as Miller takes a seat next to her, and I tilt my head at her when we make eye contact, Silently asking if she's good. She sends quick nod in my direction in answer.

There's so much we have to talk about. Me, my mom, Miller, Sawyer, Red. The list feels impossibly long. So much to process and come to terms with. But there's also so much time already lost, and as upside down as I feel, how many nights have I spent wishing and hoping for this? For my mom and me to be surrounded by family and friends and love and laughter? It feels like a lifetime.

# Chapter Twenty-Seven

*Sawyer*

I DON'T THINK Gran has let go of Melanie all day. She's been laughing nonstop and really enjoying herself. It's a sight I didn't know if I would ever see again on a day like today. Gran used to love this festival and counted down to it every year, and I thought the love for it died with my grandpa and my parents. I can't lie and pretend I wasn't nervous as all hell when I told her I was coming here today.

I shouldn't have been surprised when she only gave me that always-knowing look and said: "I'll be seeing you there, then."

Margot tries to stick around the cafe's booth to help, but Red insists she's fine on her own. And she has been. Except she hasn't exactly been on her own. I don't think I've seen Miller stray farther than a few feet for a couple minutes to check in on us with Penelope.

Penelope and Margot are like two peas in a pod. Looking at the two of them together, you'd have no idea they had just met. Especially with how much they look alike. Margot brought her camera, explaining to me that photography is just a silly hobby she has, something I strongly disagreed with after seeing the piles of hundreds - if not thousands - of pictures on her kitchen table and decorating her walls. I become even more convinced this "hobby" is more than a hobby after I get to see her show Penelope the basics of pointing and shooting and go into detail with me about the small things I would have never noticed.

She never gives herself enough credit.

We all meet back at Red's table once the sun finally starts to go down to help haul everything back inside before the fireworks start. I've been dying all day to get just a couple minutes alone with Margot, but the time just flew by, and I wasn't going to be the guy taking her away from anything. It's not my time to be selfish and as much as I'd be okay with hiding out in one of our houses, never sharing her, she really is in her element here. Everyone in town has loved seeing her outside of the cafe. She's been snapping pictures of everyone and everything. I've caught her smiling down at the display screen a few times, quietly happy with her work.

Even though I was a goddamn stumbling idiot this morning, I meant it when I said she looked beautiful. She always looks beautiful. But holy shit, the sundress did me in. Not all of my thoughts have been innocent about it either. I catch myself staring, thinking about how good it'd look hiked up while I-

*We're at a fucking family-friendly event, Sawyer. Think with your other head.*

Gran snaps me out of my train of thought. "Sawyer, need a hand with these chairs whenever you decide to stop ogling your girl." Melanie covers her mouth, snickering, while Margot thankfully remains blissfully unaware a little farther away with Red and Gus, who showed up a little later in the day.

I roll my eyes but say nothing as I grab the folding chairs out of the back of Gran's truck. She comes up beside me and snags the bottle of wine and a sleeve of plastic cups she had stashed in a bag in the truck bed.

"And what do you think you're doing?" I ask her, raising one eyebrow.

"Mel and I are gonna share this bottle of wine and then bum a ride back to my place after the fireworks to keep the party going. She's staying with me. And *you're* gonna take that girl of yours and get the hell out of here." She pokes me in the chest.

If I were drinking something, I'd have spit it out. "I'm sorry?"

"C'mon, my boy. You've had eyes on her all day, and she's been preoccupied with everything. Go enjoy some time together. I don't want the dirty details, but-"

"Please, stop." I place my hands on her shoulders. "Gran, I appreciate it. But Melanie's here to visit *with* Margot. I don't want to take away from that."

As if on cue, Melanie comes up behind me. "I want to give her space, Sawyer. I- I have a lot to make amends for, and it's not something that can be fixed overnight." She looks down at her feet. "She'd never say anything because she would never want to hurt me, but she needs time. And I want to give her that. I feel okay giving her that because she finally has someone to turn to."

I turn to where Margot is, laughing with our friends. Miller and Penelope have made their way back over, and Penelope is handing out glow stick necklaces to everyone. How has so much happened in such a short amount of time?

I look to Melanie, who's watching the same scene I am with tears in her eyes, and God if that doesn't hit me hard in the fucking chest. "She fits here," she says more to herself than anyone else, quickly swiping under her eyes.

"Yeah." I breathe. "I think so, too."

WE ENDED up staying for the fireworks. You can't come to your first Merrymount Blueberry Festival and miss the damn fireworks. Margot looked surprised and maybe a little hesitant when her mom told her she wasn't coming back to the cottages with us, but after my Gran insisted, saying she'd return her in one piece in the morning, she agreed with the plan.

The excitement of the day must have caught up to little Penelope because, somehow, she fell asleep mid-show on Margot's lap. After passing her off to Miller and saying our goodbyes, I helped Margot into my Jeep to head home.

And then I think the adrenaline of the whole day must catch up to both Margot and me because suddenly, neither of us has anything to say.

This might be the longest ten minutes of my fucking life. Margot's dress keeps riding up high on her thigh with every bounce of her knee, and I keep glancing over to see her biting her lower lip, staring out the window. Her tattoo sits so perfectly between her breasts that my eyes are fucking drawn to it. Her fingers have been drumming the armrest for the whole ride.

The radio's on low, playing whatever station I left it on. After holding back as long as I can, I reach across the center console to splay my hand over the exposed skin on her leg. Goosebumps break out under my palm as my thumb rubs soft circles. She adjusts to get closer, finally looking away from the window at me.

"So," she says through a nervous laugh. "Any plans tonight?"

"I had a few things in mind." I slowly drag my calloused hand a little higher on her thigh, and she sucks in a breath.

"Things, huh? Cool. Coolcoolcool." Her knee starts bouncing again.

I finally pull into our driveway, parking in my usual spot. I remove my hand from her leg and take the keys out of the ignition, cutting the soft music and leaving us in thick, tension-filled silence.

"I'm calling in that raincheck, Pix."

"Oh, thank fuck," she blurts out. The next thing I know, she's unbuckling herself and crawling over the center console to straddle me. Grabbing my face with her hands, her mouth is on mine in an instant. Her tongue licks across my lip, begging to be let in. I open for her, and she moans into me when my tongue meets hers. I reach under her dress that's barely covering her as it is, and cup her ass, squeezing. This draws another moan from her.

The straps of her dress fall off her shoulders and I break from her mouth to kiss down her neck to what I've learned to be one of her favorite spots. I suck and bite, and she gasps. My hands move upwards, and where I should feel the fabric, I only feel smooth, soft skin.

"You're not wearing any underwear." I mean it as a question, but it comes out more like a statement.

She leans back, staring at me with hooded eyes. "Nope," she pops the P at the end.

"All day?" My voice sounds shaky.

She shrugs her shoulders. "I hate underwear lines."

*This fucking woman.*

I slide my hands up both sides, sliding my thumbs into the crease where her thighs meet her hips, groaning into her neck. "Fucking hell, Margot."

"I thought for sure you'd notice earlier. I've been waiting *all day*." She whispers into my ear in between soft bites, slowing on the last part, enunciating each word.

I need to get us in the fucking house *now*.

"Come on, let's go." I throw the door open and swoop her into my arms. Kicking the door shut with my shoe, I march us up the stairs and bend to unlock the front door, still holding onto Margot, who's busy kissing and sucking on my neck.

"You even taste good. Why do you taste good?" she breathes into me as I walk us to my bedroom.

"I'm pretty sure I said the same thing when I had my face buried in your pussy the other night," I reply, tossing her on the bed. A wave of deja vu hits me. But this time's different. No interruptions tonight.

I make quick work of getting my shirt up and over my head, tossing it on the floor, kicking my shoes off, and unbuttoning my jeans. I manage to strip down to my usual black briefs, and I watch Margot sit up on her elbows, staring at me with those fucking hooded, sage eyes. She wants this as much as I do, and it's giving me dirty fucking thoughts.

My cock stirs in agreement when I watch her breasts pour out of the top of that fucking polka dot dress, the straps doing absolutely nothing, hanging off the sides of her arms. The bottom falls high on her legs so I can see just a sliver of that perfect, pink pussy.

"You already wet for me, pretty girl?" I ask as her hand trails down her middle, gripping at the fabric of the dress, bunching it up so it creeps higher, exposing more and more of her to me.

Pink on her cheeks is the only tell she's as nervous as I am because there's no shake in her voice when she looks me in the eyes. "Aren't you going to find out for yourself?" she playfully asks while letting those bare legs fall open.

I shake my head in disbelief. How the hell is this perfect woman mine? God, I have to make this so fucking good for her. I *want* this to be so fucking good for her. I hold my hand out until she takes it with her own, and I pull her up so she's sitting. I silently motion for her to put her arms up which she does with zero hesitation. The dress goes up and over, thrown who fucking cares where.

I let her fall back into the bed and crawl over her body, so small and soft under my own. I bring my face to hers. My arms cage her in and my hands find the tendrils of her honey hair. "I want to make sure all of this is okay."

"What do you mean? Yes. *Yes,* everything is more than okay."

"A lot happened this weekend. I just want you to know I understand if you want to take things slow or…"

She scrunches her nose and tilts her head in confusion. She places her palm on my cheek. "I want this. I want *you,* Sawyer."

I didn't realize how much I needed to hear that, that she wants me and this isn't just something to check off a list. It's not just convenient or out of routine. It's not a distraction. She wants this. She wants me.

The softness in her face disappears, replaced with pure fire. She bites her bottom lip as her fingers find the waistband of my briefs, not so gently trying to yank them down. I place my hand over hers, helping her guide them down and get them off.

Her eyes trail down, and her mouth falls open. "It's… It's not going to fit."

A devilish grin breaks out on my face, and fist myself once before climbing back over her. "We're gonna make it fit, Pixie girl."

She shudders, licking her lips and biting that plush bottom lip again. "You don't understand." She stammers. "It's been… a while." She grips the base of my cock and slowly starts stroking it.

"I know. Me, too," I tell her. I nip and kiss up the side of her neck. "But I'll be gentle."

I swipe two fingers up her middle, her hips lifting in answer, letting my fingers sink into her hot wetness. Margot gasps, and her face flushes. It's fucking beautiful to watch her come alive like this.

We continue to work each other while our kissing becomes

frantic. I curl my fingers to hit that sweet spot I know can pull dirty noises out of her, and she answers exactly as I thought she would. Learning how to play with her has already shot up to the top of my favorite hobbies list.

I hold her gaze, eyes wide, as I pull my fingers out of her and bring them to my mouth. She watches me suck them in, tasting her. I lean back and grip my cock. She places those small, soft hands over mine as I guide myself to her entrance.

I press against her and slowly, so fucking slowly, with every bit of restraint I have, sink into her. Her hands release mine and find my back, nails biting into my shoulders. She finally lifts her hips, pulling me in deeper. And as much as I don't want to look away from Margot's stunned face, I squeeze my eyes shut to let the wave of pleasure crash through me. I pause to adjust to the rush of sensation.

*Holy fucking shit. This body was made for me.*

"This is… God, Margot. You're so fucking tight. Are you okay?" I pant.

"More," she moans. "Fuck, Sawyer." Her head falls back as I give her exactly that. I pull out a few inches just to sink myself right back into her, and she cries out.

"You take me so well, Margot. You're a fucking vision." I hold her hips, the tips of my fingers digging into her skin as I fuck her. I watch a new part of her come undone with every thrust.

"Oh my God, don't stop," she gasps.

*Couldn't if I fucking tried.*

I could. If she asked. I'd give her anything she asked for right now.

She gets an arm around my neck and pulls me down so I can capture her mouth. Our tongues come together, and I keep my pace, in and out, as her muscles flex around me. Her thighs are tight around my waist as I drive into her.

Shifting back to my knees, I grab her legs and bring them

to my shoulders, loving the fuck out of the position. Margot seems to agree as her eyes flutter down, pupils widening when she sees where our bodies connect.

She cries out as I feel her muscles start to flex around the length of me, driving me closer to the edge. I look down and get lost in the pools of her eyes again. God, she's so fucking beautiful.

"I'm gonna come," she shrieks, and I lose all control. I wanted to take my time, but I lose sense of everything else in the world. It's just me and her.

"Come with me, Margot," I grunt out.

A cry from deep in her throat does me in, and I'm falling with her, spilling into her. We're both breathing heavily, our skin glistening. I look into her eyes when they finally open after her release. The look she gives me - the adoration, the lust, the care, the happiness - it all shoots an arrow straight through my heart. I am… ruined. Wrecked. Demolished. For the rest of my life.

"Wow," she whispers, and I swallow the word, kissing her again.

"You're…" I start.

"Me? You…" she breathes.

We smile at the same time and laugh together as I slowly pull out of her. "Yeah," we both say, still chuckling.

I fall beside her onto the bed, and she wiggles her way out of my arms, taking her warmth with her. And I wonder if there's a way to manly pout my way into making her come back.

As if she can read my mind, she turns that perfect, naked body to me and gives me another one of those soft smiles. She points a finger at me. "Don't move. I'll be right back." I watch her bare feet padder into the bathroom connected to my room until she shuts the door.

I lay in bed on my back, looking up at the ceiling with my

arms tucked behind my head, and sigh. I think about how I want every night to end like this and how it feels like I wasted a lot of time before. I was missing out on sharing my time with Margot LeClair. But I can't dwell in the past. It's never changing, and I have a lot of things around here that I'm ready to change as soon as the pixie in my bathroom catches up to my plans of keeping her around here forever.

Margot emerges a couple minutes later, scurrying back into the bed to crawl into my side. I find the comforter that somehow got discarded along the way, and wrap it around us. She places her hands on my chest, playing with the patch of hair there. A finger lazily twirls in a pattern. "I don't have to sleep here, you know… I can go-"

I silence her with my mouth on hers, swinging my leg so I'm on top of her again. "Don't start with me."

And true to that troublesome, up to no good, pixie nickname I gave her, Margot laughs. She cackles, actually. I'm suddenly mesmerized from watching the pure joy dance across her face.

"Don't be silly. I wasn't planning on leaving this bed until you hand over a couple more of those orgasms, Sawyer Hale."

I crash to her side again, pulling her up so she straddles me. My hands run up her thighs, squeezing along the way, and a wicked grin breaks out. "Oh, only a couple?"

"Well, if you're feeling generous…" She leans down and bites my bottom lip.

▭

"WHAT DOES IT MEAN?" Margot's head is lying on my stomach and I'm playing with her hair. She's tracing the tattoo on my thigh with her finger. Her touch is a light graze that causes goosebumps to break out on my leg.

We've just come down from the high of another round.

Sweat coats out our skin, and I'm already thinking about pinning her up against the shower wall to go again.

"My parents' wedding anniversary," I tell her.

She pauses her tracing and turns her head so the other cheek is now resting on me. "Is this your only one?"

I nod my head and continue twirling the strands of her golden blonde hair. "Mhm."

She moves to sit up on her knees and bends over to leave light kisses on each number that's inked there. It's the most intimate thing I've ever felt.

"It's beautiful, Sawyer," she whispers and traces it again. "The line work is great."

"Thank you." When she sits back up and looks up at me, I pull her into my arms. "That means a lot coming from the expert over here." I run my palm over the designs covering one of her arms.

"I'm not an expert. Most of mine don't even mean anything. I just like how they look." She shrugs her shoulders, and Margot has the audacity to look ashamed. Like I'd give a shit what she did with her own body. Like I don't think she's absolutely stunning no matter what.

"Believe me. I like how they look, too. This one's my favorite, though." I tap the bouquet of wildflowers in between her breasts.

She looks down like she forgot it was there and blushes. "Really? It was an impulsive decision a couple of summers ago. A girl I follow online was doing these flash designs, and I just showed up and pointed to this one. Daisies are my birth flower, so I normally just tell people that's why I got it. But really, I just thought it was pretty."

"Do you want more?"

She doesn't need any time to think about it. "Oh yeah, absolutely. You?"

"I had a few ideas, but I went out and got this one done the day I turned eighteen and haven't given it much thought since then."

I don't tell her that at one point, what feels like forever ago, I thought I'd get my own wedding anniversary tattooed on the other thigh to match. It's an idea long forgotten, dormant in my mind until now.

# Chapter Twenty-Eight

*Margot*

I'M DELICIOUSLY SORE.

Yep. That's my first thought of the day.

I didn't know sex was…*like that.* I was going around having mediocre sex, thinking that was the best it was gonna get. For what? To just go home and have to finish myself off after the fact?

*Never again, as long as I can help it.*

When I basically stopped dating a year ago, I raised my standards for the men I allow in and with that, brought the unplanned celibacy. The only time I've gotten off has been alone, in my bedroom, with the help of no one aside from the vibrator I have in my nightstand and an immediately cleared Google search history.

The sun's not even up yet, so I'm in no rush to disturb Sawyer, who is still knocked out under me. I don't think we've separated since we got back last night aside from me getting up to pee after every time we finished - because there were multiple times. I may have been blissed the fuck out from Sawyer Hale orgasms, but I'm not risking a UTI.

It was like we couldn't get enough of each other. We got out of bed long enough to make food when neither of us could ignore my stomach grumbling. Sawyer pulled out his dad's recipe book, sharing pages filled with their favorites, however small or simple, with me. We ended up eating very burnt grilled cheese sandwiches after Sawyer laid me out on his kitchen island, forgetting the toasting bread on the stovetop. Worth it.

When he wasn't inside of me, we were already reminiscing about the day with everyone. I had Sawyer run out to the Jeep to grab my camera bag, and he laid with me while I clicked through photos. I already can't wait to get them transferred to my laptop so I can start editing.

I plan to have them printed so I can make sure everyone gets their own copies. I can tell there are some really good ones, too. I've missed this part of me so much. I'm trying my hardest not to beat myself up for tucking it away for so long. But how much else of myself have I thrown into a box and forgotten about? And for what?

It's finally sinking in that I'm going to have to sneak out of here soon to avoid whatever morning-after conversation Sawyer and I are supposed to be having. I also need to somehow make it back to my cottage before my mom shows up.

Sawyer and I are… together, I think. But are we jumping headfirst into a relationship? Is it too soon? Is this what I need with everything else going on?

The answers to these questions are all actually obvious, given we spent the entire day with our two families together and then fucked until neither of us could move. And then I spent the night. That's another thing I've never done - Sawyer's drunken sleepover aside.

In college, it always came down to the question of why sleep in some random guy's twin-sized dorm bed when mine is only a short walk away? And post-graduation, it was: why stay in a man's apartment after a hookup when rideshare is so easy? It never made sense, and I like my space.

*Liked* my space, I should say.

Sawyer stirs, and I find myself lightly grazing his chest, my fingers intertwining with the hair there. He turns his head, and his lips find the top of my head on his chest.

"Good morning, beautiful girl," he murmurs into me. His voice is still heavy with sleep, and it vibrates down my body, sending a shiver through me.

"Hey there," I reply, swinging my leg so it lays over his.

"How'd you sleep?" he asks while rubbing my back.

I huff out a laugh. "We didn't exactly get much sleep."

"Really? I've never felt more rested," he teases and stretches one arm up.

I jokingly flick one of his nipples. "That was…" I trail off, the misplaced confidence I found last night shedding away.

"Incredible, Margot." He lifts my chin so I have to look at him. "It was incredible. *You're* incredible. And if my memory's right, I told you that last night. Repeatedly."

He did. Among other really sweet, really dirty things and I loved every second of it. I didn't take myself for a praise girlie, and yet, here I am. Tingles ripple down my body remembering how *incredible* it really was.

He kisses me, and it's sweet and slow as I melt into him. This doesn't feel like one night. It feels like I already want to do this again.

As if reading my mind, he says, "I want you to come to dinner tonight at Gran's with your mom."

I laugh lightly. "Beth probably already invited her."

His forehead touches mine. "You're probably right. But I wanted to be able to ask you. You know, properly."

The butterflies who are apparently living rent-free in my stomach start to flutter. "Well, then my answer is *I would be delighted*," I say in my most regal voice.

I kiss him one more time and move to get up, but he anchors an arm around me, pulling me back into him. "I know you're not already trying to leave this bed right now."

"My mom could very well pull into this driveway, driven by *your* grandmother, at any minute. Do we really want to scramble for clothes like teenagers *again?*" I gesture to our very naked bodies, and his eyes go up the length of mine slowly. A chill follows up my spine.

He raises an eyebrow at me. "I mean… I think it's worth the risk." His rough hands have started roaming my legs, creeping higher and higher until his fingers find the apex of my thighs.

I breathe into the side of his neck and let him continue to rub light circles around my clit. Only just barely hitting that spot, teasing me, but I'm already wet. His touches are leaving me writhing for more. "Sawyer…"

"You gonna let me play with you again?" he responds as he plunges two fingers into me, eliciting a cry. How we're both not sated after last night is beyond me.

"Oh god, *yes*," I hiss.

"I want to keep you here all fucking day."

A few minutes later, Sawyer's still fucking me with his fingers in a steady rhythm, and I'm losing any sense of control I had. We both hear the very inconvenient sound of tires on dirt.

He picks up the pace, hitting that spot deep inside while his thumb makes quick work of playing with my clit. "You're gonna come for me, Margot," he demands into my ear, and it does me in. The tingling starts at my core and scatters through my whole body. He kisses me deep to swallow my scream and slows his rhythm so I can ride out my orgasm.

I take a few seconds to catch my breath. "You really like giving those out, huh?"

"Watching you finish is one of the prettiest things I've ever seen. I can't get enough of it." He kisses my forehead and starts to peel away from me.

"Wait, no," I whine as he gets up from the bed and turns his back to me. I finally notice the scratch marks trailing down his skin. *My* scratch marks. Whoops.

He turns and throws me one of his sweatshirts, that big smile of his that I thought was only few and far between but has pleasantly surprised me by showing up more and more plastered across his face. "You're the one who reminded me who's about to break down the front door."

I fight the urge to throw a pillow over my face when I hear two snickering voices from outside. They're not even trying to be quiet. They're probably getting a kick out of how embarrassed we're about to be.

"Now, do you think they're shacked up and naked at Sawyer's or Margot's place?" Beth says through a laugh.

▭

"THAT'S IT! I'm throwing in the towel!" My mom calls out as she tosses her napkin onto her empty plate.

"I don't think I've been this full since that Thanksgiving we decided to go to the Chinese buffet instead of cooking," I say.

Mom nods her head in agreement while rubbing her stomach.

"Thanksgiving with no turkey?" Beth asks, shock on her face.

"Mhm," I respond. "I think we've only ever done a traditional Thanksgiving meal a couple of times. We try to pick a theme when cooking, or a fun place we haven't tried if we're going out."

"You can do that?" August asks, still somehow shoveling pasta into his mouth. Like, I knew Gus was a big dude. Just look at him. But I guess I didn't quite get how much he must need to eat to look like that. I tapped out after two plates. I think he's on his fourth.

My mom is the first to answer, "What do you mean? Of course, you can. No one is watching you to make sure you eat a bird on Thanksgiving. You wanna mix it up this year and get wild with us? We haven't decided on anything yet. All of you, let's plan something."

Oh, great. Nothing says clingy like combining families for a small-town festival followed up with *Join us for Thanksgiving in four months!* the very next day.

"Mom, it's barely the Fourth of July. Let's simmer down on the holiday plans."

It's Beth's turn to chime in. "Why? It's not like we're all going to be somewhere else. I'm sure that Miller and the little girl of his will be in, too."

"I'm in. As long as we can still watch the parade," Gus adds.

The three of them immediately started brainstorming, leaving Sawyer and me completely out of the plans. How Beth and my mom became inseparable best friends over the course of twenty-four hours is beyond me, but it's really nice to see my mom like this.

I want to bury my head in my hands until I finally glance over at Sawyer who's sitting across from me, a soft smile on his face, staring at me. I try to convey my apologies and embarrassment on my face, but he just shakes his head. I would pay a lot of money that I do not have to know what he's thinking right now.

I mouth, "Is this okay?"

He doesn't immediately answer. Instead, he silently gets up from his chair and picks it up, carrying it over to plop down on my left. He sits and grabs my hand to hold in his lap.

Leaning into me, he finally whispers, "More than okay." He leaves a quick kiss on the side of my head and leans back to sit up as if this is totally normal and something we do every day.

The planning committee on the other side of the table pauses their conversation to watch us, and my face heats up. I have no fucking clue how to do any of this, and I hate that I get in my head over the smallest things. It's just all really new.

I realize all of this is most likely dramatic, but I don't want my mom to think I'm jumping into things too fast, and I don't want Sawyer to think I'm rushing to stake a claim over him. I don't want Gus or Beth to feel like I'm pulling him away from them. I want to be the cool, go with the flow girl.

Beth is the first to break the silence. "Guess we'll have to rearrange the seating chart." Everyone bursts out laughing.

WE ALL PITCH in to help clean up, minus Beth because she did all of the cooking. Once we are done, I ask my mom to take a walk with me to the river. After multiple bottles of wine, she and Beth were in no state to go out last night, apparently, and I want to show her before she has to take off. She has an early private lesson tomorrow morning, so she wants to get back home tonight to get situated. I get it, but I miss her already.

We sit on the beachy area near the water, both not saying anything, watching the sunset. There's so much I want to ask her.

"You're at peace here, Margot," she says, still looking towards the water.

"I-"

"No, sorry. I'm not finished." She looks at me, tears in her eyes, and grabs my hand. "It's my job to worry about you when you're gone. Every year I moved you back into that college, I worried. When you signed that lease for that stuffy apartment, I worried. When you called me up and told me you were moving to a cottage in the middle of nowhere, I worried like never before. But seeing you here, with these people... This place. I'm not so worried."

"Mom..."

"Again, sorry, no. Not done. I was wrong, Margot, keeping your father's secret. Miller is nothing like him. And Penelope... That girl is special. I don't want you to shy away from them. It's important that they're in your life."

I nod my head, unsure what to say. She lets me sit with it for a minute and then continues, "You recognized you needed a new beginning and a fresh start. You threw your all into it, and to see it's paid off means the world to me. It's nothing like you, or I, thought it would be, and I think that's just beautiful."

I didn't realize I was crying until she wipes away a tear rolling down my face. "I don't want you to leave," I say.

"I'll be back soon, honey. I don't think you could keep me from Merrymount now." She wraps her arm around me, and I lean into her like I have my entire life.

# Chapter Twenty-Nine

*Sawyer*

IT'S gotta be the rainiest day of the summer. I feel like the past few weeks have flown by. It's like Margot and I have fallen into a new routine without trying.

We still have our laundry nights, she's started joining family dinners at Gran's with Gus, and she sleeps at my house more than her own. After I make sure I thoroughly take care of her in bed. Or in the kitchen. Or on the couch. Or in the Jeep. Or in the shower.

I have zero complaints.

Watching her get comfortable has been a real treat. She doesn't stumble over her words as much anymore, which I miss sometimes because she's fucking adorable when she does it, but it means she's not as nervous about saying the wrong thing. She meets Gus shot-for-shot with his jokes and checks in with Gran, probably more than I do at this point.

Miller and Penelope make it a point to stop by Red's almost every shift Margot has, and the way she lights up when she gets to spend time with that kid makes me think of things that have never crossed my mind before. If she told me to put a baby in her tomorrow, there'd be no shot of me turning her down.

It feels crazy. She makes me crazy. But it's in the best kind of way where I don't see the point in ever being sane again if this is how being insane makes me feel.

We've taken Miller and Penelope down the river a couple times now. There haven't been any more  boat tipping incidents, thankfully. It's been fun. Miller really is a cool guy, too. He's more of a quiet, nerdy tech guy, but Gus and I are opening him up.

Margot still insists the photography thing is a *silly hobby*, as she puts it, but I've been helping her sort through pictures, and I watch her edit at her kitchen table or sitting on my couch while I catch up on the news. She gets so into it, her eyebrows all scrunched up, and when she's done, she'll sit there looking through all of the photos, smiling at each one.

I finally convinced her to send some of the pictures from the Blueberry Festival over to the town's paper, and they ended up running an entire piece based around them. Gran framed a copy and hung it right up next to our wall of articles in the main building at the riverside. Proud as could be.

I told Gran to let Margot find it on her own, and the look on Margot's face once she did made the wait worth it. She was beside herself, hurling her whole body into Gran's, causing them both to tumble back. Thankfully, they righted themselves before they both ended up in the hospital.

Margot fits here. I'm still mad at myself for the wasted time, but I gotta figure out how to get over it.

I'm patching a hole on the bottom of a kayak in the workshop when Gus comes around the corner. "Hey, you need a hand?"

"Yeah, can you grab me that seal tape?"

He hands it to me and leans against the wall beside me. I

contemplate if now is a good time to bring up what's been on my mind for a bit now, but I haven't figured out how to get it out.

"You got plans with Margot tonight?" he asks.

"With the weather, we're probably just gonna stay in. Maybe watch a movie or something. You wanna join?"

"Thanks, but absolutely fucking not. I don't need to see you two with your tongues down each other's throats during the good parts."

"Oh, fuck off. We don't do shit like that."

"Beth had to clear her throat to get you two to stop eye fucking each other at dinner last night."

"She was exaggerating. You egg her on," I throw back at him.

"So things are getting serious then?" I can't tell if he's fishing for information.

I decide to take the bait and set down my stuff to look at him. "I think she's it for me."

He lets out a loud laugh. "Well shit, I didn't think it'd be that easy."

"What the hell does that mean?"

"Nothin'." He holds a hand up. "I just thought it'd be a lot harder to get you to admit it."

"Why?"

"Because in all the years I had to deal with Katie, you never said something like her being *it* for you. It was drama and bullshit and it never felt worth it."

"It wasn't."

He huffs out another laugh. "Yeah, you don't have to tell me that. But this is good, man. Margot's fucking great. I mean, she's got a loose screw if she saw me and still wanted you..."

"Watch it," I joke.

"But I'm happy for you," he finishes.

If I'm honest, I needed Gus' approval. He's right. The bullshit with Katie was never worth it, and I wish I listened to him or let him tell me off a couple times. I didn't realize how easy it would be to have another person in my life if they just got along with my best friend and my grandmother like Marot does. For some reason, I thought poorly juggling all of it made more sense. For a long time, I thought I was asking for too much, hoping for all parts of my life to work together. Margot never makes me feel like that.

"Thanks, man."

"I'm still not third-wheeling movie night."

I laugh and go back to my patch job. "Understood."

"Maybe I'll see if Miller's up for some company."

"Yeah?"

"Yeah, he's got that new PlayStation. He said he usually plays when P goes down for bed. He's mentioned it a couple times, so I might as well, ya know?"

The thing with Gus is as friendly as he is to everyone, he keeps to himself. His hookups don't make it to the morning, and as far as I can tell, I'm his only friend besides Gran. He'll go out with John and George or chat with Red, but it's pretty surface-level. He likes it that way, and I'd never push him to branch out. He has a hard time trusting people. I'm happy to see he's wanting to let some more people in.

"That's really cool."

"I'm gonna go check the sump pump in the basement. The rain is crazy today."

"Alright, let me know if you need help with it. Hopefully, it's working. I don't feel like hauling buckets of fucking water today."

"Don't have to tell me twice," Gus says as he heads out the door. He stops and turns to me. "I mean it. I'm happy for you, man."

With the territory of being the brooding, quiet guy, Gus

also never really gets sentimental, so I'm caught off guard. I nod my head. "Me, too," is all I manage to say.

Happy feels weird. Happy feels really fucking good, though.

I pull out my phone and tap into mine and Margot's text thread. She's closing the cafe today on her own, and I haven't heard from her too much. The last thing she sent me was a picture of her and Penelope, whipped cream mustaches on their beaming faces behind two giant coffee cups filled with what I'm assuming is P's favorite iced hot chocolate. I smile down at the screen like the sap she's turned me into and type out a quick text.

ME:

Can't wait to see you later, pretty pixie girl.

# Chapter Thirty

*Margot*

OKAY, *don't fucking panic, Margot. It's just rain.*

Yeah, that's not going to help shit. I fish my keys from my tote bag and take a deep breath before making a beeline to my car parked beside Red's. I could just wait out the storm here, but I'm sick of letting this fear completely take over me. I'm turning over a new leaf here or whatever the hell I'm supposed to be thinking. It's really not even that bad out. I just have to throw my headlights and windshield wipers on full blast and go for it.

I jump into the driver's seat and slam the door shut, listening to raindrops pelt the hood of the car. I try to keep myself from shaking as I turn the car on. The Bluetooth connects, and some type of club music starts blasting, making me jump.

*Nope.* I turn the dial completely down. I need to be able to focus.

*Breathe. In and out.*

Once I check my mirrors for the seventh time and triple-check that I'm buckled in, I reverse out of my spot to head home. I just hope I manage to beat Sawyer so he doesn't see me like this. Nothing says sane and normal quite like a crippling, irrational fear of the weather.

*He'd probably calm you down.*

That's not his job, though. I am a strong, independent woman who can drive ten minutes in some light drizzle.

Lightning cracks across the sky, and a roar of thunder barrels through almost immediately after in answer. What was a steady pace of rain turns into an all-out torrential downpour, like the sky opened right up and decided to drop its biggest buckets right over Merrymount.

I can't seem to get a full breath now, and it's hard to see through the storm, even with the windshield wipers working overtime. So, instead of risking everyone else's and my life on the road, I manage to put on my hazards, swerve to the side of the road safely, and park my car.

Instead of trying some stupid mantra again, I let the panic attack consume me. I unbuckle and rock myself through the tears and try everything to get my breathing down to a somewhat regular pace while listening to the water, thunder, and wind surrounding me. I let everything go dark as I squeeze my eyes shut.

*It'll pass. It'll pass. It'll pass.*

After a couple - maybe a few - painful minutes, my lungs feel shallow. So I find the inhaler I keep in my glove box for emergencies, puff it up, and let the medicine do its thing.

The rain finally starts to slow, and I've brought myself down to a point where I feel okay - not great - but okay about making the rest of the ride home.

By the time I pull up to the cottage, the skies have completely cleared, and I've gotten my breathing down to an almost normal pace. I still can't release my grip off the steering wheel without uncontrollably shaking, but the tears have stopped. My body feels so physically exhausted from the panic attack. I don't even want to think about looking in a mirror.

I unclick my seatbelt, grab my tote, and sprint into the cottage without stopping to pay attention to anything.

There's only one thing that's going to calm me down after that drive home that doesn't involve calling my mom like a baby. Normally, I would pick out a bathbomb and soak in the tub until the water is cold, but my only option is the closet-sized shower the cottage has to offer. I'm *definitely* not going to involve Sawyer in this meltdown. I hate how shaken up I still get just because of a fucking thunderstorm. It's such a stupid fear I've carried throughout my entire life.

The first time I freaked out about a storm was with my dad. It's actually the last time we did something together, just the two of us. We were getting ice cream like we always did. It's like he heard once that fathers are supposed to take their kids out for ice cream, and it's the only parenting lesson that stuck with him.

Not that he spent a lot of time being a parent.

I remember sitting at the picnic table of the food stand we stopped at and hearing the crack and boom of thunder and lightning and dropping my ice cream as the dark clouds rolled in. I focused on the chewed gum on the ground while my dad yelled at me for wasting his money. I tried telling him the thunder scared me, but it didn't matter. I already ruined the day. He got me back in my car seat just as the wind and rain started whipping around and coming down.

I cried the whole way home with the sky.

By the time we were pulling into our apartment complex, he had told me to shut up no less than 10 times and kept muttering about how this was going to be my mother's problem.

He was gone by the following week.

I strip my clothes as I walk into the bathroom, leaving them scattered along the way, and I queue up my favorite moody playlist and turn the showerhead to *burn my ass off* hot. Tonight wasn't supposed to be a hair-washing night, but since I'm here, I lather up the purple shampoo in my hands. I'm starting to belt the second verse of *All Too Well (10-minute version)* and twist my hair into a George Washington-style updo with the shampoo when I pause.

I think I hear footsteps in the front of the cottage, and now I'm sure I hear the clicking of a door shutting. That was definitely my front door shutting, and now there is certainly someone or maybe *something* in my house.

Okay, be fucking for real, Margot. It's not a something. *Somethings* wouldn't gently close the door behind them.

Well, since the storm didn't take me out, the home intruder just might.

Do I scream? Is it even worth it? Would anyone hear me? Now that I think about it, I didn't even notice if Sawyer's Jeep was parked in front of his house. So, even if I do manage to yell, it's possible no one will be there to hear me. I'll die naked in my fucking stand-up shower.

I grip the shower curtain and begin to peel it back to see my murderer's face before they attack. I'm preparing to shriek for my life when I see Sawyer, shirtless, fumbling to get his jeans off.

"Sawyer, what the actual fuck are you doing!?" I scream and reach out to hit pause on the music playing from my phone on the bathroom sink.

He finally frees one of his legs from his pants and looks up at me with the slyest smile. "Hey. Saw you pull in, and I was heading over to say hi, but when I got to the porch to knock, I heard the shower start running, and I thought you could use some company. You know, conserve water and shit."

There is no way this man or this day is real.

"Just because you have a key here doesn't mean you get to abuse your power to barge into a tenant's home to jump their bones in the shower. You don't want the townsfolk to start whispering." I'm trying to sound angry, but looking at this giant, beautiful man standing in my tiny bathroom in just his black briefs is causing me to lose my momentum.

But my nerves are still on edge, and there's a shake in my voice that I didn't expect to be there.

"*Jump their bones? Townsfolk?* Are you okay?" I can still see the heat in his eyes, but they also start to soften with concern as he steps forward.

"I'm fine, it's nothing. Obviously, I'm just jumpy from thinking a serial killer was just about to make me his next victim. Also, Sawyer, I don't know if you know this, but I'm fairly confident this shower was only built for Girl Scouts, and while I am vertically challenged and still fit into that category size-wise, you do not. And I am mid-purple shampoo. It's a very important step in my self-care routine." I'm talking so fast I'm tumbling over my own words.

He goes completely still. "Margot, did something happen? Did someone hurt you?"

"No, oh my God. This is so embarrassing. It's best if you just go. I'm sorry for wasting your time- You know what? No. You broke into *my* house!"

"Technically, I had a key. But that's beside the point. What. Happened."

I close my eyes and take in a deep breath while the hot water continues to fall on my back. He's not going to let this go. He's going to make me talk it out. I might as well have just called my freaking mom. I let the shower curtain fall in front of me, hiding my face.

"Imafraidofthunderstorms," I finally exhale.

"Come again?"

"I'M AFRAID OF THUNDERSTORMS. Okay? Happy?"

"No. I'm not happy. You have this fear, and you didn't think you could come to me with it. You saw my Jeep parked out front. You knew I was home, and you still ran in here to deal with it alone."

I peek my head back out. "In my defense, I actually didn't see your Jeep. I kind of had tunnel vision getting in here."

He hooks his thumbs into the waistband of his briefs and lets them fall. He ignores everything I just said about shower proportions and pushes the curtain to the side to step in.

Suddenly, Sawyer is everywhere. I mean, he always manages to take up all of the air and space around me when he's close, but this is on another level. I close my eyes and suck in an audible breath. I'm immediately hit with his familiar, piney, citrusy smell, and I feel warm for the first time all day.

"I think we both know I know how to fit big things in tight spaces," he says in a low voice as he spins me around so I can feel his hardness pressed against my lower back.

I place my hands on the shower wall, bracing for him to fuck this lingering storm anxiety out of me because Sawyer somehow always seems to know when to show up and when I need to calm down.

"You know what? I'm not mad at the breaking and entering anymore," I say as I try to pivot my thoughts from the storm, my voice still a little shaky. I try to press my ass into him for good measure.

I feel his hands slowly moving from my hips up my body. I'm ready for him to wreck me when he tilts my head back and begins to massage the shampoo out of my hair.

Oh, right. I look like a founding father. There's shampoo in my hair.

He's not trying to have sex with me. He's washing my hair.

When you're growing up, you're taught that sex is the most

intimate thing you can do with a person, but that's wrong. Because I've had sex - bad and good - and nothing has felt as exposing as this. He's being so gentle with me, as if I'm going to break at any second. He thought he was coming over here for hot, shower sex and isn't making me feel bad for not being in the right state of mind to deliver.

The tears welling up in my eyes spill over before I can stop them, and then I cry. The sobs wrack my body. I'm finally crashing from my panic attack, and this is all too heavy. I can hear Sawyer shushing me gently and letting me feel it, but I can't handle this. I try to sink to the floor of the shower, but Sawyer holds me up.

"I'm right here. I'm right here, and I'm not letting go," he whispers in my ear.

I'm about to beg him to leave me alone when he cuts off my thought.

"And don't even think about telling me to leave anyway. Margot, listen to me."

He spins me back around so I'm facing his chest as he pushes me back against the shower wall. He gently grabs my chin with his fingers and directs my head up so I have to look him in the eyes.

"You're gonna tell me what's next in this 12-step hair routine, and I'm gonna do it for you. Then we're going to dry off and get in that cozy bed of yours, naked, and I'm going to hold you. You're going to walk me through what happened tonight, and I'm going to remind you that I'm not going anywhere, and you're not alone anymore. I have no problem doing this every thunderstorm for the rest of time. There's no secret agenda or ulterior motive here, Margot. I just want to hold you through it, okay?"

I manage a shallow nod of my head, refusing to make eye contact.

I wonder what he sees when he looks down at me because

he doesn't even give me a chance to respond. His other hand comes up to cup my face, and he's kissing me. It's one of those all-consuming kisses where he's breathing life back into me, and I don't know where I end and he begins. The only sounds are the water beating against us and our heavy inhales intertwining.

I part my lips to let him further in, but he starts peppering me with soft pecks. Apparently, Sawyer meant what he said about there being no ulterior motive. He kisses the tip of my nose, and I finally open my eyes and look up to see him staring at me like... I'm not so sure.

"There's my Pixie girl."

I OPEN my eyes to darkness. I hear rain pattering away on the roof, and for the first time in a while, it doesn't affect me. Sawyer's sleeping soundly next to me on his stomach, his arm draped across my middle. My mouth is bone dry. I manage to shimmy myself out from under him and tiptoe to the kitchen for some water.

I look at the clock on the stove and see it reads 3:00 a.m. as I fill a glass from the sink. I don't remember falling asleep earlier. After our shower, Sawyer dried me off and took half an hour to carefully brush my hair. He laid me down in my bed and held me - just like he said he would. I've never been taken care of like that by anyone. I don't think I could picture anyone else doing it, either.

I jump when I hear the creek of a floorboard and turn to see Sawyer walk in, rubbing his eyes. His hair is sticking up in every direction. He squints his eyes, looking at the clock, and then at me. "Did the rain wake you?"

"No, I was thirsty." I hold up my glass before placing it on the counter. "I'm sorry if I woke you."

"Hey. None of that." He makes his way over to me and wraps me up in his arms.

My face finds the small indent in his chest, and I breathe in Sawyer's scent. He starts to sway while we're standing here in the middle of the kitchen.

"What are you doing?" I ask him.

"Dance with me, Margot."

I giggle into him. "There's no music." It doesn't stop me from starting to sway along with him.

"Remember that night I ended up here?" he asks.

"I'm surprised you do, but how could I forget?"

"I told you I wanted to dance with you. I haven't gotten the chance since, so I'm taking the opportunity now."

We use the sounds of the rain and each other's heartbeats to waltz around the kitchen and when he spins me out and back into him, capturing my mouth with his, I'm hit with a wall of emotion.

*I love him.*

I *love* him.

It's too soon. I don't know what I'm thinking. I don't know what I'm doing. But those three words bounce around my brain repeatedly, begging me to let them out as he kisses me, and I try to pour that feeling into him without letting it slip out.

# Chapter Thirty-One

*Margot*

I DON'T KNOW what I'm going to do when school starts back up and I don't get to see Penelope barrel into the cafe every morning. It's become routine for us, and I love every second of it. We have two weeks left before she starts the first grade, and I'm already trying not to mope about it.

Obviously, growing up as an only child in a total family of two, I never pictured getting the chance to be the cool aunt. There were a few fleeting times when I had hoped I'd become close enough to someone where we would be like sisters, and her kids would feel like my nieces and nephews and vice versa.

Needless to say, that never happened.

But I'm not mad. Life led me here.

"Morning, Auntie M!" Penelope yells, barely through the door. Miller shakes his head a few steps behind her as she races to the side of the counter. I meet her there, and she jumps into my arms. I do a spin around, and her laugh trills through my ears. When I set her back down on her feet, we immediately jump into the handshake she told me we *absolutely, most definitely, positively* needed to have a few weeks back.

Like I said, I really fucking love our routine.

"Morning, Lil P." I pat the top of her head, but I don't ruffle her hair. She takes her hair very seriously, and I've learned my lesson. Today, it's in two braids, falling down the front of her shoulders. She's wearing a pink matching T-shirt and shorts set with peace signs all over them. "Hey, Miller." I wave to my brother.

For some reason, having a niece doesn't trip me up, but the whole brother thing still throws me for a loop. We're a lot alike, both in looks and personality, something that I think freaked us both out. I don't ask about our shared dad, and Miller doesn't bring him up. It works for us right now. We've both been alone for most of our lives, lost in a lot of ways, and it's nice to connect with someone who really gets it. "How's it going, Margie?"

Oh yeah, there's *that.*

I side-eye him as Penelope sets up camp at the closest table to the counter. "I told you that nickname sucks."

"And I told *you* I'm making up for lost time in the little brother department. I like it. I think it suits you."

I roll my eyes as I grab a cinnamon roll out of the case to warm for P. "Whatever. Did I tell you my mom's coming this weekend?"

He throws a ten-dollar bill in the tip jar, another part of the routine because I insist on covering Penelope's breakfast every morning, and goes to sit at the table. He doesn't agree with it, but it's the least I can do. Certified cool aunt, remember?

He awkwardly clears his throat. "Yeah, umm- She told me. She texted me. To let me know. She wants to see Penelope."

This is another thing Miller does. He gets super fucking weird about talking to my mom because he thinks I'm going to flip out or something. As far as I'm concerned, he got the shit end of the stick. I can share her. I don't mind. In fact, I'm encouraging it.

The toaster dings, and I plate the cinnamon roll to bring over. "Miller, I've told you, you can have a relationship with my mom without acting like you're committing a crime."

"I know," he sighs. "I just don't want you to think I'm imposing or… I don't know."

I squeeze his shoulder on my way back behind the counter. "I know. But I'm happy to lend you the crazy woman any day."

That gets a laugh out of him. I've learned to appreciate every one, too, because this is where we differ. Miller is serious a lot of the time. Not so much with Penelope, but I think he had to grow up really fucking young, and he struggles to be a normal twenty-something-year-old guy.

Red comes through the door from the back and stops when she sees Miller. I can see the look on her face - she's about to pretend she wasn't coming out here and bolt back - but Miller happens to look over to her before she can ditch.

"Hey." He waves.

She waves back but says nothing, immediately pretending to look busy cleaning the espresso machine that's already just about spotless.

I've tried to corner her a couple times now, worried Miller said or did something to upset her or make her uncomfortable. She insists he hasn't and I believe her, but I can't pinpoint why she acts like this when he comes around. She's never rude, but she doesn't act like Red. She's quiet and keeps to herself. It's the most unlike Red I've ever seen.

Which is why I find myself standing there, with my mouth practically hanging open when Red swivels her head back to Miller and asks, "Did you get a haircut?"

Miller's hair is what I would categorize as long. It's a really dark brown and wavy, hitting just above his shoulders. It's still sitting just above his shoulders.

274

Miller's face goes beet red. "Uh, yeah. Just a trim though. Was it too much?" He self-consciously runs his hand through it.

"No!" Red yells and then lowers her voice to normal volume. "I mean, no. I think it looks nice. Penelope, you look cute as a button, as always."

"Thanks, Miss Red!" Penelope mumbles with a mouthful of cinnamon roll. A piece falls out of her mouth, and Miller reaches down to clean up, talking to P and reminding her not to talk with food in her mouth.

"How did you notice that?" I whisper shout to Red while the other two are distracted.

"What do you mean? It's shorter. It's obvious," she hisses back.

"*No*, it's fucking *not*. You're being weird."

"Just like you were weird about Sawyer, and I let you continue on like that, minding my own business?"

"One, no, you didn't. Two, I liked him, and I *was* being weird, so if that's what you're telling me…" I trail off.

Red throws her hand over my mouth. "You're done."

We both jump when we hear Miller's voice closer than it was a few seconds ago, and Red drops her hand. He's standing on the other side of the counter, watching the two of us with his head tilted. "Hey… Sorry to interrupt. Could I get a coffee?"

"Of course! This is a coffee shop. Where we make the coffee. Margot's got you. I just have to…" Red starts walking backward. "Go make a call. Have a great day! Bye!" And she disappears.

"Off day?" Miller points to the back where Red went.

I sigh as I start getting his drink together. "Sure. Let's call it that."

━━━

THE NEXT WEEKEND, as soon as my mom arrived, she insisted we get everyone together for dinner, and we quickly realized there wasn't enough room at Beth's to fit us all, so Red offered up the cafe. It took some convincing, but I got her to stick around for it too.

Sawyer and Gus threw some tables together and rearranged the chairs so we could all sit together family style and ordered pizzas and salads from George's next door. No one felt like cooking, and pizza is *always* a good idea.

Penelope has had the table in hysterics for the entire meal, entertaining us with stories, songs, and jokes. She's in her element with an audience, and it cracks me up to see it. The stress on Miller's face when she says something out of pocket is also pretty damn amusing. Beth and my mom egg her on in any way they can, so much that I think I've seen Miller try to rip his hair out a couple times.

I look out the window to see it's already dark out. The sun must have set a while ago. It's probably way past P's bedtime from the looks of her sleepy eyes while she sits in her dad's lap, playing with the ends of his hair. I've seen Red watching them every so often with a look on her face that lines up with what I suspected earlier, but I'll leave it be for now.

"I think you kids should go out," Beth declares, hitting her fists on the table to get our attention from her seat when there's a lull in conversation.

"I second that notion." My mom raises her glass of water.

"Go out where?" I ask.

"*Anywhere!*" They yell at the same time.

Gus and Sawyer both look at each other, smiles spreading across their faces. "You know what tonight is?" Sawyer asks me while his hand continues to lazily rub the top of my thigh from under the table. He hasn't let me go since he showed up. I haven't made any effort to leave his touch.

"Uh, no." I give him a confused look.

Red's eyes light up, and she slams her hands on the table, looking more animated than I've seen in a while. "Let's do it."

"Red's in!" Gus and Sawyer cheer and high-five each other as Red gets up and moves around the table to get in between them, throwing an arm around each of them.

Miller and I are looking at each other, lost to whatever the hell the others are going on about and waiting for any sort of explanation. He shrugs his shoulders at me, and I imitate the motion.

"Well, whatever it is. You guys have fun tonight. I should get this one to bed." He pulls Penelope tighter to him because she's started to slide off his lap, fully asleep now.

"Tut tut," Beth starts. "Let us mother hens take the sleeping babe. You deserve a night out. Lord knows you probably haven't had one since the night she was conceived."

Red is mid-sip of her water and chokes, coughing and waving her hand. Miller's face, once again, is consumed by a deep blush. The rest of us are trying to hide our snickers. Sawyer's leaning into my shoulder to muffle the sound.

"Oh, I don't know. All her stuff is at home, and she's never slept somewhere that I wasn't, and I don't want her to wake up confused. What if she has a nightmare…"

Suddenly Lil P's head pops up off Miller's shoulder, and she reaches out to my mom sitting next to them. "Miss Mel, we're gonna have a sleepover?"

Without missing a beat, my mom pulls the girl into her arms and snuggles her, petting her hair to shush her back to sleep. "That's right, baby girl. And Daddy will swing by bright and early to have breakfast with us. Does that sound good?"

Penelope nods her head and closes her eyes. "Mhm. Pancakes with Daddy in the morning. Got it."

"Is anyone going to tell me where the hell we're going and what the hell we're doing?" I finally ask the table, looking over at Red, Gus, and Sawyer who have their heads together, whispering. Planning *something.* But Sawyer keeps his hand on me, he has all night.

The three of them finally look at the rest of us, shit-eating grins on all of their faces, and shout simultaneously, "*Karaoke night!*"

# Chapter Thirty-Two

*Sawyer*

"SHOTS!" Gus yells as we walk into *The Bar*. It's the liveliest I've ever seen the guy. I have Margot tucked under my arm, and am enjoying watching her take everything in with wide eyes, trying to focus in the dim light. Red and Miller follow in behind us, each pretending the other doesn't exist. Clearly, there's something going on there, but that's none of my business right now.

The Bar isn't fancy, but not much in Merrymount is. It's right next door to Red's and allegedly used to be called the Village Tavern, according to the sign on the front, but I've never heard anyone call it that a day in my life.

The floors are always a little sticky, none of the stalls in the bathroom lock, and their top shelf of liquor is a supermarket special at best most days. But it's a staple. It's another version of home. Everyone in town gets their first legal drink here on their twenty-first birthday, and there's not a single bartender who would ever let anyone drive home drunk.

Margot's the first to notice Daisy sitting on a barstool and runs off to hug her, Red right behind her, squealing, as girls do at the bar. It's cute as fuck.

I turn to Gus, already prepared to see his eyes roll into the back of his head. I elbow him in the gut. "Don't go there."

"Why does she have to be here?" he grumbles.

"Because it's the local townie bar on a Friday night. Don't be a dick."

"She doesn't even fucking drink."

"That's not a requirement to be here. If you can't avoid each other in a crowd of people, go home."

"Whatever," Gus mutters. Good enough for me.

"I've seen her around. She owns the flower shop, right?" Miller asks with his hands on his hips, coming to stand next to us as we watch the girls on the other side of the bar.

"Daisy fuckin Stiles. Yeah, her yuppy uppity parents own the place, and she runs her mouth. I mean, she helps out," Gus replies, glaring at her. She looks towards us, smiles at me and Miller, and glares right back at Gus. She sticks her tongue out at him for good measure, too.

I shake my head and give Miller a look that hopefully conveys *don't ask*. Thankfully, he takes my cue. I haven't gotten in the middle of that feud in the last ten years, and I'm not about to fucking start now. They both can hold their own. Daisy proves that statement by flipping off Gus behind Red's back as the two hug.

Chris is bartending tonight. On Gus's command he lines up five shot glasses on the bartop and fills them to the brim with tequila. He waves to me, his arm flailing so much he almost hits a guy on the other side of the bar. He's a good kid. A little odd, but... a good kid.

The DJ just started setting up the karaoke equipment and the three of us guys make our way over to the women who are huddled together, paying no mind to us.

I've had this need to touch Margot all fucking day. I think I kept a hand on her the entire dinner, and I'm already itching to hold her again. I can't get enough of her, and it's nothing sexual - well, not always sexual - I just physically like to be close to her. I come up from behind and wrap my arms around her shoulders to lower myself to whisper in her ear. "You gonna put on a show for me tonight?"

She brings her hands up to rest on top of mine. "Buckle up, cowboy."

And with that, Margot LeClair, the pixie girl of my fucking dreams, reaches out, picks up the shot glass, and turns around to face me. She downs the tequila without making a face and reaches up on her toes to kiss me hard. She breaks our contact to grab another shot and motions for me to open my mouth, and she pours the liquor down my throat. She wipes the drop left on my lip and sucks her finger into her mouth, down to the knuckle. She releases it with a hard pop.

*I love her.*

The thought practically falls out of me before I can comprehend it. Can you love someone after only a couple months? When you didn't know if you'd ever even want to spend your life with someone when the year started or anytime before now?

The straight-line, logical part of me wants to say no. But then I know I'd be lying because I love this woman. I love her quirks and her passions and how much she loves the people in her life. I love her ability to pick up on moods and be exactly who and what everyone needs at all times.

She showed up here thinking she could just be a blip on the radar but has embedded herself so fast and so deeply without even trying. Margot *is* Merrymount. I hope she knows that. I need her to know that. I should tell her that - all of it.

But not right now in some dark bar after ripping shots.

The tequila burns going down. How she didn't make a face

is beyond me, but I watch the rest of our group pick up their glasses. Daisy raises her soda with everyone and cheers. The night has kicked off.

To absolutely no one's surprise, Margot, Red, and Daisy are the first to start requesting songs and writing their names down for their chance to sing. And they do. Very badly.

It kind of sounds like a group of dying raccoons. I kind of love that, too.

We've kept a steady flow of drinks going for most of the night, and after Margot's third song (this one was *Cowboy Casanova* by Carrie Underwood) she jumps off the small stage, practically skipping over to me. Her face is flushed from the alcohol and some of the front strands of her hair are sticking to the side of her face. She shed the sweater she brought a little while ago and has been prancing around in one of those ridiculously short sun dresses she owns.

When she does one of her little twirls, the dress flies up, and I catch the crease of her ass. She wiggles her eyebrows at me and winks. She knows exactly what she's doing.

I'm thinking I'd only need five minutes with her in the bathroom to hike that dress up and fuck her against the sink until I can coax an orgasm or two out of her when the biggest cock block and buzzkill walks through the door.

"Here to ruin the night already?" Gus calls out to Dean Fitzgerald as he walks up to us, out of uniform.

"If you couldn't tell, I'm off duty." He waves to Chris at the bar, motioning for a beer.

"Yeah, gathered that, dick. Doesn't mean you can't still ruin it for the rest of us," Gus says.

Dean ignores him and looks around the bar, eyes landing on Red who's on the dance floor with Daisy. Miller catches Dean's eyes lingering and stands up from his barstool.

"You're gonna leave her alone." Margot pulls away from me, landing her pointer finger on Dean's chest.

"Aren't you sick of playing house with him yet?" Dean grabs the bottle Chris left on the bar for him and takes a swig.

The thing about Margot is, yeah, she's tiny. But she's also scary as hell when it comes to defending the people she loves. Her circle is small but fiercely protected. Dean doesn't have two brain cells to rub together to see that, though.

"Are you drunk?" she snaps. "What does that even mean?"

"Are *you* drunk? Do you really think this is gonna last? The two of you? When Katie gets bored, she'll be back, and you'll be gone. You're the placeholder, sweetheart."

I don't catch Margot's reaction.

I see red. It's all I see, and then I'm moving. I need Margot out of the way so I can finally lay this piece of shit out. Gus steps in front of me, and I slam into his back, but he's not quick enough to stop Miller on Dean's other side who rears his fist back and lets it fly until it collides hard with Dean's nose.

The music stops, and there's yelling. Red and Daisy are rushing over while Dean holds his face, blood seeping out between his fingers.

"What the hell is going on?!" Red yells, her head swiveling between Miller and Dean, shock written all over her face.

"You just assaulted a police officer!" Dean screams.

Miller shakes his hand out and sticks it into a glass of ice water that Chris just placed on the bar without a word. "Nah, you're off duty. I just punched some douchebag who mouthed off to my sister."

Dean twists his head to the bar, looking at Chris. "You saw that?"

Chris puts his hands up. "Sorry, man. I was busy. Must've missed the fall. You fell, right? Need some ice?" He holds up another glass, identical to the one Miller has. I knew he was a good fucking kid.

Dean looks like he's about to start up again when Gus

slowly steps in his face. "You have no buddies here. Go home, Fitz. Now."

Surprisingly, Dean takes the advice and hauls ass out the front door. The half of the bar who watched the whole shit-show unfold, starts to whoop and holler. Some guys, Gus included, pat Miller on the back.

I don't give a fuck what anyone is saying right now. I turn to find Margot, who ran off. I see the top of her blonde hair duck behind the door to the bathroom and follow her.

I catch the door right before it shuts, head in, and lock it behind me. Margot's staring at herself in the mirror, breathing heavily.

"Pix…" I start.

"I'm fine." She doesn't turn to look at me, though. "I'm fine. He just said the quiet part out loud, right?"

I come up behind her to look into her reflection in the mirror. I want that sad look off her face right now. I want to go back to where we were five minutes ago.

"Wrong. He's a fucking asshole who will say anything to bring everyone down to his misery. I know. I've been dealing with it for years. Red has worse than all of us."

"I know. I just- Fuck." She places her hands on the sink and lets her head fall. "He knew what to say. I should go check on her."

I place my hands on her hips, massaging my thumbs into her. "I know. But Margot, everything he said was bullshit. I know that. You know that. Even Dean knows that. He'll just say anything to get his way. Tonight his way included pissing off every person he could. I was ready to hit him, but your brother took care of it."

That gets a laugh out of her. "Oh my God. Miller just punched Dean."

I duck my head into the crook of her neck, kissing up and down. "Yeah, he did. A long time coming, too. But I need you to understand every single thing he said was bullshit. I- You're-You're everything, Margot."

Now is not the time to tell her I love her. I pull myself together enough to recognize that.

She lets out a shaky sigh and tilts her head to the side to give me more access. "I was so blissed out before he showed up."

"I was thinking about fucking you in this bathroom before he showed up," I say into her skin, letting one truth slip out in favor of saving the other for a more appropriate time. Her skin breaks out in goosebumps. Her body is always so responsive to mine, and god, I fucking love it. But now isn't the time.

"But he's gone now..." She wiggles her bottom half into my groin and brings her dress up, showing me once again, there's nothing underneath. I stifle a moan.

"Margot..." I start.

She looks up at me in the mirror. Her face is flushed from the drinks, and she's trying to steady her breathing when there's a knock on the door that sounds more like someone trying to batter-ram their way in.

"Margot, I don't know if you're fucking or fighting, but your brother just punched my ex-husband in the fucking face, and I need you out here to celebrate *now!*"

Daisy chimes in next, "I heard what he said, babe. I'm sure Sawyer's in there reminding you it's a bunch of bullshit, but we need you!"

I pull myself together to help Margot smooth out her dress, knowing I'm taking her home later to rip it off. I adjust myself in my pants and turn her around to kiss her forehead. "Come on," I whisper. "Let's go finish this night on a high so I can take you home and fuck you properly."

I don't miss the way her eyes light up when I say home. Anywhere with her is home to me now.

# Chapter Thirty-Three

*Sawyer*

NOISES ARE PULLING me from the dream I'm desperately trying to cling to. I try to stay in the world of my mind's making, but the edges of the images in my head start to blur and fade. I'm fairly certain I can feel Margot waking next to me, and I think that's my phone causing the rude awakening.

"Go the fuck away," I mumble while I throw a pillow over my head.

God, how much did Margot and I have to drink last night? My head is already pounding, and the sun is already starting to shine in from behind the blackout curtains in my bedroom. I don't even know what time it is, but I'm guessing it's at least after eight.

"It's too early. I need coffee and a McDonald's hash brown before anything. Absolutely no substitutions or alternatives. Do you hear me, Sawyer Hale?" Margot grumbles.

Well, at least we're on the same page.

The phone starts vibrating again, and before I can catch who it belongs to, it crashes to the floor, vibrations continuing.

I sit up to reach for it at the same time Margot does this very sexy backbend - hanging off the bed - to grab the phone. Whoever is trying to get a hold of one of us apparently isn't going to give up.

"Unless you're maneuvering yourself to shut that fucking thing off, don't bother," I say to Margot.

I'm more than slightly distracted by the topless dream girl stretched out in front of me, remembering my morning hard-on. I hover over her, caging her in with my arms, as she grabs what looks like my phone. I start covering her stomach in licks and kisses, making my way up to her perfect breasts. I make myself busy outlining one of her tattoos with my tongue. I'm about to suck her right nipple into my mouth when she stops me.

Quietly, with almost no emotion, Margot says, "Um, Sawyer, I uh, I think you should take this."

She's being weird.

She hands me the phone and doesn't hesitate before jumping out of bed. Margot bolts to the bathroom connected to my room, taking the top sheet from the bed to cover herself with her, and shuts the door. I hear the water in the sink running, and I look down at my phone, confused about what would have caused that kind of reaction.

Everything was fine, more than fine. What just happened?

And then I see it. My phone starts vibrating again, and the caller's picture flashes across the screen. It's a picture I haven't seen in months, me on the day of my high school graduation, in my cap and gown, kissing a bleach blonde who feels like a stranger now on the cheek. She's in a matching cap and gown, and we're holding up diplomas. It's a person I haven't given a single mean-ingful thought about since Margot LeClair walked into my life.

Why the fuck is Katie St. James calling me?

Actually, who the hell cares why she's calling? I throw the comforter off and toss my phone back on the bed as I head towards the bathroom. I never put a lock on the door because it's always just been me living here. I slowly open the door and see Margot sitting crisscrossed on the counter, just watching the water run in the sink.

She must have grabbed one of my shirts from the bathroom floor because she's swimming in it, fidgeting with the hem. The top sheet is discarded on the floor.

"Tell me what you're thinking," I say as I step towards her.

"You know exactly what I'm thinking. Please don't embarrass me and make me say it out loud." She still won't look at me. The only sound is the running water.

She thinks my ex is calling to ask for another chance, and she thinks I'm going to say yes. The worst part is that I can't blame her. I can practically hear her thoughts roaring.

A little over a year ago, I said goodnight to the perfect woman in front of me after the best first date you could probably go on, after meeting through a stupid fucking app. And I stupidly walked away because I was clinging to the past, a past that I had outgrown a long time before that, but was too scared to admit. Margot made me see that, but she doesn't even realize it.

I'm not scared anymore, and I'm sure as shit not repeating that kind of mistake. I reach over and turn off the water.

"Margot," I start.

She cuts me off, "No."

"No?"

"No. I don't want to hear it. I don't care. I'm fine. I'm totally cool. Been here, done this. Read the book and returned it. This was bound to happen, right? I mean, Sawyer and Katie. It's like, written in the town handbook that you two are supposed to be together. I'm just the placeholder, right?"

I wince. That part of last night was temporarily blocked out. I'm going to punch Dean in the fucking mouth for putting thought in her head. Let his lip match the broken nose Miller gave him last night.

"Margot."

"No, Sawyer. I already told you it's too fucking early. I don't have time for the it's not you, it's me conversation *again.*" She jumps down from the counter, and I have no doubt she's about to try to run out on me. She's fucking cracked if she thinks I'm letting that happen.

"Margot, *listen to me.*" I gently grab her arm in hopes it gets her to stop for just a minute or two so I can sort this out.

"I don't know why she's calling, but I don't fucking care. I woke up to you. I want to go back to bed with you and worship your body the way I planned to. I want to take you to get that coffee *and* the McDonald's hash brown."

She has tears in her eyes. Fuck, I didn't want to make her cry. I have to fix this. I try a joke. "Please don't tell me you're crying over a hash brown."

"I'm not crying over a hash brown," she huffs, rolling her eyes while she wipes away the tears.

"Do you need me to repeat myself? I'm not going anywhere. There's nothing for me with Katie or anyone else. It's you, and it's been you. I was just too scared to take a chance. I know I put this doubt in your head, and it's killing me that I have no one to be mad at but myself, but it's you."

One tear slides down her cheek, and I wipe it away with my thumb. She shakes her head but doesn't pull away, and I'm taking that as my in.

"I'm never going to be able to erase Katie from my past. This town is small, and I've spent my entire life here. It's all tied together. But what you're missing is that I walked around on autopilot until I met you. I would trade all the years of just existing for one season with you."

She looks up at me but doesn't say anything. Tears are still swimming in her eyes. Last night's makeup never got washed off. Her hair fell loose at some point, too. She's the most beautiful thing I've ever seen. I thought I could hold out for some big, grand moment, but-

"I love you."

She gasps, opening and closing her mouth. "What?"

"I said I love you."

"No." She shakes her head. "Please don't say that." She steps away from me, and I feel the loss of her immediately, but I'm not backing down.

"I love you, Margot. I wanted to tell you last night, and I didn't because you deserve more than some half-drunk confession in a dark bar, even when it killed me to keep it in. You deserve more than this, too, but you have to know. I'm not going anywhere, and neither are you." I step towards her again, and this time she doesn't move away. I brush a strand of hair behind her ear. She doesn't need to say it back, but I'll stand her all fucking day waiting for her to say *anything.*

"You… love me." She looks down at her bare feet. Her toes are still the yellow color I painted on them last week when we were waiting for the dryers to finish.

"I love you." I cup her face.

"No one's ever… I've never…"

"It's okay." I bring her head to my chest and she leans into me as I wrap my arms around her. We stand here like this for a couple minutes, me letting her lead now. I can feel her heart beating in her chest, and the only sounds around us are our breathing and a few birds chirping outside. "It's okay. If you're not ready, there's no pressure… I'm fine with waiting."

"I think I love you, too." She says it so quietly, the smallest whisper. I could believe I imagined it. I think my heart stops. But then she looks up again, still crying, but this time there's this giant, wide smile plastered on her face, and I'm hauling her ass up. Her hands interlock behind my neck, and her mouth is on me. "I love you," She says over and over in between kisses, and I breathe it right back into her.

Fuck my phone and whatever Katie thinks she needs from me. The rest of the world can go to hell for all I care. I walk us back into the bedroom and gently lay Margot down. I'm gonna show her just how much I love her right now and then get her that breakfast. We can deal with the bullshit later, everything's going to be fine.

# Chapter Thirty-Four

*Margot*

THERE'S NOT a single thing that could bring me down today.

Sawyer made sure I saw fucking stars again this morning. He'd have given me the moon and the sun, too, if I asked for them. Then he got me those hash browns he promised and brought me to the cafe for coffee and a night-out debrief with Red, who insists I'm only here as a customer right now and can't help out even though it's been a pretty busy Saturday morning. How she's running back and forth and not milking a hangover, is beyond me. The Tylenol and caffeine have kicked in, but bright lights were looking a little hairy for me earlier.

Oh, and Sawyer Hale loves me.

I'm not going to pretend his ex calling this morning is going to magically disappear forever, but I refuse to let myself sink into a panic about it. The past exists. It's there and we'll deal with it, together. It doesn't mean it's going to repeat itself or that I'm not good enough or any other negative thing the old Margot would have let consume her.

I look over at Sawyer sitting across from me, a lazy smile on his face. "What're you thinking about there, Pixie girl?" he asks.

"I'm just really happy here," I reply.

"Happy looks good on you."

The bell on the door jingles, and it's the last noise I hear in Red's before all of the air is sucked out of the building. I look up and see a woman on a mission. She has a knowing smirk on her face as she makes her way over to our table.

The confusion lasts all but a second. And yet, it feels like time slows down around me. I've seen her in pictures at Beth's house. One night after dinner she was trying to embarrass Sawyer by whipping out his baby box. Sawyer's senior prom, his graduation day. The memory from this morning flashes through my mind - the graduation picture lighting up across his phone, the name on the Caller ID.

Stalking toward us is Katie St. James with icy, blonde hair that looks like it was just blown out at a salon. She has perfect beach waves framing her face and falling down her back. It's Katie with a makeup routine that clearly has been mastered over the years because it only brings out and accentuates her best features. It's Katie with the designer heels that add to her already model height, putting her at least six or seven inches taller than I am.

It's Katie, Sawyer's ex-girlfriend.

And while all of that would have already made me feel smaller than small and more insecure than I already am, nothing prepared me for her most noticeable feature. Her very fucking round, very fucking pregnant, belly.

My senses finally kick back in, and everything and everyone surrounding me hits me at once. Red is hopping the counter to make her way over to us, looking like she's ready to go to war. She signals to Miller, who's sitting on a bar stool eating breakfast with Penelope, to take over on orders. Book Club in the corner has apparently decided that real-life drama trumps their fictional drama because they're as silent as I've ever heard them, obviously eavesdropping. All of the color has drained from Sawyer's face.

The click-clacking of Katie's heels stops once she reaches our booth. "Nice of you to answer any of my calls, baby." She purses her lips, and her eyes jump right over me like I'm not even here.

Katie places her phone face up on our table, showcasing her recent call log of what looks like hundreds of unanswered calls to Sawyer.

I'm going to be sick. Like, absolutely, without a fucking doubt, going to yak all over this table, her phone included.

"Um, I should-" I start to push back from the table, trying to get up and get the hell out of here.

"Well, if you're the bitch sleeping with my son's father, the one keeping him from answering his phone, you might want to stay for this." She finally looks at me with a cold smile void of any sincerity.

"Talk to her like that again, Katie, and see what happens. Better yet, get the hell out of my place." Red is seething when she steps up to our table.

"A son?" Sawyer's voice is quiet and shaking.

Katie looks at Sawyer. "A son, babe. We're having a boy." She tries to place her hand on top of his because he's not moving. I don't even know if he's breathing at this point, but her hand never makes contact because Red swats it away.

"I said out, Katie," Red snaps.

I should say something or do something, but I'm just sitting here, stupid. I'm afraid to even look at Sawyer. This is all wrong. I shouldn't be here. I wasn't supposed to be here. Suddenly, this morning feels like a dream, and I don't know how to get out of the nightmare I've landed myself in now.

Katie lays her hand on the baby bump and turns to Red,

plastering that fake as fuck smile on her face again. "I'm not here to cause a scene, Red. I'm simply trying to communicate and co-parent."

Red lowers her voice so only the four of us at this booth can hear. "Save it, St. James. This town has been better off without your snake ass around. Congrats on the spawn. Get. Out."

I watch the mask fall in real time. Katie might be drop-dead gorgeous physically, but the last three minutes with her are all I need to know she's actually ugly as hell. "Careful, Red. Jealousy doesn't look good on you." She drives her dig home by rubbing her belly.

She says it loud enough for everyone in the cafe to hear, silencing all conversations again. Red freezes, blinking like she's trying to focus her vision.

"No." Sawyer suddenly stands up, his voice clear and steady again. "You're not about to drag everyone back into our bullshit. This is between you and me, Katie. You don't come in here throwing insults at Margot or Red. You wanna talk? Fine. I'll call you later, and we'll set a time and place to discuss this."

"Don't think you can just brush this off-"

"If you really think I'm the type of guy who's going to abandon my child, you're mistaken. But I'm not letting you bully anyone else today." He takes a step to angle himself slightly in front of Red.

*My child.*

The two hash browns I scarfed down earlier are about to make a reappearance. Sawyer's having a baby. An innocent little human being who's half him and half this woman. A son.

Katie scoffs. "You're being dramatic but fine. I would prefer not to get lawyers involved if we can avoid it. I'm not staying in town, but I'm nearby, so call me, and I'll meet you wherever. Unlike you, I'll answer my phone."

She digs into her purse, pulls out a small, black-and-white

picture, tosses it onto the table in front of me, and walks out before Sawyer can respond. Even if I wanted to avoid it, I couldn't. My eyes latch onto the ultrasound of a small baby. Sawyer's baby. *It's a boy!* is typed next to its little head.

I faintly hear the door jingle again, signaling her exit. I look up to see Sawyer, face still ghostly white, staring down at the scan. His fingers graze the paper, the rest of him still frozen. Red runs into the back.

"Sawyer?" I whisper. I'm afraid to touch him.

He doesn't respond. Whatever he did to get himself to stand up and talk to Katie was all the energy he had left. I reach out with my hand and wrap it around his forearm, trying to gently get him to sit back down. He does on autopilot, still staring at the ultrasound.

"I need to make a call." I get up, press a hand on his shoulder, and then pull my phone out of my pocket. Walking towards the back, I bring up Beth's contact. She's with my mom. They'll know what to do. At least, I really fucking hope they will because I'm out of my league here.

# Chapter Thirty-Five

*Sawyer*

"THERE'S nothing I can do except step up," I finally say, and the room goes quiet.

It's the first thing I've said since I got here.

I've let my gran and Gus talk and argue over each other for the last hour, discussing the situation I somehow unknowingly landed myself in. I've barely been paying attention. Actually, that's a lie. I haven't been paying attention at all. I don't really think I care what they have to say right now. There's no way to get out of this.

Katie's pregnant. With *our* son. A boy.

"Now, Sawyer…" Gran starts.

"She's having a *baby*, Gran."

"Yeah. We got that. My question is, how the hell do we know it's yours?" Gus asks.

I pull the ultrasound out of my back pocket and toss it onto the kitchen table. I haven't been able to bring myself to look at it since I left Red's. "Shows how far along she is in the top right corner. Timeline matches up." I point. The first thing I did was do the math, not trusting Katie for a fucking second.

Gran grabs the scan and her reading glasses to take a closer look. I see her eyes well up with tears that she tries to stash away before I can notice. Absolute shock and awe paint her face.

Gus grunts. "That doesn't mean shit. Could be faked, still might not be yours."

"You're forgetting I saw her. She looks like she's about to go into labor any day now. There's nothing fake about it."

"You need a paternity test, Sawyer," Gran says, not looking up, still holding the ultrasound.

I finally lose it. "You really think she'll agree to that? Since when has she ever made anything simple? I mean, look at this whole thing. Who shows up days before giving birth to drop this on someone? I haven't heard from her or even seen her in months. How am I supposed to co-parent with her? What about Margot?"

It's the first time I've let myself go there. I don't think I'm scared to be a dad. I'm not some kid anymore. I have a good job I love and a place to live. I know how to be responsible but also have a good time. I can see myself coaching baseball or soccer. I'm down for dance recitals, and taking camping trips for fishing and hiking. Puking? No worries. Blood? I can handle it. None of that freaks me out.

I've been watching Margot and Penelope together for weeks now and have thought on more than one occasion about how much I can't wait to grow a family with her.

The thought of having to do any of that with Katie St. James, though? That's an actual fucking nightmare I thought I woke up from. Letting Margot get sucked into it? Even worse.

She deserves better. Maybe she always did, and this just showed me that. Because I love her, I can't rope her into this. You know, I don't even know if she plans on sticking around because we haven't gotten the chance to talk. That's my fault, because I completely shut down. She left with her mom after dropping me off here at Gran's. I wouldn't blame her if she were home packing her shit up right now.

"She has to agree to a paternity test. I don't think that's something she can get out of if she wants you involved. I'll call a lawyer," Gran replies, moving to find her phone.

"She says she doesn't want lawyers involved," I add.

"Too fucking bad for her then," Gus says.

I sigh and drop my head into my hands. None of this is going to be easy. To think I was lying in bed with Margot this morning, thinking about everything we had ahead of us.

Gran comes to stand behind me, placing her hand on my shoulder. "We're going to figure this out, my boy. All of us. Margot included."

"I don't want her involved." My voice sounds low and detached.

"You don't mean that," she says.

"Yes, I do." I move to stand up and turn to her, yelling now, losing control again. "You know, Katie. You've seen it all. She'll rip Margot apart for fun. She called her a bitch this morning, and you know what I did? I sat there, frozen. I already failed her. I have to let her go. She came to Merrymount for a fresh start, and I was a fucking idiot to think I could have given her that."

I run my hands through my hair and pull to the point of pain. Anything to make this stop. I start pacing the kitchen.

"Sawyer, how about you sit back down? I'll call Margot back over here, and we can all figure out a plan. She has a place here," Gran says gently.

"No." I snatch the ultrasound off the table, and pull out my phone, finding Katie's contact in my missed calls, and head for the door. "Gus, I need a ride back to Red's. I have to talk to Katie without the fucking audience."

"For the record, I don't think this is a good idea," he mutters.

"For the record, I don't fucking care." I swing my head back around before shutting the door behind me.

I'm not being fair to either of them right now, or Margot, who has done nothing wrong. She's the one who called my Gran and drove me here. She held my hand the entire way and didn't say anything. She walked me to the front door like a toddler, and then brushed a light kiss on my shoulder, whispering *I love you* before she left without another word.

*She deserves better.*

I stand out on Gran's front porch waiting for Gus and hit call on Katie's number. I count the rings, half hoping she answers, half hoping it goes to voicemail and I can pretend this never happened for a couple more minutes.

"Hey, babe-"

I don't let her finish whatever bullshit sentence she was stringing together. "Can you meet me back at Red's in an hour?"

"Are you bringing your little girlfriend along?"

"No. I told you, Katie. This is between me and you. No games, got it?"

"So assertive. It's kind of hot, you know."

"Red's. One o'clock." I end the call before she can respond, and contemplate throwing my phone across the yard.

---

FOR THE SECOND time this summer, Red's apartment above the cafe is being used as a family mediation location, and if this wasn't one of the most fucked up situations I've been in, I'm pretty sure Margot and I would have a good laugh about it. I found someone who matches my dark sense of humor and it feels like it was all for nothing right about now.

I stare at Katie, sitting across from me on the couch, rubbing her swollen belly with the corners of her lips tipped up. She's waiting for me to say something. I feel like I'm going to be sick.

"How?" I finally manage.

She laughs, and it goes right through me. "Sex, Sawyer. We learned about it in high school, remember?"

"You were on birth control."

"Yes. And sometimes it's unfortunately not always reliable, so here we are."

"What took you so long to tell me? Even you have to admit that this is beyond fucked up."

Katie manages to look somewhat guilty for once. "I don't know. I was mad you didn't want me anymore, and when the test came back positive, I thought *who cares*. I was going to do it alone, and I was fine with that. Until I saw those *stupid* pictures from the Blueberry Festival the town posted."

She registers my confusion and continues, "I saw you. At the festival, looking happy as ever. I begged you for years to go to that dumb thing, and you always blew me off. I didn't recognize the name in the photo credits. And we all know everyone in town, so I looked her up. Do you know how easy it is to find pathetic Margot LeClair online?"

I forgot about the newspaper article. The one that made me so fucking proud of Margot. Now Katie's here twisting it to ruins.

She brings her phone out of her bag and pulls up Margot's profile, clicking on a picture she posted from an afternoon that we took Penelope to get ice cream and hands it to me. There's a drop of vanilla ice cream on P's nose, and sheer and Margot are both laughing at the camera. And I see why Katie is doing this. I have my arm reaching around Margot and Penelope, but I'm not looking at the camera like they are. Nope, my eyes are wholly fixed on Margot. Before I even let myself say I love you, it was written all over my face.

"You were jealous."

"Of course, I was jealous, Sawyer!" She rips her phone out of my hands and stuffs it back in her bag.

"You were jealous. I finally moved on after everything - after you cheated, after every fight. And *that's* why you decided to tell me we were *having a baby together?*" I'm trying to breathe. I'm trying to remain level-headed in a less-than-sane environment.

"I wasn't going to let you get what I always wanted with some random bitch."

"Do *not* call her that again, you hear me?"

She at least has the decency to nod her head once, and I keep going, "I don't know what you thought you were accomplishing when you blew through here but I'm gonna lay out how it's gonna go from here on out."

She opens her mouth to interrupt, but I put my hand up to stop her. "One, I'm asking for a paternity test. You don't want lawyers involved? That's your only way out of it. Let me remind you, I don't trust you at fucking all. Two, while I have every intention of being the best father I can be, it ends there. There is *nothing* between us except this baby. Whether Margot is in the picture or not, me and you are not happening."

Her face starts to fall and she slowly gets up to walk towards me. 'You don't mean that. We can be a family. A real family, like you always wanted. We can raise him like your parents raised you, here in Merrymount."

I take a step back, feeling like I was just punched in the chest.

She never stopped to think about how much Merrymount meant to me or why I wouldn't want to leave the place where most of my last good memories of them are. She spent years pretending my parents' death wasn't a big deal just to throw it in my face when it's convenient for her. It's a nasty old habit I forgot about.

"Family looks a hell of a lot different to me now," I finally say.

It clicks that this conversation isn't going the way she wanted it to, and she pivots to grab her bag and heads for the door leading down. "Well, we'll see about that."

Venom laces every word.

When she shuts the door I walk over and lock it, so she can't change her mind and come back to keep the conversation going. We've said what we needed to say today. I place my back to the door and slide to the floor, dragging my knees up to my chest.

I don't know how to fucking fix this.

# Chapter Thirty-Six

*Margot*

SAWYER DIDN'T COME HOME last night. I watched for his Jeep until he texted me and told me he was safe. Gus texted me a little bit later to say Sawyer was crashing at his place, but everything was still all wrong.

My mom's trying to help. She held me in my bed like she used to when I was younger and just let me cry until I finally fell asleep, but there wasn't anything to say. This is no one's fault. She's tried to tell me it'll all work itself out, and she's right - it will. But not in the way I wished it could. It's not like Sawyer's going to pick me over his kid and the mother of his child.

Nor would I want him to. The goodness that is Sawyer Hale is why I love him so much and why this hurts so bad. He's going to do the right thing, and I won't be able to do anything but wholly support him. I don't want to make this any more difficult for him or anyone else than it needs to be.

For once, I'm also giving myself time to think about myself. I spent ten minutes total with Katie, and it was already too fucking much for me. How could I ever picture her as a permanent fixture in my life? Sawyer's going to need to co-parent and show up for his son, and she'll obviously be around. But I don't see how I fit into that equation. And as shitty as it sounds, I don't know if I really want to.

The news, to be expected, spread through town fast. Since yesterday, my phone has been lit up with texts from everyone checking in on me and sending their support. Red insists she's ready to slash Katie's tires, and I love her for it, of course. But I just want to disappear. For the first time in my life, I'm surrounded by so much love that I don't even know what to do with it, and I want it gone.

I want to go back to my lonely little life.

I'm really trying to keep my shit together, but I don't know how.

Miller's name flashes across my phone screen, and I swipe to answer the call, immediately switching it to speaker. "Hey."

"Shit, Margot. I'm so sorry to bother you but is there any way me and P could swing by?" He's breathing heavily, and he sounds really worried.

"Wait, what's wrong? Is everything okay?" I quickly ask, looking over to my mom who picked up on Miller's voice too.

"Ah, it's complicated-" Miller starts.

My stomach drops. I cannot take any more bad news right now.

"Penelope and I are okay. Sorry, I should have started with that. But uh, ugh. It's better if I explain in person. You're home, right?"

"I'm at the cafe with my mom."

"Even better. We're two minutes away from there." The call ends.

"What do you think it could be?" I ask my mom.

"I have no clue, honey. But it's going to be okay." She tries to reassure me but it does nothing for the uneasy feeling in my stomach.

"Yeah. You've said that," I huff.

"We just have to hope for it all to work out, my girl."

She keeps saying that. Maybe one of these times, I'll believe it. I watch Miller's car park out front and see him jump out to run around to Penelope's side to unbuckle her from her car seat. She pops out and sprints to the door. She tugs on it but isn't able to get it open on her own quite yet.

My mom and I both stand to greet them, and Penelope dashes right past both of us to plow right into the front of Red, who just walked out from the back with a tray of cake pops shaped like little red apples. Penelope is Red's number-one fan. Positively obsessed with her.

"Woah, hey there, girlie pop." Red places the tray on the counter and crouches down to Penelope. "I'm glad you're here. I ordered these especially with you in mind. To celebrate school starting back up next week. Whadya think?" She pops one off the tray and hands it to her, and Penelope's face lights up. She then quickly swivels to Miller.

"Daddy, can I have one of Miss Red's apple pops?!" she squeals.

Miller nods his head and then looks to Red, who averts her gaze from him almost immediately, pretending to be focused on anything else. "Just remember to thank Miss Red."

We all hear Penelope shout her thanks to Red as she chomps down on the cake pop, making her way over to her usual spot, the coloring table in the corner. That leaves the rest of us to face Miller, anxiously waiting for him to catch us up.

He sits with me and Mom and puts his forehead right on the table. "I'm fucked," he says.

My mom scoots her chair around so she can put a hand on

his back, rubbing those small, comforting circles. "Miller, you have to tell us what's going on. We're worried."

"Our apartment flooded. The neighbor upstairs turned the bathtub on and then never shut it off. For over ten hours."

My hand flies to my mouth in shock.

"The whole fucking ceiling came down, there's water *everywhere*. It's a mess- no, it's a shitshow. I mean, thankfully, a lot of our stuff didn't get ruined. It's mostly contained to our bathroom and the living room, but our landlord says it's going to take weeks to fix, and we can't stay there. He says it's a hazard. We have nowhere to go. I don't have anyone to call. She starts first grade next week, and I have work and-"

"Miller," my mom starts. "It's going to be okay. I need you to take a deep breath for me, okay?"

Thankfully, he does. It doesn't stop the shake in his hands, but he isn't teetering into panic attack territory anymore. Another thing my mom is an expert at is diffusing thanks to lots of practice with me.

"Your landlord doesn't have anywhere you can stay?" I ask.

"I can't have Penelope staying in some sketchy motel. She deserves a home, stability. It's all I've tried to do for her." His head falls into his hands.

"And you have, Miller," I say. "She is so loved and well cared for. This has nothing to do with you as a parent."

"It's just constant. I try so hard every fucking day to give her the best life. Everything I wanted. She needs that, and she deserves it. She's the best thing that's ever happened to me."

It hurts to see him like this. The love I feel for the both of them hit me so fast and so easy it's like I can't remember what life was like before they showed up. It must be only a sliver of what Miller feels for Penelope, what my mom feels for me.

"The apartment's empty. Take it." I jump at Red's voice.

The three of us whip our heads to her. "What?" Miller says.

"Upstairs. The one you three had your pow-wow in. It's mine. Well, I don't live there. Like I said, it's empty. But I own it and it's yours if you need it."

My mom is the first to speak up. "I think that's a fantastic solution."

"No, wait. Red, I can't ask that of you. It's your space-"

"You didn't ask. I offered. Do you really think I'm going to let that little girl stay in some seedy place? I heard everything you said. You're out of options. And no offense, Margot, but you can't exactly fit the two of them in your cottage."

"None taken. I can't." I hold my hands up and agree with her, partly because she's right, there's no room. But also, Red is offering Miller a place to stay here. For Penelope mostly, I'm sure, but if this gets the two of them to hash out whatever the hell the tension is between them, I'm game.

Miller sighs deeply, looking at Penelope. A knowing look on his face says Red's right, and he's about to agree to anything for his girl. "You have to let me pay rent. And help out at the cafe."

Red waves her hand. "We'll discuss it later or something, but just say yes, okay?"

"Yes." He stands and pulls Red into a hug she wasn't expecting. I watch her back stiffen as her arms slowly and hesitantly wrap around his waist. "Thank you." I hear him say into her fiery, red hair.

She pulls away, waving him off again, slightly dazed, without saying anything to go join Penelope. She sits herself into one of the child-sized chairs and picks up a crayon to join her in coloring.

"Well, that's one way to handle things," I say.

"Do you guys mind keeping an eye on P? I need to make some calls." Miller heads to the door with his phone in hand after my mom tells him *of course*, already getting to work organizing things. He's the epitome of a dad on a mission to make things right for his daughter.

God, everything feels so fucked right now. But then I stop and look around. I wanted this. I waited my whole life for it. Wishing it away is dumb. Somehow, I've found myself surrounded by a village for the first time in my life, and the insanity of the past week suddenly doesn't feel so heavy.

# Chapter Thirty-Seven

*Sawyer*

IT'S BEEN THREE DAYS, and Margot and I still haven't talked. Both of us are unhealthily avoiding each other beyond a text here and there checking in, letting the other know we're okay. I've had three fucking days of reading through Katie's texts because she's decided to now give me a play-by-play of the last however many months I missed out on, as if it'd change my mind after our last conversation.

I can't bring myself to respond. There's nothing for me to say. I feel numb.

Melanie waited up for me the other night. I found her sitting on Margot's porch. She didn't say much aside from telling me it'll work out, grabbing me into this big hug that I wasn't prepared for, but subconsciously really needed. She ended up staying in town longer than she originally planned, and I'm grateful for it. It helps to know someone's there for Margot, even when it can't be me.

I miss Margot, more than what feels reasonable for a few

days apart. But I meant it when I said I didn't want to drag her into this. I have to stick to my word on that until things settle down.

I'm so lost in my own head that I barely hear the knock at the door. Then I hear the flop of a mat and the click of a key unlocking the door.

The door slowly creeps open, and Margot pokes her head in to see me standing in the kitchen, leaning against my small island. She silently steps in and shuts the door behind her.

Her hair is down, tucked behind her ears and she's wearing one of my sweatshirts. It's practically swallowing her, stopping right above her knees. Her legs are bare except for a pair of calf-length socks and slippers. The purple smudges under her tired eyes probably match my own. There's no smile on her face, her lips in a straight line. She's fidgeting with her sleeve while looking at me nervously.

"Hey." Her voice is low, heavy with exhaustion.

"Hey," I reply.

"I used the spare key." She holds it up.

I can't help it, I laugh. "I can see that."

"You're gonna be a dad."

My breathing turns shaky. "Looks that way."

Neither of us has moved from where we're standing.

"I'm really fucking sick of avoiding you, Sawyer." Her voice breaks, she sniffs once, and the tears fall. Before I can manage to say anything, I'm wrapping her up in my arms, smoothing the back of her hair with my hand.

"Please don't cry, Pix," I breathe into her head.

"What else am I supposed to do?" She asks into my chest.

Something in me snaps. I should walk away. It's another time that I can't be selfish. I shouldn't be hoping and wanting for more. But I can't do it. Every decision I thought I was making about the future for us is thrown out the goddamn window. I softly grab her face to wipe the tears still falling away. "We're gonna figure this out."

She looks at me with those green eyes, wet and shining. "I don't want to make things worse."

"Believe me, you being here right now is the only thing that's felt right all week."

"I don't even know what I was thinking. One minute, I'm lying in bed, staring at our awkward text thread. The next, I'm breaking into your house to… I don't know. I just wanted to be here. With you. Even if it is goodbye."

"Goodbye?" I pull away from her.

"I've gone over it all in my head a million times. I also admittedly spent too much time cyberstalking Katie. I don't see how I fit into all of this without seriously causing issues."

I let out a long breath. We're both putting ourselves through hell when neither of us deserves it. "Katie's… something we're going to have to deal with. But I want to do it together, Margot. If you want to walk away with a clean slate, I- I won't stop you. It might fucking kill me, but I understand. I want you to have it all, not this mess."

"So, we're ignoring each other because we think the other wants to walk away?"

I've held back long enough, I kiss her forehead and repeat what I said earlier. "Looks that way."

Her head tips back, and she starts to cackle. It's a wild laugh that sets me off, and we're both cracking up, holding each other in the middle of my kitchen, tears streaming down both of our faces. Letting the moment of hysteria take over to forget the world for just a couple seconds, it feels so good. It always feels good with her.

After we collect ourselves, I pull her face to mine and kiss her for the first time in what feels like forever even though it's only been days. She still smells like lavender. She still tastes like coffee. She's still my Margot, the pixie girl of my dreams, and we're gonna get through this.

I finally break our contact and grab my keys off the counter. "Let's get out of here for the day."

WE END up at the beach in this small town in Rhode Island that mostly caters to old, rich people. I've come here a couple times in summers past. There's a nice little public beach at the top of the hill next to this insane oceanfront hotel and other fucking massive properties. It's relatively quiet for the middle of the day, on what feels like one of the last good summer days before school starts back up and families wrap up their vacations.

Margot opted to run back to her place to change into her bathing suit and sandals, covered up by my hoodie again, before we hit the road. She nuzzled up on my arm on the ride over while I kept my hand wrapped around her thigh. We quietly sang along to a playlist she put on. We were just enjoying being near each other again. The physical touch was comforting.

Before getting situated in the sand, we stop at this small deli and pick up grinders to eat and some lemonade. Now we're sitting on a blanket I thankfully found in the back of my Jeep. Margot leans up against me as we watch the waves roll in and out.

"Can I ask the hard stuff first?"

"You can ask me anything, Margot."

She hesitates, and her mouth opens and closes. She looks at me and then looks to her feet, kicking around the sand. Finally, she winces and mumbles, "You're going to get a paternity test, right?"

I choke on my bite, and her eyes go wide. "I'm sorry! Can I

ask that? I shouldn't have asked that. Are you okay?" She smacks my back in an attempt to get me breathing again.

I clear my throat and laugh. "No, Pix. No, it's fine. I mean-*yes*. Yes, I'm getting a paternity test. And yes, you can ask that. I meant it. I'm an open book for you. Together, right?" I reach over and take her hand.

Her breath whooshes out. "Wow. Shit." She releases a nervous giggle. "Okay, yeah, cool. Good. Great plan. Just to be sure, right?"

"Exactly. But Margot, either way-"

"Together." She squeezes my hand and tilts her head up towards me, lips searching for mine.

"Together," I mutter into her.

My phone starts vibrating and ringing between us on the blanket, startling both of us. We look down at the same time to see Katie's name and the graduation picture flash on my screen, call incoming.

We look back up, eyes facing each other, holding our breath. I pick it up and slide to answer it before it goes to voice-mail, immediately hitting the speaker button. I don't look away from Margot as I say, "Hello?"

We both hear it. The sounds of beeping, and carts moving. Other voices are calling out in the background. We hear Katie's low voice through what sounds like clenched teeth. "You need to get here *now*."

"Now?"

"Now, you fucking asshole. The baby is coming *now*." The call ends, and a text pops up no less than ten seconds later with a screenshot of the hospital's address, and a room number in the text.

I feel the color drain from my face, and I let my phone fall. *Fuck*. I cannot freeze again. *Fuck, this can't be happening.*

Margot places her hand on top of mine, crawling into my lap. My hands instinctively wrap around her. "Hey. Sawyer.

Look at me." She then caresses my jaw, lifting it up to look at her. Those sage eyes bore into me, only love in them. And I finally fill my lungs with air. "I love you."

"I love you," I say without hesitation. Leaning my forehead in to rest against hers.

She smiles softly at me. "There you are." She moves her hand up into my hair, her fingers running through my mussed curls. "Let's get you to the hospital. I can drive. We'll come back to the beach, I promise."

I couldn't do this without her. I take another deep breath as she gets up and holds her hand out for me to grab hold of. As I pull myself up, she intertwines her fingers in mine, pulling me down to her level for a kiss.

We quickly pack up our picnic and start trudging through the sand back to the Jeep to make the journey to the hospital. I have no fucking clue what we're about to walk into, but I know if I have Margot by my side, everything will work itself out.

# Chapter Thirty-Eight

*Margot*

I HAD ABSOLUTELY ZERO - NEGATIVE, actually - intentions of being anywhere near the hospital where Katie St. James was going to give birth. But once we put the address into the GPS, it said we were over two hours away if we miraculously didn't hit traffic. And with Katie's very aggressive, urgent updates, we didn't have time to drop me off beforehand.

So, here I am. I'm sitting in the waiting room of the Labor and Delivery unit, watching Sawyer pace in front of me. We apparently missed the birth by fifteen minutes. The nursing team is in the middle of moving Katie and the baby - both healthy and doing fine - into another room. Katie also apparently requested no visitors - Sawyer included - until they were situated in the new room. It's a petty move to punish Sawyer for something that wasn't his fault or even in his control.

We're waiting for Beth and Red to get here. They should only be a few minutes out. We called them on the ride over so

Beth could stay with Sawyer and Red could take me home. I told Sawyer it would be best if I took off, and he eventually agreed after some coaxing.

Beth runs through the doors and stops when she sees the two of us. Her face is red, and she's breathing heavily. "Sawyer…"

Hearing his name breaks him. I watch Sawyer fall into his grandmother. She wraps her arms around him to hold him up. She looks so small compared to him. She shuffles them back until they're sitting on the small couch.

She rubs his back, whispering what I'm assuming are comforting words as the heavy sobs continue to wrack his body. I quietly excuse myself to call Red to check in and see when she'll be here.

I find myself aimlessly walking down the closest hallway to give Sawyer and Beth some privacy. I've never had to spend any extended period of time in hospitals throughout my life, but they still give me the fucking creeps. I can't let myself think too long about how there can be one room experiencing the happiest moment of their life, like the birth of a baby, and the room next door might be seeing someone take their last breath, sometimes with no warning. It's heavy.

My call to Red goes to voicemail, and I opt to send her a text letting her know I'm checking in. I'm sure she'll be here soon. A blonde man exits a room a little ahead of me, his head down. When he looks up - eyes red-rimmed - my brain catches up and I recognize who it is. I throw myself into the nearest open door before he sees me. I look around to see rolls of toilet paper surrounding me, so at least it's just a supply closet.

*What the hell is Dean Fitzgerald doing here?*

Talk about a jumpscare. I peek out of the doorway to see if he noticed me and see the hallway is empty. I take a tentative step out. Still swiveling my head back and forth on alert, I make my way over to the door he came out of to take note of the patient's name on the whiteboard.

It's none of my business, I could just walk back to the waiting room. I should definitely do that. But my feet have a mind of their own as I find myself standing in front of the now-closed door.

*St. James.*

Oh, what the fuck. That's just a coincidence, right? We're not adding a new layer to this soap opera, *are we?*

I know I'm going to hate the answer to that.

My phone starts vibrating in my hand, and a selfie of Red and me pops up on the screen. I swipe to answer it, still staring at the name next to the door. "Hey… you." Damn it, my voice sounds nervous. My acting skills are still shit.

Thankfully, she's too preoccupied to notice. "Hey, I'm here. I think. Jesus, this place is huge. I finally stopped at a nurses' station to get directions. I'm on my way to L&D now."

"I'll meet you there!" I practically shout into the speaker and click end, almost jogging to make it back to the waiting area.

I round the corner and almost crash into a broad back blocking the middle of the hallway. I stop short. My shoes squeak on the vinyl flooring. "Sorry!" I yelp, clutching my phone so it doesn't go flying.

Beth and Sawyer are on the other side of the broad back that I now realize belongs to Dean. Sawyer's face looks deadly. Beth looks very concerned and has a hand on Sawyer's arm.

"What the fuck are you doing here?" Sawyer asks, taking a step towards Dean.

Dean tries to take a step back and trips over my foot, falling into me. Sawyer grabs him by the front of his shirt, yanking him back up before I crash to the ground.

"I said, what the fuck are you doing here?" Sawyer repeats.

He tightens his grip on Dean's shirt and then looks at me. All of the anger directed at Dean and this mess melt away for just a moment. "You okay?"

"I'm fine," I reply.

"Okay, okay. Let's settle down." Beth tries to pull Sawyer back, but he has a one-track mind right now, and he's not letting go.

For once, Dean looks absolutely terrified. If this weren't already a shitshow, I'd probably laugh at his expense. But between whatever reason he had for visiting Katie, the state Sawyer is in right now, and the fact that Red is about to join us any second, now is not the time for jokes.

"S-Sawyer… Hey. It's all good. Calm down." Dean's nodding his head frantically, still trying to get out of Sawyer's way. Sawyer finally drops Dean's shirt, and he stumbles, quickly righting himself.

Nothing about this is right. Maybe I should try to diffuse the situation. I could try to talk Sawyer off this ledge. Be a voice of reason or something. I look at him again, trying to will him to focus on me for just a second. When he does, I pivot my plans. I see the look in his eyes. He needs someone in his corner, on his team, 100%, with no questions asked.

He needs someone to jump into the crazy with him. I walk around Dean to stand next to Sawyer.

"Why were you in Katie's room, Dean?"

The sound of two coffee cups falling and splattering on the hallway walls and floors causes all three of us to turn and see Red. Her face is as white as a ghost, and her mouth is hanging open. She must have walked up without any of us noticing.

"No," is all she says before turning around and bolting down the hallway, right out the door to the parking lot.

Beth is the first to move, and we're all standing here in stunned silence. "I'm gonna go check on her. I don't know fuck all what just happened but figure it out." She points two fingers at the three of us and, before turning to walk away, walks up to Sawyer, pulling him down to kiss him on the cheek. "I love you, my boy. I know who you are. Margot does, too, don't forget that."

# Chapter Thirty-Nine

*Sawyer*

SOMEHOW MARGOT GOT me to walk myself into this fucking hospital room.

Katie's laying in the bed with a newborn baby sleeping on her chest. Neither of us has said anything yet. Everything feels really fucking heavy, and I'm stuck here, speechless. I don't know what the fuck's going on, and the only thing I'm sure of is that the woman standing next to me is the only thing keeping me together.

I think that's my son lying there, and I don't have a single clue what I should be doing. I've never even held a baby. I've loved hanging out with Penelope this summer, but even she's just a tiny version of a grown-up. This baby is helpless, reliant on the adults around him for literally everything.

All that confidence I thought I had was wiped away as soon as I saw him.

"You need to tell him," Dean says from behind me.

And what the fuck is he doing here?

Katie's eyes go wide, and she shakes her head no. Dean doesn't let up, walking fully into the room now to Katie's bedside. "Tell him, or I will."

"You promised." Katie starts to cry and gently moves the baby from her chest to the clear, bucket-looking bassinet thing next to her.

"Promise broken. Now, Kathryn."

"Tell me *what?!*" I finally interject.

Margot's hand finds mine, squeezing once. She's looking at me with a sadness that I can't figure out. Like she knows something I don't. As a matter of fact, even Dean is giving me that same look, and I'm so fucking lost.

"He's…" Katie manages to get out in between sobs, "I don't think he's your son." She covers her face with her hands, and I take a step back, hitting the wall behind me. Margot tries her best to hide her gasp. She still hasn't let me go of me.

"I'm *sorry,*" she cries. "It got out of control. I thought I lost you forever. You didn't *care* anymore. About *anything.*"

I don't… God damn it. The room is spinning again. I look over at the baby, blissfully unaware of the mess he just landed in. I can see wispy blonde hair peeking out from under the little bonnet they put on him. It's a mirror color of Dean's and nothing like my brown curls. I should probably sit down. I *should* just walk the fuck out of here right now, but you know what? Fuck that, I need answers. I'm getting them right now.

"How long?" I ask, turning to face Dean.

"I didn't know until a few months ago." He holds up his hands.

"I meant, how long were you fucking Katie behind your wife's back," I say through clenched teeth. I'm trying to stay calm. We're in a hospital, and there's a sleeping baby in here. Innocent, regardless of who his parents are.

"I don't see how that's important now, Sawyer," Katie says.

"Almost three years." The words fall out of Dean's mouth.

I bark out a harsh laugh, and Margot tightens her grip on my arm. "Three fucking years." I shake my head in disbelief.

"It just-" Dean starts.

Katie tries to speak, but Margot cuts her off. "You're both *awful.*" She steps forward. "Just awful fucking people. But I guess that's the beauty in all of this. Because now you get to officially be awful together."

"We're not together," Dean and Katie say at the same time.

"Oh!" My sanity breaks for a second. "I'm sorry, did we misunderstand the entire affair that resulted in a fucking *child?*"

"Sawyer, please be reasonable," Katie whispers.

"Were you going to just pretend he was mine? How long did you think this was going to go on for?" I motion my hand to the bassinet. I'm trying to reign it in here. That baby didn't do anything wrong, and Katie just gave birth. But I have no patience left in me for this.

"I don't know! I don't know what I was going to do. I just- I wanted- I wanted us back. We could be a family."

"That's never going to happen, Katie. It was never going to happen. Call me when the paternity test results are in. Test Dean first, for all I fucking care. Congrats."

And with that, I grab Margot's hand, and we walk out of that fucking hospital room. We say nothing as we walk through the hallway right out of the automatic doors, and for what feels like the first time in forever, I take a deep breath of the fresh air.

"Hey." Margot tugs on my hand.

I answer by quickly turning, backing her into the brick wall. I capture her mouth with mine. The kiss is hard and deep, and I'm trying to pour every bit of love I feel for her right back into her. She meets me with the same eagerness, her hands wrapping around my neck to pull herself up, molding into me. She fits. She fits right here with me.

Nothing and everything makes sense right now. The emptiness I felt until Margot makes me appreciate the fullness of life with her. We have a future, and it's not held back by the past. It's supported by it.

I'm not worried about the paternity test. That baby's not mine. I can feel it in my fucking bones. The whole thing never felt right, and now I finally understand why. I just want to get the hell out of here and get back to Merrymount. I don't feel so lost anymore. As a matter of fact, everything looks pretty clear from here on out.

A quiet noise comes from Margot, and I tug her bottom lip with my teeth before leaving another soft kiss there. "Let's go home."

"Are you okay? I mean, that's a dumb question." She looks up at me, trying to read my face.

"What did I tell you?" I bop her nose with my finger. " No-"

"Dumb questions. I know. But Sawyer, God. That was… a lot."

"I know. But you're here. You're here for me. You found me and continue to see me." I run my hand up her neck, gripping her chin. "It's all I could hope for."

# Chapter Forty

*Margot*

"IT DOESN'T CHANGE ANYTHING," I remind him.

The paternity results came in this morning. Sawyer has had the envelope sitting on his kitchen island for an hour now, and he's been ignoring it. I'm trying to be supportive - I really am - but we kind of have to make a move here. He picks it up and then puts it back down, the same thing he's done probably eighty-five times now.

We didn't let it consume us the past two weeks, and it was the right call. After we got home from the hospital, Sawyer and I crawled up in his bed and hid out at his place for two days straight, talking everything out. We went over all the possible scenarios, even the worst-case ones that felt harder than anything.

We made love to each other. That's something I never experienced before him. We poured every emotion into our bodies, coming together, fusing as one to remind us of everything good we have, together. I mean what I said, whether

Sawyer is the father of this child or not, it changes nothing between us. I'm his, and he's mine, and we're going to walk through whatever comes our way as a team.

Some would say a season isn't enough time to know. But they're wrong. I've never been more sure of something so much in my life than how much I love the man pacing the kitchen floor next to me, except maybe how much I know he loves me back.

We are two lost, broken pieces fitting together.

"But, what if?" he asks, another thing both of us have said more times than I could count.

I get up and meet him in the middle of the room, running my hands up his muscular arms. "Then it already is. We deal. But we need to know the facts before we can do *anything*."

"Okay."

"Okay?" I ask, reaching for the envelope.

"Okay." After I hand it to him, he breaks the seal and slides his finger in to open it. He pulls out the piece of paper and holds it up. "Well, here goes nothing." He starts to unfold the paper, and I place my hand on his, stopping him.

"Wait."

"Margot, you're the one who's been telling me we need to know right *now*."

"I know." I smile at him and stand on my toes. "I just wanted to tell you I love you first." I peck a small kiss to his lips and feel him smile against me.

"I love you too, Pixie girl." I let him finish unfolding the paper, watching him scan the information, looking for any hint of what it's telling him. His face gives away nothing, and I hold my breath.

His eyes dart back and forth as he reads out, "This letter is to serve as proof that Sawyer Fern Hale is excluded as the biological father of Braxton James St. James."

He throws the paper on the floor and grabs me into his

arms, hauling me up and spinning me around. I bring my face to his, and he kisses me. It feels like there's no end to me or beginning of him, and I don't know when we both started crying but tears are falling down both of our faces. I hear him laugh. It's the most beautiful sound in the world after the silence.

"It's over." He's shaking as his hands cup my face, and he's looking at me like I'm his whole world. Just like I know he's mine.

"No." I cover his hands with my own again. "We're just getting started."

With that, he throws me over his shoulder. He carries me to the bedroom, and I'm giggling the entire time. The lingering heaviness dissipates, and I'm left with nothing but lightness in my chest as he lays me down.

I watch the softness on his face melt away, heat filling his eyes as he says to me, "Get on all fours, Pix. I'm about to show you what just getting started really fucking means."

I oblige, of course. A shiver of need courses through my body. Another one of his favorite sundresses of mine falls to my torso, exposing my bare ass to him. A bruise his hand left last night is still developing on one cheek. I wiggle backward into his hips as he starts to undress himself.

I feel him lower himself, his breath on my core as he licks me right up. I'm already wet. The anticipation is killing me, and I buck into him. "So impatient," he whispers.

"Sawyer, I need you," I whine. I don't care if he calls me impatient. I am.

A heady laugh escapes him. "I need you, too. Always will." He drives his cock home, deep inside me, in one thrust. I scream into the pillow, the pressure already building as he continues to plow into me. He fists my hair with one hand, carefully pulling my face up.

"You need to scream? I want to hear it. None of that pillow

shit again. Got it?" he says into my ear, not letting up on his pace.

I nod my head as much as I can, unable to find words right now beyond mews and moans. He's relentless, unleashing every bit of pent-up frustration and desperation of the past few weeks.

I'll take every bit of it. It's the kind of release that comes with painful build-up, only satisfied by raw feeling. He pulls out of me, and before I can register the loss, he's flipped me onto my back.

He repositions his cock at my center and takes a second to drag his head through the wetness. I thrust my hips to take the tip in, and he meets me, thrusting in again. Once he's fully seated and I've adjusted again, he brings his pace back up to a steady rhythm, hitting that spot only he can.

His thumb finds my clit, swirling circles around the sensitive bud as we both race to the end of the finish line together. I feel his cum jet inside me as I hit my climax. Sawyer pulls me in for a sweltering kiss, our tongues again tangling together as he breathes life into me.

His sweat-coated chest crashes into mine as he pulls out, and he leaves kisses all over the top half of my body, muttering *I love yous* throughout. My fingers find the curls in his hair, like they always do, and I whisper those same *I love yous* right back to him.

"So, what now?" I ask him after I gather myself.

"I was thinking you need to take that photography thing more seriously," he replies, his head falling to the side to face me.

"What?!" I almost laugh. That is absolutely not anywhere near where I thought this was headed. I don't even know what he's talking about.

"Margot, come on. You're so talented. Even before your mom showed up with your camera. You were sorting through hundreds - if not thousands - of old pictures. And since you've had that thing back, it's barely left your side." He points his hand in the direction of the kitchen, where my camera sits on the table in view from the bed.

"Yeah, so? It's just a fun hobby. They're just photographs." I try to wave him off but he's not having it.

"That's bullshit, and you know it. How much did everyone love the photos from the Blueberry Festival? Or Penelope's back-to-school pictures you did for Miller? And don't think I didn't hear Daisy talking to Gran about using you for riverside coverage."

"I don't know…" I start.

"You see people, Margot. I think you've been on the outside looking in for so long that you don't even realize what you have to offer. As much as I'm sure Red loves you at the cafe… and if you really wanted to work there till retirement, I'd support you. But I think there's more for you. Here." He holds my cheek with his palm and rubs his thumb along my chin. I lean into his touch, the feeling of home taking over my body.

He's crazy. But I kind of love following along with his version of crazy.

"What if I say I'll think about it?" I finally give in. Just a little. Because maybe he's right. I've never let myself dream about something like this and if I have someone like Sawyer in my corner? Who knows.

The surrender is worth it when his priceless smile takes over his face, and he brings his lips to mine again. "Then to that, I say, hell yeah."

"Speaking of things that come next, do you think we're going to have to intervene with Miller and Red?" I ask as I get up. I flip my head, gathering my hair to throw into a bun.

He sighs. "How bad is it now?"

"She tried giving him the silent treatment yesterday because he declared he's only referring to her as Gwen."

"I haven't heard Red be called her government name since her wedding, I think. Did he say why?"

"Nope. Because Red refuses to ask. She's content with ignoring him. While he's in the cafe. Working. For free. He won't tell me why. Neither of them will crack. It's infuriating. The only time the game pauses is when Penelope's around. Thank God for that kid."

I leave Sawyer lying in bed and run into the bathroom. I strip out of my dress and find my favorite of Sawyer's shirts to throw on after I take care of my business.

Miller and P moved into the apartment upstairs the same day Red offered. She gave him the keys, and they've settled in since. Penelope thinks it's the coolest thing ever to live *above* a coffee shop, and Miller spends his days working from a booth downstairs while P's at school. He helps with orders and cleaning throughout the day, regardless of how many times Red tried to object before she eventually gave up.

I love having him around and the extra hands are definitely helpful. It drives Red absolutely mad because she can't say no. Penelope has Red wrapped around her finger, and Miller really is great. The cafe is in tiptop shape because the three of us kind of rock together as a team. Their weirdness aside.

I come back into the bedroom to find Sawyer still lying naked with his hands behind his head. God, he's perfect. I crawl back in bed, snuggling up against him.

"Let's just… cross the bridges as they come," his lips murmur into my hair.

We lay here for a while, thinking about everything that comes next, planning for a future filled with my favorite types of quiet happiness.

I have waited my whole life to feel like there was someplace or someone out there that felt like home. Laying here tucked into Sawyer, listening to his heartbeat as he falls asleep, I feel it.

I feel it walking into my morning shifts, and at dinner when Sawyer and I go to Beth's. When Daisy, Red, and I break out into impromptu song and dance. When Gus walks by me and ruffles the top of my head.

I feel it when I see Penelope run off the bus after school and hear her yell, "Auntie M, I'm here!"

I feel it every time Miller calls me or introduces me as his sister.

I felt it when I took pictures of my mom sitting on the sandy shore of the river as the sun was setting last week when she wasn't paying attention. She has been spending a lot more time here lately. She looked so at peace. I wonder if she feels it, too.

Merrymount and everyone in it is home.

# Epilogue

CHRISTMAS EVE

*Sawyer*

"IT'S NOT GONNA FIT."

"Baby, you've said that before, and I've proved you wrong multiple times." I look at Margot next to me with my eyebrow raised.

She looks like a lightly toasted marshmallow, the puffiest white coat swallowing her right up. She has a chestnut-colored beanie with a tan, puffy pom pom looking thing on top, and matching boots that go so high they almost meet the bottom of her coat. She hasn't stopped moving, bouncing around to keep warm. Her nose is a bright pink and seems to alert everyone that this pixie does not belong in the cold. She punches me in the arm and looks back to the seven-foot-tall balsam fir standing in front of us.

"Besides," I continue. "I'm the one cutting it down, hauling it out of here, and getting it in the house. All you have to do is look cute as fuck decorating it tonight. Preferably wrapped in a bow." I nudge her with my elbow, and she bursts into laughter.

I wait for her to finally give me the go-ahead, and I march over to start sawing away at the base of the trunk.

"Oh, you're just full of 'em today, huh?"

"I can't help it. I'm a holly jolly kind of guy."

We both know that's not the whole truth, but she lets the half-lie slide.

That's not me saying I was a Scrooge or anything before. It's just… Margot got me to fall in love with life again. Nothing feels like going through the motions anymore. And, as a matter of fact, with big things like holidays and events, I feel like I'm experiencing a lot for the first time again.

"I'm kind of glad we decided to wait to decorate. It feels more magical," she says, sitting down in the grass, crisscrossing her legs the way she always does. It hasn't snowed yet but the air feels like that's going to change any day now.

"Me, too!" I call out as I cut through the trunk, sitting on my knees. After a moment, the tree falls on its side. She has no fucking idea how excited I am to decorate later.

I told Margot I was going fishing last weekend, spending the whole day up at this place up in New Hampshire called Barefoot Lake with Gus. While I *have* been to Wilcox Grove and fished at Barefoot plenty of times, this wasn't one of them.

Gus and I went into stealth mode. I parked my Jeep at his place, and we hid his truck in the trees a little ahead of the riverside. We spent the day locked up in the work shed and covered the windows so no one could peek in, building Margot a custom ring box.

We cut a hole in its side for a ribbon to make an ornament. I tucked the finished piece into the decoration box she left open for later when she was showering this morning. So, when we're decorating the tree she'll be confused by this ornament she's never seen, and I'll get down on one knee and make the speech and - you get the point.

I love her. It's the easiest thing I've ever done in my life. I spent a long time wondering how people like my parents or my grandparents could meet each other and just know. I couldn't understand how they could see their whole lives planned out. They were so sure that even if time could be cut short, it would have be worth it. There isn't a doubt in my mind now what that kind of love feels like.

So asking Margot LeClair, *the* pixie girl of my fucking dreams, to marry me? I can't wait any longer to get this ring on her finger. It's my mom's ring. I know she's happy for me. For us.

And Melanie's happy for us. And Miller. I asked both of them for their blessing because I didn't really know the proto-col, and I didn't want to offend anyone. Then I had to tell them that even if they said no, I was *still* asking Margot to marry me because I got in my head about offending *her* by thinking we needed approval or something. So, anyway, they're happy. They feel it, too.

I know it's fast. It was also fast for her to move into my cottage this fall, but once she started sleeping in my bed, I didn't want her to leave, so she didn't.

We could wait. We don't have to get married tomorrow.

*If she wanted to, I would.*

But I don't fucking care. I know this is it for me, and she feels it, too. I want it all with her. I don't see a point in holding off the inevitable.

Margot crashes into my back, wrapping her arms around my neck from behind me and plants a smacking kiss on my cheek. "Whatcha lost in your head about there, Peter Pan?"

"A pretty pixie girl who's always twittering around my ear." I reach my arm around to pull her so I'm holding her. She's writhing about, giggling as I tickle her. Her lips find mine, just as they always do and we get lost in each other. "Can I wrap you in Christmas lights tonight?" The thought leaves my mouth before I can think not to say it out loud.

Her green eyes light up, practically sparkling, nodding her head frantically. "Can you help me take pictures? This could be a good test of my boudoir skills."

*God, I love this woman.*

If you said the word boudoir to me a couple of months ago, I would have looked at you like you were speaking French. But my future wife has a passion for photography, and I have a passion for my future wife, so I'm all fucking ears when she wants to talk shop.

"You're incredible."

"Yeah. You've mentioned that a time or two." She kisses me again and then knocks my favorite beanie off my head, ruffling my hair before standing up. "Let's get this bad Larry home."

I grab the trunk and hoist it over my shoulder to start dragging it up to the parking lot when I hear the distinct click of a camera.

I turn to catch Margot's freckled face behind the lens, and hear that click again. I know when she eventually pulls that picture up on the laptop, it'll have captured me at the exact moment I saw everything I ever could have hoped for in this lifetime, and all the others.

**THE END**

*I'm too broken, too damaged, too much to let myself get lost in some fantasy with the two of them. They deserve easy. They deserve more than some messed up, mouthy, truckload of baggage redhead taking up space in their lives. I need to distance myself hard from any feeling of hope or want involving Miller and Penelope Caswell.*

**merrymount book two**

**coming winter 2025**

## Acknowledgments

First and foremost, thank *you*, dear reader. I cannot believe I wrote a whole book and now real human people are reading it. Wild stuff, I tell ya. Thank you for being here.

To B: My person, in this life and every other. Thank you for cheering me on, hyping me up, and jumping off a bridge with me in anything I do. I wouldn't want to be on the other end of anyone else's invisible string.

To HJ: My girl, my girl, you are my entire world. I'm so glad you picked me to be your mom when you were waiting up in the sky, as you say. Thank you for existing and giving me a reason to chase every dream. You can read my books when you're older.

To Marissa: I don't even know how to start a thank you to you. Thank you for inspiring me in every sense of the word. Thank you for sticking by me since the moment we met. Thank you for helping me bring Merrymount to life. Just… Thank you. I love you.

To Kim: My sister author. I would have never gotten to the point of writing chapter one, let alone getting to the acknowledgements, if I didn't have you. Thank you for your big, beautiful brain and dark humor and always being down for chaos. You're stuck with me for life, you weasel snake. (Lovingly.)

To Jessi: the co president of The World's Most Okayest Moms Club. I wouldn't have remained sane enough to do this without you.

To Cassidy: My editor. Thank you for your kindness and never judging my inability to know where a comma goes. Or just grammar as a whole.

A special thank you to my mom and dad. I don't know if I ever would have found a love for reading and writing if you didn't ground me for basically the entirety of middle school for not doing my homework. (...And failing gym.) Night-loveyaseeyainthemorning.

My friends and family, near and far. Thank you for supporting me in every way. I feel like the luckiest person in the whole damn world to have the circle I do.

Ms. Griffiths and Mr. Olson, thank you for giving a shit about the student who refused to complete a single homework assignment and definitely mouthed off more than she should have. (It's me, hi. I'm the problem, it's me.)

The Merrymount Book Club and my ARC Team, thank you for taking a chance on a debut indie author who is constantly faking it til I make it. Let's keep this going, yeah?

Finally, my soul kitty, Honey Lemon. You can't read because you are quite literally a cat. But you saved my life and I really feel it's important to thank you here, officially.

# The Spice Guide

# About the Author

Ila is a hopeless romantic who loves to write small town stories with found family, banter, happy endings, and a dash of spice.

Born and raised in Massachusetts, an overly emotional pisces, she is a girl mom to the coolest kid ever, married to the boy she had a crush on in high school, and completely obsessed with her cat.

When she's not writing, you can find her and the family checking every Disney destination off their bucket list, speaking in song lyrics, binging early 2000s tv shows, reading books that make her cry, and sending ridiculously long voice memos to her friends.